TWISTED LOVE

By Robert Bigaouette

ARCHWAY
PUBLISHING

Archway Publishing books may be ordered through booksellers or by contacting:

Archway Publishing
1663 Liberty Drive
Bloomington, IN 47403
www.archwaypublishing.com
844-669-3957

ISBN: 978-1-6657-4117-0 (sc)
ISBN: 978-1-6657-4119-4 (hc)
ISBN: 978-1-6657-4118-7 (e)

Library of Congress Control Number: 2023905677

Printed in the United States of America.

Archway Publishing rev. date: 03/22/2023

CHAPTER 1

O N A SPARKLING AND CRISP Monday morning in New York City, a young man by the name of Tommy Landis walked to a corner deli to buy a cup of coffee and a newspaper.

Ring! Ring! The door chimed as Tommy entered the deli.

"Tommy! What's up?" the turbaned Sikh Indian man who ran the place asked Tommy from behind the counter.

"Hi! I'll have the usual," Tommy said. He grabbed a newspaper from the row of papers laid out below the magazine rack above.

While Tommy put the newspaper on the counter, the Indian man behind the counter made his coffee. "Will there be anything else?" he asked Tommy.

As Tommy reached into his pocket to get the money he owed for the coffee and the newspaper, he said, "No, only the coffee and the morning paper."

The Indian man put the coffee into a brown bag. Then he put the money into the cash register as Tommy motioned at the coffee. While getting Tommy's change from the register, the clerk noticed Tommy looking at the coffee but not taking it.

"Now, look, I've been coming here for how long?" Tommy asked with half a smile as he stared at the Indian man.

"About a year, right?" the clerk said as he leaned on the counter.

"All right. Don't I always ask for two bags instead of one bag? Because—"

While smiling, Tommy and the Indian stared at each other.

Tommy continued. "The coffee will leak to the bottom of the bag, then the coffee that leaks to the bottom of the bag creates a hole, then the coffee falls out of the bag, and then I have no coffee for the morning."

"Therefore, my morning is ruined!" the Indian man and Tommy said together as they laughed.

"I should've remembered after a year," said the clerk. He pulled another brown paper bag from underneath the counter. He placed the coffee in the other bag for extra support of the coffee.

"No problem!" Tommy said. He smiled while he grabbed the newspaper from the counter. He exited the deli and made his way to the subway to go to work.

In the subway, a train arrived at the station. Tommy walked toward the train to enter. When the train made a complete stop and the doors slid open, Tommy entered, looking for a place to sit. A couple of seconds later, he found a place to sit, and the train began its journey to Manhattan.

While sitting in his seat, Tommy placed the cup of coffee down between his feet and then opened the morning paper to read it on the way to his job.

As he read his newspaper, right across from where he was sitting, he faced another commuter: a woman with long dark hair that shone from the fluorescent lights inside the train.

As Tommy came across the personal ads while reading the paper, he smelled the sweet scent of a perfume, which was overwhelming him. He lowered his paper to his nose and noticed the goddess-like brunette creature sitting across from him.

When she noticed his stare, he quickly pulled up the paper, covering his face, trying to read the paper again.

The face behind the newspaper looked somewhat like Woody Allen. He wore black-framed glasses and had a little bit of hair on his head.

As he lowered the newspaper again, he glanced over at the brunette goddess. She noticed his stare once again, and it seemed she was getting annoyed with him. When she noticed his heavy stare, he quickly moved up the newspaper, covering his face again for a second. Then he bent down to get his cup of coffee.

After taking a sip of coffee, he put down his cup on the floor between his feet again. He straightened out his newspaper and continued to read it.

A minute went by as he continued reading. Then he lowered the paper again, taking another quick glance at the beauty sitting across from him.

When he brought the newspaper down to the level of his nose, he saw her. She noticed him and appeared annoyed by his stares from behind the paper. They looked into each other's eyes. But as she stared at him, she gave him a "Go to hell" look.

With a rejected look on his face, he brought up the newspaper slowly, again covering his face and still reading the personal ads. The train entered onto the Manhattan Bridge, crossing the Hudson River, on the way to Manhattan. When the train made it to its destination, he rose from where he was sitting and exited the train.

Tommy Landis exited the subway and crossed the street in the heart of Sixth Avenue. He rushed to a typical office building not far from Times Square and close to Radio City Music Hall.

Tommy worked for a messenger company in the building. His job was to take a full cart of the day's mail and package deliveries to the upper floors.

The elevator he took from the lobby arrived at the basement level, and he exited the elevator and walked toward the messenger center. He walked through the basement, and then he arrived at the messenger center. When he entered the center, it was busy, with many items to be delivered for the day. As he walked to his locker to get ready, he noticed a couple of guys sorting out the mail. He saw Maria at her desk, conducting her secretarial duties, with old man Louie at her side, assisting her. Old man Louie was the supervisor at the messenger center. He walked around with a cigar dangling from the corner of his mouth, supervising, just making sure the day's work got done.

When Louie was done with Maria, he walked over to the counter and helped load the day's mail into the cart. Tommy put on his work smock, getting ready to start his workday. After he put on his smock, he grabbed one of the empty carts from the side near the counter.

"What's up, Louie?" Tommy asked, helping Louie load the cart.

"Nothing much, Tommy. Just working my ass off!" Louie laughed, and Tommy joined in on the laughter. "All right, Tommy, you're all set! Go! Now!" Louie said. He took a sip of coffee from his usual coffee mug.

"OK, Louie, I'm gone!" Tommy said. He left the messenger center, pushing the cart of the day's mail and packages to the upper floors.

Tommy walked to the elevator bank and pressed the call button on the wall, calling for an elevator to go up. When the elevator arrived, Tommy entered the elevator with his cart. When he entered, he noticed several people. He greeted them as the doors on the elevator slid shut.

The elevator arrived at its destination, and Tommy, among others, exited the elevator. Tommy was the last one to exit. When Tommy was out of the elevator, he pushed his cart into the reception area, going through the double glass doors. When he entered the reception area, the receptionist lifted her head, noticing Tommy with his cart of the day's mail. She stopped what she was doing momentarily as she greeted Tommy.

"Hi, Tommy! How are you doing?" the receptionist asked.

Tommy walked toward her desk with the cart, which he put to the side. "Hi, Destiny. I'm doing all right. I kind of wish it was time to go home." He stood by her desk.

"Yeah, I wish it was time too, but the day is going rather quickly," Destiny replied. She continued doing some paperwork.

"I suppose the day is going fast," said Tommy. He removed his glasses and wiped them with his smock shirt.

"I have so much to type today," said Destiny as she pointed toward a pile of papers.

"Wow! That is a lot of work. I guess I'll be going now," said Tommy. He pushed his cart into the office area of the floor.

The day went by fast at the messenger center. Louie and one of the mailroom clerks were cleaning up the center before going home.

"Louie, where's Tommy?" Maria asked. She was sweeping the floor over by her desk. The other mailroom clerks were wiping off the counters.

Louie looked over at her and smiled with the cigar at the corner of his mouth. "Tommy? He's up on the upper floors, delivering the final batch of mail. Why?" He looked quickly at his watch as he wiped off the counters.

"Well, I was just wondering—that's all," Maria replied. She emptied the dustpan into the trash can.

Louie watched Maria as she emptied the dust into the trash can. "Maria, why don't you wonder how much work you're doing for me, huh?" he asked.

Maria glanced over at him momentarily and stuck out her tongue at him. When he looked back, she quickly went back to her desk to finish her paperwork before going home.

Still on the upper floors, Tommy passed Destiny again, leaving the office area of the floor to make his way back down to the messenger center in the basement.

"Oh, Tommy!" Destiny called out.

He stopped over by the double glass doors on his way to the elevator when he heard Destiny call out to him. He turned with one of the glass doors open, facing her.

"Have a lovely day!" Destiny blurted out while still typing on her computer.

"See ya, Destiny!" said Tommy as he exited the receptionist area, going to the elevator bank. He pressed the call button on the wall, calling for an elevator. An elevator arrived, and he entered and pressed the button for the basement as the elevator doors slid shut.

Tommy made it to the basement and pushed his empty cart to the messenger center. Inside the center, Maria and Louie were sitting on chairs, talking. Tommy entered the messenger center with the cart and pushed the cart toward the spring water tank.

"Hi, Tommy!" Maria shouted as she smiled at him.

"Hey!" Tommy responded while walking over toward them. He sat down with them to join in the conversation. When he sat down, Maria smiled at him.

"Tommy, you know what?" Maria asked while she looked into Tommy's eyes.

As he looked into hers, he wondered what she was leading up to. Maria rose from where she was sitting and knelt down in front of Tommy, with Tommy still wondering what was going on. He felt a little uncomfortable with her getting too close to him. He thought to himself that she looked attractive, but he didn't want to be more than just friends and coworkers with her.

"You look all right now, but you would look a thousand times better if you would consider wearing contact lenses instead of these black-framed glasses," said Maria as she stood upright in front of the mirror that hung on the door of her locker and started brushing her shoulder-length black hair.

Tommy watched her brush her hair from behind, still sitting in the chair. "OK, Maria. What are you trying to say? I'm not attractive with the way I look?" he asked.

"Yes, you look all right now. In fact, you're freaking gorgeous! All I'm saying is that you would look a lot better with contact lenses." Maria smiled as she continued brushing her hair while Tommy pondered for a moment.

"Oh, all right. Well, I might consider it," said Tommy as he grabbed his daily newspaper and looked at the front page.

Maria walked up to him from behind and rested her hands on his shoulders. When she put her hands on his shoulders, he looked up at her.

"You know?" Maria asked, moving to his side.

"What? Know what?" Tommy asked, trying to figure her out.

"You are very handsome. Sexy. You know, a sexy Woody Allen. He's sexy—well, sort of." Maria laughed.

Louie saw what was going on. "Oh brother!" said Louie as he rolled his eyes to the side as he rose.

Tommy and Maria looked at each other, and they all laughed.

"OK, you guys ready to go? If you are, get the hell out of here!" Louie shouted while putting on his coat.

As Tommy and Maria put on their coats, Tommy looked over at Louie. "Are we ready to go?" Tommy asked, smiling.

Louie looked at him without saying a word as he swayed his hands, expecting Tommy to say what he was going to say.

"Shit yeah! I have a ton of things I have to do," said Tommy as he zipped his coat.

Maria walked over to him while buttoning her coat, came up behind him, and massaged his shoulders from behind. "Oh yeah? What things, Tommy?" she asked as Louie rolled his eyes to the side again.

"Oh shit, Tommy. Here we go again!" said Louie as Tommy looked over at Maria, who laughed quietly.

"Well, Maria, I can't really talk about the things that are going on in my life right now, so I'll see you tomorrow, all right?" Tommy walked away from her massaging hands.

"See ya, Louie!" Maria shouted as she walked out the door with Tommy behind her at a distance.

"All right, Louie! Bye, Maria!" Tommy shouted, following Maria to the elevator as they left messenger center with a few of the other workers behind them.

Tommy left the office building after another long day on the job and turned on his Discman while carrying his newspaper under his arm. After he crossed the busy city street, he entered the subway. He walked down the concrete steps and went through the turnstile. Within seconds, the train arrived, and he went down more concrete steps to meet the Brooklyn-bound train. When the train came to a complete stop and the doors slid open, he entered the train, quickly looking for a place to sit. After he found a place to sit, he opened his newspaper and began to read it as the train started its way to Brooklyn.

Looking through the paper, he rediscovered the personal ads, but he ignored them and began reading other parts of the paper, avoiding anything to do with relationships in general. The train crossed over the Manhattan Bridge, overlooking a wonderful view of the skyline, as the sun set behind them. The buildings looked like mere shadows, standing ever so tall.

When the train approached Brooklyn, he was already finished reading the newspaper, and he rested the newspaper on the seat next to him. There weren't many people on the train. As the train made its way to the Bensonhurst section of Brooklyn, he looked out the window.

"Oh, good. One more stop," he mumbled to himself as he rose from where he was sitting and went over to the doors of the train, awaiting the next stop.

As the train approached his stop, he looked over his shoulder at the newspaper he'd left on his seat. He stared at it for a second and then walked over and retrieved it before rushing back to the doors of the train. When he arrived back at the doors, the train arrived at Tommy's destination and came to a stop. When the doors opened, he exited the train with the newspaper underneath his arm.

When he left the subway, he was walking on the block where he lived, and within minutes, he arrived at his apartment building. He noticed, as he was walking up the block, his landlord putting garbage bags into the garbage cans on the side of the building, in the alley. As Tommy approached the landlord, Mr. Hill noticed Tommy walking toward him.

"Hey, Tommy!" Mr. Hill shouted as he put a lid on one of the garbage cans.

"Mr. Hill, how are you doing?" Tommy asked as he leaned with one hand against the brick wall.

"Just coming in from work?" Mr. Hill asked, wiping his hands with a cloth from the back pocket of his jeans, as Tommy wore half a smile.

"Yeah." Tommy reached into his pocket and pulled out a wad of cash.

Mr. Hill looked around. "You know, you have to be careful around here when you pull out a lot of money like that," he said as he walked back to the garbage cans and picked up another lid from off the sidewalk.

Behind him, Tommy smiled. "Now, Mr. Hill, don't worry yourself to death. Really. The moment someone tries to take my money, I'll chop him up, and then I'll feed him to the dog."

Tommy and Mr. Hill laughed while Mr. Hill lit a cigar he took out of his shirt pocket.

"By the way, how is your pit bull doing?" Tommy asked with a mysterious look on his face.

Mr. Hill gave him a half smile as he grabbed the wad of cash from Tommy's hand, which he took for the monthly rent. "Rent day is today, Tommy," he said while placing the bundle of cash in his pocket as Tommy smiled.

"Well, Mr. Hill, by a freak occurrence of nature, today is rent day and payday all at the same time," said Tommy, and he and Mr. Hill laughed. "See ya later, Mr. Hill."

"OK, Tommy," Mr. Hill responded as he watched Tommy enter the apartment building, shaking his head, noticing some weirdness from Tommy.

When Tommy entered his apartment, he threw the newspaper onto the sofa and then sat on the recliner. As he looked over to the side table, he noticed there were some messages on the answering machine; the machine's light was blinking on and off. He reached over and pressed the message-retrieval button.

Beep! The answering machine responded and played a message.

"Hi, Tommy! It's your sister, Michelle. Do you remember I told you I was going to Los Angeles? I'll be out here for two weeks. I'll send you a postcard. I love you. Goodbye."

Beep! The next message came on.

"Hi, Tommy. It's your mother. Why don't you ever call me? I'm starting to forget I have a son. See ya later. Bye."

Beep! Click. The answering machine tape was rewinding.

By that time, Tommy was in the kitchen, looking into the refrigerator. He reached inside and pulled out a can of cola. While opening the can, he walked back into the living room and jumped onto the sofa, careful not to spill the soft drink. He set the can of soda on the side table near the sofa and pulled out the newspaper from under him. He opened up the newspaper while he lay down. After skimming through the pages, he lost interest and threw the paper to the other side of the sofa.

Still lying down, he slowly closed his eyes.

"I'm so bored and so fucking lonely! I'm thirty-four—almost thirty-five—years old, and I have no kids, though I wish I had a couple of them," said Tommy as he smiled. Then he quickly came back to his reality.

Hell, I'm not even engaged or married! he thought as he sat upright on the sofa.

"I don't have a goddamn girlfriend!" he shouted out, looking toward the window in his living room.

After pacing around, when he calmed down, he lay back down on his back on the sofa. Slowly, he shut his eyes, and he fell asleep.

An hour later, Tommy awoke from the small nap he'd had. He sat upright on the sofa, noticing the newspaper at the other end of the sofa and remembering the personal ads he'd read earlier on the train ride home from work. He rose, reached out and grabbed the newspaper, and opened it up to the personal ads. He began to read the personal ads eagerly while walking to the recliner. He sat down and quickly looked at the top of the page to the 900 number for responding to a particular personal ad. As he continued to read the instructions on the top page, he noticed how much it cost to respond to an ad.

Two dollars and ninety-nine cents a minute. That's not too bad, considering my situation at this moment, he thought as he went back to the sofa. He lay back and crossed his legs, making himself comfortable, while he continued reading. He saw a pen on the side table and grabbed it. He slowly continued reading the ads, circling all the ones he was interested in. At the end of his journey, he chose the best circled ad.

"Here we go!" he said to himself.

> Single white female, five foot five, slender. Long blonde hair and blue eyes. Marriage-minded, no kids, totally responsive, nonsmoker. I like going out at times and sometimes staying at home and renting a DVD. Looking for a single male, five foot six or taller, slim to medium build, nonsmoker, social drinker, twenty-five years old or older. My box number is 00123.

Tommy read the ad to himself.

He rose from the sofa, picked up the receiver of the cordless phone, and dialed the 900 number from the personal ads to leave a message in box number 00123.

⋅⋅✦✦✦✦⋅⋅

The next day arrived. Tommy rode the train, drinking his coffee, on his way to work.

An hour and twenty minutes passed, and Tommy made it to his workplace at the office building and took the same elevator down to the basement. He walked through the basement and entered the messenger center, where he noticed his coworkers sitting in a group, in conversation.

"Hey, Tommy! Good morning!" Maria shouted as she quickly ran up to him.

"Hi, Maria! Good morning to you!" Tommy shouted in response to her with a half smile upon his face.

Louie, their supervisor, walked over to the refrigerator in the corner, near the spring water tank, and reached for a carton of orange juice. Tommy walked over to his locker, took off his coat, and hung it up in the closet next to his locker.

"All right, Tommy, take this load of deliveries up to the twentieth floor," said Louie as he continued helping one of the workers load one of the carts while Tommy put on his smock.

"All right, Louie," Tommy responded, pushing the cart full of the day's mail through the doorway and out of the center, on his way to the elevator bank.

Tommy's day came to a quick end, and as Tommy entered his apartment when he got home, he noticed the light on the answering machine flickering, awaiting a response. He shut the door behind him, locked it, walked over to the answering machine, and pressed the button to retrieve the messages.

Beep! The answering machine responded.

"Hi. My name is Crystal. I received your response to my ad in my voice mailbox, along with your phone number, and I thought I would give you a call. I can see you're not home yet, so I'll call you back. Bye."

Click. The answering machine tape rewound itself as Tommy sat there stunned, feeling somewhat numb. Then his face lit up with excitement and relief at Crystal's message.

"Yes!" Tommy shouted, and he went to the kitchen, whistling a happy tune.

Thirty minutes later, Tommy was still in the kitchen. He was warming up some macaroni in a pot, stirring it. As soon as the macaroni was sizzling, he added some extra tomato sauce while he continued stirring the pot. Suddenly, the cordless phone rang from the kitchen table. He quickly walked over to the table to answer the phone.

"Hello?" Tommy answered.

"Hello. My name is Crystal. May I speak with Tommy, please?"

"This is Tommy," Tommy responded nervously.

There was a moment of silence between the two.

"Oh yes, Crystal, I received your message when I arrived home from work. How are you?" he asked as he removed his glasses, rubbing his eyes.

"Hi, Tommy! I'm all right. My full name is Crystal Farnsworth, and I received your message in my voice mailbox from the personal ads. You have a very interesting voice." Crystal laughed slightly.

"Oh yeah? I listened to your message on my answering machine, and you have an angelic voice," said Tommy as he sat on the sofa. "So, Crystal, why don't you tell me some things about yourself?" he asked as he rushed off the sofa and went back into the kitchen to turn off the stove pilot as he remembered the food he was warming up. After he turned off the stove and moved the pot to another burner, he went back into the living room and sat on the sofa.

"Well, I work as a receptionist in a big office building. I work in the lobby. It's a huge building on Madison Avenue. I've been working there for a few years. How about you?" she asked, feeling a little bit nervous.

"I work for a brokerage company, in the mailroom, or messenger center. I deliver all kinds of deliveries. I'm a mailroom clerk, or messenger. I work in a big building too. Located on Sixth Avenue, close to Radio City Music Hall. It's a very interesting area, and I've been there for several years now," said Tommy, feeling somewhat anxious.

Silence crept in once again between the talkative two.

"So, Tommy, what do you look like?" Crystal asked, not feeling fascinated with what she was hearing so far.

"Well, I'm five foot six exactly. My hair is short, and I have blue eyes. I wear black-framed glasses. I have a slender build." Tommy took a sip of soda as there was a slight pause in the air between the two again. "So, Crystal, what do you look like?" he asked.

"I stand at five foot five. I have really long blonde hair. My hair reaches all the way down my back. I have blue eyes," said Crystal.

As she was describing herself, Tommy sat back down on the sofa, wide-eyed and amazed, as he thought he was dreaming. Neither one said anything for a moment.

"So, Tommy, what do you think?" she asked as she sat on her recliner in her apartment on the Upper East Side in Manhattan as Tommy sat on the sofa in his Brooklyn apartment.

"What do I think? Well, I'll tell ya." Tommy smiled. "I think we're going to get along wonderfully," he said as he sat up straight, placing his right hand over his right cheek.

"Tommy, do you look like any celebrities, actors, or singers?" Crystal asked, trying to get a visual of what he might look like.

Tommy hesitated for a moment, because he remembered what Maria had said about looking like Woody Allen, and he didn't know what to say for the moment.

"Well, let's just say that when you meet me, I'll let you be the judge," he said finally.

"All right, Tommy. Do you have any hobbies?" she asked.

"I love to bowl, play tennis, listen to music, watch movies, and try different foods from all around the world. I would like to travel one day in the future. I love to write poetry, go fishing and swimming, and watch and play sports." Tommy drank the last bit of his cola that he had resting on the side table.

"Tommy, you sure have many hobbies. My hobbies are shopping, tennis, traveling, knitting, and cooking," said Crystal as she sat on the recliner, making herself comfortable.

"You have some interesting hobbies. As far as days off, I'm off on the weekends. So why don't we meet for coffee at the coffeehouse located on Forty-Ninth Street in the heart of Hell's Kitchen in Manhattan?"

"Oh yeah. I know where it is," she responded.

"Yes, they have sofas and recliners; it's like you never left your apartment," said Tommy.

"Sounds good to me," said Crystal as she wrote down the address of the coffeehouse. "Well, Tommy, I have something to admit. I am a coffee addict." She and Tommy laughed.

"Oh yeah? I'm definitely one too," Tommy said. They continued laughing as he walked into his bedroom and lay down on his bed.

Crystal was already lying in her bed, wearing nothing except a long black T-shirt and panties. "Coffeehouses are definitely great places to hang out. I mean, they have such nice recliners and sofas. It's really a comfortable atmosphere. Nice wooden tables and all of the different-flavored coffees," she said, still lying in bed, crossing her long legs over one another, while she and Tommy laughed and yawned together because of the amount of time they'd been talking over the phone. It was getting late.

"All right, great. So I'll see you there on Friday night—say, around seven?" Tommy asked, yawning quietly, as he rose from the bed and walked to the kitchen.

"Friday night at seven would be fine," said Crystal.

"Crystal, is it all right with you if we meet in casual clothes since we're just meeting each other?" Tommy asked as he stirred the lukewarm macaroni still in the pot.

"That is fine with me. So I'll see you there," said Crystal.

"All right, Crystal. See you there. Bye," said Tommy, and they hung up their phones.

After Tommy hung up his cordless phone, he placed it on the kitchen table and went back to the macaroni and sauce on the stove. As he continued stirring the pot of macaroni, he lost his appetite while he thought about Crystal and their coffee date on Friday night. He put the macaroni and sauce in a bowl and placed the bowl in the refrigerator, and then he placed the pot underneath the faucet, ran hot water into it, and left it in the sink to soak overnight.

CHAPTER 2

FRIDAY NIGHT ARRIVED. TOMMY WAS in the messenger center, finishing up the duties of the day. Maria entered the center and noticed Tommy was in a cheerful state of mind.

"We're in a cheerful mood today," said Maria as she went up behind him and put her hands on his waist while he looked at her.

"Hi, Maria. Yes, I'm in a cheerful mood today," said Tommy as he smiled at her, directly in front of her.

"So what's going on?" Maria asked as she moved over by the counter and leaned up against it as Tommy looked over to her.

"Well, let's just say it's going to be an eventful evening." Tommy smiled and then giggled as Maria wondered what was going on in his life.

At the coffeehouse where Tommy and Crystal were supposed to meet, Tommy arrived fifteen minutes early. When he entered, he browsed the place, looking at the trinkets and the giant coffee mugs with the company logo on them.

As he continued looking around, a blonde-haired, blue-eyed woman entered the coffeehouse. She wandered about the place, and then she thought she saw Tommy. She walked over toward him but then walked past him, not sure it was him, because he had his back facing her. He noticed her from the side of his eye but thought it might not be her, so he declined to investigate any further, allowing her to make the first move.

Tommy took a step back, and as he stepped back, the blonde turned around quickly just as he turned around. Their eyes met. Neither said a word at first as he put a mug back on the shelf slowly.

He quickly walked toward the blonde woman in question.

"Are you Tommy Landis?" Crystal asked, feeling a little shy, as he approached.

"Yes, and you must be Crystal," he responded, and they both laughed.

Tommy gave her a single long-stemmed red rose while they shook hands. Crystal smiled because of the rose, and they quickly walked over to the counter to order something from the cashier. They decided quickly what they wanted.

After they paid for their coffees, they retreated to a table in the corner of the seating area. As they placed their coffees on the table, Tommy smiled at her, and they sat down as she smelled the rose.

"You really didn't have to do this," she said about the rose as she put it aside at the side of the table as they added sugar to their Irish cream coffees. "So, Tommy, what made you decide to look into the personal ads?" she asked while taking a sip of her coffee.

Tommy looked down at the table, half smiling, before answering her. "Well, it was just another technique for how one meets others. Like going out to clubs or going out to singles' events. This was just one of those ways of meeting others," he said, a bit tense.

"This is one of those techniques?" She wondered out loud.

"Well, yes. As I mentioned earlier, the club scene, singles' parties, parks, music events, and things like that draw people together. You and I chose, like millions of others in the world, to do the personal ads."

"Out of those techniques, you chose the personal ads?" she asked. She took another sip of her coffee as she watched Tommy take another sip of his.

"Ah, yes. How about you? Why did you place the personal ad in the paper?" he asked while he added more sugar to his Irish cream coffee.

"Well, like for you, it was a way to meet others, and it's pretty interesting. And plus, before I was involved with the ads, I knew someone who was involved with the ads. She's been doing this for a while, and for me, it seemed pretty interesting." Crystal smiled.

"How long have you been involved with the personal ads?" he asked as he gripped his cup, taking another sip of his coffee.

"I've been doing this for about six months now," she said, wiping her mouth with a paper napkin. When she wiped her mouth, she took a little bit of her lipstick off. They continued to drink their coffees and enjoy their conversation.

An hour later, they were still at the coffeehouse, and more people were entering the coffeehouse.

"Tommy, it's been nice meeting and speaking with you, but I have some things I have to take care of at home," said Crystal while she drank the last drop of her coffee.

"Well, I definitely had a great time speaking with you too. Would there be a chance of us maybe taking in dinner and a movie—say, tomorrow night?" he asked while helping her put on her coat.

Crystal smiled, thinking about it without saying anything for a moment. "Sounds great to me, but as far as the time, get back to me on that. Or better yet, I'll call you, and we'll discuss the time, all right? Let me give you my phone number, and if I don't call you by eleven or twelve in the afternoon, call me, all right?" she said as she walked toward the coffeehouse.

Tommy, from behind, watched her approach the glass doors, going to the street, as he put on his coat. "Sounds good to me, Crystal. Bye." He waved at Crystal, and she waved back from behind the glass door at the front entrance.

As she walked away from the coffeehouse, Tommy, partially out of the glass door, watched her walk toward the subway, never taking his eyes off her.

I can't believe how beautiful she looked, he thought as he continued watching her walk down the block on her way to the subway. He stared, now standing fully outside the coffeehouse, watching her walk, until he couldn't see her anymore.

The next day arrived. As the morning sun rose to greet the new day, Tommy awoke, and the first thing he saw was the other apartment building outside his bedroom window, across the alley.

He sat upright in his bed, with his feet on the floor, and turned around, looking at the side table, at the clock. It was eight thirty in the morning.

He rose from his bed, went into the kitchen, and pressed the button on the coffee maker to make some coffee. After starting the coffee maker, he walked into the living room and sat on the recliner, and as he sat there, he fantasized about Crystal.

Tommy imagined he and Crystal were lying on white sands in the Caribbean, making passionate love, as the waves of the ocean hit the beach. They heard the collision of the waves hitting the sand as the sun beamed down its rays from above. A warm wind blew gently across their sweaty bodies as their bodies were tangled in a moment of passion.

All of a sudden, the telephone rang, and he jumped, startled. His heart beat quickly, as he was frightened by the sudden ringing of the phone. After he arrived back into reality, he picked up the receiver, answering the call, just as the phone rang for the third time.

"Hello?" Tommy said, wondering who it might be.

"Hello, Tommy."

"Oh, hi, Mom. How's everything?" he asked.

"OK, I guess. How are you doing, Son?" his mother asked with a whining voice.

"OK. I met this girl, and—"

"Here we go!" his mother said, interrupting.

"Mom?"

"Son, I was only kidding." His mother laughed a little.

"I know, but that kind of gets on my nerves," he replied, feeling somewhat annoyed.

"I'm sorry, Tommy. Tell me about this girl," said his mother, and she listened.

"Well, this girl—"

"Another one!" His mother interrupted again.

Tommy felt frustrated with his mother, so he said nothing back for a moment while he removed his glasses, which were fogging up from the frustration steaming up within him. He rested the black-framed glasses on the side table.

"Mom!" Tommy shouted.

"Well, you go through more girls—"

"It's not my fault things don't work out!" Tommy shouted, frustrated with the conversation.

"Tommy, I didn't call to fight or argue with you. You know that I love you, Son," said his mother.

"I love you too, Mom. Anything new I should know in the family?" he asked while he went into the kitchen.

"No, nothing much around here happening. Oh, wait. The family is having a barbecue next Saturday. You want to come over for the barbecue?" his mother asked.

"All right. Well, you know I love barbecues," Tommy responded, smiling.

"All right, Tommy. Everyone in the family will be bringing something to the barbecue, so what are you going to bring?"

Tommy thought about it for a moment. "How about my world-famous potato salad?" he asked while reaching for a carton of orange juice from the refrigerator.

"All right, I'll put you down for potato salad. And, Tommy? When you come over, don't fight with everyone in the goddamn family, all right?"

"Yes, Mom. Just tell everyone to leave me alone," Tommy said, putting his glasses back on.

"Are you being antisocial, Tommy?" his mother asked, feeling a bit annoyed with his sarcastic voice.

"No. I interact with everyone fine, but someone always manages to press my buttons," said Tommy.

"Well, Tommy, I don't think that will happen. Let's just have a good time, all right?" his mom said with a slight whine in her voice.

"Yes, Mom." Tommy was starting to feel he had been on the telephone too long with his mother.

"OK, Son, I love you, and I'll see you soon."

"I love you too, Mom. See you soon." Tommy hung up his cordless phone, put it back into the charger on the side table, and sat back down on the recliner. He grabbed the remote control to the stereo and turned it on. He turned on the CD player, not remembering which CD was still in there, and pressed the Play button. The song "Lovely Rita" by the Beatles played. He shut his eyes in deep thought while listening to the song.

After a while, Tommy awoke after falling asleep, still on the recliner, still listening to the Beatles CD, realizing he had five Beatles CDs playing. He glanced at the digital clock that hung over the television on the wall. It was twelve noon.

He rose from the recliner quickly, still wearing a sweat suit, and paced about the living room in anticipation of the phone call he was supposed to make at noon. The way he was pacing back and forth, one would have thought he was expecting a baby and pacing around in the waiting room.

He glanced over at the clock once again; it was five minutes after twelve. He approached the side table, picked up the cordless phone from the charger, and dialed Crystal's phone number. He waited for Crystal to answer the call.

"Hello, Crystal. It's Tommy."

"Oh, you want Crystal? Hold on," said Darlene, Crystal's sister and roommate, and she went to see if Crystal was in the apartment.

"Sure. No problem," said Tommy as he smiled, waiting for Crystal's voice to appear over the telephone waves. He pressed the phone to his ear to hear in the background what was going on.

"Crystal! There's a phone call for you!" Darlene yelled out while standing in the living room, leaving the cordless phone resting on the arm of the sofa.

Tommy smiled as he waited patiently for the beauty queen.

"All right, here she is," said Darlene as she picked up the cordless phone, and then she passed it to Crystal as she stood near the sofa, by the side table.

"Tommy?"

"Hi, Crystal."

"Hi, Tommy. How are you?" Crystal asked as her sister and roommate giggled in the background. Crystal looked at her sister with a weird facial expression.

"I'm doing great," he responded, and he smiled when he heard her roommate giggle again.

"That's good. Tommy, can you pick me up tonight around six?" Crystal asked.

Tommy's smile widened as his eyes lit up. "Sure, six would be perfect. We can go out to dinner and afterward maybe take in a movie if you want. We'll be in the Times Square area," he said with a tone of hope.

"All right, that sounds great. I guess while we're at the restaurant, we can decide which movie we're going to watch, right?" she asked while giggling.

"Yeah. I have a newspaper, so we can look at it on the way to the restaurant."

"OK, Tommy. So for now, I'll give you my address. Do you have a paper and pencil?" she asked. She wore an uncertain look on her face while Tommy looked for the paper and pencil.

"All right. I'm ready to write down your address," he said as he grabbed the pad and pen from the side table.

"OK, this is my address." Crystal gave her address.

"All right. You live on the Upper East Side in Manhattan, in the upper nineties. OK, I know where you are," Tommy responded as she gave him the address. He wrote down the address as he repeated what she was saying. "Crystal, may I give you my address?" he asked as he stood by the living room window.

"Ah, sure," Crystal responded, feeling a bit odd that he would suggest giving his address. He gave her his address. "Oh, where is that in Brooklyn?" she asked as she wrote it down on a piece of paper she got from the side table near the sofa.

"I live in Bensonhurst in Brooklyn, over toward Coney Island," he said.

"OK, I know where you live. I have a friend who lives in that area."

His smile disappeared, and a concerned look on his face appeared in regard to Crystal's "friend" who lived in his area in Brooklyn.

"So I'll see you tonight," said Tommy while he walked into the kitchen.

"All right, Tommy. See you tonight. Bye," said Crystal.

"Goodbye." Tommy and Crystal hung up their phones.

Tommy placed the cordless phone on the kitchen table while he smiled with disbelief as his eyes glistened with excitement.

"Yes! Yes! Yes! I did it! I actually found the love goddess of my life!" Tommy shouted while he walked into the bedroom to get ready for his big date with Crystal. He shut the door.

* * * * * * *

Meanwhile, at Crystal's apartment on the Upper East Side in Manhattan, Crystal sat at the kitchen table, resting her head on top of her arms, which were folded on the table. Crystal's sister entered the kitchen and noticed Crystal with her head on her arms on the table as though she were a preschooler in the middle of nap time.

"Crystal, are you feeling all right?" Darlene asked with some sisterly concern.

Crystal lifted her head midway from off her folded arms. "No. Actually, I'm not all right. I'm just a little depressed right now, and I don't know what to do about it," Crystal said with a withdrawn look on her face.

"Want to talk about it?" Darlene asked as she sat down on a chair on the other side of the table, facing Crystal.

"Well, li'l' sis, it's like this," said Crystal. Then she stopped speaking, thinking momentarily with a smile upon her face that she had just made a rhyme. She and Darlene both started to laugh.

"Pretty good," Darlene said as she and Crystal continued laughing, coming up to the moment of seriousness.

"All right, in all seriousness, here is the problem I have," Crystal said as Darlene listened closely. "The guy I'm going out with tonight—his name is Tommy Landis, and well, I met him through the personal ads. He answered my ad I placed in the personals."

"OK," Darlene responded, still listening to her sister intensively.

"Well, we decided we would meet for coffee, you know, before going out on a date. This way, we're more at ease when and if we go out on our first date," Crystal explained, hoping her sister would understand.

"Good for you! Now, that's smart! Because you never know what weirdo you're going to meet." Darlene rose from her chair, walked over to Crystal, knelt down by her, and put her left arm around Crystal's shoulders.

"Yeah, that's smart, but you also meet each other before dating, so you can check each other out," Crystal said while Darlene looked at her weirdly as she stood upright.

"All right," Darlene responded, trying to understand her elder sister and roommate.

Crystal noticed the weird expression of her young sister. "You know what I'm trying to say. You know, to see if there's any attraction there when you meet the guy, and vice versa." Crystal placed her hands over her face in frustration.

"So is this guy Tommy attractive to you?" Darlene asked.

Crystal removed her hands from in front of her face and looked over at her sister. "He seems like a really nice guy. And he did treat me well that day at the coffeehouse over in Hell's Kitchen, but—"

"But what?" Darlene asked with growing interest.

"But, well, you know who Woody Allen is, right?" Crystal asked.

"Yes, I know who Woody Allen is. He's that famous actor and director in the movies." Darlene smirked.

"Yeah, well, he's sort of cute, except he's missing some hair," said Crystal, and she and Darlene started laughing. "I like Tommy. He's really a nice guy, but I don't feel attracted to him. Not only am I not attracted to him, but we don't have anything in common." Crystal laid her head on top of her folded arms on the kitchen table again.

"Crystal, it's never one hundred percent cut clear that a person you go out with will have the same interests you do, but opposites attract," said Darlene as she smiled at Crystal.

Crystal lifted her head from her arms and looked at Darlene with a weird expression, with a half smile creeping in. "Who the hell told you that lie?" Crystal asked. She felt more annoyed and restless than before. "Darlene?"

"Yes, Crystal?"

"Tommy Landis is not the man in my life. I'm not attracted to him, and it's not just the way he looks, but it's his personality and everything else. No, I have to tell him the truth, but I don't know how to without hurting his feelings." Crystal stared at the wall behind Darlene.

"Well, just tell him. Get it over with. The longer you wait, the deeper you and Tommy are going to go, the more you'll get involved, and the more Tommy will be hurt—and look out with the problems from all of that." Darlene removed her eyeglasses to clean them with a paper napkin from the napkin holder in the middle of the table.

"Darlene, he's already crazy about me. I saw the look on his face when we met at the coffeehouse. Not once did he take his eyes off me. I never saw any man act that way after meeting me. But I saw how Tommy reacted, and to be honest with you, it's a bit scary," said Crystal as Darlene put her glasses back on.

"Crystal, aren't you jumping the gun a bit?" Darlene asked.

"What?" Crystal felt taken aback by what Darlene had asked.

"I mean, so what if he's attracted to you this soon? That doesn't mean that he's saying he loves you or that he's in love with you."

"Yeah, but, Darlene, even though he's a gentleman, attraction has to be there as well," said Crystal.

Darlene sat back in her chair and thought about what Crystal was trying to say. "I suppose you're right. Attraction should be there as well as the type of person and everything else."

"That's what I'm trying to say," said Crystal. She and Darlene put their heads between their hands and thought about it as they stared at each other.

———————— ✦✦✦✦✦ ————————

Meanwhile, back at Tommy's apartment in Brooklyn, Tommy exited the bathroom after getting out of the shower, with a towel wrapped around his waist. While he walked to his bedroom, going through the living room, a thick cloud of steam followed him on the way. The moment he stepped into his bedroom, he removed the towel from around his waist and put on his black robe. He then went into the living room and sat down on the sofa, and as he laid his head on the back of the sofa, relaxing, he thought about his date with Crystal. He looked over to the side table near the sofa, making sure Crystal's address was still there on the table.

I sure hope I don't forget the address on the way out, Tommy thought to himself as he kept his head tilted back.

———————— ✦✦✦✦✦ ————————

Crystal and Darlene were in their living room, watching television.

"Crystal, are you going to tell Tommy about what we were talking about? You know, what we discussed in the kitchen?" Darlene asked, biting into an apple.

"Actually, I've been thinking about how I'm going to do that. On the subway, on the way to dinner, I'll tell him how I feel. Now, if I chicken out before we reach Times Square and we end up having dinner, I'll insist I pay half of the bill for dinner, and then on the way to the movies, I'll have to tell him." Crystal looked confident that she was going to do what she said.

"All right. I just hope he doesn't take it too hard. After all, you said he was really into you already." Darlene bit into her apple again.

"I don't think he'll take it that hard. There are a lot of lonely women out there. Look, I'm being totally honest with him," said Crystal. Inside, she was hoping he wouldn't do anything crazy to her. "Well, I have to be happy too!" Crystal shouted, feeling a bit guilty as she waited for Tommy to pick her up at her apartment.

"It's cool. I mean, it's not like you're knocking him or something," said Darlene as she took another bite of her apple.

"True, true. Oh shit. It's one hour until he arrives! I have to get ready!" Crystal rose from the sofa, and Darlene watched her run into her bedroom while she continued eating her apple.

+ + + ◆ + +

"Hey, Tommy! What's going on?" Mac the florist asked as Tommy approached the counter.

When he arrived at the counter, Tommy leaned on the counter, smiling at Mac. "Oh, I have a date with this beautiful blonde-haired, blue-eyed goddess."

Mac looked surprised, as he never had expected Tommy would end up with someone who sounded incredibly beautiful. "No shit. Who would've thought that guys like you and me would ever have that kind of luck?" Mac asked as he went to the side of the counter and put an arm around Tommy.

Tommy felt a little uneasy with Mac's big, fat arm on his shoulders, bearing the weight, so he slid away from his arm and then walked around the flower shop, looking around at the different kinds of flowers, as Mac went back behind the counter, ready to do business.

"So, Mac, how's business?" Tommy asked while smelling one of the flowers he was looking at.

"Oh, it's going," said Mac as Tommy looked at the vast array of roses he could choose from, admiring all the different colors and shapes.

"I'll take these three long-stemmed roses. One red, one yellow, and one pink, please, Mac." Tommy imagined himself giving Crystal the three multicolored roses as Mac walked over to the refrigerator where the roses and other flowers were kept.

"OK, Tommy. One of each color like you just mentioned, right?" Mac asked while showing him the roses.

"Yes, one of each color." Tommy smiled.

"All right. This is a very interesting set of roses you picked. One question," Mac responded as he walked with the roses in hand behind the counter to start wrapping them in paper and then plastic.

"All right, what's the question?" Tommy asked as he followed Mac as Mac went behind the counter.

"Why the multicolored roses?" Mac asked while wrapping the roses at his wrapping station at the side of the counter.

"Why? Well, why the hell not?" Tommy replied.

Mac looked up, trying to figure him out, while he continued wrapping the roses. Tommy wore a cold look in his eyes.

"Well, Mac, to answer your question, it's different. And different is better. And that means my chance of being with her is increased," said Tommy as Mac turned around smiling with the three long-stemmed roses wrapped and laid them down on the counter.

Tommy, on the other side of the counter, smiling, took some money from his pocket to pay him.

"Tommy, I wish you a little luck tonight, and that will be six dollars, please," said Mac.

Tommy took out of his pocket a wad of cash. "Here you go. Six dollars." Tommy laid six dollars on the counter.

"Tommy, have a wonderful evening," said Mac, and he took the money from the counter as Tommy took the three multicolored roses from Mac.

"Let's hope so," said Tommy with a concerned look on his face as he left the flower shop with the roses. He proceeded to the subway, which was around the corner.

CHAPTER 3

A<small>T</small> C<small>RYSTAL'S APARTMENT</small>, D<small>ARLENE WAS</small> sitting on the sofa, while Crystal was in the bathroom, blow-drying her hair while looking in the mirror.

"Hey, Crystal! Are you ready yet?" Darlene asked as she kept switching channels on the television.

"Yeah! I'm just about ready, but I'm not really looking forward to this evening." Crystal walked toward the living room, brushing her long blonde hair. "I mean, it would be one thing if I were attracted to him and if we could see where we fit together, but it's another thing when you have to tell someone you're not attracted to him." Crystal was fully dressed, and she laid the brush down on one of the side tables near the sofa.

Crystal was wearing a sweatshirt with the logo FUBU on the front, and she also wore a comfortable pair of jeans that showed off her beautiful, sexy physique and a pair of sneakers.

"Hey, Darlene!" Crystal yelled out, and Darlene looked over toward Crystal. "Where's your boyfriend?" Crystal asked as she sat down on the recliner.

"He's boxing tonight at the YMCA," said Darlene.

"So why didn't you go to see him? You could've been sitting at the corner of the ring and watching him fight tonight." Crystal sat back comfortably in the recliner as she put up her feet.

"Now, Crystal, you know when he and I first started going out, I was at most of the boxing matches he was in. And then, after a while, it got kind of boring. And besides, I'm into baseball a lot more." Darlene put up her feet and lay on the sofa while watching television.

"Well, it's getting close to that time," said Crystal. She and Darlene looked at the clock that hung above the entrance to the kitchen, and Crystal noticed the time passing.

Five minutes later, the doorbell rang, startling Darlene and Crystal. Crystal walked over to the intercom in the kitchen, near the door.

"Who is it?" Crystal asked, knowing who it might be.

"It's Tommy Landis."

"All right, I'll buzz you in." Crystal reached for the button to let him in from downstairs at the main door.

When the buzzer sounded, Tommy opened up the main door, entered the building, and proceeded up to Crystal's apartment. As he walked through the lobby, he found the elevator. He entered the elevator and pressed the button for the third floor, the elevator doors slid shut, and the elevator proceeded to the third floor.

When the elevator arrived on the third floor, he stepped off and looked for apartment 3I. Walking around, he found the apartment. He approached the front door of the apartment with the long-stemmed multicolored roses in hand. Right before he knocked, the front door of the apartment flew open. It was Darlene.

"Oh, hi. Come in," said Darlene as she stepped aside, allowing Tommy to enter the apartment.

After Tommy entered, Darlene shut the door behind him, and he looked around as he walked slowly through the kitchen into the living room. Darlene followed.

"Tommy, I'm Darlene," said Darlene as Tommy turned around. "I'm Crystal's sister and roommate." Darlene put out a hand.

"Hi," Tommy responded as his hand met Darlene's hand slowly, and they shook hands in greeting.

Crystal walked into the living room and saw Tommy wearing a black Notre Dame sweatshirt and a pair of blue jeans. He also wore a blue jean jacket.

"Hi, Tommy," Crystal said as she stood by the sofa, smiling.

"Hi, Crystal. These are for you," said Tommy as he walked over to her. He gave her the roses as he smiled.

Crystal gave a half smile, and he looked over toward Darlene as she smiled.

"Tommy, the roses are so beautiful!" said Crystal as she looked over to her sister, who stood by the entrance of the kitchen, smiling at her.

Tommy looked over at Darlene again, and Darlene smiled at him again. He grew a little nervous, trying to see how Crystal was feeling.

"Well, are you ready?" he asked Crystal.

"Sure. OK, Darlene," said Crystal as she walked across the living room, and then she stopped. "Oh, I'm sorry, Tommy, Darlene. I never introduced you to each other." Crystal smiled.

"That's all right, Crystal; we already met." Darlene smiled.

"All right. I'll see you later, Darlene," Crystal responded as she took her coat out of the closet in the hallway.

"All right. Have a good time, you two," said Darlene as she walked them toward the door of the apartment.

As soon as Crystal and Tommy entered the hallway, Darlene shut the door behind them. She smiled at Crystal while closing the door slowly.

Crystal and Tommy walked toward the elevator bank as he looked over at Crystal from the sides of his eyes.

"You really look great tonight, Crystal," said Tommy as she pressed the down button for the elevator.

"Thank you, Tommy." Crystal smiled as an elevator arrived on the third floor.

They entered the elevator, and Crystal pressed the button for the lobby as she smiled. The doors slid shut, and the elevator car went down.

When they arrived in the lobby, they exited the elevator and proceeded through the lobby and out the entrance of the building. They proceeded to the subway.

When they went through the turnstile in the subway, Crystal looked over at Tommy. They arrived at the platform and awaited the train.

"So where are we going to eat?" Crystal asked as they continued walking around the platform while waiting for their train. She smiled.

"I thought about going to this barbecue place on Forty-Third Street. Do you like barbecue food, or would you rather go someplace else?" Tommy asked as they walked up to a wall. He leaned up against it with his hands in his pockets as he smiled.

"No, barbecue food would be fine." Crystal smiled while she looked away for a quick second.

"I was also thinking about which movie we could see after we're done eating," said Tommy.

Meanwhile, she was thinking about what she was going to say to him after dinner, wondering if she should've just called him before he left Brooklyn to cancel the date, because going out to dinner was just encouraging him. Crystal quickly turned around, facing him, deciding she was going to tell him how she felt.

Just as she was going to tell him, the train arrived at the station, along with the wind as the train went by them. When the train came to a screeching stop at the platform, Crystal declined to tell him at the moment. As the doors of the train slid open, Tommy and Crystal, among others, entered the train.

"Passengers, can I have your attention? This train will be going express all the way to Times Square!" said the conductor as the doors slid closed, and the train exited the station, on its way to Times Square, while they found a place to sit.

The train arrived at the Times Square station in Manhattan, and after Tommy and Crystal exited the subway, they walked about Times Square. They walked around without holding hands but enjoyed each other's company, the summer scenery, and the flashy, lit-up atmosphere in the heart of the Big Apple.

While they continued walking about, Tommy felt as though he were on top of the world. It was a beautiful summer night, he was in

Times Square, and he had a beautiful blonde-haired, blue-eyed goddess by his side. They walked toward the restaurant.

They walked along Forty-Third Street, and Tommy saw the restaurant not far from where they were.

"Here we are," said Tommy as he and Crystal crossed the street and arrived at the restaurant. At the entrance to the restaurant, Tommy held the door open for her. Crystal entered the restaurant, and Tommy followed. Tommy and Crystal smiled at each other as a waitress walked toward them with a couple of menus under her arm.

"Hi. My name is Shelly. Welcome," said the waitress as she escorted them to a table.

When they reached an empty table, the waitress placed the two menus on the table, and Tommy pulled out the chair for Crystal to sit down and then went to the opposite side and sat down as they both smiled.

"Here are your menus, and I'll be back with your iced waters," said Shelly.

"All right, thanks," said Tommy. He smiled at Crystal while the waitress went to get the waters, and Crystal smiled back. "So what do you think?" Tommy asked as he and Crystal looked around.

"This is nice. I've never been here before. I guess there are many restaurants I haven't been to yet," said Crystal as the waitress returned with their waters.

"All right, here are your iced waters. Are you ready to order yet?" Shelly asked as she smiled.

"No, can you give us a little while longer, please?" Tommy asked as he and Crystal picked up their menus from the table. They opened the menus to see what they would order.

"All right, no problem." Shelly smiled pleasantly as she momentarily left to tend to another table while they decided what they wanted.

Ten minutes later, Shelly returned, ready to take their orders.

"Hi. Ready to order now?" Shelly asked as she took out her pen and pad from her waitress apron.

"Yes, I'm sorry it took a little while to order," said Tommy as he smiled at Crystal. Crystal returned a half smile to him as the waitress watched them smile.

"Oh, that's quite all right," said Shelly as she smiled at them.

"Well, it's easy to be distracted by beauty when it's right in front of you," said Tommy as he smiled at Crystal again, and she smiled again halfway, feeling a bit nervous and embarrassed but a little flattered by his impulsive comments, as she laughed slightly.

"All right, what will y'all order?" Shelly asked.

Tommy looked over at Crystal for her to order first, and the waitress looked to Crystal.

"I'll have the barbecue shrimp," said Crystal as she smiled while still looking over the menu.

"All right, barbeque shrimp. Will that be with french fries, mashed potatoes, or maybe a baked potato?" Shelly asked.

"I'll have a baked potato," said Crystal as Tommy watched her from over the top of his menu. Crystal didn't realize she was being watched.

"With soup or salad?" Shelly asked.

"I'll have the house salad, please," said Crystal as she placed her menu down on the table, near her plate, and smiled. "With oil and vinegar, please," Crystal added as she looked over at Tommy, who was looking over the menu to decide what he wanted.

"All right, what would you like to drink?" Shelly asked as she smiled.

"I'll have a Diet Coke, please," said Crystal.

"And you, sir?" Shelly looked to Tommy.

"I'll have the barbecue chicken without the skin on it," said Tommy as he put down the menu over his plate.

"All right, barbecue chicken with no skin," said Shelly as she wrote the order on her pad.

"And with the chicken, I'll have mashed potatoes and a cup of soup." Tommy smiled at Crystal.

"And what kind of soup do you want to have?" Shelly asked.

"What kind of soup do you have?" he asked as he opened up the menu again, looking over it.

"We have New England clam chowder, cream of broccoli, Manhattan clam chowder, chicken noodle, green pea, and cream of chicken," said Shelly.

"I'll have the cream of chicken, and to drink, I'll have an orange juice. A large orange juice, please." Tommy closed the menu.

Shelly took the menus from the table. "All right, will there be any dessert tonight with your dinner?" she asked as she smiled at Tommy and Crystal.

Tommy looked over at Crystal, seeing if she wanted some dessert with dinner.

"No, thank you," said Crystal, and she smiled gracefully as she shook her head.

"No, thank you, Shelly," said Tommy as he smiled at Shelly.

"All right, your orders will be ready shortly. If you need anything else, let me know. Y'all know my name," said the sassy redheaded waitress, about to leave their table.

"Oh, Shelly?" Tommy called out.

"Yes?" Shelly responded as she quickly turned around toward Tommy.

"I've noticed your accent. You're not from New York, right?" he said as he smiled.

"Actually, I'm not. I'm from Norman, Oklahoma. I'm a student. I transferred to NYU from the University of Oklahoma. I'm in the medical field," said Shelly as she smiled at Tommy and Crystal, and Crystal nodded.

"All right, that's pretty cool," Tommy responded as he smiled.

"OK, your orders will be ready soon," said Shelly as she went to the cooks to place the orders.

Tommy and Crystal smiled at each other while looking around the restaurant as country music played in the background.

"This is really a nice place. How did you hear of this place?" Crystal asked as she took a sip of her iced water, as most of the ice was melting, and the water in the small glass was rising.

"I used to work at an office a few blocks away before we moved to Sixth Avenue," said Tommy as he took a sip of his iced water.

"What kind of company did you say you work for?" Crystal asked.

"The company I work for is a brokerage firm. You know, stocks, investments—that sort of thing. My position in the company is in the mailroom department. I'm a mailroom clerk, but soon I will be starting school. Possibly starting in November, in time for the winter semester," said Tommy as he moved in his chair, trying to get comfortable.

"Oh yeah? What school are you thinking about going to?" she asked as she looked around the restaurant a little bit.

"Well, I'm thinking about taking some computer courses at a school I choose. I would like to be a computer repairman eventually. It's a pretty good career in the high-tech industry." Tommy smiled, believing what he was saying, even though he knew it was not true.

"Yeah, that is a decent career for you to choose. That's good," said Crystal, running out of things to say, hoping the evening would end soon.

"I've always believed it's good to have goals in life," said Tommy as he took another sip of his iced water.

"That's true. At the marketing company I work for, I plan on moving up in the company," said Crystal as she smiled.

"Oh yeah?" Tommy responded.

"Yes, most definitely," Crystal replied as she took another sip of her water.

"You sound like you have a lot of ambition," said Tommy.

"I do. It's the only way to accomplish what you want," Crystal said as she saw, behind Tommy, at a distance, the waitress getting the food together.

"That's true." Tommy smiled.

Shelly arrived with the food on a huge, circular tray, holding it right above her head. She brought the huge tray of food down onto a stand next to the table and then set the food on the table.

"All right, enjoy your food. If you need anything else, let me know," said Shelly as she smiled.

"Thank you, Shelly. Everything smells and looks so good," said Tommy as he and Crystal looked at the food on the table.

"All right," said Shelly, and she went to the next table to assist her other customers as Tommy and Crystal started eating their food.

After a while, they were through with dinner, and as Crystal was laughing because of a joke Tommy was telling her, the waitress walked toward their table.

"All right, may I remove your plates?" Shelly asked as she smiled.

"Sure," Tommy responded, and she started picking up the plates while he and Crystal looked into each other's eyes. Tommy wished to know what Crystal was thinking at the moment.

I'm just not attracted to him. He's such a gentleman, and he's so kind, but I'm just not attracted to him. And attraction does matter. No doubt about it. I have to tell him right after dinner how I feel and be honest with him and, more importantly, with myself, Crystal thought. As she and Tommy continued looking into each other's eyes, she started to feel more and more uncomfortable.

"So, Tommy, I—" Crystal stopped as the waitress arrived back at their table and rested the dinner bill on the table, in a black leather casing, next to Tommy.

"Thanks, Shelly. You were great, and we appreciate your services," said Tommy.

"Thank you. And the two of you have a wonderful evening," said Shelly, and she smiled while walking toward the next table.

"Tommy, I'll pay half of the bill," said Crystal as she went into her purse.

"Are you kidding? This is our very first date. I've got it," said Tommy as he rose from where he was sitting and walked up to the cashier to pay the bill.

When Tommy arrived back at the table, Crystal was just standing up as she took her jacket from the back of her chair.

"Are we ready to go?" Tommy asked, helping her with her jacket.

"Sure," said Crystal, buttoning her jacket. "Thank you, Tommy."

Tommy put on his jacket, and as they walked toward the entrance of the restaurant to leave, they saw Shelly by the doors.

"Thanks for coming," said Shelly as Tommy left her a tip on the table as he and Crystal were leaving the restaurant.

"The food was really great, right?" Tommy asked as he and Crystal crossed Forty-Second Street, walking toward Broadway, the middle of Times Square.

"Yeah, the food was really great," said Crystal.

Tommy tried to hold her hand as they walked up Broadway, looking for a movie in the theaters they walked by, but she declined his hand and pulled back her hand.

"I'm sorry. I just feel a little uncomfortable right now," Crystal said as she realized it was time to be honest, hoping it wasn't too late.

"That's all right. What movie would you like to watch?" Tommy asked, smiling, hoping she wasn't angry with him, as they crossed the street.

In the middle of Times Square, Crystal stopped walking abruptly. Tommy didn't expect the sudden stop between Broadway and Seventh Avenue on Forty-Fourth Street.

"Actually, Tommy, why don't we talk first?" she said.

Tommy wore a concerned look on his face as the lights and glitter of Times Square flashed all about on the perfect summer night. "OK, we could do that," he said, facing her, as people were all around them, going about their business.

"Tommy, I had a great time with you tonight, and you're so much fun, but—"

"But?"

"But I'm not attracted to you," said Crystal as they walked across the street back to Broadway, still on Forty-Fourth Street. Crystal continued as she and Tommy walked along Broadway toward Forty-Second

Street. "You see, there are a lot of things to consider when two people start going out, dating, and maybe getting into some type of relationship, and attraction is a part of it." They stopped walking on the corner of Forty-Second Street and Broadway, facing each other, with the lights in the background flickering on and off.

"All right, fine. I got the hint. May I take you home?" Tommy asked.

"No. No, that's all right," said Crystal as she smiled slightly, and she turned around and walked away toward a subway nearby.

As she walked away down Forty-Second Street, Tommy watched her until he couldn't see her anymore, until she disappeared into the crowd as she made her way home.

Feeling abandoned, he crossed the busy street and entered the subway. He went through the turnstile and onto the platform to await his train back to Brooklyn. He walked up and down the platform, trying to make sense of everything that had happened from the time he'd met her at the coffeehouse up to now, their first and last date. While still waiting for the Brooklyn-bound train, he thought about how beautiful she'd looked that night and how in love with her he was.

A train arrived as he leaned up against a beam on the platform, and when the train came to a complete stop and the doors slid open, he entered with others onto the train. The doors slid shut, and the train left the station, on its way to Brooklyn.

But when he looked out the window when he sat down, he noticed the train was going uptown instead of downtown.

When the train stopped at the next station, he exited. As he got off the train, he noticed, to his left, Crystal. She was about twenty feet away, boarding another car of the train, in the midst of a small group of other commuters. Upon seeing Crystal enter the train, Tommy quickly jumped back into the train, even though it was still going uptown. As the doors slid shut, he was breathing hard because he'd just made it inside before the doors closed. As the train exited the station, Tommy went to the door that would take him to the next car of the train. He opened the sliding door at the end of the car and walked between the two cars, wanting to get inside the next car. Before entering, he looked through the glass of the other door and saw Crystal sitting there listening to her Discman headset.

"Good luck to you—and me," Tommy whispered to himself with his face up against the glass of the door of the next car of the train, staring at her from a distance.

The train approached the Eighty-Sixth Street station on the Upper East Side and made a complete stop. Most of the commuters exited the train, and Crystal was among those people. Tommy exited behind the group of people, waiting for some people to get between himself and Crystal. He slowly walked behind the group of people, making himself almost invisible, still following Crystal from behind, though she didn't notice his presence. When the group of commuters from the train dispersed to their own destinations, Tommy kept following her from a distance.

When Crystal made it to her apartment building, she entered while Tommy, at the corner of the block of where Crystal lived, hid behind a parked car and looked through the car, watching Crystal enter the building.

After Crystal went into her building, she went to her mailbox and looked over some mail she'd received. As Tommy sat on the curb behind the parked car, where he was hiding, a tear rolled down his cheek. He wished he was with her that night as Crystal went through the second door. When he could no longer see her, Tommy decided it was time for him to go home, and he walked toward the subway with both hands in his jacket pockets.

CHAPTER 4

MONDAY MORNING ARRIVED WITH THE sun, and Tommy rose out of bed. All he could think about was how much he wanted to be with Crystal. When he walked into the living room, he noticed the telephone on the side table. Prior to getting ready for work, he stared at the telephone momentarily, wondering if he should call Crystal and beg her to reconsider her decision and to be with him and be his girlfriend, but he declined. As he walked away from the telephone, he felt a struggle to change his current desire to call to get ready for the work instead.

After a while, Tommy was at his workplace. He entered the messenger center in the basement level of the building and saw old man Louie, his supervisor, along with his coworker Maria preparing the mail of the day.

"Hi, Tommy!" Maria shouted as she walked up to him. She kissed him on the cheek gently.

"Hi, Maria," he responded. He felt a little taken aback by Maria's surprise kiss on the cheek as he went into his locker and hung up his jacket inside the locker.

"All right, you guys, time to go back to work!" said Louie as he dumped some of the office mail into two carts. Tommy helped Louie as Maria went to her desk to answer the suddenly busy telephones and do some paperwork of the day.

"Louie?" Maria called out from her desk.

"Yes, Maria?" Louie answered.

She looked over at Tommy and smiled. Tommy had his back turned toward her, and she checked him out from behind. "Could Tommy and I have lunch together today?" Maria asked while looking at Louie, and then she looked over at Tommy as she smiled, checking him out still, nodding slowly with an expression of approval.

Louie walked over toward Maria. "If it's OK with Tommy, it's OK with me. All right?" Louie asked as he and Maria looked over at Tommy, who was brushing his hair in front of the mirror that hung on the back side of the door of his locker, not knowing what was going on.

Tommy slammed the door of his locker closed and then secured the lock on his locker. When he was ready, he turned around, facing Louie and Maria.

"Well, Tommy?" Louie asked.

"Yeah, fine," Tommy responded, not really sure what was going on, thinking Louie had meant to get the mail out now rather than later, as he grabbed his delivery cart full of the day's mail. "Louie, I'm outa here!" Tommy yelled out while he pushed his cart.

"All right, Tommy!" Louie yelled out.

Tommy looked over at Maria as he pushed the cart toward the doors of the center, on his way to the upper floors. On his way out of the messenger center, still looking at Maria, he crashed his cart into the corner of the doorway.

"Tommy!" Louie yelled out as Maria turned and laughed, hoping he might be attracted to her.

Later on, Tommy came back down from the upper floors after delivering the morning mail to the offices; he entered the messenger center, getting ready for his lunch break.

"OK, you guys are having lunch together today, right? So do not come back late, all right?" Louie shouted from across the center as Maria stood behind her desk, smiling.

"Huh? What?" Tommy responded while he looked at Maria and Louie. "Louie, what joke are you pulling now?"

"It's no joke, Tommy. I asked you earlier, right before you took the morning mail, remember?" Louie asked, approaching Maria's desk.

Tommy thought for a moment as he looked over at Maria. Maria looked down at the floor and then looked back at him from the side of her eyes as she smiled shyly, as though she were saying he should remember, but he really didn't.

"So, Tommy, enjoy your break with Maria, and I'll see you two in an hour, all right?" said Louie, walking with Tommy and Maria to the double doors of the center with his arms around Tommy and Maria and a cigar dangling from the corner of his mouth.

On the way to the elevators, Maria tried to hold Tommy's hand, but he declined her advances. When Tommy pressed the button to go up, one of the elevator cars opened up. He and Maria entered the elevator, and he removed his clip-on tie from his shirt and then unbuttoned the first button as Maria pressed the button for the floor they wanted, going to the employee cafeteria.

When the elevator arrived on the floor where the cafeteria was located, Tommy and Maria stepped out of the elevator among others and went to the cafeteria.

They got in line in the cafeteria, picking out the food they wanted and placing the food on their trays. When they stepped off the line, they found a place to sit and sat down to eat their lunch. Maria was having tuna salad on a roll, and Tommy was having a cheese sandwich. As they ate, they slowly started to have a conversation.

"Tommy, this day is going by so fast, isn't it?" Maria asked as she drank some milk from her glass.

Tommy was in a daze, and Maria noticed.

"Hello? Tommy?" Maria leaned over the table.

Tommy didn't hear Maria, no matter what, and if he did, he really didn't want to. It was as though he were in some kind of trance. All he could think about was Crystal and how beautiful she looked. Why had she walked away from him? Would he ever see her again? He thought of how much he wanted her.

"Hello? Hello, Tommy? Earth to Tommy," Maria said as she sat back in her chair, ready to walk out of the cafeteria.

Tommy smiled as he finally snapped out of it. "Oh, I'm sorry, Maria," he said, smiling halfway.

"Yeah, whatever!" Maria replied, looking elsewhere, as she felt annoyed with him.

"No, really. I'm sorry. I really am. It's just that my brain is someplace else right now." Tommy bit into his cheese sandwich.

"All right. OK," said Maria as she bit into her tuna salad sandwich. "Tommy, can we talk?"

"OK, let's talk," said Tommy as he gave her all the attention a friend could give.

"All right, Tommy, I know we're just coworkers and friends, but during the time we've worked together, I—" Maria paused, trying to find the right words to express what she felt.

"Maria, you are, without a shadow of a doubt, the best coworker I've ever worked with. I mean that." Tommy interrupted her, smiling.

"Thanks, Tommy, but you see, I was—"

"I couldn't find a better coworker!" said Tommy, interrupting again and reassuring her, hoping he was being nice to her as much as he could, while he ate his cheese sandwich.

"But, Tommy!" Maria put down her tuna salad sandwich on the plate.

"What?" Tommy wondered what all of this was leading to.

Maria took a deep breath while she collected her thoughts as she picked up her sandwich again. Then she put the sandwich back down on the plate and rose from where she was sitting. She smiled halfway as she walked over to the salad bar and grabbed a celery stick. After she took a celery stick from the salad bar, she went back to the table, rejoining Tommy, and sat back down in her chair.

"OK, Tommy, what I'm trying to say is that I—"

Tommy interrupted again as Maria put the celery stick into her mouth and bit off a piece, as she was still frustrated with the situation.

"Maria, what in the world do you want to say? Just say it, and get it over with!" said Tommy, feeling some frustration with what was going on.

"All right, Tommy. What I'm trying to say is that I'm in love with you," said Maria as Tommy sat there stunned, not sure what to say. "I've known you for a few years now, so I don't think I'm rushing anything," Maria said while drinking her glass of milk.

Tommy sat there thinking how beautiful she looked, but compared to Crystal? He wanted Crystal. He chewed on a celery stick after sprinkling some salt onto it as his eyes widened in disbelief at the situation.

"So, Tommy, what I was trying to say was that I want to be the woman in your life," said Maria.

Tommy sat there in awe as he removed the celery from his mouth and put the remaining part of the celery stick on his plate. "Maria."

"Yes, Tommy?" Maria wore a hopeful expression on her face.

"Maria, we are coworkers and friends. Good friends. You are definitely a sexy, beautiful woman, but I don't want to go beyond friendship, because I always thought of us as coworkers and, of course, good friends. And besides, I'm currently in love with someone else at this time."

Maria was in a moment of panic. She had not expected the conversation to turn out the way it had. "You have a girlfriend? You never said you were seeing someone." She was trying to turn things around in her favor.

"Well, she's not exactly my girlfriend yet," Tommy responded as he picked up his glass of milk to drink the last bit of it.

"And what's that supposed to mean?" Maria asked as tears welled up in her eyes.

"It means I'm currently working on being involved with someone I want to be with. Maria, I like you an awful lot. I see you as someone I like very much. You are attractive, but I am pursuing someone else right now. And that's it! I just don't like you in the way you want me to." Tommy wiped his mouth with a paper napkin.

"Fine," said Maria, disappointed, with her hands partially covering her face as her elbows rested on the table. "All right. You said what you wanted to say. Now may I be alone?" she asked, still covering her face with both hands and looking at Tommy with one of her partially covered eyes.

"All right. I was about to leave now anyway," said Tommy as he pushed back his chair and rose. He walked over to the trash can, emptied the remains of his lunch into the trash can, and rested the tray on the conveyer belt as he looked over at Maria. Then he walked toward the entrance of the cafeteria and exited.

Maria watched him leave and saw him enter an elevator. She stared at him until the doors slid shut, and she couldn't see him any longer.

Tommy, I'm going to be your woman, even if I have to kill the bitch you are pursuing. I've had my eye on you for a long time, Maria thought as she rose and walked toward the trash cans and conveyer belt.

The end of the workday finally arrived, and Tommy exited the freight elevator with his empty cart, on his way back to the messenger center.

Maria was at her desk, finishing up the paperwork. Louie was cleaning up the center before closing the doors for the day and making sure all the deliveries had been sent out. Tommy entered the center.

"Hey, Tommy!" Louie yelled out while sweeping the floor.

"Hey, Louie!" Tommy yelled back as he returned the cart, putting it with the other carts in the corner of the messenger center.

"All of the day's mail is delivered, right?" Louie asked, bending over with the dustpan to pick up the dirt and dust he'd swept into a small pile. Tommy grabbed the broom and swept the dirt and dust into the dustpan for Louie. "Thanks, Tommy," said Louie as he dumped the dirt and dust into the trash can by the counter.

"All right, Louie," said Tommy. Then he saw Maria at her desk. "Hi, Maria," said Tommy as he put the broom in the closet near the counter.

"Hey, Tommy," Maria responded as she finished up the day's paperwork at her desk.

"Tommy, finish cleaning up. I have to go upstairs for a minute before we shut down, all right?" Louie said as he rushed out of the center.

"All right," said Tommy, and he took a rag on the counter and began wiping down the counter.

As Tommy wiped down the counters, Maria watched him from the side of her eyes, and then she turned around and watched him, getting him to acknowledge her stares while she was still at her desk.

"Tommy?"

"Yes, Maria?" Tommy responded, wiping down the next counter.

"Tommy, I really wish you would reconsider what we talked about at the cafeteria," Maria said while filing the last of the papers from her paperwork.

Tommy looked over at her. "Reconsider what?" he asked while wiping down another counter.

"Reconsider you and I going out together. Reconsider that maybe there could be a possible connection between us." Maria rose from her desk and walked over to him.

Tommy stopped what he was doing as he looked down at the counter. "Now, Maria, I told you that I'm still in love with this other girl," he said, and he continued wiping down the other counters.

"Who is this other girl?" Maria asked.

"Maria, that's none of your business," said Tommy as he threw the rag onto the corner of the counter by the carts. He went into his locker to get his jacket, getting ready to leave the job. He looked over at Maria while putting on his jacket. When he had his jacket partially on, he slammed shut his locker. After he secured his locker, he exited the messenger center as he looked over at Maria.

"Tommy!" Maria yelled out, putting on her jacket. She slammed shut her locker and ran after Tommy as Tommy continued walking toward the elevators.

Louie stepped off the elevator, walked straight, and then turned the corner, passing Tommy as Tommy rushed toward the elevators around the corner.

"Good night, Tommy!" Louie shouted, wondering why he was in a rush.

"Good night, Louie!" Tommy shouted, approaching the elevators.

"Good night, Maria!" Louie shouted.

Maria was walking fast toward the elevators. She didn't say anything, pursuing Tommy, wondering who the girl he was pursuing was.

When Maria arrived at the elevators, she saw the elevator car Tommy was in as the doors were sliding shut. She jumped toward the elevator to put a hand in between the doors, but the doors continued sliding shut. When the doors slid shut completely and the elevator car went up, she quickly jumped into the next one and pressed the lobby button.

Louie stopped midway to the messenger center, wondering what was going on with Tommy and Maria. As he shook his head, he decided to walk fast back toward the elevators.

When Louie arrived back at the elevators, the doors of the elevator car Maria was in had just slid shut, and the elevator car was on its way up. *Well, shit,* Louie thought while scratching his head, walking back to the messenger center, wondering about Tommy and Maria and what was going on between them.

Tommy walked across the lobby and left the building. Maria stepped out of the elevator and walked through the lobby, following not far behind Tommy as he continued walking without knowing he was being followed at a distance.

Where's Crystal's job located? he thought to himself as he pulled out a piece of paper on which he'd written the address of her job. *Hmm, all the way in the West Village part of Manhattan,* he thought while looking at his watch. *She gets off her job an hour from now.*

He went down the concrete steps of the subway with Maria not far behind. Tommy went through the turnstile and onto the platform to wait for the train's arrival. Maria walked down the same concrete steps of the subway slowly and then walked toward the token booth as she watched Tommy. With his back facing her, he looked straight ahead. Tommy didn't feel anyone watching him from behind.

Within minutes, the train arrived, and a group of commuters walked up behind Tommy as they waited for the train to stop.

Maria went through the turnstile and walked to the other end of the platform, getting ready to board the train, a few cars from where Tommy was going to be, hiding in the midst of the crowd, careful not to be discovered. The train's doors slid open, and the commuters entered the train, including Maria and, a few cars down, Tommy.

The car of the train was packed from one end, and when the train had all the commuters on board, the doors slid shut. After the doors shut, the train left the station, on its way to the next station. Maria quickly went through the crowd of riders, going from one car to the next, always looking through the glass before going into the car she was entering. Finally, she looked through the glass and saw, among the groups of riders and the thick waves of people, Tommy standing against the exit doors of the train.

Tommy was looking in the opposite direction, so she entered the car where Tommy was and continued to hide among the other riders, careful not to let Tommy see her.

The train arrived at Tommy's destination: the West Village, close to Lower Manhattan. Tommy and some of the other passengers exited the train, and Maria carefully followed behind.

As the crowd dispersed and everyone went his or her own way out of the subway, Tommy walked over to where Crystal's job was located. Maria followed from across the street.

"Five minutes," Tommy whispered to himself as he looked at his watch. Maria, hiding on the side of a building across the street from where Tommy was hiding, watched Tommy while he awaited Crystal's exit from the building where she worked.

Maria didn't know why Tommy was waiting near a building and just standing by or why he'd arrived at that particular place.

Five o'clock arrived, and people started to exit the building. Tommy looked for Crystal among the homebound crowd. Maria watched from across the street, still hiding on the side of the building, wishing he would be with her.

Patiently, Tommy waited, and out of nowhere, Crystal exited the lobby of the building. She walked out of the building, wearing her Discman headset on her head, on her way to the subway to go home, with a small crowd forming behind her. As she continued walking, Tommy tailgated, walking along the small crowd, careful not to be discovered by Crystal.

Maria watched Tommy follow a crowd, trying to figure out whom he was following. She crossed the street and followed at a distance as she saw Tommy blending into the crowd. While Tommy followed Crystal, Maria followed Tommy. Looking over the sea of heads, she saw a blonde lady walking ahead of the small group of people. Tommy stared in her direction from behind, and Maria thought the blonde could be the girl he'd said he was in love with. It was obvious because the blonde was a little ahead of the quickly shrinking group of people, and Tommy was staring in her direction from behind as he got closer but stayed at a distance.

Crystal entered the subway, going down the concrete steps, with Tommy following not far behind. Maria crossed the street quickly, not far from Tommy.

When Crystal went through the turnstile, Tommy walked down the concrete steps of the subway in a hurry. As he approached the turnstile, a train was just arriving at the station.

Tommy went through the turnstile, and Crystal was twenty feet away from him, listening to her Discman headset. Maria heard the train's arrival and rushed down the steps of the subway as Tommy went through the turnstile. He was now on the platform, with his back facing Crystal. He walked among the crowd, looking for Crystal.

The train made a complete stop, the doors slid open, and the crowd entered the train slowly. Tommy moved in with them, looking for Crystal, as everyone entered the train. At the last moment, he jumped over into the next train car, as he thought he saw her go into that particular car. Maria went through the turnstile quickly and rushed into a crowded car of the train, barely making it into the train as the doors slid shut.

Maria took a deep breath as she slowly looked around the train, and she saw Tommy enter the car she was in. He entered from the back sliding door, coming in from another car, frantically looking around for Crystal, the woman he was pursuing.

Looking around, Tommy realized she was not present in that car. Maria panicked as she saw him moving closer in her direction.

"Oh my God," Maria whispered to herself as she knelt down on the floor of the train, not touching the floor with her hands, so as not to be discovered. She noticed a newspaper underneath the seats, and she looked up from the side of her eyes and saw Tommy. She slowly reached out for the newspaper under the seat as she turned herself to face another direction, with her back facing Tommy. She was able to grab the paper, and then slowly, she rose straight up with the newspaper in her hands and opened up the paper. She turned around slowly, facing Tommy, with the newspaper open between them, hiding behind the newspaper.

After staying in one place while looking for Crystal, Tommy walked slowly about the train, still looking for Crystal.

"Excuse me. Pardon me," Tommy said as he walked through the zombie-like after-work crowd. He walked toward the sliding door at the end of the train and then, feeling a bit worried, went back in the other direction. Maria quickly raised the open newspaper, covering her face.

As he walked by a few other riders, he was within inches of Maria. Maria watched Tommy through a little hole in the paper as he walked right by to the sliding door at the end of the train car. He opened the door and walked out of the car. Between the two cars of the train, he looked through the glass of the sliding door and saw Crystal in the next car. He rode between the two cars of the train for a while as he stared at her. Then he entered the car to be closer to Crystal, to satisfy the hunger of his obsession, which once had been love. Maria, still holding up the newspaper, saw him go into the next car of the train.

Maria lowered the newspaper, giving her aching arms some relief from holding it up, feeling a bit annoyed over the whole thing and a bit jealous. She continued pursuing Tommy from a distance, and she folded the newspaper up while walking to the door at the end of the car. She opened the door, walked between the two cars of the train, entered the next car, and saw Tommy, with his back facing her. As Maria stood near the sliding door, she unfolded the newspaper and opened it up, shielding herself from being discovered, watching Tommy through the hole in the paper. As Maria looked around through the paper, keeping an eye on Tommy, she noticed that there were still a lot of people on the train but not as many as before.

Even though she longed to be close to him, she knew that for now, she must keep her distance from Tommy as she satisfied her hunger of obsession, which had been love at one time. Maria remained at a distance while Tommy kept his distance from Crystal as he watched her from the side of his eyes, careful not to be discovered by her. Crystal sat back in her seat, enjoying the music she was listening to on her Discman and reading a paperback novel, unaware of what was going on in the world around her, unaware of the obsessive impulses that surrounded her.

Within fifteen minutes, Crystal realized she would be getting off at the next stop, so she rose from where she was sitting. Tommy turned around with his back facing her as she looked his way. She did not notice the back she glanced at as she walked toward the doors, awaiting her stop.

When the train arrived at its destination and came to a complete stop, the doors slid open, and Crystal exited, unaware of Tommy's presence, as his back again was facing her. He quickly followed her from behind among the crowd. Behind Tommy, a small crowd stepped off the train. Maria was behind the crowd exiting the train, following at a distance from Tommy.

Crystal quickly walked down the metal steps of the elevated subway, with other commuters behind and in front of her. In the midst of the crowd of commuters, Tommy was present within a few feet of her, while Maria was hiding in the midst of a handful of commuters behind him.

On the street, the small crowds dispersed in different directions, and Crystal walked in the direction of her apartment building, but she was walking slower than usual. Tommy was about twenty-five feet from her, and Maria was about twenty feet away, across the street, from Tommy. She kept an eye on him while the double pursuit continued.

All of a sudden, Crystal stopped walking and turned to the side, facing a window of a department store. She saw something in the window she liked that caught her attention. Tommy didn't expect her to stop, so he froze in place and then slowly turned his body, with his back facing her, hoping she didn't notice him. Her total attention was on the display behind the window as she still listened to her Discman.

With his back turned toward her, he leaned up against the wall with his eyes shut, hoping he wouldn't be discovered. As Crystal continued looking at the display in the window, Tommy continued standing, not knowing what to do, wishing she would walk away. Meanwhile, Maria was watching from across the street, wondering if she and Tommy would ever be together in her future.

⁺⁺✦✦✦✦⁺⁺

Later, Tommy arrived home, and as he entered his apartment, he noticed, when he entered the living room, the flickering light on his answering machine. He rushed to the answering machine, which rested on one of the side tables near the sofa, and pressed the message-retrieval button on the top of the machine.

Beep! There was a short pause, and then somebody hung up.

The answering machine tape rewound itself back to the beginning and then went back to the normal mode as Tommy sat down on the sofa, wondering who might've called. He didn't have caller ID, so he dialed *69 to find out who had called. An operator came on and gave the number that had called. "You can reach this party by dialing one for instant callback," said the recording.

As soon as Tommy wrote down the telephone number, he hung up the telephone. "Who the hell called me?" he said as he anxiously dialed the unfamiliar number.

A pay phone somewhere in Manhattan rang, and a passerby noticed the ringing and picked up the receiver.

"Hello?"

"Yes, I'm Tommy. I received a phone call from this phone number. Did you call?" Tommy asked, still wondering who'd called.

"Sorry, Mac. This is a pay phone. Bye." The passerby hung up the telephone.

All right, it's a pay phone, but who the hell called me? Damn it, Tommy thought as he sat down on the sofa and put his cordless telephone back on the charger.

◆◆◆◆◆

"Hey, Crystal!" Darlene shouted.

Crystal was watching television in the living room, sitting on the recliner with her legs curled up. "Hey, Darlene!" Crystal yelled back as she ate a peanut butter and jelly sandwich.

Darlene entered the living room and sat down on the sofa with her feet up on the coffee table. "Crystal, are you feeling all right?" Darlene asked, feeling a bit concerned about her sister.

"Yes, I'm fine. I'm just feeling a bit strange right now."

"Strange?"

"Yeah. Do you remember that guy I went out with the other night? It was only once."

"Yeah, I remember—the one who answered your personal ad in the paper."

"Yeah! That's the one." Crystal put down her sandwich on a small plate on the coffee table in the middle of the living room.

"All right." Darlene wondered where her sister was leading with this.

"Well, I remember the strangest look on his face. And on the way home from work today, I felt as though someone was following me home. I feel like I'm being followed." Crystal rose from the recliner, went to the sofa, swung Darlene's feet from the sofa, sat down next to Darlene, and folded up her legs.

Darlene looked at Crystal, feeling concerned. "Crystal, you're letting your imagination run away with you. You do this every time you meet someone from the ads. You go out with him once, and if you're not too crazy about him, you feel as though he's stalking you. You feel as though some nut is stalking you." Darlene took Crystal's hands as she rose from the sofa.

"Maybe you're right. You're probably right, Darlene. But somehow, I feel that this situation between Tommy and me isn't over. What if I'm right and he has been stalking me?" Crystal stood up from the sofa.

"Crystal—"

"No, Darlene, this is different! I really felt his presence, and it was strong. When I was on the subway, on my way home! I'm telling you: it's different this time! It wasn't like the other guys, where I dated them once, they followed me once, and then I never heard or saw them again. This guy Tommy—I don't know!" Crystal went into the kitchen, in a daze, walking with Darlene.

All of a sudden, the telephone rang, and Crystal walked back into the living room to answer the phone.

"Hello?" Crystal answered. Silence fell over the line. "Hello?" Crystal said again, feeling a little frustrated and frightened.

"Hello. Crystal?" the caller responded.

"Yes, this is Crystal. Who am I speaking to?" Crystal asked. There was another pause of silence on the telephone line.

"This is Tommy," Tommy responded slowly.

"Tommy?" said Crystal as she thought of what to say next. She began to feel nervous.

Darlene walked into the living room from the kitchen, in disbelief, as she continued listening to the conversation in the living room.

"Yeah, this is Tommy. I was wondering if we could try again. You know, if we could go out again maybe one more time. Did I do something wrong the first time we went out?" Tommy asked.

"But I—" Crystal felt as if she were having a nightmare.

"Is there anything I could do to somehow get us to start over?"

Tommy asked. He was shaking, feeling a bit anxious, as silence fell upon them for a moment.

"Tommy, we only went out once on a date and met once before at a coffeehouse. There was no relationship here, so I don't know why you feel the way you do. And I already told you why we couldn't see each other anymore! I was very honest with you right from the start." Crystal shook while speaking with Tommy.

Darlene was by her sister's side, comforting her, as she knelt next to her.

"I know, Crystal, and I really do appreciate your honesty, but I find myself very much in love with you." Tommy closed his eyes, fearing the outcome.

"What?" Crystal asked in disbelief at what she'd just heard as her eyes widened with horror. Feeling as though she were living a nightmare, she felt as if she were going to faint.

"If I'm making you a little nervous, I—"

"A little nervous?" Crystal yelled.

"Well, I—"

"Tommy, don't call me ever again. Don't come near me!" Crystal shouted, and she hung up the telephone.

Tommy heard the dial tone and put the receiver down on the charger on the side table near his bed.

He went underneath his blanket in his bed, reached over to the side table, turned out the light, turned over, and went to sleep.

CHAPTER 5

THE NEXT DAY ARRIVED, AND Tommy arrived at the messenger center for another day at his job.

"Another day, another dollar!" said Tommy as he walked toward his locker.

Maria and Louie were standing by Maria's desk, and they smiled at him when they noticed him.

"Hi, Tommy," said Maria as she picked up the telephone to answer an incoming call.

"Another day, another half of a dollar, huh?" Louie asked as he gathered the day's mail on the counter.

"Uncle Sam takes his fair share, right?" Tommy asked as he slammed shut his locker, locked it, and then grabbed an empty cart from the corner of the center.

"Yeah, and then some!" said Louie as he dumped some of the day's mail into Tommy's cart and into other carts.

"All right, Louie, I'm outa here!" said Tommy as he pushed the day's mail out the door of the messenger center.

When he went into the hallway of the basement, he straightened out the mail in the cart while Maria watched him from the side of her eyes, still at her desk. He had his back facing her while she stared at him with a deranged look on her face and smiled.

At Crystal's place of employment, it was business as usual in the lobby of the office building.

"Shane and Fender Properties. How may I help you?" Crystal answered the phone at the reception desk.

"Crystal?"

"Yes, Darlene. What's up?" Crystal asked. She was behind a long lobby desk, wearing a headset attached to the main switchboard.

"Are you busy?" Darlene asked.

"For the moment, no. Why?" Crystal asked as she looked around the lobby, making sure she wasn't going to get busy until she was done speaking with her sister.

"Well, Crystal, I'm worried about you. Lately, you're not your usual self. And that phone call you received last night—I'm assuming that was Tommy, right?" Darlene asked.

"You assume right. It was Tommy," Crystal responded, wondering where this conversation was going.

"All right, so what did he say that made you shake like that?" Darlene asked.

"Well, he said—hold on. I have another call. Hold on." Crystal placed Darlene on hold and answered the switchboard.

Tommy arrived back at the messenger center an hour later.

"Hi, Tommy!" said Maria with a wide grin on her face.

"Hey, Maria!" said Tommy as he parked the empty cart alongside the counter, with his back facing her.

"Tommy?" Maria called out from her desk.

Tommy turned around, facing Louie, who was also by Maria's desk, as Maria talked on the telephone.

"Why don't you take a fifteen-minute break and then, at one, take your lunch break?" Louie asked.

Tommy looked at his watch: 10:45 in the morning. "All right, I'll be back at eleven," said Tommy, removing his smock. He laid it on one of the carts by the counter.

"Can I go too, Louie?" Maria asked as she rose from her desk slowly as Tommy exited the messenger center quickly.

Louie looked up at the ceiling, trying to deal with her whining voice. "Go! Go!" Louie yelled to Maria, feeling a bit annoyed with her whining, as he pointed toward the double doors at the entrance of the center and smiled.

Maria exited the center quickly, hoping she could catch up with Tommy, as Tommy proceeded toward the elevators.

As Tommy was approaching the elevators, Maria was catching up with him. As she walked quickly around the bend, she saw him pressing the call button on the wall, waiting for an elevator.

"Tommy!" Maria shouted, catching up with him, getting closer to the elevators. When she reached Tommy from behind, Tommy turned around.

"Oh, hi," said Tommy as one of the elevators arrived at the basement level, and the doors slid open.

Tommy and Maria both entered the elevator.

"So, Maria, I guess you're on your break now?" he asked as the elevator doors slid shut. Maria and Tommy looked into each other's eyes.

"Yes, I am, Tommy," said Maria as she smiled. She grabbed his left hand and held on to it tightly, as though she were afraid to let go.

As soon as the elevator arrived in the lobby and the doors slid open, Tommy went forward, letting go of her hand and exiting the elevator, making sure he was ahead of her, trying to avoid her further. Leaving her behind, Tommy went forward to the outside of the building while Maria tried to keep up with him from behind.

◆◆◆◆◆◆

Back at Crystal's place of employment, Crystal was just finishing the call that had interrupted the conversation with Darlene.

"I'm sorry for keeping you on hold like that, but we had a little rush," said Crystal as she took a deep breath.

"That's all right, Crystal. You're at work. There's no need to apologize. Now, getting back to what we were talking about," said Darlene.

"Oh yeah. When he called last night, he said he loved me. Or that he was in love with me. And he asked if there was anything he could do to make things right between us," Crystal said.

"I guess he really has problems, huh?" Darlene asked.

"Yes, he does. Major problems, girl. I don't know, but I feel like he won't call again after what I told him last night. I told him never to call me again or come anywhere around me ever again." Crystal laughed.

"I remember. You go, girl!" Darlene shouted into the telephone as she laughed along with Crystal.

Crystal quickly quieted her laughter, remembering she was still at work.

＊＊＊＊＊＊

Back at Tommy's place of employment, Tommy and Maria were sitting by the big fountains along Sixth Avenue, on the side of the building where they worked.

"Do you know what I like about walking around Rockefeller Center?" Tommy asked Maria as they looked at the shooting waters of the big fountains.

"What?" Maria asked as she smiled while she moved closer to him. They were sitting on a cement bench between two trees.

"These beautiful, big water fountains on a clear, cool, sunny day," said Tommy as he rose from where he was sitting. Maria rose as well. Tommy started walking away from the fountains, and Maria followed behind, tugging at his arm. Tommy stopped walking momentarily and turned around quickly as she stood behind him with a half smile.

"Look, Tommy, I have to tell you something. I don't know this girl Crystal. I think that's her name," said Maria, and Tommy nodded.

"All right, so?" Tommy responded, trying to be patient.

"I don't know this girl Crystal, the girl you talk about, but I want to let you know that I still want and need you in my life." Maria looked into his eyes as a slight pause came between them.

"Well, Maria, I want Crystal in my life, and like I told you once before, we can be friends, and that's it. All right, Maria?" Tommy looked at his watch.

"Yes, Tommy, but—"

He walked toward the entrance of the building. "Maria, we have to get back to the messenger center. We are about to be late in getting back from break, so let's go."

Tommy and Maria rushed back into the building and back into the elevator, on their way back down to the basement.

When the end of the workday arrived, Tommy was the last messenger clerk to enter the center with his cart, which he pushed from behind.

"Tommy! Time to go home!" Louie shouted as he put the broom back in the closet.

While Tommy took off his smock, he looked at the big clock that hung over the doorway; it was 4:05. "Oh shit. I'm going to be late," Tommy whispered as he began to panic while putting on his sneakers and his long-sleeved black turtleneck shirt. "Good night, everyone!" Tommy shouted as he exited the messenger center with Maria behind him at a distance.

Louie sat on one of the stools, scratching his head, wondering where Tommy was off to in a rush with Maria trailing him from behind.

"Tommy! Tommy!" Maria shouted, walking fast, trying to keep up with him, as he walked toward the elevators. He turned the corner in the basement with Maria several feet behind.

Hearing Maria, he stopped midway to the elevators. "What, Maria?" Tommy responded angrily.

"Tommy, you know that you don't have to go on with this stupid thing!" said Maria as she thought about the time he'd followed Crystal while she'd followed him. She grabbed his left arm.

Tommy shrugged off her hand, and a moment of silence fell between them. Then, all of a sudden, Tommy was possessed with an evil, demented grin she was familiar with as he slowly turned around and proceeded toward the elevators.

Louie was walking right behind Maria. When Tommy smiled, Maria had a chill up her spine, and she became frightened. She and Louie just stood there looking at each other, because Louie had heard and seen what Tommy sounded and looked like before Tommy proceeded toward the elevators.

"Jesus Christ, what the hell was that all about?" Louie asked. He never had seen Tommy react like that with anyone.

"I don't know. I really wish I knew," said Maria as she turned around with her hands covering her beautiful Peruvian face.

The elevator approached the lobby level, and after the doors slid open, Tommy walked out of the elevator, through the lobby, and out the door, on his way to Crystal's workplace.

+ + + + + +

At Crystal's workplace, Crystal was sitting on her chair, conversing with coworkers, at the reception desk.

"So, Crystal, how's your social life?" one of her coworkers asked.

Crystal smiled as she thought about her current situation, tallying up all the calls she'd had all day. "Don't ask," said Crystal as she continued her work at the desk with one of her coworkers, Sally, looking over her shoulder. Crystal looked up at her, smiling. "So, Sally, how did you do today?" Crystal asked as she stood up and started putting on her blue jean jacket.

Sally looked at Crystal as she walked toward the back behind the desk. "Don't ask," said Sally as she covered her face with both hands, laughing, and soon after, Crystal joined in the laughter.

"Bye, Sally. Have a nice night," said Crystal as she walked away, on her way home, walking toward the elevators to go to the lobby level.

When she approached the two elevators, one opened up, and she entered and pressed the button to go down to the lobby level.

+ + + + + +

Tommy waited on the side of the building for the exit of Crystal Farnsworth like a tiger waiting for its prey.

When the elevator arrived at the lobby level, Crystal walked out of the elevator and then left through the Fifth Avenue side entrance. She walked toward Madison Avenue. Tommy saw her approaching the area where he was, and as he turned around quickly, she walked right by him, not noticing his presence. He held his breath in fear of being discovered by her.

Suddenly, she stopped and turned around, feeling as if she were being followed. Tommy had his back still facing her as he continued holding his breath with his eyes shut as she wore a weird expression on her face.

Crystal quickly turned around and continued her walk toward the subway to go home as Tommy followed her.

When Crystal arrived at the subway, she again stopped walking and stood still in place. Tommy was just few feet away, staring at her from a distance. He slowly turned around with his back facing her as she turned around and walked into a women's shoe store. The subway was only ten feet away from the store.

After she entered the shoe store, Tommy followed her inside. He noticed he still had his shirt and tie underneath his jacket; he hadn't changed before leaving the messenger center. Thinking for a moment, he came up with an idea. While Crystal was browsing various shoes on the shelves against the wall, Tommy went back toward the front of the store and used the big mirror on the side to make sure his appearance was neat and salesman-like while looking around, making sure he wouldn't be discovered by Crystal as she continued browsing the many shoes on display.

He noticed the store was starting to get a little crowded, filling up with the after-work crowd. He used the crowd to his advantage as he approached Crystal from behind.

"Crystal?" Tommy called out.

As she heard her name called out by a familiar voice, she jumped.

"Tommy?" Crystal responded as she turned around abruptly, not believing her eyes.

"Yes," Tommy answered as he smiled sheepishly.

"I thought I told you I didn't want to see you or hear from you anymore," she whispered, trying not to make a scene in the shoe store.

"Well, Crystal, I know what you said, but you see, I work here," said Tommy, still smiling.

"You work here? I thought you said you work in an office building. In a messenger center," she said, feeling a bit nervous.

"I still work there at the office building. See?" said Tommy as he showed his work ID with his picture on it.

"So why do you work here?" she asked as she looked around the shoe store as he put the ID back in his wallet.

"This is my part-time job I have on the side." Tommy smiled while looking around the store. "So may I help you find a pair of shoes?" he asked with an innocent expression.

"Well, I don't know. I remember the last conversation on the telephone we had, and I—" Crystal looked around the store, not sure whether to trust him or not.

"I'm sorry for being so persistent. I really am sorry. I promise I'll be good," said Tommy as he smiled, and soon she smiled back, regaining some trust.

"Oh, all right. No, maybe I should ask someone else to help me," said Crystal as she looked around the store.

"Well, all right, I understand." Tommy looked down at the floor with a frown. Then he turned around, looking up, acting as if he were trying to find another salesman to help her.

"Oh, wait. All right. You can help me. No trouble, right?" she said.

"I promise. No trouble. Thank you for this opportunity, Crystal," said Tommy as he turned around with a wide grin on his face.

"And if you step out of line," Crystal responded, pointing her finger at him.

"Don't worry. I'll treat you right," said Tommy as he smiled, trying to reassure her.

"If you don't, I'll report you to your manager in the store, all right?" said Crystal as she walked the aisles of shoes as Tommy followed behind.

"All right, let's see. What particular brand are you looking for?" Tommy asked while she looked at the numerous brands on the shelves.

"Do you have Sade brand?" she asked, looking at the other brands on the shelves.

"I believe we do. Let me check in the back stockroom," said Tommy, and he went to the back of the store to see where the stockroom was.

"Hey, dude!" someone in the back called out behind the double doors, where the backstock was.

"Yeah?" Tommy responded when he went behind the double doors into the back area. He turned around, facing one of the clerks of the store.

"How come I've never seen you around here before, man?" the store clerk asked as he approached Tommy.

"Well, you probably haven't seen me because this is my very first day here." Tommy smiled, trying to convince the employee.

"That might be true, dude," the clerk responded as he smiled.

"It's true. And your name?" Tommy asked as he put his right hand out.

"Oh, right. The name is Wilson, but everyone calls me Will." Will put out his right hand to meet Tommy's right hand, and they shook hands.

"All right, Will. I need a pair of Sade shoes," said Tommy as he smiled halfway while looking around.

Crystal was still next to the shelves where Tommy had left her, waiting for Tommy to return to help her with a pair of shoes. She felt a little doubt about his employment with the shoe store.

"No, we don't sell Sade here. I wish we did. Sorry, man," said Will.

"That's all right, man. Later, dude." Tommy went toward the double doors, going back to Crystal, who was still waiting for him.

"Yeah, it's been great meeting you, man. Rock on!" Will shouted as Tommy went onto the selling floor.

"Yeah, cool," said Tommy as he walked toward Crystal. "Crystal, we don't sell that brand of shoes. Sorry for the long wait. How about these shoes, or how about these?" Tommy asked, starting to really feel like a salesman.

From the other side of the store, a cashier noticed Tommy as Tommy was dealing with Crystal, but she didn't recognize him as an employee of the store.

"Well, all right, let's see how it feels. I'm a size six and a half," said Crystal as she sat down on one of the chairs to try on the shoes after taking off her shoes.

Tommy held up two different pairs of shoes, letting her choose which ones she wanted, as he smiled, not believing what a great time he was having.

"All right, I'll choose that pair." Crystal pointed toward the ones in his left hand, and he put the ones in his right hand back on the shelf.

"Here we go," said Tommy as he put the box of shoes underneath his arm, not paying any attention to the cashier, who was suspicious and was watching him from behind. He'd forgotten he didn't really work there.

Crystal, waiting to try on the pair of shoes, began feeling a little annoyed with him, but she wanted to tough it out, get her shoes, and then go home.

Tommy's face lit up as he stood with the box of shoes under his arm and stared at her feet. Her feet were covered in coffee-toned stockings. She moved them slowly in a circular motion, stretching them a little bit, as she waited for him. He was thinking that he was going to be the lucky guy who sold shoes to this beautiful woman. He had a demented look on his face as he walked in front of her. She looked up at him with a half smile on her face, somewhat frightened.

He knelt down in front of her and took Crystal's left foot gently. Crystal felt wary of his touch, while he felt as if he were dreaming and then became optimistic about them possibly coming together in the near future.

He stared at her left foot while holding it as Crystal wondered what in the world he was doing as she stared at him.

"Tommy, I meant what I said earlier," said Crystal. She felt like leaving the store.

"I know, I know. Don't worry," said Tommy as he put the new shoe on her left foot as one of the assistant managers walked over toward them from the other end of the store.

When Tommy stood up abruptly from kneeling, Crystal rose too.

"So how does it feel, Crystal?" he asked her as he watched from the side of his eyes as someone walked toward him.

"It feels really good," said Crystal as she put the other shoe on the other foot and began walking around. She continued walking around, feeling the shoes, making sure they felt right for her feet, as Tommy noticed the woman approaching closer.

"Well, keep walking around, and see if this pair of shoes is what you really want," he told Crystal as he smiled halfway, looking around the store, feeling a little pressured.

Crystal looked at him without saying anything.

"All right?" Tommy asked as Crystal continued walking around, trying to feel the comfort of the shoes.

"This really feels good on my feet. I think I'll buy this pair of shoes," said Crystal.

Tommy turned his head and saw the woman walking their direction stop midway because the security guard was speaking with her for a moment. Tommy began breathing easier, relieved at the time he had now to escape. As the security guard spoke with the woman, who was the manager of the shoe store, they both stared at Tommy. The security guard had had his eye on him the moment he entered the store. By that time, Tommy was panicking. When he looked over toward the cashier and saw the expression on her face, he knew she knew what was going on.

"You're going to buy these shoes, Crystal?" he asked her as she removed the shoes and put on her sneakers, sitting where she had sat before.

"Yes, I will buy this pair of shoes just as soon as I put back on my sneakers," said Crystal. Tommy walked slowly backward toward the swinging doors in the back of the store as Crystal tied her sneakers' laces.

When he went through the swinging doors to the other side, Crystal stood up and looked around, trying to find out where Tommy was.

As Tommy turned around after going through the back doors, he walked into Wilson in the stockroom.

"Whoa!" Wilson said as he and Tommy bumped into each other. Wilson was carrying a few boxes of shoes, and they fell onto the floor.

"Oh, I'm sorry," said Tommy as he quickly turned around. He hadn't known there was someone standing behind him.

"That's all right. Going home already?" Wilson asked as he and Tommy picked up the shoes, placing them back in the right boxes.

"Yeah, leaving early today because I have a dentist appointment," said Tommy as he gave two of the boxes back to Wilson on top of the box he was holding.

"Oh yeah?" Wilson smiled.

Tommy gave a half smile of his own, feeling a bit edgy, while walking toward the outside back door, which would put him out of the store. "So I'll see you tomorrow!" Tommy shouted as he exited through the back door.

"OK! See you tomorrow! Take care!" Wilson shouted as he went through the swinging double doors onto the selling floor of the store with the three boxes of shoes he was carrying. As Wilson walked toward the shelves to restock the shelves with more shoes, the cashier at the front of the store waved him down to come to the front while she was taking care of Crystal at the register. Wilson noticed the cashier, so he put the boxes of shoes down on the floor, near the shelves he was working with, and walked to the front of the store, to the cashier.

"Wilson, did you see anyone suspicious today posing as a salesman?" the cashier asked as she was placing the pair of shoes Crystal had purchased in a plastic bag as Crystal gave the cashier her credit card.

"Well, I did see a new salesman in the back stockroom earlier today," Wilson said as the cashier gave Crystal her credit card back.

Crystal listened to what had been going on.

"Wilson, the new supposed salesman you saw today was not a salesman. The salesman who's normally here was out to lunch," said the cashier as she gave the plastic bag to Crystal, along with a receipt for her to sign and her credit card.

As Crystal signed the receipt, she wore an expression of wariness, not sure what had taken place there at the shoe store.

"Excuse me, ma'am. Did you just say that the gentleman who was helping me earlier was not a salesman?" Crystal asked as she grabbed her bag of shoes.

"Yes. As I just said to our stockman, the man who was helping you was posing as one of our salesmen but was not one of our salesmen. I don't know who the hell that guy was," said the cashier. The assistant manager listened to the conversation at a distance as everyone wondered who the man was, except for Crystal, who knew what was going on.

"Well, I know who it was," said Crystal. She felt annoyed as she took her bag of shoes and proceeded to the front doors of the store as the cashier and the salesman watched.

As she approached the front doors of the store, the assistant manager ran up to her before she exited the store. "Oh, ma'am? Miss?" the assistant manager called out.

Crystal stopped at the open door and turned around partially. "Yes?" Crystal responded, holding her bag of shoes.

"I am the assistant manager of the shoe store. I and my staff here at the store want to apologize for what happened. I want to promise you that this will never happen again. We've never had a situation like that before. It's crazy, but let me just give you a coupon for fifty percent off on your next purchase, all right?" The assistant manager reached into her pocket, pulled out the coupon, and handed it to her.

"Thank you." Crystal took the coupon and put it in her bag.

"I am truly sorry for this. And I hope you'll come back again," said the assistant manager as she smiled and extended a hand.

"Yeah, it's all right. Thanks for the coupon. And I'm sorry this happened too." Crystal smiled halfway as she exited the store. The assistant manager looked a bit worried as she looked around the shoe store behind her.

Crystal proceeded to the subway, thinking about and being conscious of Tommy lurking around with each step she took, going down the concrete steps of the subway, underground, underneath the city, on her way home.

She looked around as she went through the turnstile and onto the platform, making sure Tommy wasn't around. As she looked around, some of the people waiting for their trains looked back at her. Some whistled at her, and some of them looked down at her. She wanted so much to be at home, where she was safe and warm, she thought.

As she walked around on the platform, waiting for her train, she was perspiring a little on her face. As she walked to the end of the platform, she wanted to turn back and walk toward the middle of the platform, but as she turned around to walk toward the middle, behind her was a cement stairway, and Tommy was watching Crystal from behind the cement stairway. He'd put on his sunglasses to disguise himself from a distance. As a train arrived at the station, Crystal rushed to the middle of the platform, and Tommy rushed to catch up with her at a distance while putting on his favorite New York Yankees cap.

Tommy, at a distance from Crystal, hid within a small crowd of commuters. Crystal and two others stood near the yellow line of the platform as the train stopped at the station. When the train made a complete screeching stop, the doors slid open. Crystal and the crowd of commuters, with Tommy in the back, entered the uptown train, all longing to be at their homes as they rode through the rush hour. The doors slid closed, and the train proceeded to the next station. Crystal went all the way to the end of the car to sit, while Tommy went to the other end to sit, watching from a distance the woman he wanted more than anything in the world.

When the train finally made it to Crystal's destination, she exited the train, and Tommy exited too, with his back facing her. Within a few feet of her, slowly, he followed her as Crystal went through the turnstile, on her way home to her apartment building. As Crystal exited the subway, Tommy followed at a distance.

As Tommy was following Crystal, someone was following him as well. When Tommy exited the subway, pursuing Crystal from a distance, Maria exited the subway, following Tommy from a distance. Crystal only lived a couple of blocks from the subway. As Crystal proceeded to her apartment building with Tommy walking behind, Maria was behind Tommy at a distance.

Crystal walked up the block and then turned a corner. Tommy, a few feet away from her, turned the same corner, and when he turned the corner, he was face-to-face with Crystal!

"Tommy! How could you?" Crystal asked, feeling angry and, at the same time, frightened and shaken somewhat by the drama taking place.

"Well, Crystal, if you would just calm down, I could explain why I'm here," said Tommy as he held both his hands up.

"Don't explain! And as far as what happened at the shoe store, why did you have to deceive me like that, saying you work there part-time, when I would've eventually found out the truth?" Crystal asked with tears in her eyes. She was scared, showing a frightened expression on her face.

Tommy looked down at the concrete sidewalk, and then he looked up. "I'm sorry for lying to you and saying I was a salesman, when in fact, I'm not. I just wanted to be near you." Tears formed in his eyes, and Crystal began to feel sorry for him.

"Tommy, you are a nice guy. Despite the way you treated me the night we went out, I really had to be truthful about the way I feel. This isn't going to work between you and me, with us being together." Crystal looked down at the sidewalk.

"Why not? What did I do so wrong?" Tommy asked as his glasses started to fog up from perspiration.

"Tommy, like I told you before, you didn't do anything wrong on the night we went out. I'm just not attracted to you. I just don't like you like that. There's no chemistry here between us. It's just not going to work, all right?" Crystal said.

Tommy looked down at the sidewalk again. The sidewalk was partially covered with city soot and asphalt. Then he looked up at her. "All right. You won't see me again," he said as he looked into her eyes.

"Tommy, if you come anywhere near me again, I will get an order of protection against you, and that means the police will be involved in this," Crystal said as she threw her long blonde hair back.

"Yeah, but, Crystal, I can't go on without you," said Tommy as he removed his black-framed glasses and stared at her, begging with his eyes for her affections.

"What! You are obsessed! Oh my God. You need help!" said Crystal as she started walking away from Tommy.

"Crystal!" Tommy yelled out, partially whispering, because he didn't want to draw any attention, and she turned around quickly while he looked around.

"You answered my personal ad, we met at the coffeehouse, and then we went out once! Get it? We only went out once! Only one time! You don't even know me!" Crystal shouted, annoyed. Passersby stared, noticing the tension between them. She didn't want to make a scene. She was starting to feel sorry for him, but at the same time, she didn't want to be with him or continue this bizarre situation.

He put back on his glasses after wiping them. "I know, I know. I know I don't know you, but I know I'm in love with you," said Tommy as he stared at her as though he'd known her for years.

Crystal's eyes widened with discomfort as she felt his obsession grow with each minute they were together. "In love? But you don't even know me! How could you be in love with me?" Crystal asked, feeling frustrated about the situation.

"I don't know. I don't know! All I know is that whenever I'm around you, I—" Tommy stopped speaking as he closed his eyes while he smiled, in a daze, as though he were drunk.

Crystal wore a disgusted look on her face. "Wait! Wait right there! I don't want to see you anywhere around me, and next time, I will call the police! I will call the cops! Do you understand?" Crystal shouted as tears flowed down her cheeks. She looked around, trying to draw attention now, because she was becoming frightened by his weird expressions on his face, which showed signs that this situation wouldn't go away anytime soon. Tommy backed up a little bit while looking into her eyes with a serious look on his face. He had tears of his own streaming down his face, and his glasses were fogging up again.

"Fine. Bye. No problem," said Tommy, and he walked by, shoving her with his shoulder as he walked away.

Crystal turned around and saw him turn the corner on his way to the subway. She walked toward a deli, and when she arrived at the deli, she leaned up against the brick wall, taking a deep breath and letting it out with a sigh, relieved that nothing serious had happened and feeling exhausted over the drama in her life, as she looked up at the evening sky. The stars glowed brightly in the dark sky.

As Tommy went up the steps into the subway, Maria was waiting for his arrival. She stood right behind the token booth. She saw him walk down the steps. Maria continued watching Tommy as he approached the turnstile, but instead of going through, he stopped.

He looked over his shoulder for a moment with an expression of concern, feeling as though he were being followed. But then he shrugged it off, thinking he was probably thinking about Crystal, and he walked through the turnstile, laughing to himself a little bit.

Maria was still behind the token booth, breathing heavily, still worried that she would be discovered, as he walked onto the platform.

With his hands in his pockets, as the train arrived in the station, he walked up to the train, near the yellow line on the platform. As Maria noticed the train and where Tommy was going, she hurried through the turnstile and onto the platform, staying behind the small crowd of commuters, with Tommy in the front of the small crowd.

When the train made a complete stop and the doors slid open, she entered the car of the train with the small crowd. Tommy walked fast into the next car ahead of that car.

When everyone was inside the train, the doors slid shut, and the train proceeded to its next destination. Maria looked through the glass on the side door at the end of the car and saw Tommy in the next car.

At that moment, Tommy happened to look toward the next car, toward Maria, as Maria stared at him from the other car. Tommy couldn't believe his eyes. He thought he saw Maria in the next car of the train, looking at him through the glass of the side door of the car.

Maria realized Tommy had discovered her. She knelt down, hiding herself, immediately when Tommy turned his head, and she moved forward through the crowd, crawling. She felt embarrassed while moving forward to the other side of the car.

Tommy rose from where he was sitting, rushed to the side door in his car, and quickly entered the next car, looking for Maria among a large number of riders.

When the train stopped at the next station and the doors slid open, Maria quickly rushed out while bent over. Within seconds, Tommy was at the end of the car of the train. As the doors slid shut, he turned around and saw a woman with her back turned toward him. She had long black hair midway down her back and light brown skin, and she looked exactly like Maria from behind. Tommy couldn't believe his eyes and approached her from behind.

"Maria? Maria!" Tommy called out angrily.

The woman turned around, and he quickly realized she was not Maria. He felt embarrassed.

"Excuse me?" the woman responded, wondering, as he stood in front of her looking apologetic.

"I'm sorry. I thought you were someone else. Sorry," said Tommy as he looked around the train. The other commuters looked at him strangely as he walked away and into the next car through the side door, where he had been before, where he wished he'd stayed. After he entered the car, he found a place to sit, and when he sat down, he covered up his face with his hands in frustration over Crystal's grim rejections earlier that evening, not realizing that several people down from where he was sitting, Maria was sitting there staring at him.

-◆◆◆◆◆◆-

The next day arrived in New York City. Tommy arrived at work at the messenger center. When Tommy entered the messenger center, Louie was lining up the carts, getting them ready for the day's deliveries of mail, as usual, and Maria was sorting out the day's paperwork at her desk.

Tommy walked over to his locker and put on his work smock as he curiously watched Maria from behind. With her back facing him, Maria felt his wondering stares while he was getting ready.

"So, Tommy, how was your evening?" Louie asked, and Maria looked up at Tommy from the side of her eyes while filing away some of her papers as she held her breath.

"Well, I—" Tommy looked at Maria and then looked back at Louie. "Honestly, I had an interesting evening, Louie," said Tommy as he looked over at Maria again. She was at her desk, and she was a little embarrassed, feeling a little uncomfortable with the conversation between Louie and Tommy.

"How about you, Maria?" Tommy asked Maria.

"Huh? Me? I was in my apartment, watching *Seinfeld* and then the news. And after the news, I went straight to bed," said Maria as she went back to her paperwork, hoping the topic of what she had done last night would end quickly.

"That's wonderful! Everybody had something going on last night except for me!" Louie shouted as he continued working.

Tommy walked over to him. "Oh yeah? You were bored last night?" Tommy asked as Maria looked over to see what was going on, listening to their conversation, as she was concerned about Louie. Tommy helped him put the mail in the carts.

"Did I have a boring evening last night? You could say that my night sucked!" Louie shouted as he threw the last of the mail into the last cart while he looked at Tommy.

When lunchtime approached, Tommy walked over to a pay phone and dialed the number to Crystal's apartment. Her answering machine picked up the call.

"I know you're not at home yet. I just wanted to ask you if we could talk. I've come to a realization that I need you in my life, and I was thinking maybe, deep down inside, you might have something in your heart for me. Well, hopefully we'll talk soon. Bye." Tommy hung up the phone.

After hanging up, he turned around and rushed away from the line of pay phones. As he left the area, Maria was on the side, near the line of pay phones. She'd overheard him leave his message on Crystal's voice mail. She stepped out from the side and watched Tommy walk away from the area. He never noticed her presence near him, as his thoughts were on Crystal. Maria continued watching him from a distance as she walked around the side of the building to meet with Tommy. As he turned around the bend, Maria was walking by in the opposite direction.

"Tommy!" Maria called out to him, and his concentration broke, as he had been thinking about Crystal.

"Oh, hi, Maria." Tommy smiled, trying to be nice.

"Tommy, how about lunch on me?" Maria asked as she approached him.

"Maria, actually, I have something I have to do right now. So I'll see you later, all right? Sorry." Tommy walked away, waving a hand while he left.

"Oh, that's OK," said Maria as she again watched him walk away. As she stood there alone, feeling frustrated, she covered her face with her hands.

When it was time to go home once again, Tommy removed his work smock and hung it up on the hook in his locker as Maria observed him from behind.

"So, Maria!" Tommy shouted to Maria as he turned around. Maria jumped nervously, not expecting him to shout, as he quickly turned around.

"Yes, Tommy?" Maria responded, not knowing what to expect, as she smiled nervously.

"Maria, I'll see you tomorrow! Be good!" said Tommy as he smiled on his way out of the messenger center.

Maria watched him leave from behind. She was behind her desk, sweeping the floor. "Someday. Someday it will be you and me," she mumbled to herself.

Louie overheard her mumble from behind. He just stood there without her noticing his staring as he wondered about her.

Tommy arrived home at his apartment after a quick day at work. He entered his apartment and saw his answering machine light flickering as he closed the door of his apartment.

He entered the living room, turned on the light, and anxiously walked over to his answering machine. He pressed the message-retrieval button.

Beep!

"Tommy, I told you I didn't want to be with you. I appreciate the fact that you're interested in me, but I'm not the least bit interested in you. Now, I have to insist that you never call me again. If you call me again or come anywhere near me or where I live or work, I won't hesitate in calling the police. If you persist in interfering in my life, I will call the police next time. I mean it. So help me God! This is harassment, and I won't take it!" Crystal shouted, and then she hung up the phone.

There was a short dial tone. *Beep!* The answering machine sounded as the tape rewound itself to the beginning.

Tommy looked straight ahead in the living room, and then he looked at his stereo while he walked toward it.

When he arrived at his stereo, he reached for a Beatles CD as he turned on the stereo. He placed the CD in the CD player of the stereo and pressed the button. He chose the song "I Want You (She's So Heavy)," and it began to play.

As soon as the song started to play, he turned off the lights in the living room and then walked into the kitchen and turned on the light in the kitchen. He then went back into the living room and sat down on the recliner, sitting all the way back and looking spookily straight across the living room into space, while he sang the words to the song while he thought about Crystal.

"Crystal. Crystal." He slowly repeated her name as the classic rock song continued playing on the stereo as he faded away into the evening.

——————— ✦✦✦✦✦ ———————

A new day dawned, and Tommy entered the messenger center, ready for a new day at work. Maria was at her desk, doing some paperwork, and noticed Tommy enter the messenger center.

"Hi, Tommy!" Maria shouted as she cleaned out her desk.

"Hi, Maria," said Tommy as he opened his locker and reached inside for his work smock.

"Hey, Tommy!" Louie shouted, taking a sip of his morning coffee.

"Hey, Louie! What's up?" Tommy asked as he smiled while putting on his smock.

"Oh, nothing much but SOS," said Louie as he bit into a bagel smeared with butter.

"SOS?" Tommy asked.

"Yeah, SOS!" said Louie while he looked at Tommy with a weird expression on his face.

"OK, Louie," Tommy responded with a concerned look on his face while smiling continuously as he slammed shut the door to his locker.

"Tommy, don't you know what SOS means? Same old shit! You dumb shit!" Louie shouted out, laughing with a few other workers from the center.

"Yeah, and a different day, right?" Tommy asked while laughing too.

"Right!" Louie said, still laughing, as he started to load up one of the carts for the morning deliveries to the upper floors.

As Tommy entered the elevator with a cart full of the day's mail, he walked into a messenger from the outside accidentally.

"Whoo!" the long-haired messenger said, wearing sunglasses, listening to his CD headset.

"I'm sorry," said Tommy as he pulled back his cart, fitting the cart into the elevator, going around the messenger. As the elevator door slid shut, Tommy stared at the tall, lean, long-haired messenger.

The messenger started bopping to the music from his CD player, back and forth. He didn't smile. Tommy smiled, feeling a little uncomfortable, as the elevator filled with many people, and he was tucked into a corner of the elevator. The messenger was chewing on bubble gum, and he blew bubbles with his gum.

The elevator reached its destination, the top floor of the building, and Tommy exited the elevator with his cart full of the day's mail.

He walked over to the sliding glass doors of the office space and placed his access card through the card reader, and the glass doors slid open. He entered the reception area, and Desiree, the receptionist, looked up from her paperwork and noticed Tommy as she took a bite of her cinnamon roll and then placed it on a plate next to her morning coffee.

"Hi, Tommy," said Desiree as she gathered some of her paperwork at her desk.

"Hi, Desiree," Tommy responded while taking a few envelopes out from the cart.

"So, Tommy, how's everything?" Desiree asked while taking a sip of her coffee.

"Everything is fine, except for—" Tommy laid some of the day's mail on her desk.

"Except for what, Tommy?" Desiree asked as she smiled at him, also wearing a concerned look on her face, as she leaned forward at her desk.

Tommy moved in closer to her and whispered near her ear. "Well, actually, I'm trying to go out with this girl I know, and I—"

"No kidding? Our little Tommy's in love?" Desiree asked.

Tommy stood straight up at the front of her desk while he looked around, making sure no one had heard their conversation. "Sh!" he said as he held her hands at the top of the desk and looked around the reception area nervously.

Soon after, he left with his cart to deliver the rest of the day's mail, covering his lips with one finger, silently telling Desiree not to say anything. Desiree copied the gesture, covering her lips with her index finger as well, as she smiled.

As he went into the inner office area, Desiree watched him as she shook her head.

Tommy completed the day's final mail delivery on the upper floors of the building and then reentered the messenger center, as it was time to get ready to go home.

"Hey, Tommy!" Maria shouted from her desk as she waved to him.

"Hey, Maria!" Tommy shouted, waving back, as he walked toward his locker while removing his work smock. Then he opened up his locker.

"Tommy, it's going to get very busy tomorrow, so get some rest tonight, all right?" said Louie with one hand on Tommy's shoulder from behind.

"All right, Louie," said Tommy as he hung up his smock, and he put on his shirt and looked over at Louie. "Look, Louie, I'll be all right tomorrow, all right?" Tommy responded while putting on his sneakers.

"All right, Tommy. Just make sure—that's all," said Louie as he wondered why Tommy was so touchy.

"See you guys tomorrow," said Tommy, and he exited the messenger center and went to the elevators to go up to the lobby level of the building.

Tommy pressed the call button for an elevator's arrival and waited. An elevator arrived, and when the doors slid open, he entered with a few others and pressed the button for the lobby level.

When the elevator arrived at lobby level and the doors slid open, he exited the elevator and then exited the building, on his way to the subway.

When Tommy arrived at his apartment, he went into the kitchen after closing the door. He opened the refrigerator and pulled out a can of beer. He shut the door of the refrigerator, walked into the living room, sat down on the recliner, and laid his head back, feeling good that the workday had come to an end. He removed his black-framed glasses and rested them on the side table, next to the lamp, near the answering machine.

He smiled, took a sip of his beer, and then rested the can of the remaining beer on the side table, next to his glasses. Then he laid his head back against the back of the recliner as he covered his face with both hands.

Tommy thought back to high school. He was walking through the dimly lit halls of the school, on his way to the next class. On his way, he saw a girl standing by her locker with a man who was rather tall, at least six foot five.

"Hey, Julie!" Tommy yelled out as he waved to her while he smiled.

"Yes, Tommy?" Julie responded as she looked up at the tall man standing next to her, and he looked down at her. She had her arm around his waist. As the tall man noticed Tommy, he became annoyed with his presence.

"What's it to you, punk? Julie was always mine! I think you're obsessed or something, dude. You're never going to be with this beauty queen ever in your life. You're such a fucking loser!" said the tall man as he put his arm around her shoulders as she placed her arm around his waist once again.

Back to reality, Tommy removed his hands from his face slowly, and his eyes opened wide and then became smaller as his disappointment grew. He looked around his apartment. He led a lonely life in a lonely apartment, and he still wasn't with Crystal. He looked quickly at the clock that hung over the television and noticed the time. He picked up the receiver of the cordless phone desperately and called Crystal.

At Crystal's residence, the telephone rang and rang. As Crystal heard her telephone ringing, she rushed out of the shower with a big towel wrapped around her, and a cloud of steam above and all around her followed her as she left the bathroom door wide open. When she entered the living room, she rushed over to the telephone, still with the big towel wrapped around her tanned nude body and with a small towel wrapped around her hair.

"Hello?" Crystal answered as she held on to the telephone receiver tightly.

"Crystal? Hello, Crystal," Tommy responded with hopeful intentions.

"Who's this?" Crystal asked with dread in her voice, hoping it wasn't who she thought it was.

"Hi, Crystal. It's Tommy," said Tommy, and the moment was coated with a thick layer of silence. "Crystal? Hello? Are you still there?" he asked as the silence crept in between them.

"Yes. I'm still here," Crystal responded as she sat down on the sofa, covering her face with one hand, as she was beginning to lose patience with him.

"I know that you told me not to call you ever again, but I—"

"But fucking what? Yes, I told you not to fucking call me ever again!" Crystal shouted, and then she hung up the telephone.

"Crystal? Crystal!" Tommy called out, and he realized when she didn't respond that she had hung up the phone on him.

He slowly put the receiver of the cordless phone back on the charger on the side table near the recliner. While still sitting on the recliner, he took the can of beer from the side table and drank the rest of the beer, allowing his thirst to take over the consumption of the beverage. When he was finished with the beer, he rested the can on the side table and looked toward the kitchen. As he smiled a devilish grin, he rose from where he was sitting, walked into the kitchen, opened the refrigerator, pulled out a six-pack of beer from the second shelf in the refrigerator, and then shut the door of the refrigerator. He began his journey back into the living room but stopped midway and then went back into the kitchen, opened the refrigerator, and reached for another six-pack of beer. When he had the other six-pack of beer, he shut the door to the refrigerator, exited the kitchen, and went back into the living room. He sat back down on the recliner as he rested the two six-packs of beer on the carpeted floor next to the recliner.

As he lay back in the recliner, he reached for the first can of beer from the first of the two six-packs.

A couple of hours later, Tommy lay on the carpeted floor in the living room, full of beer, feeling really drunk. As he slowly passed out, he began to dream of the time when his mother had abandoned him when he was six years old.

"Mommy? Mommy!" little Tommy shouted while looking around.

"Yes, Tommy?" said his mother as she put on her coat.

"Where are you going?" six-year-old Tommy asked, walking toward his mother slowly, while his mother stood by the front door of their apartment. Tommy's eyes shone with innocence. As Tommy approached his mother, she quickly knelt down to him.

"Now, look, Tommy, I'm going to the store to buy you a surprise, and with the surprise, would you like Mommy to buy you some ice cream?" his mother asked as she smiled.

"Yes, Mommy!" Tommy responded as he hugged her quickly and then looked into her eyes.

"What flavor of ice cream would you like?" his mother asked, and Tommy took a moment to think about it.

"I know! I know!" Tommy shouted with a big smile upon his face, and his mother knew which flavor he wanted.

"Chocolate and vanilla fudge swirl!" said both Tommy and his mother together, and they laughed while hugging each other by the front door.

Back to the present, Tommy was still lying on the floor, still passed out drunk, on his back, while he mumbled to himself. As he turned over onto his stomach, he slipped away into his ongoing dream.

Six-year-old Tommy sat on the sofa alone in a dimly lit, almost dark living room as the day came to an end, with the sun setting as the skies became dark.

As Tommy waited for his mother's return to their apartment, it was apparent that his mother wasn't coming back. At six years old, Tommy was starting to realize that scary reality. Suddenly, tiny whispers and almost silent cries came from the six-year-old boy.

The telephone rang, and Tommy was startled by the loud ringing. He climbed over the sofa and reached for the telephone to answer it.

"Hello?" Tommy said while crying quietly as he wiped his eyes with his damp sleeves.

"Tommy, this is your aunt Sylvie. Let me talk with Mommy," said Aunt Sylvie.

"You want Mommy?" Tommy asked, holding the big receiver of the phone to his small ear.

"Yeah. Let me talk to Mommy," said Aunt Sylvie.

"Hold on." Tommy slowly looked around the darkened apartment while standing on the sofa. Then he sat down on the arm of the sofa, feeling hopeless because of his mommy's absence in the apartment. "Aunt Sylvie?"

"Yes, Tommy?" Aunt Sylvie responded as she wondered what was going on.

"Mommy is not here," said Tommy as he started to cry again silently.

"Mommy isn't there? Where's Mommy?" she asked.

"I don't know. Aunt Sylvie, I'm scared," said Tommy as he continued to cry.

"Tommy, it's going to be all right. Aunt Sylvie is coming over, all right?"

"All right, Aunt Sylvie. Aunt Sylvie?" Tommy called out as he stood up on the sofa.

"Yes, Tommy?"

"Is my mommy coming home? She's been away for a long time

now. I'm so scared!" Tommy cried out as he looked around while holding on to the back of the sofa.

"All right, little Tommy, Aunt Sylvie is on her way, OK? I'm on my way. Bye for now, Tommy," said Aunt Sylvie as she put on her coat with one hand.

"All right, Aunt Sylvie. Hurry," said Tommy as he continued crying.

"All right. I'm on my way. Bye," said Aunt Sylvie, and she hung up the telephone and rushed out of her apartment.

Little Tommy realized, as he was still holding on to the receiver of the phone, that Aunt Sylvie had hung up the phone and was on her way over to his apartment. He continued looking around the darkened apartment while listening to the dial tone.

In the realm of reality, Tommy woke up as the telephone rang. Tommy rose from the floor on his knees and crawled to the side table to answer the telephone. He rose up and grabbed the receiver of the phone.

"Hello?" Tommy answered the phone, still partially sleeping, thinking it was his aunt Sylvie from his dream. Out of a moment of silence came a familiar voice.

"Hello. Tommy?"

"Yes, this is Tommy. Who's this?" Tommy asked, struggling to hold on to the side table, still intoxicated. He swayed back and forth.

"Tommy, this is Maria. Are you all right?" Maria asked.

"Maria, I'm not feeling very well tonight, so I'll see you at work tomorrow morning," said Tommy, holding his head because he felt dizzy.

"All right, Tommy. I'm sorry," said Maria.

"That's all right. Bye," said Tommy.

"Bye, Tommy," said Maria, and they both hung up their phones.

As Tommy hung up his phone back on the charger, he rubbed his face while looking up at the clock above the television; it was twelve thirty in the morning. He let go of the side table, fell onto the floor, and crawled to the sofa. When he arrived at the sofa, he climbed onto it, and wasting no time, he fell back to sleep.

Falling into a deep sleep due to his intoxicated state courtesy of his two six-packs of beer and depression, he slid back into the past through his dream.

Little Tommy sat alone on the sofa in the dark, cold, and lonely apartment with a stream of light coming from a lamppost outside. His mother never had returned home. There was knock on the front door. Little Tommy rushed off the sofa with tears in his eyes, thinking his mother finally had arrived home, and approached the door of the apartment.

"Who is it?" Tommy asked while placing his ear on the door. He was shaking and feeling vulnerable.

"It's your aunt Sylvie!"

"Who is it?" Tommy asked, still shaking from uncertainty, as he stood near the door.

"It's your aunt Sylvie," she responded once again.

"OK, wait a minute!" said Tommy. He ran into the kitchen, to the kitchen table. He took one of the chairs and dragged it to the door. He placed the chair next to the door, climbed up onto the chair, stood straight up, looked into the peephole, and saw that it was his aunt Sylvie. He jumped down from the chair, pushed the chair away from the door, unlocked the door, and opened the door. As soon as Aunt Sylvie entered the apartment, she took Tommy into her arms, and they embraced and kissed each other. He was shaking but glad to see his aunt's arrival. At the same time, he hoped his mother would return instead.

"Where's Mommy?" Aunt Sylvie asked Tommy as she closed the door.

"I don't know, Aunt Sylvie. My mom was supposed to buy me some ice cream at the store, but she never came back from the store." Tommy's tears flowed down his cheeks.

"It's all right, Tommy," said Aunt Sylvie as she embraced him.

"When did Mommy go to the store to buy you ice cream? Do you remember when?" Aunt Sylvie knelt down near Tommy.

"Mommy said she was going to the store to get some ice cream, but when Mommy went to the store, she never came back home," little Tommy said.

"I know, but when did Mommy leave the apartment?" she asked as she picked him up from the floor and sat him on the sofa. She sat next to him with her arm around him as the moonlight shone through the window, and she and Tommy continued talking about his mother.

"All right, Tommy. Try to remember when Mommy left the apartment when she went to the store. Try to remember," she said, hoping he would remember.

"Ah, I don't remember. I don't remember!" Tommy cried out as he looked down at the carpeted floor in the living room.

"Was it still sunny outside when Mommy went to the store?" Aunt Sylvie asked.

"Yes! Yes, it was, and then the sun went down real fast! And the apartment went dark," said Tommy.

"All right, Tommy," said Aunt Sylvie, and as she thought about it for a moment, she knew what was going to happen.

"Aunt Sylvie, is my mommy coming back home?" he asked as he pulled back, looking into the eyes of his only aunt as she looked into his eyes.

"I don't know, Tommy. I'm not sure. But for now, we'll pack up some of your clothes, and you can stay with your aunt Sylvie, all right? Would you like to stay at my house?" Aunt Sylvie asked.

Little Tommy didn't say a word while he looked into his aunt's eyes again with tears streaming down both cheeks. Then they embraced each other.

Morning arrived with the morning sun, and as the sunshine blared through the window, Tommy awoke to the sound of the alarm clock. Tommy sat up on the sofa while looking at the clock, trying to wake up from the sleep and the dream.

"Oh shit! I'm going to be late for work!" he shouted as he got off the sofa. He quickly went into the bedroom to get dressed.

While he was getting dressed in his bedroom, the telephone rang. With only one leg in his jeans, he hopped back into the living room to answer the telephone.

"Hello?" Tommy said while trying to keep his balance as he slid his other leg into the other leg of the jeans.

"Tommy? Are you all right? Usually you're in at this time!" Louie shouted into the telephone while sitting at Maria's desk at the messenger center.

"Yeah, Louie. I'm just running late this morning. I'm sorry," said Tommy while tightening his belt.

"All right, OK, Tommy. Just hurry, and get your tired ass in, all right?" said Louie as he looked at load of the day's mail. A pile of bags sat on the floor next to the carts.

"OK, Louie. I'm truly sorry about this," said Tommy as he went back into his bedroom, putting on his sneakers.

"All right, fine. But didn't I tell you yesterday that it was going to be busy today?" Louie asked as he threw his unused cigar into the trash can next to Maria's desk.

"I know, I know," said Tommy as he tied his shoelaces.

"Yeah, you know! Tommy, just get your ass in!" Louie shouted, and then he hung up the telephone. "Fucking lousy workers!" Louie shouted while covering his face with both hands as Maria walked into the messenger center.

Tommy walked into his bathroom to wash his face and to wake up quickly, and when he was done, he rushed out of the apartment.

An hour and twenty minutes later, Tommy entered the messenger center in the basement, and Louie glanced over his shoulder and noticed his arrival to work.

"Well, if it isn't Sleeping Beauty!" Louie shouted as he smiled with a cigar dangling from the corner of his mouth.

Without saying a word, Tommy approached his locker. When he opened up his locker, he stared at Louie, hoping he wasn't too angry at his late arrival to work, and he saw Maria at her desk. Tommy smiled at her and then smiled at Louie, who stood by the carts at the counter, while getting out his work smock and putting it on. As it grew quiet in that part of the messenger center, Tommy grew more and more annoyed by Louie's earlier comment.

"All right, Tommy. Enough. Here's your load of today's mail. Let's go," said Louie as he pushed the cart full of the day's mail. Tommy grabbed the cart and proceeded out of the messenger center without responding, on his way to the upper floors throughout the building.

Another day came to an end, and Tommy reentered the messenger center with an empty cart. Maria was at her desk, doing the usual final paperwork of the day, while Louie was talking to someone on the telephone. Tommy pushed the cart toward the corner with the other carts and then proceeded to his locker without saying a word to anyone. As Tommy was taking off his smock, Maria glanced at him. She noticed him walking behind her as he was taking off his smock.

"Tommy?" Maria called out softly.

"Yes, Maria?" Tommy responded while hanging up his smock in his locker and tucking his shirt into his pants.

"Tommy, I know this nice barbecue restaurant in Times Square, so why don't we go there tonight? It's on me!" Maria said while smiling at him.

"Maria, thanks for the offer, but I have something I have to do tonight. Maybe another time, all right?" said Tommy as he smiled.

"Fine," Maria responded as she looked down at her desk, silently sighing.

"Bye, Louie!" Tommy yelled out as he left the messenger center, and Louie waved at him.

Meanwhile, Crystal was just getting off her job.

"Goodbye, everyone! Be good!" Crystal said while walking out of the reception area. Then she walked through the lobby on her way out of the building, on her way home.

Meanwhile, the thought of lust was just a couple of blocks away, as Tommy was walking fast, catching up with time, going to where

Crystal worked, as his train had arrived late. He saw her barely at a distance as she walked toward the subway. He walked a little faster, trying to catch up with her, while Crystal continued onward to the subway, unaware of who was behind her at a distance as she entered the subway.

After she went down the concrete steps of the aging subway, she went through the turnstile and onto the platform to wait for her train's arrival to the station. Tommy reached the subway entrance, wondering if she had gone down already, because he hadn't seen her go down. He thought about it for a moment, and then he went down the concrete steps, skipping down the steps. At that moment, Crystal was entering the train that had arrived at the station.

As the doors slid shut on the train, Tommy went through the turnstile, only to find the train leaving for uptown Manhattan with Crystal on board. He stared at the back of her head. Tommy just stood there, frustrated because he hadn't arrived at the train in time.

After a moment of thinking, he went back through the turnstile, depressed that he couldn't get near Crystal that night. He left the subway and walked toward Sixth Avenue to catch another train to Brooklyn.

When Tommy arrived at his apartment, he turned on his living room light. He walked into the kitchen, turned on the kitchen light, walked over to the window, and heard a cat meowing below, near some garbage cans in the alley. He opened the window and stared at the talkative cat below in the alley that separated his building from the next building.

"Here, kitty, kitty!" Tommy whispered loudly as he continued watching the hungry cat. He felt a bit hungry too, so he went back into the kitchen and walked toward the refrigerator to look for something to eat. When he opened up the refrigerator, the telephone rang. Tommy shut the door to the refrigerator and rushed into the living room to answer the telephone.

"Hello?" Tommy said, not expecting the call.

"Tommy, it's Maria. So what's up?" Maria asked.

"Well, Maria, I'm looking for something to eat at this time, but anyway—"

"Oh, I'm sorry. Did I call at a bad time?" Maria asked.

"It's OK. I can look for something while I'm talking to you. So what's up?" he asked while he went back into the refrigerator, looking for something to eat.

"Nothing much. A little bored and maybe a little bit lonely," said Maria.

Silence filled the air momentarily, as Tommy was still looking for something to eat in the refrigerator, not paying attention to her.

"Hello? Tommy?" Maria called out as she wondered if he'd been listening.

"Yeah, I'm still here. I'm just looking for something to eat," said Tommy, growing frustrated because he couldn't find something he wanted to eat while listening to his lovesick coworker on the telephone.

"Tommy?" Maria again called out.

"Huh?" Tommy responded. He was ready to give up and just go to bed and call it a night.

"Tommy, what do I have to do or say to be able to go out with you?" Maria asked, frustrated.

Tommy stood upright and shut the refrigerator door. "Maria, listen up! I like you. I like you, Maria. I'm not in love with you! I'm not into you like that. I'm not in love with you, nor do I love you. Understand?"

"Yes. Yes, I understand, Tommy. I hope you enjoy whatever it is you're having for dinner," said Maria.

"OK, Maria. You have a good night. Bye, Maria."

"Goodbye, Tommy."

"Bye." Tommy hung up the telephone.

After hanging up the telephone, he walked into the living room and lay down on the sofa. Then, suddenly, he rose from the sofa, walked over to the side table, and reached for the cordless telephone to dial Crystal's number. However, before dialing the number, he hesitated for a moment. Then he continued dialing. In the middle of dialing the number, he stopped, thinking to himself for a moment again, hesitating, and then he redialed the number and went through with it.

"Hello?" Crystal answered the phone anxiously, not knowing who it was but hoping it wasn't who she didn't want it to be.

"Hello, Crystal! I thought I would give you a call, and—" Tommy stopped, realizing she'd disconnected herself from the call. He hung up the telephone receiver on the charger.

He went back to the sofa, sat down, and stared straight ahead at the wall. Then he rose and began to pace back and forth about the living room, from one end to the other.

"I don't know what I'm going to do. I'm in love with her so much. I know I don't know her, but I feel deep down I do, in a way." He thought out loud while he continued pacing, and then he turned around. "I've got to have her. I'm going to have her! And I don't care what I have to do!" Tommy faded into the darkness, into his bedroom.

CHAPTER 6

A NEW DAY DAWNED. CRYSTAL WAS at her place of employment. She entered the reception area, and her coworkers all greeted her.

"Hi, Crystal! Congratulations to you!" said one of her coworkers as she excused herself from the desk.

"Yeah, congrats, Crystal, on your new position in the company, at the reception area. So what's up?" Jackie, one of the coworkers, asked as she and a couple of other receptionists were signing in guests at the desk.

"Oh, hi," Crystal responded as she put her purse in one of the desk drawers by her chair and then locked it.

"Are you feeling all right, Crystal?" Jackie asked as she noticed Crystal's expression as she sat down on a chair near Jackie.

"Yeah, you look a bit down this morning," said Tyler, another coworker at the reception desk, who was sitting on the other side of Crystal, as she and Jackie were getting their paperwork together for the day.

"I'm fine. Really. Maybe a little on edge. You see, this jerk called me up last night—"

"Who's the jerk?" Jackie asked, interrupting Crystal, feeling concerned for her coworker, while she looked at Tyler.

"The jerk who answered an ad I put in the personal ads a while ago," said Crystal while she took a sip of her coffee.

"Uh-huh," Tyler said as she bit into a toasted bagel smeared with cream cheese.

"His name is Tommy. He seemed to be a nice guy when we met, but—"

"But what?" Jackie asked.

"Well, he's a nut," she responded. She wished she hadn't said anything.

"Crystal, all men are nuts. My man is wonderful, sexy, and a nut," said Jackie as she drank some of her coffee while looking up, smiling.

"That's not what I'm saying. Not all men are nuts. He seemed like a nice man when we met, but I wasn't attracted to him. I just didn't feel anything for him, then and now. We just don't click," said Crystal, drinking some of her coffee.

"Do you think he's in love with you?" Tyler asked in a whisper while snickering.

"Well, he said he was in love with me. He told me so. But now it's slowly turning into obsession, I believe," said Crystal with an expression of concern on her face.

"Obsession?" Tyler asked.

"Shit, Crystal. You need the police involved right away," Jackie said as she was signing in someone.

"Yeah, I know. He still continues to stalk me and call me up on the phone. Maybe I will have to get the police involved, and somehow, I'll have to make the time to do this," said Crystal as she was finishing up the paperwork for the day.

"You mean to say you've been stalked by this guy before, he continuously calls you, and you haven't called the cops yet?" Tyler asked, stunned by Crystal's lack of action in the matter.

Crystal's facial expression turned serious. "I'm not really in any danger—yet."

Crystal, Jackie, and Tyler looked at one another.

At Tommy's place of employment, Tommy was on the upper floors, pushing the cart of morning mail. As he entered the office space and started handing out the mail, he thought back to when he first had had a crush on a girl.

He was in junior high school, and he was sitting behind a girl, who was busy doing her work according to the assignment the teacher was instructing that day. Tommy was right behind her in his seat, writing a love letter to her.

Dear Zena,

I want to take you out to the junior high school dance this weekend on Saturday night. I really, really like you a lot! Please let me know soon!

Tommy Landis

When Tommy finished writing the love letter, he folded it neatly and threw it over the girl's right shoulder. It landed on her desk, right on top of her social studies book.

When she noticed the piece of paper land on her book, she looked over her shoulder and saw Tommy. She picked up the letter and read it. As she read it, she glanced over at Tommy with no expression on her face. He smiled at her, hoping she liked him as much as he liked her.

As she read the letter again, she started to giggle. Tommy noticed her giggle and joined in. As Tommy joined in the laughter, she turned around again, still giggling. Then she realized the teacher was walking in her direction, so she turned around quickly, facing the front of the class, and Tommy sat up straight in his chair, not smiling. The teacher stepped back toward the front of the class as she looked over at the clock that hung high above the blackboard.

"All right, class. I have to go to the principal's office for a moment, but I'll be back shortly. Everyone, please behave while I'm gone," said the social studies teacher as she was leaving.

Zena, the girl Tommy had a crush on, looked over at Tommy, who was still sitting behind her and staring at her, and she smiled at him devilishly as she slowly turned around in her chair. Tommy responded with a half smile, not sure how to react, because he wasn't sure how she felt toward him or what she was going to do.

All of a sudden, Zena stood up and, holding the love letter, walked to the front of the class. Tommy watched, sitting firmly on his chair, fearing what was about to take place. At the front of the class, she turned around gracefully in a sarcastic way.

"Excuse me, everyone!" Zena shouted, and everyone in class focused on the front of the class as Zena held up the love letter he had written her. "I have in my hands what appears to be a love letter written by Tommy!" Zena shouted, pointing at Tommy with her other hand.

When she pointed at him, the whole class stared at him from all around the classroom as he turned red from embarrassment. Feeling embarrassed, he covered his face with both hands as he slid down in his chair. His glasses were fogging up due to perspiration. Zena smiled, getting ready to read the love letter. As Zena began to read the letter, tears came down Tommy's cheeks. He couldn't believe she would be so cruel to him. The whole class laughed as Zena continued reading Tommy's love letter.

He was hopelessly in love with Zena, and at the same time, he was hurt and humiliated. He wanted to die.

When she finished reading the letter in front of the class, she grinned at him, and Tommy, in a fit of rage, stood up near his desk.

"How could you, Zena?" Tommy shouted with teary eyes as the whole class watched in amazement. Amid Tommy's explosive tone of voice, the laughter died down. Zena tried to recreate the laughter by laughing at him, about to read the love letter again.

"What? What do you feel bad about?" Zena shouted.

"That letter was between you and me! I didn't mean for the whole class to know about this!" Tommy shouted as he walked over to her at the front of the class.

"So what are you going to do now?" Zena shouted as she smiled at

Tommy and the class as she looked around the class. "Are you going to propose to me or something?" Zena asked sarcastically with a cocky smile while looking around at her classmates.

"No, I don't think so," Tommy responded.

She began to laugh while tearing up the love letter into little pieces of paper that meant something to him. She threw the tiny pieces of paper at him, and he watched the pieces come down like snow on a cold winter day. The bits of the letter fell slowly over him while he watched in agony, embarrassment, and shame.

Back to the present, Tommy was standing still in the office space as an office worker had her hand out for her mail.

"Well, Tommy, am I getting mail today or maybe sometime tonight?" she asked.

"Oh, I'm sorry, Mrs. Klondike!" said Tommy as he realized what was going on. He realized he had been daydreaming again, and he handed her mail to her and went onward with the rest of the morning mail, continuing the deliveries.

Crystal's place of employment was busy. All the receptionists' desks were packed with visitors signing in from all around the world.

When the morning rush was dying down, Crystal got ready for a fifteen-minute break.

"Hey, Crystal, that was some crowd, huh?" Jackie asked as she smiled.

"Yes, was it ever!" Crystal responded with a quick laugh.

"Are you ready for your fifteen-minute break?" Crystal's relief asked her as she approached Crystal from behind the long desk.

"Yes. Are you relieving me?" Crystal asked as she went into her drawer at her desk and took out her purse.

"Yes. Even though I'm your supervisor, I'm the one who is relieving you and everyone today," said the supervisor as she sat down in the chair, as Crystal was already standing up.

"Oh, I hope everything will be all right. I heard we're supposed to be busy today," Crystal replied.

"We're going to be just fine, Crystal. Enjoy your break," said the supervisor as another visitor went straight over to her.

"All right, see you in fifteen minutes," said Crystal as she left the reception area and went on her break.

Crystal stepped off the escalator and walked toward the rotary doors at the front entrance of the building to go outside, and on the way, she looked to her right and saw a man going up the escalator from the lower level underneath the building. The man looked like Tommy. But she wasn't sure. He had a little bit of hair, and he was wearing a pair of black-framed glasses. He looked like Woody Allen, and he was an average height. As the man came up the escalator, he appeared to be tall, but he looked unbelievably like Tommy for a moment. As the man walked by, Crystal held her breath, and as she sighed with relief, he walked right by her again.

She walked cautiously toward the rotary doors in front of the building on Sixth Avenue and exited the building to get some air, trying to relax.

Fifteen minutes later, she went back to the reception area, wondering about her fears about Tommy. Crystal arrived back at her seat at the reception desk, and her supervisor relieved the next person over for a break. Crystal didn't even notice her supervisor sitting next to her; her mind was on her fear.

"Crystal?" her supervisor called out.

"Yes?" Crystal responded as she smiled at her, and her supervisor smiled back at Crystal.

"Are you all right? You seem sort of out of it," said the supervisor.

"I'm all right. Actually, can we talk privately somewhere before I go home today?" Crystal asked, fighting back tears.

Her supervisor saw the unhappy and tense expression on her face. "Sure, we can talk today. Why don't we have lunch today in my office, all right?" her supervisor asked.

"All right." Crystal felt relieved to lay some of the burden on someone else.

"Come have lunch with me in my office, and we'll discuss whatever is bothering you, all right?" the supervisor said, as she noticed Crystal was a little shaken up as they spoke.

"All right. Thank you, Ms. Wallenford. I would like that," said Crystal as she smiled, acting as if she were fine, while signing someone in at the desk.

———————— ·•✦✦✦•· ————————

At Tommy's place of employment, Tommy entered the messenger center; he brought an empty cart, looking for more mail for the day to deliver.

"Hey, Tommy! Got another load for your cart!" Louie shouted from the counter in the corner as he laughed.

"Another load of shit, Louie?" Tommy asked with a demented grin on his face as he walked toward Louie.

"OK, Tommy, dummy up and listen!" said Louie with an unlit cigar dangling from the corner of his mouth. "We have tons of mail for today and tomorrow, all right?" Louie removed the unlit cigar from his mouth.

"All right," Tommy responded, ready to reload his cart, as he leaned up against the counter.

"We have to bust our asses today and tomorrow, or we are going to hear some shit from the top, and I don't have to mention the names, right?" Louie asked. He looked serious and annoyed. "And you know that when they drop their shit, it's nothing but a mess!" said Louie as he put the unlit cigar back into his mouth and then took it back out.

"Yeah, I know," Tommy responded as Maria stared at him from the side of her eyes.

"All right, here's more of the load we have. Take care of this, and when you arrive back here, take your lunch break for an hour," said Louie as he and Tommy reloaded the cart.

"All right, Louie. I'm gone," said Tommy as he exited the messenger center with his cart full of the day's mail and proceeded toward the elevators to go to the upper floors.

———————— ⊹⊹⊹⊹⊹ ————————

Crystal arrived at her supervisor's office. She took a deep breath while she knocked on the partially open office door.

"Hi, Crystal. Come in," said Ms. Wallenford, and Crystal entered the office, shut the door behind her, and then walked toward the desk. "Have a seat, Crystal. You mentioned earlier—oh, I ordered some Chinese food for lunch. Is Chinese food all right with you?" Ms. Wallenford asked, sitting behind her desk.

Crystal sat down on one of the chairs in front of the desk. "That would be fine, Ms. Wallenford." Crystal gave a half smile.

"All right, Crystal, you mentioned earlier today, when you arrived back at the desk from break, that something has been on your mind," Ms. Wallenford said, feeling Crystal's tension.

"Yes." Crystal nodded as she tried to smile, which was becoming increasingly hard.

"Does this problem pertain to your job? Is someone here at the job bothering you?" Ms. Wallenford asked.

"Oh no. No, it has nothing to do with the job. Everything here is going great at the job. My personal life is a different matter," said Crystal.

"Crystal, sometimes when our personal lives are in shambles, we tend to take it to the job. Even though we don't want to, it happens anyway," said Ms. Wallenford as she looked concerned.

"Ms. Wallenford, I have a problem in my life, and I don't know what to do, and yes, it is affecting my job. I know I need to not bring it to my job, but sometimes it gets hard with my situation," Crystal said.

"All right, anything that you tell me or that we discuss won't leave this office. You can depend on me, all right?" Ms. Wallenford said.

"I know," said Crystal as she noticed a fish tank against the wall behind Ms. Wallenford, toward her left.

"Well, Crystal, why don't you tell me about your situation? Look, no one will ever know about whatever it is you want to talk about here today," said Ms. Wallenford, reassuring Crystal.

For a moment, silence ruled the air in Ms. Wallenford's office as they stared at each other.

"Ms. Wallenford, I really appreciate this. OK, this is what's been going on. I met a guy who answered a personal ad I had put in the personals. In the beginning, we didn't even date. We decided that before going out on a date, we would meet in a local coffeehouse here in Manhattan. You know, so we could meet and get to know each other first," Crystal said, feeling a little uncomfortable talking about it.

"All right," Ms. Wallenford responded as she listened intently.

"Well, this man answered my personal ad in the newspaper." Crystal repeated herself, as she was feeling a bit nervous.

Ms. Wallenford nodded as she listened to Crystal's story. "Uh-huh," Ms. Wallenford responded as she continued listening intently.

"We met at the coffeehouse, and we drank some coffee while talking and getting to know each other. When we met and began to talk, I saw him as an average guy. He has a job, and he seems to be relatively a responsible kind of guy—like I said, he seemed to be just an ordinary guy. When we met, he was very nice to me. A complete gentleman. At the end of that meeting, we decided we were going to go out, and we were picking a night to go out. We thought about dinner and a movie—the beginner's date. Just a typical night on the town. And that's all right." As Crystal was explaining, she became more open.

"So the two of you went out?" Ms. Wallenford asked.

"Yes. We went out for dinner, and we were just about ready to go to the movies. As we were walking through Times Square, we stopped midway to the theater. I thought that before we went any further, I should be up front with him, which I'd wanted to do before we had dinner. I told him he was a real gentleman and a nice guy, but I was not attracted to him, so I didn't see the point in us going to the movies, continuing the night out, or going any further and wasting his time.

Plus, I didn't want to give him the wrong idea if we proceeded with the night," Crystal said.

"Well, I'm sure in the long run, he will appreciate that. But why didn't you just tell him in the beginning, before he went to pick you up for the date after the coffee meeting?" she asked.

"Well, it was a combination of not wanting to hurt his feelings and not knowing what to do in time. It was a last-minute decision. When I realized what time it was, it was right then I made my decision," Crystal said as Ms. Wallenford served the food on paper plates on her desk. "And yeah, I would think that in the long run, he will appreciate the honesty I had with him," Crystal added as she bit into an egg roll from her plate.

"Right." Ms. Wallenford put a forkful of pork fried rice into her mouth.

"You would think that, but he says he's in love with me, and he keeps calling me. And now he's even stalking me," said Crystal as she put a forkful of brown rice into her mouth.

"He's stalking you?" Ms. Wallenford asked in disbelief, choking on her fried rice. She immediately grabbed her can of diet cola and drank some quickly without the straw to stop the choking.

"Oh! Are you all right?" Crystal asked as she leaned forward with concern.

"Yeah. I'm fine. You just caught me by surprise," said Ms. Wallenford as she bit into her egg roll.

"I'm telling you the truth about this guy. I told him a few times already to leave me alone, but he doesn't get it. On my fifteen-minute break, I was going out to the front of the building to get some air and relax—you know, at the Sixth Avenue side entrance. And when I was there, I thought I saw Tommy, this guy." Crystal put down her fork for a moment.

"Tommy. That's the guy who's been stalking you?" Ms. Wallenford asked as she took another sip of her diet cola, this time through a straw.

"Yeah. But when this guy walked through the lobby, coming off the escalator, I soon realized it wasn't Tommy. So I was a little shaken up. Unbelievable," said Crystal as she picked up her fork and began to eat again.

"I know. I noticed your expression when you arrived back from your break at the desk."

"Ms. Wallenford, I don't know what to do about this situation. I'm really afraid of this guy. I believe he's really obsessed with me. He's so obsessed in wanting to be with me. I don't want to wake up one morning with a gun to my face," said Crystal, eating some brown rice.

"Crystal, I understand that. That's why right after work, you're going to the nearest police station around where you live. And when you get to the police station, you're filing an order of protection against this nut. I mean it. Nothing is more important than this. I mean it! Crystal, right after work, go straight to the police station, and file a complaint," Ms. Wallenford said strongly, wiping her mouth with a paper napkin, leaving a little lip gloss on her napkin.

"All right, but what's an order of protection?" Crystal asked while finishing her peppered steak and brown rice and part of the egg roll.

"An order of protection is a form that says this person who is stalking you and calling you numerous times on the telephone cannot do these things to you. The phone calls are considered harassment. The form also says that he cannot come within so many feet from you, your place of residence, or where you work. Now, you'll probably receive one for a couple of months. But there are some orders that last for six months or a year, depending on your case."

"Oh yeah? That is good. Well, I know I have to do something about this. Because I feel that it's getting out of hand, and it could get worse," said Crystal. She was finished with her food and was drinking the last of her diet cola.

Ms. Wallenford drank the last of her diet cola, placed the empty can on her desk, and leaned a little forward. "Crystal, I hope and pray that you do something about this crazy situation. Everyone at the job has noticed that you haven't been quite yourself lately. Take control, and hang this guy Tommy by his balls!" Ms. Wallenford smiled halfway.

———————— ✦✦✦✦✦ ————————

Tommy and one of his coworkers from the messenger center were in the cafeteria. They took their trays of food to a corner table and sat to eat their food.

"Tommy, have you heard the latest rumor around the messenger center?" Keith asked before biting into his tuna club sandwich.

"Uh, no. What's the rumor?" Tommy asked while eating some of his potato salad.

Keith looked down for a moment, and then he looked up at Tommy. "You mean you haven't heard the rumor?"

Tommy was getting annoyed with Keith and with the rumor he said he'd heard. He put his fork down for a moment while leaning over the table, smiling halfway. "Keith, do you mind letting me in on this rumor that's all over the messenger center?" Tommy asked while biting into his grilled cheese sandwich.

"OK, OK, but you have to promise me that you didn't hear it from me. All right?" Keith took a sip of his orange juice from a straw.

"All right. It'll be like we never spoke about it. So tell me. What the fuck is this rumor?" Tommy asked abruptly, startling Keith a little bit, as he put his grilled cheese sandwich down on the plate and then grabbed the paper napkin, wiped his hands with it, and threw it down onto the table.

"All right, all right. The rumor is that you—" Keith paused, as Tommy's eyes looked worried. "You and Maria have a thing going on. So is this true?" Keith bit into his tuna club sandwich, smiling halfway, not sure how Tommy was going to react to the rumor.

Tommy froze where he was sitting, looking down at the table. His grilled cheese sandwich was getting cold, and the cheese looked like plastic. Wide-eyed from what he'd just heard, he started eating the cold grilled cheese sandwich.

"Man, are you feeling all right?" Keith asked with concern, thinking that maybe he should've never told Tommy the rumor.

"No, I'm not all right. I am really starting to hate that bitch," said Tommy, thinking about how Maria was acting. It was similar to the way he'd been acting with Crystal, but then he justified himself as doing nothing wrong.

"Oh, you don't like her?" Keith asked, finishing his orange juice.

"No. No, I don't like her. As coworkers, we're mad cool, but as boyfriend and girlfriend, no way. It's not like that!" Tommy yelled out, not realizing he was being loud and drawing attention to himself and Keith.

"You mean that it's—"

"Exactly!" said Tommy, interrupting, and a moment of silence crept around them.

"Exactly what?" Keith asked, trying to understand Tommy's point, as Tommy stared at him with an expression of annoyance on his face.

"You schmuck. It's a rumor that bitch is passing around to everyone at the center," said Tommy as he drank some of his orange juice.

"Oh shit. Are you going to talk to her about this?" Keith asked as he drank the rest of his cola.

"Yes, I am. I have to talk to her about this. I am not in love with her. I only like her as a coworker and a friend," Tommy said while finishing his orange juice as they looked at each other. "But lately, she's been acting weird," Tommy added in a whisper.

"Weird?" Keith whispered.

"Yeah. I told her that I didn't like her that way and that we were just friends and were fine just working together," Tommy said while finishing his glass of orange juice.

"Yeah, but, Tommy, she is good looking. You can't deny that." Keith smiled.

"I know. I know she's good looking, but I'm not in love with her. I'm in love with someone else," said Tommy as he thought about Crystal.

"Oh yeah? Who is she?" Keith asked, looking interested.

"Well, I answered this girl's ad in the personals in the newspaper. And man, is she hot." Tommy wiped his mouth again with another paper napkin.

"How long have you been seeing her?" Keith asked as he smiled.

"Well, I'm not exactly seeing her right now." Tommy looked around quickly from the side of his eyes.

"Huh?" Keith said, not understanding Tommy.

"You heard me. We're not seeing each other exactly," said Tommy as he smiled halfway while looking from his table.

"What's that supposed to mean?" Keith asked with a concerned look on his face.

Tommy looked down at the table for a moment. "She's acting like she's not interested, but I know deep down inside, she loves me."

"How many times have you been out with her?" Keith asked.

"Only once." Tommy sat back in his chair.

"Only once?" Keith asked in disbelief.

"Yeah, we went out once for coffee, but she keeps coming up with reasons why she won't go out with me again." Tommy's tone of voice was of denial and frustration with Keith for asking too many questions.

"Sounds like she's not into you, man," said Keith as he pushed his tray aside with his left hand, brushing it to the right side.

"No, no. She really does want to be with me. And I really want to be with her," said Tommy under his breath while he looked up at the ceiling.

"Fine. All right. But did she say that the two of you were going out again?" Keith asked as he leaned forward a little over the table.

"Well, no, but I'm so in love with her. I'm so into her, man," said Tommy.

"Man, I don't know about you." Keith snickered.

"Let me describe her to you. Her eyes are so blue. When you look into her eyes, it's as though you're looking at the sky on a clear, sunny day." Tommy visualized Crystal in his mind as he described her to Keith.

Keith shook his head at Tommy's detailed description of Crystal.

"Her hair is blonde—golden. It's naturally blonde. It's as though she came down from the sun." As Tommy described her, Keith wore a concerned expression on his face, as Tommy spoke with obsessive overtones. "And her heart is as big as the moon." Tommy finished describing her to Keith, still visualizing Crystal in his mind, while Keith sat there quiet and still for a moment.

"Yeah, but that's nothing! Maria isn't so bad looking. Let this other girl go. I know she's probably beautiful by the way you described her, but let her go. And I'm sure she doesn't need any problems with you right now. And you sure as hell don't need any problems right now in your life," Keith whispered over the table, and then he again sat back all the way in his chair with his arms folded.

Silence again fell on the cafeteria as Tommy looked into Keith's eyes, wide-eyed, as though he were looking right through Keith.

"I can't, Keith. I'm too much in love. I need her, and she needs me," said Tommy. Only he and Keith were left in the cafeteria.

"Tommy, you're not in love, not anymore," said Keith, shaking his head.

"What!" Tommy stood up.

"I said you're not in love!" Keith shouted, and a few of the cafeteria employees looked to see what was going on. "Oh, you might've been in love before, when you two first met, but she rejected you. You've been trying to get acceptance from her, but she still rejects you, and now the love you had for this girl has turned into obsession. You're obsessed with this girl! Face it!" Keith shouted out with concern and care for his friend and coworker.

Tommy just stared at Keith, feeling shocked by his realistic response to the issue.

"Here. You want me to spell it out for you? Fine! You are not in love with her! You are obsessed with her!" Keith wrote it on a paper napkin and then slammed down the pen on the table.

Tommy's eyes grew large with anger, surprise, and bewilderment, but he was still in denial as he read what was written on the paper napkin. "I have to go." Tommy rose, picked up his tray, and left the table.

Keith picked up his tray and followed right behind him. When Keith caught up with him, he held the tray with one hand and grabbed Tommy's arm with the other hand, and they stopped walking momentarily.

"Look, man, you have to deal with this sooner or later. If you don't deal with this obsession thing, it's going to eat you up inside. And if you have problems with the cops, because sooner or later, that girl is going to get tired of your phone calls and the—"

Tommy interrupted, pulling away from Keith and placing his tray on the conveyer belt, as Keith was right behind him. "Stalking?" Tommy said as he quickly turned around after setting his tray down on the belt.

"Huh?" Keith said. He had not expected that response from Tommy.

"I said *stalking*. I mean, sooner or later, she'll get tired of the stalking too, right?" said Tommy.

Keith just stared at him, not sure if the man before him was the coworker he had known for three years or someone else he had just met.

"I have to go. See ya," said Tommy as he walked toward the front entrance of the cafeteria.

Keith placed his tray down on the conveyer belt and quickly walked after Tommy. When Keith was right behind Tommy, he tugged at his arm, trying to get his attention, and Tommy stopped. Tommy turned around, facing Keith, as they both stopped at the front entrance doors of the cafeteria.

"Hey, look, Tommy, I've known you for a few years now, and you know I would never say anything to hurt you, but I want to lay some heavy advice on you. Admit that you have problems, and then seek some counseling. I hope you don't take this in a bad way. I'm your coworker, but I'm also your friend, and that's why I'm suggesting this advice to you. You need to take some kind of control over your life," said Keith.

Tommy smiled while he looked straight ahead down the hall from the cafeteria and then looked back at Keith from the side of his eyes. "That's what you think," said Tommy, and he walked away from Keith and left Keith by himself while Keith watched him walk down the hall.

⋄⋄⋄⋄⋄⋄

The workday came to an end, and Crystal was getting ready to go home.

"Hey, Crystal!" Crystal's coworker called out to her as she entered the reception area to relieve her of her duties and walked up to the reception desk.

"Hey, Tiff. What's up?" Crystal asked while gathering her belongings before going home.

"I can see you're ready to leave," said Tiffany, taking off her coat.

"I'm just about ready to go but not quite. First, I have to brief you on what went on during the five-to-one shift," said Crystal.

"All right," Tiffany responded as she settled in for another workday behind the desk and smiled as Crystal rose from where she was sitting. Crystal and Tiffany discussed the day's events before and prior to the five-to-one shift.

⋄⋄⋄⋄⋄⋄

At the messenger center, the mailroom staff called it a day.

"All right, everyone! Have a lovely night! Good job to one and all!" Louie yelled out as the staff were walking out, waving goodbye at the entrance of the messenger center.

Louie, Maria, and Tommy were the only ones left at the messenger center. Tommy walked over toward Maria, who was still at her desk. Maria rose, getting ready to leave.

"Hi, Maria," Tommy called out as he approached her.

"Hi, Tommy," Maria answered as she smiled.

"How was your day?" Tommy asked as he smiled back.

"My day went real nice," said Maria as she started putting on her coat.

Tommy helped her with her coat. "Maria, what would you say if I walked you to the subway? I would also say let's take the train together, but I have things to do tonight."

Maria's face glowed with excitement, and her eyes enlarged. "You want to walk with me to the subway? May I ask you why?" she asked, wondering why he was showing interest in her all of a sudden but, at the same time, feeling excited for the moment she'd been waiting for.

"Well, I don't blame you for feeling a bit suspicious, but I feel we should talk. That's all," Tommy said slowly.

Maria turned around facing him and took his right hand with both of her hands as she quickly grabbed her Discman from the top of her desk. Then together, holding hands, they walked out of the messenger center.

Louie waved to them. He'd expected that to happen eventually, with the rumors all around the center.

Tommy and Maria entered the freight elevator, as though the elevator had been awaiting their arrival to go up to the lobby level. The doors slid shut, and the freight elevator was on its way to the lobby. Maria stared at Tommy from the side of her eyes, not believing he was still holding her hand. Her dream was finally coming true. Tommy was feeding into her obsession.

When the elevator arrived at the lobby level and the door slid open, Tommy and Maria exited hand in hand and walked through the lobby, on their way to the subway. As they walked out together, Maria looked over at Tommy. When Tommy noticed her heavy, wondering stares, his eyes turned to her, and he smiled pleasantly.

"So, Maria, how really was your day?" Tommy asked as they walked toward the corner, still holding hands, across the street from the subway.

"Oh, it was good, as I mentioned earlier at the center. How was your day?" Maria asked, smiling, trying to figure him out. She felt a wave of discomfort all of a sudden.

"My day was actually pretty good, as I also mentioned earlier at the center, except for one thing," he said as they walked across the street and approached the subway. They went down the concrete steps of the subway together, smiling at each other.

"Oh yeah? What's that one thing?" she asked as they approached the turnstiles. When they reached the turnstiles, they stopped walking and turned to face each other, smiling.

"I've been hearing rumors about us being together romantically, but we don't even exist. And we never will," said Tommy as he backed up Maria against the brick wall close to the turnstiles.

"Tommy, hold it. I can explain. Let me explain," Maria said as she was up against the wall.

"OK, start explaining," said Tommy as he held his forearm against her neck, pinning her up against the wall.

"All right, what happened was, a few of the guys at work and I were hanging out on our fifteen-minute break about a week ago," Maria said.

"And?" Tommy pressed her harder up against the wall.

"And I just mentioned to them that it would be great for us—you know, you and me getting together. We would go out to the movies and dinner or do something else, and we would have this relationship, being that we already know each other."

"A relationship?" Tommy responded, feeling angry.

"Yes, that's exactly what I'm talking about. That's how I feel, Tommy," said Maria as she shrugged off his forearm, took Tommy's right hand, and kissed it softly and slowly.

"Maria!" Tommy pulled away from her invading hands. "Look, I already told you that I'm in love with Crystal! Why don't you face up to reality and just find another guy?"

Maria looked around, hoping no one was noticing Tommy yelling. "Tommy, all I want is you, God damn it! I want you! All I ever wanted was you. I haven't been with another guy in so long, because in my foolish mind, I'm always thinking that someday you might give us a chance." Maria knelt down on her knees and began rubbing his left leg, underneath his pants.

Tommy walked backward a couple of steps. "Maria, you have to stop passing around these rumors. It must stop right now!" Tommy said, and then he walked away as Maria was still in the kneeling position on the concrete floor next to the brick wall near the turnstile.

As Tommy went through the turnstile, Maria stood up. "But, Tommy, I need you! We need each other!" Maria shouted as she leaned against the brick wall. She just stared at him as a train approached the station, and when the train made a complete stop and the doors slid open, she saw Tommy enter the train amid people coming and going. Maria kept watching as people went through the turnstile, coming and going from behind and in front of her. She saw Tommy sit on the train, and the doors slid shut. The train exited the station.

Maria smiled with a devilish grin, as she was gone from the depths of reality. "Tommy, Tommy, Tommy, as long as you are able to breathe, I will forever believe we will be together one day soon. Come hell or high water, we will be together!" Maria whispered loudly to herself amid the commuters coming and going around her. She slowly walked away from the turnstile and left the subway.

CHAPTER 7

A TRAIN ARRIVED AT ANOTHER SUBWAY station, and when it made a complete stop, the doors slid open. Crystal Farnsworth was in the midst of the crowd of riders, on her way home, going uptown. When she entered the train, she quickly found a seat. She sat down and shut her eyes as the train left the station, on its way to the next station.

Even though she had her eyes shut, she wasn't sleeping. She was just relaxing after a long day at work—a nerve-racking day on the job. While she had her eyes shut tightly, a homeless man wearing a pair of black-framed glasses walked toward Crystal. The train was semifull, with most of the seats taken. The homeless man walked up to Crystal, who still had her eyes shut, and moved in closer, near her face, as some of the commuters watched. Now the homeless man and Crystal were face-to-face, just a couple of inches apart.

Crystal began to feel uncomfortable, as though someone were watching her. She slowly opened her eyes, and she saw the homeless man in her face.

"No! No!" Crystal screamed as she pushed him back.

The homeless man fell backward to the floor and just sat there on the floor, staring at her strangely. He hadn't expected the strong push from this beautiful, attractive young lady.

After wiping her hands with a couple of baby wipes from her purse, Crystal covered her face with both hands as the people on the train watched her. She tried to relax, hoping to arrive at her destination soon.

When the train arrived at her destination, she exited and went down the steps of the subway, thinking to herself. Before going straight home, she stopped midway.

I wonder if I should go to the police now that I have a chance, she thought as she crossed the street. She walked a couple of blocks in the opposite direction of where she lived, on her way to the police station.

Meanwhile, in Brooklyn, Tommy entered his apartment. He shut the door and noticed there were no messages on his answering machine as he walked into the living room. He sat down on the recliner, thinking to himself, drowning in deep thought.

All of a sudden, the telephone rang. Tommy jumped, feeling startled by the unexpected ringing and still in deep thought. He reached for the telephone and answered it.

"Hello?" Tommy said, but there was no response from the caller. "Hello?" he said again, but there still was no response. "Hello!" Tommy shouted, feeling frustrated because of the silence of the caller, not knowing who it was. He finally hung up the telephone. He went to sit on the sofa.

While sitting on the sofa, he wondered who might've been on the telephone.

"Maria. It was Maria," he mumbled to himself as he rose from the sofa and began to pace about in the living room. "I sure do love Crystal. Why doesn't she see that I care for her?" Tommy continued mumbling to himself as he continued pacing about in the living room, thinking of Crystal.

Crystal entered the police precinct, feeling nervous, not knowing what to do or what her next move would be. She approached the front desk of the station.

"Hi, ma'am. How may I help you?" the officer at the desk asked while doing some paperwork.

"Oh, hi. My name is Crystal. Crystal Farnsworth," said Crystal. "I have a problem with this man who keeps calling me and stalking me after I told him to stop. And I keep on—"

The officer interrupted her. "Is this guy your ex-boyfriend?"

"No, he's not an ex-boyfriend. We only went out one time, and I told him a relationship wasn't going to work with him and me, because we didn't have much in common," Crystal said.

"Uh-huh." The desk officer put down his pen.

"So I would like to apply for an order of protection or find some way to stop him from interrupting my life," said Crystal as tears formed in her eyes.

"Uh-huh. All right, I'll have your paperwork ready in a few minutes; also, I'll have you talk with one of our officers who handle these types of complaints," said the desk officer.

"Yes, sir," Crystal responded as she looked around the police station while standing in front of the desk.

"So, ma'am, in the meantime, why don't you have a seat? But first, sign in on the register over here at the desk," said the desk officer as he went back to his paperwork.

After a short while, a female police officer entered the waiting area, and she noticed Crystal sitting alone in the corner seat at the end of the row of chairs, looking straight ahead with her eyes wide open, not blinking, as though she were in a trance. The female officer walked over toward her.

"Crystal Farnsworth?" the female police officer called out within a few feet from her.

"Oh yes," Crystal responded as she stood.

"Hi. I'm Officer Clemens," said Officer Clemens as she extended a hand to her.

"Hi, Officer Clemens. Nice to meet you," said Crystal as her hand met the officer's, and they shook hands, greeting each other.

"All right, Miss Farnsworth," said Officer Clemens as she looked at her clipboard, but Crystal politely interrupted.

"Officer Clemens, you can call me by my first name—Crystal." Crystal smiled.

"All right, Crystal, if you would come with me, we'll go to my office, past the front desk, down the hall, and toward the left."

Crystal and the officer proceeded to her office. When they entered the office, Officer Clemens shut the door behind them. Crystal sat down on the chair in front of Officer Clemens's desk, and Officer Clemens sat down on her chair behind her desk. The officer looked over Crystal's paperwork again as Crystal looked around her office.

"OK, Crystal. I read your paperwork prior to seeing you, and now I need to hear it straight from you also," said Officer Clemens.

"All right, Officer Clemens. This is the situation. I put personal ads in the personals once in a while, in the newspapers, and this guy Tommy answered my ad. He left a message and his phone number in my voice mailbox, and I responded to his message by calling him," Crystal said.

"All right, you placed an ad in the personals, and this guy Tommy responded to your ad in the newspaper, and he left a message in your box and left his telephone number?" Officer Clemens asked, writing everything down on her pad.

"That's right. So I called one night, and we talked for a while and made plans to go out one night. We agreed to meet at a coffeehouse. When we met at the coffeehouse, we made plans to go out on a date on a night we agreed on."

"OK, you and Tommy met at the coffeehouse, and that was strictly to see if there was any attraction between the two of you, right?"

"Yes. I mean, attraction isn't everything, but it is important. Plus, you have to feel to see if there's any chemistry between you and the other person. And that was why we met at the coffeehouse in the beginning."

"Uh-huh," Officer Clemens responded, writing things down on her pad.

"We met for coffee, and it went pretty well, but I just wasn't attracted to him. I mean, he was really nice in the beginning, when we went out for dinner. We were supposed to go to the movies afterward, but on the way to the movies, I told him I didn't think this was going to work. I was totally straight up with him and said I was not attracted to him. I told him in the most honest and sincere way. I was only being honest, rather than leading him on. I was up front with him—the whole nine yards. I don't know. I never have been involved in these kinds of situations before," said Crystal.

"All right, so you haven't gone out with him since then, right? But let me ask you a question. If you weren't attracted to him, then why did you have dinner with him and then decide you weren't attracted to him?"

"Well, I liked the way he was treating me—you know, being a gentleman and all of that. I made up my mind that it was going to be just for dinner, and that was going to be it, because it was too late to call him to tell him I didn't want to go out with him. So I went out with him and decided I would tell him on the way to the movies, before getting to the theater. So on the way, I did just that. And then I went home," Crystal explained as she remembered leaving him in the middle of Times Square.

"All right, so you haven't been with him since then?" the officer asked, still writing in the pad.

"No. I only met him at the coffeehouse, and then we went out that one night, having dinner," said Crystal, feeling tired and frustrated.

"OK, and he's currently stalking and calling you, and of course, you would like this to stop as soon as possible?" the officer asked as she smiled halfway.

"Yes, ma'am. I would greatly appreciate it. I told him to stop calling me and to stop stalking me, but he still continues to, not accepting that I don't want to be with him," Crystal said with tears welling in her eyes.

Officer Clemens noticed and slammed down the pen on her desk. "OK, Crystal, this is the situation before us. Based on my experience in these types of situations, he definitely fits the description of someone who is obsessed. He is, in fact, obsessed with you. The ongoing phone calls and the stalking—this is a classic case, and you are definitely not alone. Many women—and even men, if you can believe it—have the same problem you have. You're not alone. So here's what we're going to do. Right now, I'm going to prepare an order of protection, and I will explain the procedure and the things that Tommy cannot do to you, all right?" the officer said as she was preparing the paperwork on her desk.

"All right," said Crystal, feeling relieved.

The officer passed her a box of tissues because of her tears and started writing out the order of protection.

+ + + + + + +

Tommy was at his apartment, still pacing back and forth in the living room, mumbling to himself, contemplating if he should call Crystal. He looked over at the telephone.

"No! I shouldn't! I can't do it, because she doesn't want to be with me."

There was a moment of silence.

"Damn it! Deep down inside, she must love me, because if she didn't, she would've gone to the cops. If she actually felt like I was harassing her." Tommy convinced himself while pacing about the living room floor, and then he placed his hands over his face. "I don't know, God! I don't know what I'm going to do!" Tommy shouted with his hands still over his face. He went to the window, which overlooked the street in front of the apartment building.

+ + + + + + +

"All right, Crystal, here's the order of protection. If he violates it, it will most likely land his ass in jail," said Officer Clemens, showing Crystal the forms and talking her through the papers of the order of protection. They were still in her office. "This order of protection is good for twelve months. He can't come within one hundred feet of you. He can't come near you at home, at work, or anywhere else. Anywhere where you are, he cannot be. He can't call you on the telephone at your home or at your job."

"All right. He has my home phone number but not my work number," said Crystal, still reading the order of protection.

"Right. Well, it's never a good idea to give out your work number in the beginning."

"We met at a busy coffeehouse, a very busy public place," said Crystal as she smiled halfway.

"I know, but you still have to be very careful out there. This is not the land of Oz. Know what I mean?" the officer asked as she laughed, and Crystal joined in with the laughter. "Like I said, if this guy violates the order of protection, we'll lock him up. We take harassment very seriously here in New York." Officer Clemens took another sip of her coffee, which had turned cold, as she gave Crystal a copy of the order of protection.

"All right," said Crystal as she took her copy of the paperwork from the officer.

"And as for his copy, we'll physically send him a copy of the order of protection from the police station in his local area where he lives. Oh, by the way, do you have his exact address?" Officer Clemens asked as she smiled.

"Actually, I do. This was kind of strange. When we met at the coffeehouse, he gave me his address just like that. And he didn't even know who I was. Unbelievable," said Crystal as she gave her the piece of paper with Tommy's address on it.

The officer took the piece of paper from Crystal.

"This is great. I really hope it works," Crystal said, folding the paperwork and putting it in her purse.

"Crystal, look at this man. Tommy has a serious problem. It's not just personal, but it also affects your whole life as well. And I don't want to worry you, but in some cases, it could get fatal. I tell you this so you will be aware of the seriousness of this situation. Just don't have any connection with him. All right? If you see him on the streets—which would be rare unless he was following you, as we live in a big city—look the other way, and stay as far away from him as possible." Officer Clemens unwrapped a Tootsie Roll lollipop and stuck it in her mouth. She offered Crystal one, but Crystal declined as she and Officer Clemens smiled.

"Oh, I don't know. I just feel in some way, he's not going to give up so easily," said Crystal.

"Crystal, a good majority who are obsessed will not stop without a fight, and that's when the NYPD steps in. All right, so you have your copies of the forms, and like I said, we will personally serve these papers to him—I believe as early as tonight, because it's still early enough right now," said the officer as she looked at her watch while she rose from behind the desk. She and Crystal exited her office and proceeded to the front desk down the hallway.

When they arrived at the front desk, where the desk officer was still doing his paperwork, Officer Clemens and Crystal shook hands, and then Crystal exited the police station and continued her journey home to her apartment.

+ + ♦ + + +

Two hours later that evening, at Tommy's apartment, there was a knock on the door. Tommy was eating a sandwich while watching a Tom and Jerry cartoon on television. When Tommy heard the knock, he lowered the volume of the television with the remote control, rose, and went to the door.

"Who is it?" Tommy asked at the door, but there was no response on the other side of the door. "Hello! Who's there?" Tommy asked again as he looked through the peephole.

When Tommy saw who was at the door through the peephole, he walked back into the wall in the hall. There was another knock on the door.

"Mr. Landis, it's the police. Are you Tommy Landis, or is Mr. Tommy Landis home, sir?" one of the police officers asked.

Tommy opened the door and saw two police officers in full uniform standing at the doorway of his apartment.

"Are you Tommy Landis?" the other police officer asked.

Tommy froze, not knowing what to say for a moment. "Yes. Yes, I am Tommy Landis. Why do you ask? Am I in trouble or something?" Tommy asked as he let the two police officers into his apartment, getting them out of the hallway so the neighbors wouldn't see them. After the officers entered the apartment, Tommy quickly looked into the hallway, making sure no one had seen the officers, and then he shut the door. Tommy took a deep breath as he began to panic, but he was careful not to let the police see him in that state.

"I'm sorry. Where are my manners? Would you like something to drink?" Tommy asked as the three stood in the kitchen.

"No, thank you," said one of the police officers.

"All right," Tommy responded, and he waited to see what was about to happen.

"Mr. Landis, a woman by the name of Crystal Farnsworth has put an order of protection against you," said one of the police officers as he handed Tommy his copy of the order of protection in an envelope.

"An order of protection?" Tommy asked as he looked at the envelope, and then he took out the forms.

"The order of protection says you cannot come within one hundred feet of Crystal Farnsworth. Also, you cannot call her at home or at work. And stalking in New York is against the law, and you've been accused of it, as well as calling and harassing her at her place of residence. All right? You are not to call or stalk her. Failure to comply with this order of protection will result in time in jail. All right, Mr. Landis?" one of the police officers said.

"Yes, I understand, but you don't understand. She loves me," said Tommy as he stood there with tears in his eyes, and the two police officers looked at each other.

"Look, pal, we're sorry things didn't work out with this lady, but if she were in love with you, she would be here with you, instead of my partner and me being here with the order of protection," said one of the officers.

"So do yourself a favor, guy. Accept the situation as it is. All right? Move on. And maybe get some help. All due respect, all right?" said the other officer.

A few of the neighbors were in the hallway near Tommy's apartment as the two police officers walked out of the apartment. As Tommy walked the officers out of his apartment, he saw a few of his neighbors looking at him. He closed the front door.

When Tommy was back inside his apartment, he began to read the order of protection on his way back into the living room with tears streaming down his cheeks and falling onto the papers. He picked up the can of beer sitting on the coffee table and took a drink. Then he turned around, facing a mirror, and threw the can, with the remaining beer, at the mirror across the living room, shattering the mirror with a crash. He watched the shattered pieces of glass fall as if in slow motion onto the carpeted floor.

CHAPTER 8

THE NEXT MORNING IN THE subway, as the train screamed by, Tommy had his newspaper and coffee in hand as he prepared to board the train to go to work along with others doing the same.

When the train came to a screeching stop, the doors slid open, and as a few of the commuters were exiting the train, Tommy and others boarded the train. It was a typical rush-hour morning. When he found a place to sit, he sat down quickly and closed his eyes for a moment, thinking about the order of protection Crystal had had the police serve him at his apartment. He recounted what had happened yesterday at his apartment with the police officers.

An hour and a half later, Crystal's train came to a stop, and she exited the train, on her way to the office building where she worked.

Today is just another day. It's a day with a new beginning, with the hope that the order of protection will protect me from Tommy, she thought as she entered the building where she worked. She walked into the lobby with her head held high, along with her hopes, and a brand new look of confidence in whatever might come her way as she walked toward the desk.

"Hey, Crystal!" Gina, her coworker, called out.

"Hey, Gina!" Crystal called out, and they hugged and greeted each other.

"So what happened with the boss yesterday? As I was passing by her office, I noticed that the door was closed, and I overheard you and the boss talking. Usually, that means you've been fired or are getting a promotion or something." Gina smiled.

"Well, Gina, I didn't get fired or promoted again. We discussed something I can't really explain right now. Maybe I'll tell you more about it in the future, all right? So I'll catch you later," said Crystal as she quickly declined to discuss what she and her boss had discussed in her office yesterday and went to the stairway to go down to the locker room underneath the building.

+ + + + + +

As Tommy entered the messenger center, he realized he was early. He saw only Maria inside the center. As soon as he saw Maria at her desk, he casually walked by her. Maria noticed from the side of her eyes that Tommy was present as he walked to his locker.

"Hi, Tommy!" Maria called out, and he glanced over his shoulder while facing his locker.

"Hey, Maria. Where's everyone this morning?" Tommy asked, putting on his work smock.

Maria walked over toward Tommy as he put on his smock near his locker. "So, Tommy, I thought about you last night," she said as she smiled.

"Oh yeah?" Tommy responded, taking off his sneakers and putting on his shoes.

"Yeah. Did you think of me last night?" Maria asked with the longing for love she felt she needed from him.

He turned around, facing her. "Maria, actually, I did think of you last night. What is it going to take for you to understand that I'm not in love with you? I told you: I'm in love with Crystal," said Tommy as he finished brushing his hair as he looked into the small mirror that hung on the locker door. When he was done, he slammed the locker door shut and got in Maria's face, and she hoped he was going to kiss her. "I love Crystal. Got it?" Tommy asked.

"Yes," said Maria.

"Good!" said Tommy as he smiled.

Maria turned around as Tommy went around her, and he put his face in her face again. Maria turned around again, with her back facing him.

"Whatever. She doesn't even love you," said Maria as she giggled a little.

Tommy was still behind her, with her back still facing him. All of a sudden, she turned around, facing him. Eye to eye, they stared into each other's eyes, and Maria felt he might give in this time and kiss her.

"You know that it's true. Yet you keep calling her, and you try to convince her that you two are meant to be together," said Maria.

"Crystal and I are meant to be!" Tommy shouted with tears in his eyes. His eyes looked as though they were going to explode with rain.

"Give me a fucking break!" Maria shouted as she turned away, with her back facing him once again. Then she walked back to her desk as she cried silently. When she arrived at her desk, she slowly turned around, facing him again. "You know something, Tommy? You're really fucking twisted," said Maria as she smiled halfway.

"Say what?" Tommy responded in disbelief.

"I said you are twisted!" she shouted while walking slowly toward him. The messenger center was dim and empty, with only Tommy and Maria present.

"Twisted?" he asked while he put his hands in his pockets, leaning up against the lockers.

Maria walked closer to him till she was just inches from him. "Yeah, twisted! You know the Spanish term Spanish people use? *Loco*! Or in English, *twisted*!" Maria shouted.

Tommy just stared at her.

"Say, are you on drugs?" Maria asked as she went near his face.

Tommy just continued staring with an expression of concern, yet he admired her determination, because it reminded him of himself in pursuit of Crystal. "Ah, no. I never took any drugs anytime in my life. And by the way," said Tommy, close enough to Maria for them to kiss each other on the lips but not touching her, "you say I'm twisted because I'm in love, and—"

Maria interrupted. "No! I never said you were twisted because you were in love with this woman. What I mean is, you were in love, but now you're obsessed with her! Oh, by the way, she's not in love with you," said Maria as she placed her right index finger on his lips gently.

Tommy removed her finger from his lips, and he was tempted to kiss her but declined to. "Well, she isn't in love with me right now, but soon she will be. And I really do believe she and I are meant to be, but she just doesn't realize it yet. And how do you seem to know so much about how she feels about me? You act as though you were right there when I was with her."

Maria didn't respond; she turned around slowly, walked back to her desk, and stood behind her chair as she looked down at her desk.

Tommy, tucking his shirt into his pants, walked over to Maria, who was still standing behind her chair at her desk. "Maria?" Tommy called out, and she turned her head toward the doorway of the messenger center, the opposite of where Tommy was. Tommy walked around to where she was looking and stood in front of her. "Maria?" Tommy said again.

"What?" Maria shouted as she pushed her chair into her desk with her right foot.

"I asked you how you know so much about how Crystal feels about me, when you were never even there. Plus, you've never even spoken to her before," said Tommy as he started feeling a bit concerned about his privacy.

As other messenger center employees entered for work, there was a moment of silence as Tommy and Maria noticed everyone coming in. Behind the employees, Louie, their supervisor, entered.

"What the hell is going on around here? What's this?" Louie asked as he entered the center and looked around.

"Nothing much," said Tommy as he continued getting ready for work.

Louie looked over at Maria, who was at her desk, doing her paperwork. "All right, everyone, let's get busy! Tommy, get the cart, and let's start loading up!" Louie yelled out.

Tommy grabbed the nearest cart and together Louie and Tommy began loading the day's mail into the cart.

<hr />

At the reception desk, Crystal was gathering her paperwork for the day. The lobby was calm. She took a sip of her coffee.

"Hi, Crystal," Ms. Wallenford called out, approaching the reception desk.

"Oh, hi, Ms. Wallenford."

"Did you do what we discussed yesterday in my office?" she whispered in Crystal's ear.

"Yes, I did. Right before I walked home, I went to the nearest police station, and when I arrived there, a police officer who deals with these kinds of problems helped me prepare an order of protection. When she was done questioning me, she gave me a copy of the order of protection, and I was told to carry my copy with me in my purse at all times." Crystal took out a copy of the order of protection from her purse.

Ms. Wallenford took the copy of the order of protection from Crystal as she passed it on to her. "Way to go, girl! It's possibly not news to you, but I'm very proud of you," Ms. Wallenford excitedly whispered, as she didn't want to cause an echo throughout the lobby area. She and Crystal hugged each other.

"I'm so glad we talked in your office. I really do appreciate that. Thank you very much," said Crystal as they parted ways from their embrace.

"No problem, Crystal. Anytime you need to get something off your shoulders, come talk to me, all right?" Ms. Wallenford then rose from where she was sitting next to Crystal, smiled, and began to sign in a visitor at the desk.

The day ended, with the sun going down, and as the sun set behind the tall and mystical heights of the Manhattan skyline, the everyday people of New York City were on their way to their homes, getting ready for the weekend.

Tommy stood by the side of the building where Crystal worked, patiently waiting for her to pass by.

Meanwhile, at the reception desk, Crystal was present, talking to a few of her coworkers before leaving the job to go home.

"Hey, Nancy, look, you have to put yourself first. For Pete's sake, you're not married to this jerk! Why put up with this abuse when you don't have to?" Crystal asked her coworker.

"You know something? You're absolutely right. I'm letting him go. I am letting him go!" said Nancy as she smiled with her coworkers all around her. "And I really appreciate you talking some sense into me and encouraging me," Nancy added as she slammed her pen down on the desk, agreeing with Crystal in what she was saying.

"All right, everyone, have a great weekend! See everyone next week," said Crystal as she slowly walked toward the twin glass doors at the entrance.

As she walked out of the building, Tommy saw her. She passed him at a distance and walked toward Sixth Avenue while Tommy still hid on the side of the building.

About fifty feet away, Tommy began to follow her from behind. Among the crowds, Crystal didn't notice him as he violated the order of protection as he continued the pursuit of her. She continued to walk toward Sixth Avenue, and at the corner, she stopped and looked behind her. She saw a mass of people behind her; it looked like another ordinary day in Manhattan after work before the weekend.

But in the midst of the crowd, like dirt that got between the fingers of a person's hand without the person realizing it was there, Tommy wasn't far behind, watching Crystal's every move.

As she continued her journey to the subway, Tommy followed as though he were hypnotized, almost in an induced trance. She walked quickly down the concrete steps of the subway, and Tommy followed quickly, hoping not to get caught, because this time, he could end up in jail, he kept reminding himself while he continued his pursuit.

As Crystal approached the turnstiles, Tommy stood behind the token booth, watching. She went through the turnstile and fell into a large group of commuters on the platform, waiting for the train to arrive.

Within minutes, the uptown train arrived and came to a complete stop at the platform; the doors slid open; and as people were getting off, Crystal and other riders entered the train. Tommy walked as fast as he could through the turnstile and entered the train car behind the one Crystal was riding in. Just as Tommy made it onto the train, the doors slid shut. People looked at him because he rushed in abruptly. He held on to one of the poles on the train.

The train began its journey uptown as the train conductor was on the loudspeaker.

"Please don't lean on the doors! You are holding up the train, and you are holding up many people who want to go home! Thank you!" said the conductor on the loudspeaker as the train exited the station through the tunnel, going uptown.

Tommy walked over to the side door and looked through the glass into the next car of the train. He saw Crystal sitting and listening to her Discman as she looked straight ahead, moving her head in time with the music she was listening to. Tommy's eyes never left Crystal. He never blinked, not once. It was as though he were in a hypnotic state, in a trance. As he continued watching Crystal from a distance, he slowly drifted into a daydream. His body felt numb all over, and his mind was free as he continued to stare. Tommy and Crystal were inside his apartment in Brooklyn. When they entered his apartment, Tommy turned on the light in the living room, and she looked around the apartment while standing still.

"Crystal, would you like something to drink?" Tommy asked as they took off their coats.

"No, thank you, Tommy," Crystal responded as she took off her coat and gave him her coat to hang up. Then she went farther into the living room and sat down on the sofa.

Instead of hanging up the coats, he laid them neatly on the recliner, because the closet was a little unorganized. He walked over to Crystal and joined her on the sofa as she smiled at him. He couldn't believe he finally had her in his apartment. When he sat down on the sofa next to Crystal, he placed his right hand on her upper right leg and placed his left arm around her on the back of the sofa. As Crystal turned her head, her eyes met Tommy's. Their eyes locked on each other as their faces drew closer as their passion rose. As their faces drew closer, Tommy kissed her on the cheek softly. Then he moved down, kissing her on her neck. She tilted her head to the left, feeling high from his passion.

When their eyes met once again, Crystal removed his black-framed glasses, folded them, and placed them on the floor near the corner of the sofa, toward the window. Afterward, their eyes met again, and their lips burned at a fever pitch as their lips drew nearer. When their lips met and they kissed, Tommy was in ecstasy. They kissed with their tongues intertwined while the heat and the passion were on the rise.

Back to reality, back on the train, Tommy was somewhat in a daze. Someone walked into him as he was coming out of his daydream. He partially opened his eyes and looked at the passenger.

"Hey!" Tommy said as he hung on one of the poles to save himself from falling onto the floor of the train.

"Sorry, man," said the passenger who'd run into him and almost knocked him down.

Tommy just looked at him, and then he quickly looked through the glass of the side door and saw Crystal approaching the doors of the train, getting ready to exit at her stop. He also noticed some of the other passengers going behind her.

He entered the next car of the train, where Crystal was. Without Crystal noticing him, he slid into the crowd of riders as though he were invisible and hid within the crowd of passengers behind Crystal as she stood in front of the doors, waiting for the train to stop.

When the train came to a complete stop and the doors slid open while the train conductor called out the name of the station, Crystal and the crowd of passengers, with Tommy in their midst, exited. Tommy walked slowly behind the rushing crowd. Crystal was in front of the crowd, and he carefully made sure he didn't lose sight of his love interest. Everyone went down the steps of the subway, dispersing in different directions, with some crossing the street. Tommy stayed behind some of the other commuters, still keeping his eyes on Crystal, as he crossed the street. While she continued her journey to her apartment, she made plans to herself about what she was going to do over the weekend. Within sixty to seventy feet away, Tommy continued his pursuit of Crystal. He crossed another street slowly.

As a few other passengers were exiting the subway from another arriving train, Maria separated herself from the crowd, walking frantically, hoping to catch up in her pursuit of Tommy.

When Tommy had followed Crystal on the same train, Maria had missed the train, so she'd had to catch another train to continue her pursuit. As she approached the steps of the subway with the crowd behind her, she saw Tommy just across the street. She rushed down the steps of the subway, and when she was on the sidewalk, she saw him across the street. She crossed the street, keeping her distance, as she pursued her love interest.

When Crystal was about to turn the corner near where she lived, she turned her head slowly partially and then turned her head all the way forward. She saw no one behind her. Tommy was hiding behind a car.

As Maria walked at a distance across the street, Crystal noticed her across the street. Crystal wondered if she was being followed by the woman, but she didn't recognize her, so she ignored her and continued walking home. Maria noticed Crystal from across the street as she followed Tommy from behind.

Seeing the woman across the street, Crystal thought, *Maybe that woman is just walking home too.*

Even though Crystal did not know the woman across the street, Maria knew who Crystal was.

She's so beautiful. No wonder Tommy is so much in love with this blonde-haired, blue-eyed goddess! Maria thought as Crystal turned back around and continued her journey home.

As she turned the corner, Tommy walked out from behind the car and continued his path behind Crystal as he kept a distance of sixty to seventy feet from her.

Maria saw Tommy walking behind Crystal and picked up the pace behind Tommy from across the street, hoping Tommy would not notice her.

Crystal arrived at the entrance of her apartment building. Before she entered through the doors, she looked one more time over both shoulders, as she had the chills. She saw a few people walking by her—nothing out of the ordinary and, best of all, no Tommy Landis. But little did she know, Tommy, though not visible, was present. He stared at her from the side of the apartment building. Maria was hiding behind a black van parked across the street, on the corner of the block where Crystal lived, behind where Tommy was hiding.

Crystal entered the apartment building, and Tommy walked fast across the street to a pay phone as Maria watched from across the street, behind the van.

When Tommy arrived at the pay phone in front of the apartment building, he took a deep breath as he looked up at the windows, trying to remember where Crystal lived. He finally found the right window. He remembered picking her up for their first and last date, and he remembered looking out the window in the living room and seeing a heavy plant that hung outside the window.

Crystal entered her apartment, turned on the light, and entered the living room, and Tommy saw a silhouette on the pulled-down shade of the window in the living room. He watched the silhouette as she moved about surrounded by light coming from the fixture in the living room.

As Tommy watched her from across the street, he wanted to be with her just like in the daydream he'd had on the train. While staring at her through the window shade, he reached for the pay phone, put a quarter into the slot, and dialed Crystal's phone number. As Maria watched from across the street, she noticed where Tommy was looking and saw where Crystal lived. Then she looked back at Tommy as he dialed the number on the pay phone.

At Crystal's apartment, her telephone rang once and then twice. Crystal walked to the side table and answered the phone.

"Hello?" Crystal said, wondering who it might be.

"Crystal, it's me—Tommy." Tommy felt nervous and gasped for his next breath as anticipation rose from the fear of being arrested for violation of the order of protection.

"Tommy? Didn't you receive your copy of the order of protection?" she asked in disbelief.

"Yes, but—"

"But nothing! Do you know I could put you in jail right this minute?" Crystal shouted as she looked at her caller ID on her telephone. There was a slight pause in their conversation.

"Crystal, I'm sorry. I'm really, truly sorry that you're upset with me. You see, I'm not just in love with you, but I'm not sorry for being in love with you. And I'm sorry that you are unable to see things my way. For that, I really am sorry," Tommy said while swaying side to side in front of the pay phone.

"Tommy, hold it! Stop talking for a moment!" Crystal shouted, still looking at the caller ID.

"What?" Tommy asked.

"Tommy, I'm looking at my caller ID on my telephone, and the first three numbers are the same as mine. Are you calling from somewhere in my neighborhood? Because if you are, I'm going to eventually find out, and then my next move will be to call the police," said Crystal.

There was another moment of silence, and then Crystal heard a click.

"Hello? Hello! You son of a bitch," Crystal whispered to herself as she hung up the telephone while writing down the number from the caller ID. She thought for a moment as she walked to the window. She opened the window to get some air and to air out her apartment while thinking about where Tommy might've called from. When she pulled up the shade, she noticed, across the street from the apartment building, a pay phone with the receiver dangling loose off the hook. The receiver swayed back and forth with the wind.

Oh shit! God damn it! she thought to herself as she went to the closet and reached for her coat. While rushing downstairs, she put on her coat. She had the phone number in her pocket, as she thought the call might've come from the pay phone across the street.

As Crystal rushed down the steps of her apartment building, Maria was still kneeling behind a van parked near the corner of the block Crystal lived on. Maria had seen Tommy run from the pay phone across the street from where Crystal lived, and she was thinking about going home too, since Tommy had exited the area. As Maria stood upright, considering going home, she saw Crystal come out of the building. She watched Crystal cross the street as she knelt down again behind the van. Crystal walked toward the pay phone Tommy had used. Crystal reached the pay phone, looked at the top of the number pad, and saw the phone number of the pay phone in black numbers on white tape. The phone number of the pay phone was the same number that had popped up on her caller ID when Tommy called. As soon as Crystal saw that the numbers were a match, her eyes grew with horror. She ran across the street and back into her building. When Crystal was back inside her apartment building, Maria walked back to the subway quickly to go home.

Crystal reentered her apartment and saw her sister and roommate, Darlene.

"Hey, Crystal! Just getting in?" Darlene asked, sitting on the recliner in the living room with her legs up on the arm of the recliner, sideways.

Crystal entered the living room while taking off her coat. "No, I've been home. I came home a little while ago," said Crystal as she hung up her coat in the closet. Then she sat down on the sofa.

"Oh yeah! I'm so glad the weekend is here! It's finally here!" said Darlene as she began to peel a banana while still sitting sideways on the recliner.

"I am too. I have to speak with you for a moment." Crystal pulled out her copy of the order of protection from her purse. "Tommy called," said Crystal, unfolding the document.

Darlene spun around, sitting straight upright, listening to Crystal. "When did he call?" she asked while eating her banana.

"He called about ten minutes ago. That bastard called me from across the street!" Crystal cried as she walked over to the open window, pulled up the window shade, and pointed across the street at the pay phone.

"You mean he used that pay phone across the street? Right here?" Darlene asked as she put down her half-eaten banana on the coffee table, stood, and walked over to Crystal at the window. "That asshole! Call the cops! What in the world are you waiting for? Call them now, Crystal. If you don't, that weirdo won't take you seriously, and then he'll be likely to do anything in the future! And you'll be allowing him to get away with anything!" Darlene placed her hands on her hips, surprised at how Crystal was dealing with the situation.

"I know, I know. And I know this may look kind of crazy, but I'm going to give him one more chance," said Crystal as she walked away from the window.

Darlene stood there dumbfounded at what her sister had just said, and then she walked up behind her. "What! Are you crazy? What if he decides that if he can't have you, then no one else will? That's how a lot of these obsessed people think! And this is how most of them act. I read it in a magazine," Darlene said while pointing upward with her index finger.

"I don't think he's going to throw away his whole life all because he won't be able to have me in his life! Get out of here!" Crystal shouted as she went into the kitchen with Darlene following behind. Then Crystal turned around quickly and was startled because she hadn't known that Darlene was right behind her. "I actually believe he will eventually leave me alone. This won't go on forever," said Crystal as she leaned against the kitchen sink.

Darlene shook her head, as she didn't agree with her sister. "I don't know about you, Sis!" said Darlene as she clapped her hands once in frustration while she walked into the living room.

Crystal took an apple from the fruit bowl on the kitchen table and then walked back into the living room to rejoin her caring sister. "Hey, I thought about even changing the telephone number," said Crystal as she sat down at the end of the sofa, biting into her apple.

"Yeah? Well, if I were you, I would make that call to the police. I mean, this nut will eventually make his move on you, and then what?" Darlene asked as she finished her half-eaten banana and then laid the peel on the glass coffee table across from her.

"What?" Crystal responded sarcastically, eating her apple while smiling.

Darlene went over to her and knelt down in front of Crystal as Crystal remained seated on the sofa. "Look, Crystal, I'm not just your roommate. I'm also your sister. We're sisters! And I don't want to lose you!" said Darlene.

Crystal continued smiling at Darlene with little tears forming in her eyes, and Darlene started to cry. They embraced each other in a caring way. As they wrapped themselves in sisterly love, they started laughing.

"Little sister, I know you care about me, but I want to wait, and if he calls again, then I will call the police," Crystal promised Darlene as she wiped her tears.

"All right. All right if you think you have to wait, but I really believe you're making a mistake. Big sis, just be very, very, very careful. All right?" Darlene said.

"I will," said Crystal as she smiled at Darlene, reassuring her sister that it was going to be all right.

Darlene shook her head again, not agreeing with her big sister. "I mean it. I don't want to buy the newspapers and find out that this bunghole sicko pervert murdered you! Know what I mean, Vern?" Darlene asked, and she and Crystal laughed while hugging each other as only sisters could.

CHAPTER 9

TOMMY ARRIVED HOME AT HIS apartment after a long day at work and spending some time on Crystal. He entered his apartment, shut the door, entered the living room, and turned on the light while taking off his coat. He opened the closet in the hallway and hung up his coat. He walked over to the sofa and sat down, staring straight ahead into space as he tilted his head to the right slightly with his eyes open wide.

"Crystal, why do you avoid me? All I ever wanted was a woman who is everything you are," Tommy whispered to himself as he brought his head upright and continued looking straight ahead. "I need you in my life." Tommy rose from the sofa and began to pace about the living room floor, back and forth, continually mumbling to himself.

The weekend began, and Tommy exited his apartment to do a little food shopping at the local supermarket. He walked down the block, and he noticed a camera store. Before doing the food shopping, he decided he would stop at the camera store first.

He entered the store and noticed a display in the corner of the store. He saw cameras of all different kinds. He was looking for one in particular he could use. He picked one of the cameras with ease. He looked into the eyepiece at the back of the camera. He held the one he'd picked while looking at the others on display. He looked through the eyepiece again.

As Tommy looked through the eyepiece, he saw Crystal leaving her apartment building. While hiding behind a car, he focused on her and snapped a picture. He followed her all morning at a distance and continued taking pictures of her.

With each picture taken, he had a freeze-frame shot of a beautiful woman—a woman Tommy was very much in love with.

Saturday night arrived, and Tommy was in bed, underneath the blanket. He turned out the light on the side table as he smiled to himself.

Sunday morning arrived, and Tommy left his apartment to do some personal errands. At a distance, Maria was close by. As Tommy ran all around Brooklyn, so did Maria, not far behind, as she smiled.

Tommy arrived back at his apartment after running around all over Brooklyn. He sat eating a peanut butter sandwich and drinking a can of beer in his living room. He sat on the sofa, looking at all the pictures he had taken of Crystal. He spread the pictures all over the coffee table. He was amazed at Crystal's beauty.

When he finished eating his sandwich, he picked up all the pictures on the coffee table and took them to the bedroom, where he hung up all the pictures one by one around the edges of the big mirror on his dresser. When he was through, he stepped back and stared at them while sitting slowly on the bed, continuously gazing at them.

＋＋＋＋＋＋

Another day and another week began as Crystal brushed her long blonde hair in front of the bedroom mirror, getting ready for work.

She left the apartment and rushed off to the subway down the street, around the corner.

＋＋＋＋＋＋

Tommy exited the train and walked to another week at work, where he'd been for the past three years.

Tommy entered the messenger center, and as he walked through the center, Maria noticed him from the side of her eyes. She smiled halfway as he walked by her toward his locker.

"So, Tommy, how was your weekend?" Maria asked while doing some filing at her desk as he was putting on his work smock next to his locker.

"It was all right, I guess," Tommy responded, wondering why she was so interested in his weekend, while tying his shoelaces and making sure the shoes were nice and shiny. When he was done with his shoes, he walked over to Maria at her desk. "How was your weekend?" he asked while standing right behind her.

"My weekend was great. I kept myself really busy," Maria responded as she nodded as she told Tommy about her enjoyment over the weekend.

"Oh yeah? What did you do?" Tommy asked.

"What did I do?" Maria asked. She hadn't expected that question to come up.

"Yeah. What did you do over the weekend?" Tommy asked again as he placed his hands on his hips, wondering why he was having this conversation with her.

"Well, let's just say I was in pursuit of my dreams, and it's only a matter of time before I—"

Louie entered the messenger center and saw Maria and Tommy talking. "OK, are we ready to work?" Louie shouted.

Maria went back to her paperwork at her desk quickly, and Tommy went toward the empty carts in the corner while Louie grabbed the clipboard off the nail on the wall on his way to the work counter. When he arrived at the work counter, he assisted Tommy in sorting out the day's mail, putting it into the carts, and getting the carts ready for the day's delivery, while Maria started the day's paperwork, getting it ready for the week.

++++++

Crystal was on the escalator, going up to the reception area.

"Hey, everyone!" said Crystal as she arrived at the desk, and she went around the desk, where the chairs were.

"Hi, Crystal! How's everything?" Dawn, her coworker, asked as they kissed and hugged each other.

"Oh, I'm all right, I guess," Crystal responded as she put her purse in one of the drawers at the desk.

"How was your weekend?" Dawn asked, getting ready to go home. She smiled.

"My weekend was all right, I guess. How was your weekend, Dawn?" Crystal asked as she removed her uniform jacket and rested it on the back of the chair.

"What weekend? Ah, I worked all weekend." Dawn laughed, and Crystal laughed along with her.

"Hey, all that overtime! That's why I can't get any overtime! Now I know where to get some money whenever I'm broke!" said Crystal as she and Dawn were laughing.

"Oh yeah, right!" Dawn responded as she rose from where she was sitting with her purse swung over her shoulder as they continued laughing together.

"Have a great day, Dawn," said Crystal as she sat down in the chair.

"I will, and you do the same, Crystal. Cheers," said Dawn as she left the reception area, coming off the night shift.

Crystal and her two coworkers began their shift immediately, signing some people in for meetings on the upper floors.

Meanwhile, back at the messenger center, while Tommy and Louie were still loading the day's mail into the carts, Maria stared at Tommy from the side of her eyes. She watched him bend down to pick up items for the morning deliveries and load them into the carts.

"Now, take them to the upper floors, Tommy. Take all of this to the upper floors, and remember, you get your lunch break at one o'clock today, all right?" Louie said while he held on to an unlit cigar.

"Yeah, all right," said Tommy as he pushed his cart full of mail out of the messenger center into the hallway. As he exited the center, Maria kept her eyes on him till she couldn't see him any longer.

When Maria could no longer see Tommy, she quickly turned around and was startled by Louie's presence right in front of her suddenly.

"Whoa!" Maria yelled as she jumped out of her seat and away from the desk.

"What is this? When Tommy leaves the center, why are your eyes always on him?" Louie asked with an unlit cigar at the corner of his mouth, dangling.

"I don't know." Maria turned with her back facing Louie as she continued doing her paperwork, feeling slightly embarrassed.

When the day came to an end, like on any other day, Tommy and the other workers got ready to go home. He opened his locker, removed his work smock, and then hung it up in his locker, on a wire hanger. He reached for his sweatshirt and put it on. It had a picture of the Brooklyn Bridge on the front. Then he put on his sneakers after taking off his shoes. When he was ready, he slammed shut his locker. After he secured his locker, he walked over to Louie, who was sweeping the floor.

"Hey, Louie," Tommy called out as he approached him.

"Yeah, Tommy?" Louie responded as he momentarily stopped sweeping and looked over at Tommy.

"I'm going now. Have a good night. I'll see you in the morning," said Tommy as he exited the messenger center.

Maria looked from the side of her eyes. She was ready to leave and go home too. She waited for Tommy to leave first. As soon as the time was right, she exited the center and hid from the elevator bank. As soon as Tommy entered an elevator and the doors slid shut, she walked over to the elevator bank. As soon as she arrived at the elevators, another elevator was ready to go up. When the doors slid open, she entered, and she pressed the lobby button as the doors slid shut.

When she arrived in the lobby, she exited the elevator. She walked through the lobby, looking frantically for Tommy, while walking quickly toward the front entrance. She turned her head all around, looking for the man of her dreams.

When she exited the building at the front entrance, she saw Tommy about one hundred feet away, at the corner down the block, waiting for the light to change so he could cross the street. She walked fast to catch up with him, but as soon as she neared him, she hid behind a small crowd of people waiting to cross the street.

As soon as the light changed and the busy traffic stopped, Tommy and the small group of people, with Maria behind them, crossed the street. In the middle of crossing the street, he stopped dead. The Don't Walk light appeared. He went back to the corner as he checked his watch. Maria broke away from the small crowd and began to follow Tommy from behind. Walking behind him at a distance, she noticed him pull out a camera from his small backpack. She wondered why he had a camera as she continued pursuing him.

When Tommy arrived closer to the building where Crystal worked, he could see her through the glass windows of the rotating doors as he viewed the lobby. He saw Crystal walk away from the reception desk and toward the glass doors, toward the street.

Tommy backed away to the side of the building to hide himself. Maria was hiding on the side of a building across the street, full of curiosity, wondering why he had a camera and why he continued his pursuit of Crystal.

Crystal exited the building and journeyed toward the subway, going home. Twenty feet away, Tommy noticed her walk by. While hiding at the side of the building, he started to take pictures of her.

As Tommy took pictures from the side, Maria watched in amazement. It was as though he were a starving wolf watching his prey walk by.

"I can't believe it! He would rather look at pictures of some girl who doesn't want anything to do with him than be with me, someone who loves him. Someone who cares about him!" she mumbled to herself, watching him from across the street.

As Crystal continued walking, with her shapely buttocks following the rhythm of her walking, Tommy continued taking pictures of her incredible physique. She was unaware of Tommy's pursuit and picture taking. Her shapely buttocks truly defined beauty, and her long blonde hair, which reached down her back, almost hitting her buttocks, swayed with the bounce of her walk. It freely flowed with the gentleness of the breeze that rushed over her as Tommy continued taking pictures on their journey to the subway.

Maria continued following Tommy from behind at a distance, still numb, taken over by seeing how Tommy was behaving in this situation. She felt appalled and a bit jealous and envious of Crystal and the attention she was getting from Tommy. As Crystal entered the subway, going down the concrete steps, Tommy, at a distance of twenty feet away, wondered what to do, since he had the pictures taken. Maria panicked. She had not expected Tommy to stop suddenly, and she quickly looked around for a hiding spot.

As Maria hid close to a department store entrance, Tommy walked down the concrete steps of the subway, careful not to be discovered, as he decided to go home. Maria continued her pursuit from behind, also trying not to be discovered at a distance.

When Tommy was in the subway, he put the camera back into his backpack. Maria walked down the steps of the subway. Other people walked around her because Maria was walking slowly and cautiously. One step from the last step, she hid up against the wall, watching Tommy. Tommy went through the turnstile, onto the platform, and down the concrete steps to the Brooklyn-bound section of the subway station as Maria watched from a distance.

Within a minute, Maria heard a train arrive at the Brooklyn-bound area downstairs. Maria went through the turnstile, and as Tommy entered the train, she rushed down the concrete steps to the Brooklyn-bound side. Right before the doors on the train slid shut, she ran and leaped, hoping she didn't enter the car where Tommy was. She made it inside the train just as the doors were starting to close, barely making it in time.

As the train left the station for Brooklyn, Maria looked around the car, as she was still pursuing the man of her dreams. She walked to the other side of the car, approached the door at the end of the car, slid it open, walked through, and entered the next car, looking for Tommy. Before entering each car of the train, she would look through the glass of the sliding door into the next car.

Finally, she saw him in the next car. She slid the door open, walked out of the car she was in, and stood between the two cars, just watching Tommy.

In the next car of the train, Tommy was reading a newspaper, relaxing, sitting. Maria grew more and more frustrated as she continued staring, as she wanted badly to be near him. As he was still reading the newspaper, Maria entered the next car of the train. She walked through a mass of commuters who were standing and holding on to the poles that hung above the seats; some were right in the middle of the train. She continued walking slowly until she found someplace to sit.

She sat down across from him, knowing she was taking a major risk of being discovered. But he hadn't discovered her yet, because he was still reading the newspaper. She grew nervous, wondering why she was doing what she was doing.

A gentleman sitting next to Maria was getting off at the next stop. He rose and left his newspaper on his seat as he walked to the doors of the train. Maria noticed the newspaper the gentleman had abandoned. She grabbed the newspaper slowly, opened it up, and hid behind the newspaper, lowering it every now and then, staring at Tommy.

Every time Tommy turned the page of his newspaper; Maria would raise her newspaper, covering her identity. As she stayed behind the newspaper, covering herself, she decided to read the newspaper as she continued her pursuit of Tommy. When Tommy was finished with the newspaper, he folded it once and placed it on the seat next to him.

After a while, Maria glanced across to see if Tommy was still reading his newspaper, but all she saw was an abandoned newspaper lying on the seat where Tommy had been sitting moments ago. She became frantic. She rose and looked all over the car as she held on to a pole in the middle of the car as the train was approaching a station.

It appeared that while Maria had been reading her newspaper,

Tommy had exited the train at his desired stop. She looked out the window of the train. The train was still at the station, with its doors wide open. She rushed to the slide doors and thought for a moment.

He probably already made it home, she thought as the doors began sliding shut as she looked through the glass.

• • • • • • •

Tommy never went home; instead, he walked into a one-hour photo shop near where he lived.

"Hi, Tommy!" Harry shouted from behind the counter.

"Hi, Harry! What's new?" Tommy asked while he took his brand-new camera from his backpack. He removed the film from the back of the camera.

"Oh, nothing much. Just staying busy. Know what I mean?" Harry said. He smiled as Tommy approached him at the front of the counter.

"Can I pick up the film tomorrow?" Tommy asked as he put the film on the counter. Then he reached into his front pocket and took some money out.

"Sure. Tomorrow would be fine," Harry replied as Maria was just getting out of a cab one block away from the photo shop.

"All right, Harry. See you tomorrow," said Tommy as he exited the shop.

· When he exited the shop and continued on his way to his apartment, Maria was only half a block away.

While Maria was walking, she looked straight ahead, and she couldn't believe her eyes. She saw Tommy as she continued walking up the block.

Oh, thank God, she thought, walking faster, trying to catch up with him but staying at a distance. As she continued walking, she placed her hands into the front pockets of her long black trench coat as Tommy turned the corner on the street where he lived.

As Tommy walked up the block, he decided he wanted to buy a couple of cheeseburgers instead of having to cook, so he turned around and walked back to a fast food restaurant near the camera store. When he entered the restaurant, Maria rushed to a wall near the restaurant, watching. Maria watched him buy some food at the front counter.

After he purchased the food, he started making his way to his apartment building. Maria quickly hid behind a car parked near the curb as Tommy came from around the corner. He quickly walked up the street to where he lived as she followed him slowly from at a distance.

Maria went on the side of a neighboring apartment building into an alley between Tommy's apartment building and the neighboring building, and she watched Tommy enter the building.

"I can remember the party Tommy held one night a few months ago," she mumbled to herself as she walked through the alley, looking at the windows of the apartments, trying to remember which window was Tommy's.

"Ah, here we go. Bingo! There's one of Tommy's windows," she mumbled to herself as she discovered Tommy's silhouette through the window shade, which was already pulled down, covering the whole window. "And there he is." She continued mumbling to herself as she noticed the fire escape, with a rusty old red ladder. Seeing that the ladder was reachable with just one jump, she reached for the ladder and brought it down. When the ladder was all the way down, she began to climb it. She looked at her hands, and some of the rust coloring was on her hands. She continued climbing up.

When she climbed up the fire escape near Tommy's window, she could see him through the crack between the window shade and the window. She could see him in the bedroom. She saw him taking off his blue jeans while still wearing a black T-shirt. After he took off his jeans, he walked to the mirror while in his underwear, looking at the pictures of Crystal that hung on the edges all around the mirror. He stared at them as though worshipping them. *A God. Or in this case, a goddess*, Maria thought.

As Maria continued staring at Tommy's sick obsession, she slipped on something, falling back, and she almost fell off the fire escape.

With the little noise Maria made, she lowered down onto her stomach below the window, hoping she wouldn't be discovered. Tommy looked toward the window, as he felt a bit startled. Maria noticed that she'd gotten his attention. She remained lying flat on her stomach below the window.

He walked toward the window, and Maria grew more nervous by the minute, thinking she might be caught. However, as he was nearing the window to investigate the noise, the telephone rang. Instead of continuing toward the window, he turned away and entered the living room to answer the telephone.

While Tommy went into the living room to answer the telephone, Maria took advantage of the time that was offered and started climbing back down the fire escape via the ladder. When she made it down off the fire escape and onto the sidewalk in the alley, she ran away quickly from the apartment building. While someone watched from a window of the neighboring apartment building across the alley, Maria continued running from the building, until she was away from the alley. Then she walked fast, on her way to the subway.

"OK, OK! I'll call you more often. See you later. All right, Mom! You are a pain in the ass!" Tommy shouted as he hung up the telephone.

After he hung up the phone, he walked back into the bedroom to see what had made the noise on the fire escape. When he arrived at the window, he lifted it open and looked out the window and looked around. By that time, Maria was already twenty feet away from the apartment building, and she entered the subway, going through the turnstile. Tommy never found out the source of the noise he'd heard earlier, but as he looked down, he noticed that the ladder from the fire escape had been pulled down. He stood there as he thought about it for a moment. When he went back inside the bedroom, he closed the window, walked to the light, and turned it out as he walked out of the bedroom. He went into the living room and turned on the television. On the television, he saw a psychiatrist being interviewed on a talk show. As he sat down on the recliner to watch it, he increased the volume on his remote.

"Yes, well, being an obsessed individual is a major problem in today's society, in today's modern world," said the psychiatrist on the talk show, and Tommy laughed.

At Crystal's apartment, Crystal was also watching television as she relaxed from a long day at her job. All of a sudden, the telephone rang. The sleepy Crystal answered the phone from the side table.

"Hello?" Crystal said. The sound of silence widened her eyes, and then she hung up the telephone as she looked at the caller ID. She saw the telephone number, and she lay back in the recliner with both hands covering her face.

Tommy hung up the telephone and placed it back on the pay phone down the block from where he lived. He slowly walked away as the pay phone rang. As he walked back to his apartment building, the pay phone continued ringing. When Tommy reached the front entrance of the building, the pay phone was still ringing. He entered the building.

Crystal hung up her telephone back on the charger and lay back in her recliner, closing her eyes, as she rocked back and forth, trying to forget about what was going on. She knew Tommy must have been calling from another pay phone.

Maria was still in the subway to go home, but she had a change of heart. She decided she needed to be near the man she loved. So she exited the subway through the turnstile, on her way back to Tommy's apartment. She walked quickly to the alley and back to the fire escape.

She saw that the ladder to the fire escape was still down on the sidewalk, and she began to climb the ladder up to Tommy's bedroom window.

When she arrived at the window, she slowly opened the window and entered the bedroom quickly as the neighbor from across the alley watched her, petting his cat, who sat next to him at the windowsill.

When she was in Tommy's bedroom, she slowly and quietly shut the window. She walked over to the door and shut it partway as she turned on the light while she looked around. She saw his bed, and she imagined Tommy and herself making passionate love. She walked over and sat down at the foot of the bed at first. Then she lay there on her back with her eyes shut tightly. She felt relaxed as she continued her fantasy. She saw Tommy on top of her as they continued making love.

Back to reality, Maria opened her eyes wide as she rose from where she was lying and looked around the bedroom. She walked toward the dresser, pulled open the top drawer, and saw skimpy underwear. She picked up a couple of pairs and embraced them, noticing the texture of the material. It was satin.

"So soft," said Maria, and she quickly placed them back in the drawer and turned around, looking toward the bed. All of a sudden, she felt strange, so she followed her feelings and turned around quickly back toward the dresser. She noticed the pictures that hung on the edges all around the mirror. She walked slowly toward the mirror and saw a blonde-haired, blue-eyed young lady.

"Oh, that's the woman Tommy is hopelessly in love with," she whispered to herself while she continued looking at all the pictures hanging on the edges of the mirror. When she had seen enough, she abruptly walked away from the decorated mirror. She turned out the light, walked into the living room, and looked about the place.

At that time, Tommy entered the apartment. Maria turned around quickly as she heard the door of the apartment open.

When Tommy entered the apartment, he took off his coat, and he noticed a sweet scent of perfume. The aroma was familiar, as though he had been around that scent before, but he couldn't remember where. After he laid his coat on one of the chairs in the kitchen, he reentered the living room—and saw Maria standing by the window. While he stared at her, he couldn't believe whom he was seeing.

"Maria?" Tommy called out, trying to figure out how she had come in.

"Yes, Tommy?" Maria responded as she grew nervous, hoping he wouldn't call the police.

"How the hell did you get into my apartment?" he asked, standing near the couch, as Maria approached him slowly.

"I'm so sorry, Tommy. Well, no, I'm not so sorry!" said Maria as she embraced him. "I want to be near you, Tommy. I need you. And you need me!" Maria embraced him tighter, as though her life depended on him, while he stood there numbly, not believing that this was taking place. She took him by the hand, led him to his bedroom, and opened the door to his bedroom. When they entered the bedroom, she turned on the light. They looked at his bed, and he looked at her.

"Maria, I can't! I'm not in love with you! I'm in love with Crystal! Crystal is the woman I want to spend my life with," said Tommy as he released his hand from hers and walked to the door of the bedroom.

Maria walked over to the foot of the bed and sat down. Tommy turned out the light and hoped she'd walk out of the bedroom without any problems. While she sat there at the foot of the bed comfortably as some light from the living room entered, Maria stared directly into Tommy's eyes without smiling, wearing a seductive look on her face, hoping she could convince him to see things her way. The moment was bathed in silence throughout the apartment and the bedroom.

"Tommy?" Maria called out.

"Yes, Maria?" Tommy responded as he looked at his watch.

"What's the sense in loving or thinking you will be with Crystal, when she has no intention of ever wanting to be with you?" said Maria as tears welled up in her eyes.

Tommy looked back at the bedroom after looking toward the

living room. He looked toward Maria. His shadow was over her as he stood closer to her.

"Maria, I need you to understand something. I will always love and be in love with her. Not only is she very attractive, but she's smart, easygoing, and outgoing, and someday soon she'll be in love with me too! Do you understand, Maria?" Tommy asked as he knelt down in front of her while she sat at the foot of the bed.

"Tommy, I see and understand what you feel and what you're saying, but she is not in love with you. And this love you say you have for her is nothing but obsession. Your love turned into obsession," Maria said.

Still kneeling on the carpeted floor, he moved in closer to her, as though they were embracing, but they weren't.

"In the beginning, I'm sure it was love—maybe love at first sight," said Maria as she rose from the foot of the bed, and he rose from where he was kneeling in front of her.

"Maria, that's bullshit! A load of bullshit!" said Tommy as he and Maria stood close, with their faces almost touching. She flinched because of his shouting but remained calm.

"Tommy, I believe that love can turn into obsession. But somewhere down the path of love, along the ways of love, when she rejected your love right in the beginning and turned you away, you continued pursuing her, not paying attention to the fact that she doesn't want to be with you. Your love turned into obsession! Face it! God damn it! I wish I could make you understand!" Maria was in front of his face, shaking, feeling a bit nervous and frustrated.

When she calmed down, she and Tommy were quiet. She walked over to the dresser mirror and the pictures.

"And this! Do you really think Crystal gives a shit about this shrine?" Maria asked as she pointed from one side to the other side of the mirror.

Tommy grew annoyed and angry with her. "Shut up! Just shut up, Maria!" Tommy shouted as he stood by the foot of the bed, covered his face with both hands, and turned around, facing the bedroom window.

"Oh, you don't think that love can turn into obsession, Tommy?" Maria shouted as she grabbed his arm and dragged him to the front of the mirror as she stood behind him. "Look! Take a good look! Not only can you see the obsession within you, but look at the two of us together in the mirror! We were meant to be, damn it!" said Maria as she embraced him from behind.

While he stood in front of the mirror, he looked deep into the mirror as Maria embraced him, holding his arms, and he heard Maria's heavy breathing from behind. After hearing her lecture about love and obsession, feeling somewhat aroused by the ongoing heavy breathing, he turned his head and looked into Maria's eyes. He still smelled the sweet aroma of her perfume.

As she kissed him on the back of his neck gently, she thought she might have a chance of being with him that night in his bed. She thought he was slowly becoming hers.

"Maria, I will never give up my chance of being with Crystal. And I know somewhere deep within her heart, she feels the same," said Tommy as he walked away from the mirror and Maria's embrace. He walked about the bedroom as Maria stared at him while standing near the mirror.

"Crystal does want to be with me, and yes, she does love me," said Tommy as he faced the window and the fire escape, seeing the ladder all the way to the ground.

"What do you mean? She doesn't love you, and she doesn't want to be with you. Because if she did want to be with you, she wouldn't walk away from you every time you come around her. And all of these foolish pictures you took of her and hung on the edges of this fucking mirror to jerk off to on a nightly basis!" Maria shouted as she stood next to him, holding both his hands.

Tommy immediately dropped both her hands; grabbed her upper arm; and took her out of the bedroom, through the living room, and to the front door of the apartment.

"Maria, you need to leave, and if you enter my apartment again, I will call the police. And before you go, you need to tell me how you knew about me approaching Crystal every now and then. How did you know?" Tommy asked as Maria shrugged off his hand from her arm.

"Well, Tommy, right now, I'm not at liberty to say how I know, but one day when you and I come together, maybe I just might tell you," said Maria as she turned away, and then she exited Tommy's apartment. Tommy stepped out of his apartment, watching her go downstairs. She paused before continuing the rest of the way down.

"Hey, Tommy!" Maria shouted as she blew him a kiss, and then she continued the walk down the steps.

"Yeah, whatever," said Tommy as he quickly reentered his apartment and slammed the door shut.

CHAPTER 10

THE NEXT DAY ARRIVED WITH a crack of thunder as a thunderstorm arrived in the city as Tommy entered the building where he worked in Manhattan. He walked toward the elevators at the end of the lobby.

An elevator arrived in the lobby, and when the doors slid opened, Maria walked fast into the elevator in front of Tommy. He went in behind her, with a couple of other people following behind him. Maria pressed the button for the basement level as the doors slid shut. The elevator was on its way down to the basement. Maria looked over at Tommy from the side of her eyes as he looked down at the floor of the elevator, feeling somewhat uncomfortable with Maria. She turned her head in the other direction, also feeling uncomfortable, as the elevator reached its final destination, the basement level. When the doors slid open, Tommy motioned for Maria to leave the elevator first, as she was a woman, and he was being gentlemanly toward her in spite of what had happened last night at his apartment.

When Maria exited the elevator, not looking back at him, Tommy followed right behind her. They were on their way to the messenger center. Suddenly, Maria stopped and unexpectedly turned around, facing Tommy, as she put both her hands up. Tommy stopped walking and stayed still.

"All right, Maria, what the hell do you want from me?" Tommy whispered abruptly, feeling annoyed.

"Look, Tommy, you can go around me and ignore me while I tell you exactly what I'm thinking. I know you don't really give a shit how I feel," Maria whispered back.

"OK, so you have ESP. Shall I call *National World Record Magazine*, or are you going to make the call?" he asked with a sarcastic look on his face.

"Tommy, stop being a smart-ass. You know how I feel about you. I'm really sorry I upset you. Especially sorry for last night. I really am sorry." Maria looked directly into his eyes as she moved in closer to him while holding on to his waist with both her hands.

Tommy backed up step by step and released her hands from his waist. "Look, you say I'm obsessed with Crystal, and maybe I am. I don't know, but I do know in the end, I will be with Crystal. But you see, you must know a little something about obsession, because you're convinced that I'm in love with you and that we are meant to be to-gether, even though, I tell you I don't want to be with you." Tommy looked at his watch, making sure he wasn't going to be late.

"Yeah, but, Tommy!" Maria shouted as he turned around and started making his way to the messenger center with Maria be-hind him.

"But nothing! Just leave me alone!" Tommy shouted while he walked faster toward the messenger center, trying to separate himself from Maria. She stood there feeling stranded.

Tommy entered the messenger center quickly, and a few seconds later, Maria rushed in. She walked to her locker while Tommy was at his locker. The coworkers all watched them from the sides of their eyes as they got ready to come on the job. Louie watched, wondering what was going on with Maria and Tommy as they were getting ready while he put an unlit cigar at the corner of his mouth. Maria went over to her desk as Tommy was still at his locker. Louie walked toward Tommy from behind.

"Good morning, Tommy!" Louie shouted as he smiled with the unlit cigar at the corner of his mouth.

"Morning, Louie," Tommy answered as he put on his smock.

"The whole messenger center and I would like to wish you and the lovely Maria a happy and glorious morning!" Louie shouted. Maria looked over her shoulder, wondering what Louie was talking about, as all the workers stopped what they were doing. All the attention was on Louie and what he was saying as the others observed the conversation at the front of the center.

Tommy glanced over at Louie as he was putting on his shoes and tying them, smiling halfway at Louie. "Louie, I know I was ten minutes late, but I—"

Louie interrupted him. "You were twenty minutes late!"

Tommy pointed at his watch. "OK, twelve minutes late, and I'm truly sorry. But I've been here for three years, and I came in late only one other time. So two times in three years. That isn't bad. And again, I am sorry. Because of certain elements"—Tommy looked over at Maria and then back at Louie—"I arrived late. When I arrived in the basement, just around the corner at the elevator, technically, I was on time, but like I said, certain elements—" Tommy glanced over again at Maria and then looked back at Louie as Maria slammed down her pen on her desk, frustrated.

"OK, fine, Tommy. Whatever you do, just don't become a fucking prima donna! Got it?" Louie shouted while pointing a finger within inches from his face.

"I got it," said Tommy, and he finished getting ready and slammed the locker door shut.

"Well, if you two lovebirds are having problems, keep those problems outside these doors, please!" Louie shouted as he continued playing with his unlit cigar while walking toward the carts in the corner. When Louie arrived at the carts, he began to load up the day's mail into the carts, and Tommy walked up from behind to help Louie.

"Louie? I need to tell you something, if it's all right," Tommy said.

"All right. Work while you talk, all right?" Louie said, and Tommy grabbed a handful of envelopes.

"Louie, I am not romantically involved with Maria. I wish you would stop saying things like that in front of everyone, because it's not true, and it's embarrassing," Tommy said, feeling a bit upset and embarrassed, as Louie looked at him.

"All right, Tommy boy! I got it. So let's get busy. We have a big load today to sort out." Louie smiled and rested his unlit cigar in the astray on the counter while Tommy loaded up the rest of the day's mail into another cart.

——————— ·+◆◆+·· ———————

Crystal was at the reception desk, drinking coffee, as a tall dark-haired man with dark eyes entered the reception area in the lobby. He stopped for a moment, looking at his watch, and then he approached the reception desk. All three female receptionists noticed him walking toward them, and Crystal looked at Dawn, smiling.

"Dawn, this one is mine! I'm going to sign him in, all right?" Crystal asked while she smiled at her.

"Crystal, you go, girl!" said Dawn, and she and Crystal laughed.

The tall dark-haired gentleman reached the desk, and all three receptionists held their breath because of his handsome appearance.

"All right, which of you do I speak to about going up to the meeting?" the gentleman asked as he placed his leather briefcase on the carpeted floor next to the desk.

"Hi. Are you going to the meeting on the thirty-third floor?" Crystal asked while looking at her list of expected guests and getting her guest sheet ready.

"Yes! That's the one," said the gentleman as he smiled at her.

"Great. I'll sign you in, and as you're going up, I'll call Mr. Meyers on the thirty-third floor to inform him of your arrival and that you're on your way up," said Crystal, and she dialed Mr. Meyers's number while she smiled at the gentleman. "Your name, sir?" Crystal asked.

"Connors. Jim Connors. From the Golden Eagle Life Insurance Group from Dallas, Texas," said Jim as he smiled.

"Mr. Connors, the voice mail is coming up. I'll leave a message on it, all right?" she asked as she smiled.

"No problem, Crystal," he said while looking at her nameplate on her jacket and then continued staring at her.

"Mr. Meyers, hi. This is Crystal from reception. We have a special guest, and his name is Mr. Jim Connors. I'm sending him up to the conference room on the thirty-third floor for the meeting. All right, bye." Crystal hung up the telephone while she stared at him as he stared back at her.

"All right, Mr. Connors, you can go up now. You know where you have to go, right?" Crystal asked while she hung up the telephone again.

"Yes, I know where to go. I've been here before. But how come I've never seen you before?" he asked while leaning forward with both arms on the top of the desk.

"Well, I used to do reception on the twenty-first floor. And then I was promoted, and they sent me down to this desk." Crystal smiled.

"That's a good deal." Jim smiled at her, and he noticed the other receptionists were staring at him.

"All right, Mr. Connors, you can go up, and you have a great day," said Crystal as Jim picked up his leather briefcase from the floor. She didn't want to be in trouble for keeping a guest down in the lobby because she was speaking with him.

"I will. Oh, Crystal?" Jim called out before leaving the reception desk.

"Yes, Mr. Connors?" she responded as Jim looked over her his shoulder and smiled.

"If you like, you can call me Jim," said Jim as he turned his whole body, facing the desk again. "And would I be forward in asking you out to dinner sometime?"

Crystal smiled as she looked over at Dawn, who was shocked but happy for her.

"Sure. All right. Allow me to give you my home number," said Crystal, and she wrote it down on a piece of paper and gave it to him.

"All right, Crystal, I will definitely give you a call. Have a nice day," said Jim.

"All right. Bye," said Crystal as she waved goodbye to Jim and smiled while staring at him as he went up the escalator.

"You bitch," said Dawn while she smiled at Crystal, as she and Crystal started laughing.

+ + + + + +

It was time for lunch once again, and Tommy clocked out for his lunch break and went up to the employee cafeteria, while Maria was clocking out for her lunch break too. After clocking out, she ran to catch up with Tommy at the elevator bank.

Tommy entered an arriving elevator, and Maria rushed toward the elevator and, as the door was sliding shut, jumped in, just making it inside the elevator, as Tommy held the door from closing all the way.

"Going up?" Tommy asked as he smiled, and Maria was stunned by his sudden kindness as the doors were closing.

The elevator stopped on the lobby level before proceeding to the eighteenth floor, where the employee cafeteria was. A few people exited the elevator, and then the elevator proceeded to the eighteenth floor.

When the elevator arrived on the eighteenth floor, Tommy, Maria, and other workers from the building exited, leaving in the elevator one other person, who was going up.

Tommy and Maria entered the cafeteria, picked up trays, and joined the line of employees who were ready to pick what they were going to eat for lunch. They stood in line with the others, looking at the various kinds of foods on display.

They chose their food, placed it on their trays, paid for it at the cashier, and then walked around the cafeteria to look for a place to sit. As they looked around for a table, Maria ate a carrot stick from her tray, smiling because of an idea she had.

When they found a table, they rested their trays on the table and sat down on their chairs. It was a table big enough for only two persons, tucked away in the corner, near a window overlooking the city's magnificent buildings.

"Well, not only did we find a cozy table for two, but we have this wonderful view of the city," said Tommy as he and Maria looked out the window at the skyline as they began to eat their lunch.

"Yes. It's pretty refreshing to see a view of the city from above ground," said Maria as she continued looking out the window as she smiled at him.

As Tommy was eating his tuna sandwich, he kept looking out the window, and as Maria was eating a slice of cheese pizza, she stared at him from the side of her eyes while looking out the window.

While they were gazing out the window as they ate their lunch, she took a carrot stick from her tray and rested it in her mouth while holding on to it. She started to slide it in and out of her mouth, between her upper and lower lips, while looking directly at him. But as usual, Tommy didn't pay any attention; he continued to look out the window at the people below on the streets and sidewalks of the city.

She then kicked off her right shoe and rubbed her right foot up and down Tommy's leg while still sliding the carrot stick in and out of her mouth and lowering her head a little bit forward as the carrot stick was between her wet lips.

Tommy glanced over at Maria as she kept doing what she was doing, and she smiled with the passion of seduction on her face. Her face was a bit flushed from her own excitement in the heat of the moment.

"Stop, Maria. Stop right now," said Tommy as he picked up his sandwich. Tommy was almost falling for her.

"Stop what? I'm just feeling you out, Tommy," she said, still rubbing her foot up and down his leg as he looked back at her, and she placed the carrot stick back in her mouth.

"You need to stop right now," he whispered as he leaned forward over the table, and she removed the carrot stick from between her lips.

"Fine!" She bit into her carrot stick and then threw the carrot onto her half-eaten pizza and rested her head on her left hand as she looked out the window. "Tommy?" Maria said while looking at the beautiful skyline.

"Yes, Maria?" Tommy responded while he looked out the window as she turned and looked at him.

"Why do you hate me?" she asked while she stared at him, and then she looked back out the window as he turned his head and looked at her.

"Maria, I don't hate you. I just don't have any interest in being with you romantically. That's all," he said while eating the other half of the tuna sandwich.

"I'm not unattractive, and I—" Maria put down her pizza.

"Look, I never said you weren't good looking. In fact, I think you're very good looking. You're hot," said Tommy as he thought about when she had been in his bedroom the other night before he threw her out. "It's just that I'm in love with someone else. I have feelings for you only for friendship, and we're close on the job." He looked at his watch. "Oh, it's time to go back to the center," said Tommy, and he and Maria cleared the table and dumped their remaining lunch litter into the trash can from their trays.

⟡⟡⟡⟡⟡

At Crystal's place of employment, the big meeting on the thirty-third floor between Mr. Meyers and his guest Jim Connors had come to an end. Jim Connors took the elevator down, and when he arrived at the lobby, he walked toward the reception desk.

"Crystal?" Jim called out as he approached the desk.

Crystal turned around and saw Jim at the desk. "Hi, Mr. Connors—oops! I mean Jim," said Crystal, and she and Jim laughed. "So how was your day?" asked Crystal as she smiled.

"My day went fine. The meeting went fast. Faster than I thought it was going to go. We covered a lot of ground," Jim said as he smiled back at her.

"Good. That's good." Crystal looked him over as he was looking her over, and both smiled at the other.

"So, Crystal, can I call you tonight?" he whispered to her as he leaned over the desk.

"Sure, that would be fine," she responded, feeling numb but not looking numb, as she smiled. She couldn't believe this tall, dark, and handsome surprise package was going to call her that night.

"All right then. I'll call you tonight," said Jim as he walked toward the end of the desk while looking back at Crystal. "Eight o'clock tonight. Bye for now." Jim walked away from the reception desk, and she watched him leave the desk and the reception area. He went down the escalator and toward the glass rotary doors at the entrance of the building and exited the building.

After Jim exited the building, Crystal froze in place where she was sitting. She couldn't believe this was happening to her. All she could do was look at her coworkers in amazement, and her coworkers were just as amazed.

"I can't believe it! He's so hot!" said Crystal as she smiled, excited.

"Yeah, he's hot all right, but so are you. Now, calm yourself, girl," said Dawn, and she and Crystal laughed.

"Did you see his dark hair? And his dark eyes?" Crystal asked Dawn.

"Yeah, those dark eyes. The way they would pierce right through you. Oh yeah, I saw them!" said Dawn, and she and Crystal laughed again.

"He's so gorgeous! This is going to be one enchanting evening!" said Crystal as she got ready for her break as she and Dawn continued laughing.

"I believe I'm getting a bit jealous, mate!" Dawn joked with a slight British accent.

"Ah! Poor baby!" Crystal shouted while she, Dawn, and her other coworkers at the desk all laughed.

———————

Louie and Tommy did the final paperwork to call it a day, while Maria was finishing her paperwork for the day at her desk.

"Tommy, I'll see you and Maria tomorrow, all right? I have to leave a little early today because I have something I have to do. So you and

Maria close up shop tonight, all right?" Louie said while putting on his coat from his locker.

"No problem, Louie. You can count on us. We'll take care of it," said Tommy as he was getting the paperwork ready for tomorrow morning for Maria.

"How many more deliveries do you have to do before you go home today?" Louie asked while he stood by the entrance of the center.

"I have one more load for the lower-level floors and the rest of the paperwork before I call it a day," said Tommy while loading up the cart with the rest of the day's mail.

"Goodbye to one and all!" Louie yelled out while he exited the center as Tommy continued loading up one of the carts.

The other coworkers in the center were coming and going, continuously working. Maria was at her desk, working feverishly on the rest of the paperwork and, at the same time, watching Tommy load up the last cart with the final delivery of the day's mail.

"Hey, Tommy," Maria called out, and Tommy looked over his shoulder at Maria.

"Yes, Maria?" he responded as he placed one last big envelope onto the cart and placed the bag on the counter behind him.

"I'm not giving up on us, Tommy," said Maria as she was finishing up her paperwork.

Tommy just stared at her as he turned around, facing her. "Maria, what the hell are you talking about?" Tommy asked while leveling the mail in the cart so nothing fell off the cart.

"Well, right now, there is no situation between us, but I believe we are destined to be together," said Maria as Tommy pushed the cart toward the entrance of the center. Before reaching the doors, he stopped by Maria's desk.

"Maria, I hate to burst your bubble you live inside of, but by the time those men in white uniforms pick you up and size you up for a custom-made straitjacket, the kind with the sleeves that go around to the back, Crystal and I will be together. And that's one story you can believe in." Tommy laughed as he pushed the cart out of the center and toward the elevators to go up to the upper floors.

As he exited the center, Maria watched with a deranged look on her face. When he was finally out of view, she rose from her desk, and in a fit of rage, she threw an empty coffee cup at the doors. The cup shattered as she yelled. A few of the coworkers looked at her with wonder as she calmed herself down and sat back down at her desk. She covered her face with both hands as she leaned forward over her desk slowly, feeling defeated and pushed aside on a shelf of forgotten people.

The evening arrived, and a full moon shone over the city. At Crystal's apartment, Crystal was washing the dishes. She noticed the time on the clock that hung above the kitchen sink while thinking about the gentleman she had met earlier that day, Jim Connors.

All of a sudden, the telephone rang, and she quickly dried her hands with the towel over her shoulder and ran into the living room to answer the call. She thought it might be Jim Connors and hoped it wasn't Tommy, the man she wanted to forget she ever had met. The telephone rang for the third time, and she picked it up.

"Hello?" she answered.

"Hello. Crystal?" the caller asked.

"Yes, this is Crystal," she responded as she sat on the recliner.

"This is Jim Connors," Jim said as he sat on his recliner, near a window.

"Hi, Jim. How are you?" Crystal asked, relaxing on her recliner.

"The rest of my day went smoothly. I'm enjoying my stay in New York, like usual. I come to New York a few times a year for meetings and whatnot," said Jim as he went into the bedroom, sat on his bed, and removed his shoes, still wearing his Calvin Klein buttoned shirt, slacks, and black socks. He placed his shoes on the side of his bed and then reclined on the bed, sitting up with his back against two pillows, comfortable in his hotel room with an evening view of the skyline.

"Are you staying at a hotel right now?" she asked as she took a sip of the glass of milk she had on the side table, next to the all-glass lamp.

"Yes, I'm staying at a hotel near Central Park. Actually, the hotel is across the street from the park." Jim looked out his window overlooking the greenery of Central Park.

"Wow! That must be so beautiful!" said Crystal as she smiled.

"Yes, it is. It's very beautiful. My room has windows that overlook Central Park and another window overlooking some other buildings," said Jim as he went underneath the blanket.

"It must be very nice to be at a place like that. So you work for an insurance company, right? Let's see how good my memory is." Crystal laughed, and Jim joined in on the laughter.

"Actually, I'm one of four owners of the company, but I'm usually the one who travels all over for the company," Jim said while setting the alarm clock on the side table.

"Oh yeah?" Crystal responded as she drank the rest of her milk.

"Yeah. We've been in business for the past five years now."

"Well, you're very professional. I figured you had been in business longer than that." Crystal rose, walked into the kitchen, rinsed out her glass under the kitchen sink faucet, put her glass under the faucet of the spring water tab to fill her glass with spring water, and drank some on her way back into the living room. In the living room, she sat back down on the recliner.

"I wish we had more years in the business. But so far, everything is relatively all right. We're doing quite well right now. So why don't we talk about you now, Crystal Farnsworth? Are you married, and if not, how come?" Jim asked, and he and Crystal started laughing.

"Well, Jim, I'm not married, nor have I ever been married. Maybe sometime in the future I would like to be. Are you married?" she asked, and she held her breath.

"No, Crystal, I am not married, nor have I ever been married. I had a girlfriend I lived with for ten years, and we were going to get married, but things didn't work out. She was trying to be an actress, and she picked up and moved out of Texas to Hollywood, California.

So we never really had a chance. But one day, like yourself, I do plan on settling down—at the right time."

"That's good. You seem to have a slight accent. You said this morning and just now that you are from Texas. You said Dallas, right?"

"Yes, I'm from and currently live in Dallas."

"Oh yeah? Do you like New York?" she asked, and she again held her breath.

"Yes, I do! Even though I live in Dallas, Texas, I come to New York as often as I can. Especially when I'm seeing a lovely woman such as yourself," said Jim, and Crystal exhaled while giggling. Jim joined in with the laughter. "So how about you and I having dinner this Friday night?" he asked, hoping she wouldn't decline his invitation. There was a moment of silence over the telephone line. "Oh, I'm sorry, Crystal. Did I move too quickly?" Jim asked, thinking he might've blown his chance to meet with her.

"Oh no. No, it's not that," Crystal responded as she halfway smiled.

"You're a little bit nervous?" he asked, looking down at his bed.

"A little bit," said Crystal.

"I guess in a way, I am too. I haven't been with anyone since my ex-girlfriend went to California to pursue her acting career a couple of years ago. I haven't been involved with anyone in two long years. I've just concentrated on the business for two years." Jim sat up, crossing his legs.

"Yeah?" Crystal responded as she folded her legs while still sitting on the recliner.

"Well, I pretty much distance myself from serious relationships. Every once in a while, there's a fling here and there and dating but nothing romantically serious," Jim said.

"How long were you and your ex-girlfriend together before the breakup?" Crystal asked, hoping she wasn't making him uncomfortable with the personal questions she was throwing at him.

"We were together for ten years before she went to Hollywood. I heard from mutual friends that she was seeing someone, and she and this other guy went together to Hollywood." Jim sighed but quickly covered it up by laughing.

"Oh shit. I'm sorry to hear about that," said Crystal.

"Yeah, well, she had to do what she had to do. She broke my heart, but I moved on with my life. Life goes on." Jim began pacing around the hotel room.

"I'm sorry about the struggles you had to endure," Crystal replied.

"It's all right, and I'm fine now. You see, I went to counseling, and I learned a lot about myself. I also learned that I must live for myself, and I went on with my life," said Jim as she thought about her own life.

Again, the moment grew silent, and Jim wondered what Crystal was thinking as she wondered what he was thinking.

"So, my dear, are we still on for Friday night, or do you have someone else in your life?" Jim asked Crystal, lying on the bed, on his back.

"I am not involved with anyone at the moment, so Friday night would be great." Crystal smiled while she walked toward the window in the living room.

"All right. Do you live in Manhattan?" Jim asked as he grabbed the hotel pad and pen on the side table next to the bed.

"Yes, I live on the Upper East Side," said Crystal, and she gave Jim her address as Jim wrote the information down on the pad.

"OK, I'll rent a car, and I'll pick you up, all right? Sound good?" Jim asked.

"All right. Sounds good, Jim." Crystal smiled while she looked out the window in the living room.

"I'll pick you up around, say, seven thirty?" he asked while he smiled as he looked at her address on the hotel pad.

"Seven thirty would be fine," said Crystal as she walked away from the window, smiling.

"All right, Crystal, what would you say if we saved the rest of the conversation for dinner on Friday night?" Jim asked, trying to face the reality that he was going on a date on Friday night with this beautiful, magical goddess.

"All right, Jim. See you on Friday night," said Crystal, walking toward the side table near the couch.

"All right, Crystal. Have a nice night. Good night," said Jim.

"Good night, Jim," said Crystal, and she and Jim hung up their telephones.

After hanging up her phone, she sat back down on the recliner, stunned, not believing she was going out with this tall, dark, and handsome Texas stud. She felt as if she were going to burst into a fireball of excitement.

"Yes!" Crystal shouted as she jumped up off the recliner with excitement, and she went to her bedroom to get ready for bed.

As Crystal was thinking about the new man in her life, whom she was going out with on Friday night, Tommy was in his apartment, pacing about in the living room, plotting his next move to get with Crystal and ultimately make her his.

"What am I to do? I tried so many ways to get Crystal to be with me, but each time I tried, she denied her love for me," said Tommy as he turned around, still pacing about the living room. "I must be with her. I have to be with her. I don't want anyone else but her," he mumbled to himself, still pacing about.

Friday arrived, and the city was getting ready for another weekend, depending on what was going on in one's life. Tommy arrived at Crystal's place of employment, several blocks from where he worked, and waited for the presence of Crystal Farnsworth as she left work on her way home.

"All right, everyone, have a great weekend!" Crystal shouted as she waved goodbye.

"You too, Crystal!" said Diane and Dawn as Crystal was leaving the reception area.

Crystal continued waving good night to Dawn and Diane as she walked toward the front entrance of the building to go home.

"Oh, Crystal!" Diane shouted, and Crystal turned around before going through the rotary doors, facing the reception area, as she stood by the rotary doors at the entrance.

"Have a good-o time!" Dawn shouted in her heavy British accent.

"I shall! Cheerio!" Crystal shouted, and she and her other coworkers laughed as she exited the building.

On the way out of the building, she put on her CD player headset. On her way to the subway on Sixth Avenue, Tommy walked behind her at a distance of twenty feet. As she walked to the subway, she thought of her date that evening with Jim Connors as she listened to her Discman, blind to the presence of Tommy behind her.

At the subway, the uptown train arrived at the Eighty-Sixth Street station, which Crystal lived a few blocks from. Tommy was in the car behind Crystal's, watching her the whole time.

When the train came to a complete stop, Crystal exited her car, and Tommy exited his, following behind. After she exited the subway, she walked up the block and turned the corner as she hurried, looking at her watch, noticing she was running a little behind.

Trying to keep up with Crystal, he noticed her speed and thought maybe she knew he was right behind her, though he was being careful.

When Crystal entered her apartment building, Tommy was across the street, over by the pay phone. He noticed a car he could hide behind for the moment. While watching Crystal's apartment building, he saw Crystal's silhouette on a shade that was pulled down as she moved about the apartment. He wondered what she was doing while she was getting ready for her date with Jim Connors.

One hour later, a car drove up to the front of the building slowly, and when the person in the car, Jim Connors, saw the number on the building, he pulled over near the curb, double-parked between two other cars. He pulled out his cell phone and called Crystal.

Crystal's telephone rang, and she ran out of the bedroom to answer the call as Tommy watched her silhouette.

"Hello?" She held her breath.

"Hi, Crystal. It's Jim. I'm out front of the building," said Jim as he smiled.

"Hey, Jim," she responded as she sat on the couch.

"Hey, Crystal. I couldn't find a parking spot," said Jim, looking around, while seated in his rented BMW.

"That's all right. Stay where you are, and I'll be down in a moment," said Crystal as she smiled.

"All right. See you when you come down. Bye," said Jim.

"Bye," said Crystal, and they both hung up their phones. As she looked out the window, she moved the window shade for a moment, and she saw Jim's car he was renting: a shiny black BMW.

Tommy, still across the street, noticed the shiny black BMW double-parked in front of the building and wondered if the car and the man inside had anything to do with Crystal.

"I know this guy can't be waiting for Crystal," he mumbled to himself.

Just then, he saw Crystal come out of the building. She walked over to the passenger side of the car. Tommy, hiding behind another car across the street, watching, couldn't believe his eyes as she entered the shiny black BMW and slammed the car door shut.

As Jim and Crystal smiled at each other, Tommy watched the flashy black BMW drive away, leaving behind Tommy. He stood upright from behind the car, hopelessly watching the BMW leave with the woman of his dreams with another man. The BMW stopped at the corner of the block at a red light. When the traffic light turned green, the car drove away. Tommy walked in the other direction, on his way to the subway, going home to Brooklyn.

Later, when Tommy made it to his apartment building and entered his apartment, he didn't even turn on the light in the living room as he shut the front door. Because of his dark mood, he walked through his apartment in the dark. Then he turned around and walked to his kitchen and opened up the refrigerator. As some light from the refrigerator shone through the darkness throughout the apartment, he reached inside and took out a can of beer. As he opened it, he shut the door of the refrigerator and went back into the darkness abyss, through the living room, and into his bedroom. He shut the door without turning on the light as he drowned in the darkness.

CHAPTER 11

O NE WEEK LATER, IT WAS Friday night, and Tommy was following Crystal. She was on her way home, rushing as usual, as she was thinking about that night, which was going to be her second date with Jim. Tommy had a plan this time.

As Crystal entered her apartment building, Tommy hid behind a parked car across the street, near a pay phone.

Thirty minutes later, a BMW showed up in front of the building as Tommy watched from behind the car, knowing who it was. While Jim was thinking about his second date with Crystal, he noticed a parking space a couple of cars down from the front entrance of the building, and he drove down and parked between two cars. After he parked the rented BMW, he stepped out of the car with a dozen long-stemmed red roses in his hand. He locked the car doors, and then he entered the building, with Tommy looking on from across the street. The front doors on the car were locked, but the two back doors were not. Jim didn't notice.

When Jim entered the apartment building, Tommy came out from behind the parked car across the street and walked over to the BMW. He checked the passenger-side door and saw that it was locked. While looking around, making sure no one was noticing him, he checked a back door of the car, and he discovered the door was unlocked.

He looked around again before he bent down, entered the BMW's backseat, and crouched down, shutting the door slowly and gently.

"All right, I'm ready for you, Crystal," Tommy whispered to himself as he stooped low in the backseat, on the floor of the BMW.

By that time, Crystal and Jim were exiting the building, and they walked toward the car. Jim took out his remote control and unlocked the car and then walked around the car with Crystal to the passenger side. Jim opened the door and held it open for Crystal as she entered the car. When she was fully inside the car, he slammed shut the door, went around to the driver's side, entered the car, and slammed the door shut.

As Jim and Crystal smiled at each other, the shiny black BMW drove off. As they drove off on their second date together, Tommy was still on the floor in the backseat.

As Tommy lay there quietly, he listened to them talk while Jim drove the car.

"Jim, I just love this car," said Crystal as she smiled at him.

"Oh yeah? I'm just renting this BMW, but back home, I own a BMW similar to this one and a Labagene," said Jim as he smiled while looking in his rearview mirror while driving.

"Wow! That's pretty cool. And thank you for the roses." Crystal leaned over and kissed him on the cheek as he smiled at her.

"Uh-huh," Jim responded as he smiled.

"It must be nice to have such beautiful cars to drive," said Crystal as she cuddled next to him, holding his right arm while he continued driving with his left arm.

"Well, it feels good. I work hard, so I like to play hard as well," said Jim, and they laughed.

"Jim, I had such a good time with you last Friday night," said Crystal as she laid her head on his right arm while still holding on to it.

"I had a great time with you also, but tonight you are in for a treat. Tonight we will be dining at this nice, fancy restaurant on Central Park, Sam's Place in the Park. And after dinner, maybe we can park the car and walk around Midtown a bit. Maybe take a ferry ride on the Hudson River or something," said Jim as he continued driving.

"Sounds great. But, Jim?" said Crystal as she looked at him.

"Yes, Crystal?" Jim answered as he looked into rearview mirror.

"I was wanting to ask you a question last week, but it slipped my mind. Please don't get offended by my question, all right?" she said while looking at him.

"All right. I'm ready," said Jim as he smiled.

A moment of silence filled the car while Tommy listened. Crystal was trying to work up her courage to ask him the awaited question.

"Go ahead, Crystal. I'm listening," said Jim as he smiled. They were about to be stuck in traffic, as they were going to the west side of Manhattan, to Central Park.

"All right, Jim. I'll tell you my age if you tell me your age," said Crystal as she looked straight ahead while looking at him from the side of her eyes, smiling.

Jim laughed as the car moved slowly due to the heaviness of the traffic. "Well, Crystal, I'm glad you told me that," said Jim as he smiled at her.

"You are glad?" Crystal asked, feeling relieved.

Tommy felt a bit uncomfortable listening to their conversation and felt a bit jealous and envious of Jim.

"Yes, because I was wondering how old you were. Not that it really matters."

"And you're so good looking and mature, and you're established in your life," said Crystal as she smiled, feeling attracted to him while he spoke.

"All right, I'm thirty-five years of age, and I didn't say thirty-five years old, because I haven't received my first winkle yet," said Jim as he looked over at Crystal, into her eyes. She looked into his eyes, smiling, as the car came to a stop due to the slow-moving traffic.

"So, lovely Crystal, how old are you?" Jim asked as he put his right arm around Crystal's shoulders above the seat and looked into her eyes while she looked back into his eyes as she positioned her body to face him.

"I'm twenty-two years old—oh, I mean twenty-two years of age!" said Crystal, and they laughed while looking into each other's eyes.

As they looked into each other's eyes, the heat of the passion rose. Tommy continued listening on the backseat floor as he grew more jealous by the second.

As they moved closer toward each other while waiting in traffic, they both unbuckled their seat belts the higher the heat was turned up. When they were close enough, their lips slowly met. As their eyes were closed, Tommy rose slowly from behind in the backseat and watched in disgust and rage, feeling frustrated. He watched Jim and Crystal kiss slowly, gently, and with passion while his mouth opened with envy.

As soon as their lips parted slowly, Tommy immediately went down, hiding behind the seat, as cars behind them honked, signaling for them to move their car and go on. Jim and Crystal looked at each other and realized they were holding up traffic, and they started laughing as they held hands while Jim continued the drive to the restaurant.

When they arrived at the restaurant, Sam's Place on the Park in Central Park, Jim parked the car, and he and Crystal got out of the car and walked to the entrance of the restaurant. Jim forgot to lock the car with his remote. Within a few feet of the car, Crystal turned around quickly, and Tommy, who was still inside the car, ducked down onto the backseat floor to avoid getting caught.

"Shit," said Tommy as he lay hidden from Crystal, kneeling on the floor behind the backseat.

"What's wrong?" Jim asked, looking in the same direction as Crystal, toward the car.

She had the feeling she was being followed by Tommy. "Did you lock the car doors?" she asked while looking back toward the car again.

"You know, I completely forgot this time." Jim took out the remote control and locked the doors. After he locked the doors, he turned on the car alarm. They heard a squeak, which was the sound of the car alarm securing the car.

Then they continued their short walk to the front entrance of the restaurant as Tommy lay there on the backseat floor. Because the car alarm was turned on, he knew he was going to have a hard time getting out of the car, and he panicked.

"Well, shit! How the hell am I going to get out of here?" Tommy asked himself as he lay there on the floor of the car.

Meanwhile, in the restaurant, Jim and Crystal walked toward the host's podium near the dining area, just outside the doors.

"Hello. How may I help you this evening?" the host asked as he smiled.

"We have reservations for two under the names of Jim Connors and Crystal Farnsworth for eight forty-five tonight," said Jim as he and Crystal held hands. She held on tightly to his hand while the host searched for their names on the reservation list at his podium.

"Here we are. Jim Connors and Crystal Farnsworth." The host picked up two menus and placed them under his right arm.

"Excellent," said Jim. He and Crystal were still holding hands as the host led them into the dining area. When they arrived at their table, the host took their coats; placed the coats on his left arm; and, with his right hand, pulled out a chair for Crystal. When she sat down, the host slid her into the table, and Jim sat down once she'd sat down.

"All right, a waiter will arrive shortly to take your orders," said the host.

Jim stood up from the table while reaching into his pocket. When Jim's hand came out, he gave the host a five-dollar bill for a tip.

"Thank you, sir," said the host.

"Thank you," said Jim as he sat back down in his chair.

Jim and Crystal stared into each other's eyes. Then Crystal looked around the dining area. In the middle of the dining area, a crystal chandelier hung from the ceiling, and a man was playing a piano softly. Everyone eating at the restaurant looked beautiful and first class.

Jim stared at Crystal's blue satin dress with spaghetti straps over her shoulders. He wore a black buttoned shirt with a light blue tie and a black suit jacket.

The reflection of the lights from above shone on the marble floors, beaming with the accent of Italy.

"This restaurant is so beautiful. I've always wanted to come to this place," said Crystal. Her eyes sparkled as she looked at him from across the table.

"I come here every now and then. You know, for meetings. When there are certain people I meet, like business associates, I bring them here for dinner and cocktails," said Jim as he looked deeply into her baby-blue eyes.

Tommy was still in the BMW's backseat, thinking of a way out of the car. He rose up onto the seat in the back, looked around the parking lot, and saw that it was clear. No one was around. Once he saw that no one was watching or noticing anyone in the car, he unlocked the car door and opened the door slowly—and the car alarm went off. Quickly, he exited the car, shut the door, and ran behind three big bushes in front of the car, just outside the parking lot. A couple of people walking toward the entrance of the restaurant noticed the car alarm sounding off.

Meanwhile, inside the restaurant, a waiter was taking Jim and Crystal's order.

"Will that be all, sir, ma'am?" the waiter asked as he smiled at them.

"Yes. That will be all. Thank you," said Jim as he closed the menu.

Crystal gave her menu to the waiter, who also took Jim's and then went back to the kitchen to give their order to the chefs.

The host of the restaurant reentered the dining area, walked up to the podium near the doors, and turned on the microphone. "Ladies and gentlemen, may I have your attention, please? If you own a black BMW, your car alarm is sounding off," the host said, and he read the license plate number from a piece of paper.

"Crystal, the BMW the host was speaking about is mine, I believe. I have to check it, all right? I'll be right back," said Jim as he rose from the chair.

"Don't be long," said Crystal, and they smiled at each other as he went to check on the car in the parking lot.

When Jim arrived at the BMW in the parking lot, he checked all the doors, seeing if any had been tampered with, as he turned off the car alarm with the remote control on his key chain. Tommy watched from behind the bushes. As soon as Jim was done checking the car for a possible break-in, he walked away and back into the restaurant as the car alarm made a squeaking sound as he reset the alarm with his remote, making sure the doors were locked and secured.

When Jim reentered the restaurant, Tommy stood up from behind the bushes; he walked slowly toward the entrance of the restaurant. When he entered the restaurant, he saw the podium just outside the dining area, where the host was going through a list of the evening's reservations. He walked toward the podium slowly and noticed the glass doorway to the dining area. He stopped by one of the glass doors and looked inside through the crack in the doorway. He saw Crystal at her table, sipping a drink from her wineglass, with the new man in her life. She was laughing, smiling, and at peace with herself, enjoying her time with the new man in her life. Staring at Crystal led to staring at Jim, and again, he felt envy. Jim was where he wanted to be. As they continued to laugh and enjoy each other's company, Tommy began to feel like he was wasting his time, and he thought about giving up the whole idea of ever being with Crystal, but as much as he wanted to walk away, he wanted to be with her more. So he continued staring at them from afar. The host noticed Tommy's presence by the glass door.

"So this is Jim," said Tommy to himself in a whisper as he noticed his piercing dark eyes and dark hair that was brushed back, almost touching his shoulders. Jim smiled, showing perfect, straight pearly white teeth.

"Excuse me. Sir?" the host called out to Tommy, still at the podium.

Tommy looked away from the glass door and toward the podium. "Ah, yes. I wanted to ask you if you have any job openings at this time," Tommy said while glancing over at Crystal and Jim's table through the small opening in the glass door.

"All right. Here's an application you can fill out over there at that table," said the host.

Tommy walked over to the host at his podium to receive the application. The host had a pen and the application ready, but before giving the pen, the host tested the pen on a piece of paper first. The host realized the pen wasn't working.

"This pen seems to be out of ink. I have many pencils but no extra pens. Do you have a pen on you?" the host asked.

"No, I don't have a pen. Actually, this was a last-minute thing, asking for a job, so I'm not really prepared. Sorry," Tommy responded, feeling and looking hopeless.

"Hmm." The host looked Tommy up and down while thinking to himself. "I'll be right back. I'll get a pen from the back closet inside the restaurant," said the host, but then he went about ten feet away, to a closet close to the podium, instead of going into the restaurant closet. "I believe we have some extra pens inside this closet, instead of the one inside the restaurant," said the host, not paying attention to Tommy's presence by the glass doors to the dining area.

Tommy kept staring at the host, who kept searching for an extra pen, while he entered the dining area. He quickly and quietly walked with his back facing Crystal and Jim, and Jim and Crystal never noticed him walking toward the back of the restaurant.

When Tommy made it into the back hallway of the restaurant, he noticed a clean white apron hanging on a nail on the wall. He grabbed the apron and walked farther toward the back of the restaurant, into the kitchen. He saw a baseball cap on the floor in the corner at the entrance of the kitchen. He picked up the baseball cap, cleaned off the collected dust by brushing it against his leg, and placed the cap on his head while he walked back down the hall to the kitchen as he put on the newly found apron. When he came up to the two swinging doors of the kitchen, he removed his glasses and put them in his front pocket in his blue jeans while entering the kitchen. In the kitchen, he noticed a busboy dish bucket, something he could place dirty dishes in. He grabbed the bucket and walked back into the dining area, disguised as a busboy. He began collecting dirty dishes left over on deserted tables.

The host of the restaurant slammed shut the door at the entrance, wondering what had happened to the young man who wanted a job. As he was walking back toward the podium, while passing the glass doors at the dining area entrance, he looked through the glass. He stopped, opened one of the glass doors, and entered the dining area. Tommy noticed the host's presence in the dining area, and he slowly turned around, standing behind two tables so the host wouldn't notice the blue jeans he was wearing.

Meanwhile, at Jim and Crystal's table, they were eating fillet of sole and salad.

"The food is so good," said Crystal as she took a sip of her sparkling water, which had pieces of lemon and lime inside the glass.

"Well, Crystal, you're eating at one of the world's best restaurants." Jim smiled at Crystal.

Jim's and Tommy's eyes met briefly while Tommy stood two tables away. As Tommy turned his head away, still listening in on their conversation while doing his busboy duties, with each word he heard, he grew angrier and more envious by the moment as he watched from the side of his eyes.

While eating the rest of his salad, Jim noticed the busboy a few tables away, without knowing who the busboy really was.

"Oh, excuse me," Jim called out to the busboy almost in a whisper while waving to him. As he tried to get his attention, he stood up from his chair, reached into his pocket, and pulled out a five-dollar bill.

Tommy turned his back on their table, pretending he didn't hear the man who was at the table with the woman he wanted to be with.

"Can you get another bottle of sparkling water, please?" Crystal asked as she looked over her shoulder barely, smiling. Then she turned back to face Jim, unaware of whom she had been smiling at.

With his back facing them, Tommy, feeling nervous, replied quickly and carefully. "Sure," said Tommy while he walked over to their table backward. When he was next to Crystal, he turned quickly with his back facing Crystal, now facing Jim.

As Jim's eyes locked onto Tommy's eyes for a few seconds, Jim had an eerie feeling. Tommy took the five-dollar tip Jim offered for the favor he wanted the busboy to do.

"Now, this is service," Jim said while he held his glass, with some sparkling water still in it, in the air above his plate, making a toast.

Crystal joined in by holding up her glass of sparkling water and meeting Jim's glass in the air above their plates while he smiled half-way. As she watched the busboy, from his back, she didn't know it was Tommy. He quickly walked backward, and when he passed Crystal, he quickly turned around and walked back toward the kitchen in the back of the restaurant.

Why would a busboy in a posh restaurant like this wear a baseball cap and blue jeans? she thought while smiling halfway at Jim as she lowered her glass back to the side of her plate on the table. She looked at Jim, wondering if she should ask him.

"Ah, Jim?" Crystal looked down at the table.

"Yes, Crystal?" Jim smiled at her.

"Why would a busboy who works in a restaurant like this wear a baseball cap, blue jeans, and sneakers?" she asked as she took another sip of her wine.

"Hmm, good question. Not only a good question but an interesting one. Maybe they are getting a little casual around here," said Jim as he looked around.

In the back of the restaurant, Tommy reached for a bottle of sparkling water from the refrigerator. The host was also in the back in the kitchen, on his break, getting something to eat at the steam table. As the host was walking by the chef's steam table, preparing his plate, he saw a busboy who didn't look familiar. And the busboy was wearing blue jeans, a baseball cap, and sneakers. He wore a T-shirt, not a buttoned shirt, with a tie.

"Now, that's weird," he whispered to himself as he walked over to him.

Tommy walked out of the walk-in refrigerator with a bottle of sparkling water in his hand, shut the door, and then looked up and saw the host approaching him. While talking to someone at the pastry table, the host took his eyes off the unfamiliar busboy for a moment. Tommy took advantage of that moment and quickly walked away from the walk-in refrigerator. As Tommy walked away from the area, he heard the tapping of shoes approaching him from behind. The host took a shortcut, went around, and walked in front of Tommy, stopping him by the entrance's swinging doors.

"Who are you? Do I know you? Do you even work here?" the host asked.

Tommy, silently panicking, looked down at the tile floor, trying to use the baseball cap to cover most of his face by looking down.

"What's your name?" the host asked, wondering who he was, thinking he seemed familiar, trying to see most of his face underneath the cap.

The restaurant manager walked into the kitchen because he'd overheard what was going on, and the host took him toward the walk-in refrigerator.

"What's going on? Who's this guy?" the manager asked, looking Tommy up and down with his hands on his hips, feeling a bit frustrated, as it was starting to get busier in the dining area.

"Ah, yes, I believe this same chap was applying for a job a short time ago," said the host as he put a hand over his face, feeling a little embarrassed, while the manager kept staring at Tommy.

"What's your name?" the manager asked Tommy.

Tommy looked up at the host and then the manager. "My name is Tommy. I just wanted to see what it was like working for a fancy restaurant such as this place. I believe in on-the-job training for experience, and I wanted to prove myself to the establishment." As the host looked down at Tommy, Tommy felt embarrassed by the situation, as the host wasn't believing anything Tommy was saying.

"Well, Tommy, there's a right way to do things and a wrong way to do things, and this way was definitely the wrong way. Now, this is a five-star restaurant, and you can't do things in this manner. Take him to the front, and get him out of here," the manager told the host.

After the restaurant manager walked away, Tommy ran away while removing his apron, still holding the bottle of sparkling water and wearing the baseball cap. When he exited the kitchen and entered the dining area, he walked quickly toward Jim and Crystal's table, covering his face with the cap, and placed the bottle of sparkling water on the table gently. They were amazed at how long it had taken for the sparkling water to arrive at their table.

Jim and Crystal watched in amazement as the questionable busboy exited the restaurant with the host following right behind him. All the patrons at the other tables were looking at the spectacle as well.

"What the hell was that all about?" Jim asked, wondering, as he smiled.

"I don't know," said Crystal. She thought it might've been Tommy. She thought he'd looked a little familiar, even from behind, when he was next to her, even while wearing a baseball cap.

After Tommy ran out of the restaurant, the host stood outside the entrance doors, watching him run away. After the incident, the host reentered the restaurant, feeling confident he wouldn't see Tommy again.

When Tommy saw the host go back into the restaurant, he walked back into the parking lot, went back to the BMW, and hid again behind the three bushes in front of the car as he put back on his black-framed glasses.

Back inside the restaurant, at Jim and Crystal's table, Crystal was wiping her mouth with a cloth napkin, as dinner was almost over.

"So, Crystal, how do you like the restaurant and the food?" Jim asked, also wiping his mouth with a cloth napkin.

"I like it. It's definitely not boring around here," said Crystal, and she and Jim began to laugh. "Oh, Jim?"

"Yes, Crystal?" Jim responded as he was finishing the last drop of sparkling water from his glass.

"I have to tell you something. It's not really important, but it's something I want to get off my chest." Crystal put her cloth napkin on her plate.

"All right. I'm listening, Crystal," Jim replied, hoping it wasn't bad news. Perhaps she was about to go back to her ex-boyfriend or something like that.

"All right, before we met, I was involved in a crazy situation. In fact, it's still going on right now as we speak. And I'm really afraid," Crystal said with tears welling up in her eyes as she thought about the busboy and how it could've been Tommy.

There was silence in the air as Jim looked down at the table, and then he looked up into her eyes. "Is there someone else you didn't tell me about?" Jim asked as he took a deep breath.

"No, there isn't anyone else in my life." Crystal tried to explain as Jim tried to understand with a confused look on his face. "You see, before we met, I placed an ad in the newspaper, in the personal ads section, and this guy answered the ad."

"All right," Jim responded, being patient with her as he continued listening to her.

"Well, like I said, this guy answered my ad, and we made arrangements to go out for coffee and meet before going out on a date, and—"

"Your bill, sir." The waiter interrupted as Crystal and Jim stared at each other and then smiled at the waiter. "Will there be anything else?" the waiter asked as a busboy came to remove dishes from the table. Jim and Crystal looked at each other, as there was a different busboy at their table.

"No, no. We're fine. Thank you. The food was absolutely great. And we loved the service here," said Jim as he held on to Crystal's hand on the table.

"Yes, it was great," said Crystal as she smiled.

"All right. Have a good night," said the waiter as he placed the bill on the table and then walked away.

After the waiter left the table, Crystal and Jim got ready to leave. On the way to the cashier, Jim took out his wallet from his front pocket.

"Jim, I would like to pay half," said Crystal as they approached the cashier.

"No way. This is on me," Jim said as he put the bill on the counter where the cashier was.

"No, Jim, I insist," said Crystal as she went into her purse.

"All right, I'll give the waiter a tip," said Jim, and he went to the table and placed a ten-dollar tip on the table for the waiter.

"All right," said Crystal as she gave the cashier her part of the bill.

"Thank you, sir," said the waiter as he picked up the tip from the table.

"Thank you," said Jim as he walked back to the cashier and to Crystal, who stood by the glass doors at the dining entrance.

"Are you ready?" Jim asked as he pulled out his credit card to pay for his part while putting on his coat.

"Yes, Jim, I'm ready," said Crystal, and they walked past the host at his podium and out the front doors. They walked through the parking lot hand in hand, walking toward the car.

When they arrived at the car, Jim turned off the car alarm with the remote and unlocked the doors. Suddenly, Crystal pulled Jim closer toward her, and they embraced. Their eyes were locked on each other as their faces drew closer. Their lips felt the warmth as they moved in closer, and they smelled each other's cologne and perfume. The heat of passion got hotter as their lips drew closer to each other, almost touching, as they got ready for their moment. Gently and slowly, they kissed, with their tongues being exchanged in and out of each other's mouth passionately.

Tommy was behind the bushes, watching them kiss. Jealousy, rage, and tension filled his heart to the brim. He wanted Crystal for himself.

When Jim's and Crystal's lips parted, they came back down to reality, and they opened their eyes and looked into each other's eyes. Jim opened the car door for Crystal, and she entered the car. When she was in the car, he slammed the car door shut. He walked around to the driver's side and entered the car. He slammed the car door shut, and before starting the car, Jim leaned over toward Crystal, placed his index finger under her chin, and looked into her baby-blue eyes.

"Crystal, why don't you finish what you were trying to say to me in the restaurant?" Jim asked as he smiled with his cheeks flushed.

Crystal tried to remember where they'd left off when they were talking at their table. "Oh yeah. I wanted to tell you about this guy I met when he answered my ad in the personals. Well, we agreed we would meet over coffee at this coffeehouse. As we were talking, I realized we had nothing really in common; plus, I wasn't really attracted to him. But I thought that attraction wasn't everything, so I went out with him once. We went out to dinner, but we never made it to the movies, because I cut it short. I told him I didn't think it was going to work out. To make a long story short, even though he knows the way I feel—and I told him over the telephone that I wasn't attracted to him several times in the past—he still refuses to acknowledge the way I feel." Crystal put a small stick of gum into her mouth and passed a stick of gum to Jim.

"So does this guy still call you?" Jim asked as he took the stick of gum, unwrapped it, and put it into his mouth.

"Every now and then. And when he does, I just hang up on him. You see, I have this order of protection. He has a copy of it, and if he violates it, he goes to jail." Crystal pulled her copy out of her purse and showed him. "I had to do this because all he does is harass me. I mean, it's pretty obvious he has an attraction for me, but I don't have any attraction for him. He's very obsessed with me. I keep on telling him, but he just doesn't get it," said Crystal as Jim was looking over the order of protection.

"Crystal, be very, very careful," said Jim as he gave back the document. "This man won't stop at anything until he has you. This is his one thing in life he wants to commit himself to. He won't stop until he gets what he wants."

Crystal put the order of protection back into her purse. "The police gave him a copy of the order of protection, and so far, I haven't seen him, except one time. And every now and then he calls me but not from his home phone. From a pay phone because he knows I have caller ID."

"Do you have a tracer on your telephone?" Jim asked as he turned the ignition, started the car, and pulled out from the spot where he was parked.

"What's a tracer?" she asked as the car exited the parking lot, and they drove onward.

"A tracer is something the telephone company puts on your line with help from the police. If this guy should call back, the tracer would provide the exact location he was calling from. You must call the police, and since you already have the order of protection, the police are well aware of your situation and already have a file on this guy," Jim said, looking somewhat concerned, keeping his eyes on the road while driving.

"All right, I'll look into that," said Crystal.

"Crystal, when you looked at your caller ID the times he called from the pay phone, do you think he was calling from your home area, in your neighborhood?" he asked while driving and looking at her.

"One of the times, he was using a pay phone across the street from my apartment building," said Crystal as she looked straight ahead.

"He called from across the street?" he asked as they were approaching light traffic ahead. They were on the Upper East Side, leaving Central Park.

"Yeah," Crystal responded as the car stopped with the traffic ahead of them.

"Where does he live?" Jim asked.

"He lives in Brooklyn, but when he calls, usually, he's in the area where I live. I know because on my caller ID, the first three numbers are the same as mine. When I realized he was calling from somewhere in the neighborhood, I looked out the window in my living room, which overlooks the street in front of the apartment building, and noticed the pay phone across the street. The receiver of the pay phone was just dangling off the hook. When I saw that, I wondered," Crystal said as Jim drove up the street and entered the Upper East Side.

"So what happened next?" Jim asked.

"Well, I grabbed a piece of paper and a pen from my side table and wrote down the phone number from the caller ID, and then I ran downstairs and across the street to the pay phone, and—"

"And it was the same number?" Jim asked as he interrupted her politely.

"Well, yeah. When I saw that it was the same number from the pay phone, I became numb. I actually had chills run down my spine," said Crystal.

"Shit. It's amazing you never wrote a novel from this situation," said Jim as he smiled.

"I know. I should, right?" Crystal and Jim laughed as she thought maybe the situation with Tommy finally had come to an end, or was she being naive about the situation?

"So are we going to ride around Manhattan tonight?" Jim asked as he smiled again, and his eyes gleamed. She smiled.

"Hey, don't be surprised if I start writing my novel soon," said Crystal, and she and Jim started laughing. "I'm sorry, Jim—you were asking me if we were riding around tonight?" she asked, hoping she wasn't being rude.

"Yes. Unless you have something you have to do at home tonight?" Jim asked while he continued driving and briefly looked back at her.

"I don't have anything to do tonight at home, but I have a better idea. How would you like to come over tonight?" Crystal asked as she placed her left hand on his upper right thigh and smiled.

Tommy entered the subway, going back to Brooklyn after a disappointing, long day, as Jim and Crystal continued the drive to Crystal's apartment.

"So what about that book?" Jim asked, laughing quietly.

"No way. No one would ever believe it. And besides, I don't want to write it and have to relive it, because in writing it, I'd have to remember what happened. Being a victim of someone who is obsessed—well, it's a little scary," she said as they held hands. She squeezed his hand a little bit, and he realized she was frightened by her experience. He saw the scared expression on her face.

"Crystal, everything is going to be all right. Really, it will." Jim tried to comfort her as he firmly held her hand, showing he cared about her, while they smiled at each other. They were minutes away from Crystal's apartment, still holding hands.

✦✦✦✦✦✦

The morning sun rose to a new day as pigeons flew off the arches of the Brooklyn Bridge. It was a cold, brisk morning. The morning sun was still rising from behind the skyline as a train came out of the tunnel and entered the Manhattan Bridge.

Many people were on board the Manhattan-bound train, on their way to work, as always. Tommy sat among the morning crowd, drinking coffee, while he listened to his CD Walkman radio, listening to a talk show, as he shut his eyes. While the train continued traveling over the Manhattan Bridge, he slowly faded into a dream.

In his dream, he was entering his apartment after a long day at work. He noticed that the lights were dim throughout the apartment. As he walked into the kitchen, he saw two lit candles in the middle of the dining table, as well as two floral-designed china plates, one on each side. Two crystal wineglasses reflected the light from the candles. On the side of the table was a canister of ice filled to the brim, and a bottle of wine lay deep in the ice at a tilt, staying chilled. While walking closer to the table, he smelled the aroma of his favorite dish cooking: trout amandine. He walked out of the kitchen into the living room and then went into the bedroom.

When he entered the bedroom, he felt a little bit nervous that he was going to find Maria rather than Crystal, but to his surprise, it was Crystal. Crystal was sitting at the foot of the bed, wearing vanilla-colored lingerie, awaiting his arrival.

"Crystal?" Tommy said.

"Yes, Tommy?" Crystal responded as she rose and stood there wearing her silky lace lingerie straight from the Frederick's of

Hollywood catalog. Her long, soft blonde hair lay to one side, over her shoulder, and her baby-blue eyes glimmered with brightness. Her fingernails and toenails were painted red.

Tommy felt as though he were dreaming. Crystal walked over toward him slowly. He still didn't believe this was happening to him as she approached him. When she arrived in front of him, as their bodies were almost touching, she removed his black-framed glasses, threw them onto the bed over her shoulder, and put her arms over his shoulders as she moved in closer toward him. She began to kiss him on his neck, giving little kisses here and there. Then their lips came together in a long and wet kiss. As the kissing simmered down, she parted her lips from his slowly, and seductively and passionately, she took him by his hand. They walked over toward the bed.

She sat him down at the foot of the bed, knelt down in front of him, and removed his shoes from his feet. She then removed his socks, stood him up, and unbuckled his belt. She removed the belt and threw it onto the floor, and then she unfastened his jeans, took off his jeans and undergarment, and placed them on the floor near the bed.

As he stood there completely nude, she removed her lingerie and also stood there nude. She took him by the hand to the bathroom. When they entered the bathroom, Tommy was stunned. There were candles lit all over the bathroom, and the bathtub was filled with what smelled like peach-scented bubble bath in hot water.

Crystal entered the tub, still holding on to Tommy's hand, and when she was fully in the tub, he followed. Tommy sat down and sat back against the end of the tub as she lay down, leaning her back against Tommy's chest, as they smelled the fresh fragrance of Peaches in the Summertime bubble bath.

Time passed, and Tommy was still dreaming. He dropped his cup of coffee onto the floor of the train while dreaming.

Tommy and Crystal sat at the kitchen table, facing each other, while they stared at the two lit candles, ready to eat their dinner. Before they ate their meal, Crystal reached for a bell and rang it at the table. Tommy thought it was odd that there was a bell at the table.

Maria came out with a large serving plate of trout amandine, Tommy's favorite dish, with a serving fork on the plate. As she looked over at Crystal, Maria looked over the lingerie she was wearing, while Crystal looked over at Maria. Maria was wearing a sexy black lace maid's outfit. Tommy panicked momentarily upon seeing Maria and Crystal in the same place, until he noticed Maria was not interfering and was only there to serve the food.

Maria served the fish onto their plates with the big serving fork without saying a word. It was as though she didn't know him or never had had a thing for him. Maria looked antisocial. She looked at him every now and then, but when she stared at him, she looked as if she wanted to kill him. He constantly stared at her, not believing it was Maria serving dinner. Crystal wondered why he was staring at Maria all the time.

Tommy slowly came back to reality, waking up from the short trip in his dream, still on the train. He looked down and noticed the coffee all over the floor, and some of the riders were looking at him because of the spilled coffee.

"The next and last stop on this train is Two Hundred Fifth Street!" the train conductor said on the intercom as the doors of the train were closing.

"Shit! I'm late going to work!" he said to himself out loud as he rose from where he was sitting and waited to get off the train to call Louie, his supervisor, on a pay phone.

When the train made it to the last stop, Tommy exited, found a pay phone on the platform, and called his supervisor to inform him that he was running late. When he called, there was no answer, so he left a message on the voice mail. He then hung up quickly and reentered the train, which was preparing to go back downtown. He sat down, thinking about the dream he'd had, as the train doors slid shut.

I was having a candlelit dinner with Crystal, and we were being served dinner by Maria, he thought to himself over and over as the train left the station.

Crystal was at the reception desk, thinking about the night before and also thinking about the weird busboy she and Jim had seen at the restaurant.

Could that have been Tommy? I mean, he did try to be a shoe salesman at that shoe store I went to. I wonder, she thought as she sat there at the desk, looking as though she were in a self-induced trance.

A person approached the desk. Even though the guest was in front of her, Crystal didn't notice her presence at the desk.

"Hi, and your name must be Crystal," the female said as she smiled pleasantly.

Suddenly, Crystal snapped out of her thought. "Oh, I'm sorry. I was thinking about something. I'm sorry. How may I help you?" Crystal asked while she took a pen from the drawer and smiled, feeling embarrassed.

"That's quite all right. I'm going up to the thirty-third floor," said the female guest as she smiled.

"All right. I believe we can take care of that," said Crystal, and they laughed as she picked up the receiver of the phone to announce the guest.

◆◆◆◆◆

It was lunchtime once again, and Tommy and Joey, one of his co-workers, were together in the employee cafeteria. They were in line, deciding what they wanted.

After they chose what they wanted for lunch, they found a table and sat down, ready to eat their lunches. Maria was at another table, at a distance from them, and Tommy didn't notice her.

"Joey, I went out last night, and I saw Crystal out with this guy," said Tommy as he took a spoonful of tomato soup into his mouth.

"Tommy, you're still stuck on that situation? Man, get over it. I'm sure you could use your time a lot smarter than that," said Joey as he bit into his peanut butter sandwich.

"I knew you were going to say that!" Tommy whispered.

"Well, then why don't you get over it?" Joey asked.

"Well, because maybe I don't want to. I know deep down we are meant to be." Tommy showed confidence in his belief.

"Meant to be? What's this 'meant to be' shit? Man, I'm sorry, but I have to get away from you. You're a bit weird for me!" said Joey as he picked up his tray.

Tommy looked on, not understanding why he was moving. Joey looked at him before he walked away.

"Bye," Tommy said with a demented smile on his face as Joey went to another table, where he ate alone for the remainder of the lunch period.

Maria was watching what was going on. She picked up her tray and walked over to Tommy's table.

When Maria arrived at Tommy's table, he looked up and noticed her standing there as he bit into his grilled cheese sandwich.

"Hi, Tommy. May I?" Maria asked as she pulled out the chair from the table and smiled at him, being friendly.

"I don't care," Tommy responded, sipping his soup from the bowl.

"Be that way," said Maria as she sat down across the table and gave him half a smile as Tommy gave her a deranged look. "Tommy, what's bugging you?" she asked while eating her chicken salad sandwich.

"Nothing. Well, this morning, I had this wonderful dream on the way to work. You happened to pop into it, and then you turned it into a nightmare," said Tommy, finishing his soup, as Maria stared at him with concern.

"Tommy, I wish you would start looking more toward reality and start seeing things as they are instead of how you think they are. Now, take you and me, for instance. I'm so much in love with you, and you say you don't feel that way about me. Well, Crystal doesn't feel that way about you, but you still persist in pursuing her, and—"

"And you keep on pursuing me!" Tommy interrupted her as he whispered abruptly, leaning a little bit over the table.

"As though she will give in at any time and say to you, 'Darling, I love you! I want to be with you!'" Maria ignored what he'd said when he interrupted her, finishing what she had been saying before she was interrupted. She leaned across the table, and Tommy's and her faces were almost touching.

There was a moment of silence as Tommy and Maria went back into their chairs slowly. When they sat back down, Tommy wiped his mouth with a paper napkin as Maria looked at Tommy and frowned.

"I know deep down you really want to be with me. Look at me. I'm a good-looking girl, and I've been told by many men that I have a sexy body and a good way about myself," said Maria as she stood up again, but Tommy didn't say a word as he rested his head on top of his arms, listening to Maria as she spoke. "So, Tommy, what do you say? I know deep down inside you have some feelings for me and for us to be together." Maria sat back down. She felt worn out by doing most of the talking, and she looked down at the table.

"Maria," Tommy said as he lifted her chin till she looked directly at him, "I need for you to understand something." Tommy rose with his tray in hand, walked over to Maria, and stood near her as she continued sitting at the table. "We are not meant to be. And I have no intention of ever being with you. But that doesn't mean you are not attractive. You are definitely attractive, but I'm used to us being coworkers and friends, all right? That's the way it is." Tommy looked deep into her eyes, and she gave a half smile as Tommy gave her a demented grin in return. Then his demented grin turned into something alien toward her: he grabbed her bottom jaw with one hand as he wore a look of anger on his face. "Now, understand one thing, Maria," said Tommy, still holding on to her jawbone tightly.

"Tommy, you're hurting me," said Maria as tears welled up in her eyes.

"Please understand just one thing. I intend on being with Crystal for the rest of my life—as soon as she accepts the fact that she and I are meant to be."

Tears rolled down her cheeks. "But, Tommy, I—"

"Sh! Now, you talk about me facing or dealing with reality? What about you? Huh? Yes, you are very good looking. You're a hot Peruvian woman," Tommy whispered into her right ear, and then he let go of her jaw. "Do you hear me, Maria?" Tommy whispered in her ear.

"Yes. Yes, I hear you," said Maria, quietly crying, being careful not to draw attention to their table, as he looked deep into her eyes again. She turned her head, avoiding his stare, because she was upset with him and his actions.

"You are very, very good looking, Maria. And I bet you're fucking excellent in bed too. But I have different goals in mind. Do you understand?" Tommy whispered into her right ear as he grabbed her jaw again, holding on to it even tighter, as she cried.

"Yes. I understand, Tommy," she responded as she slowly nodded, and he let go of her jaw.

Tommy rose from bending down near her and looked into her eyes as he stood her up from her chair, tightly embracing her with one arm. He rubbed her upper lip and then her lower lip with his index finger. Then, slowly, his lips drew closer toward Maria's lips, and he kissed her. They were the only ones in the employee cafeteria.

When their lips parted, he let her go, picked up his tray from the table, and smiled at her as she sat back down on her chair. She was shocked and confused and didn't know what to think.

"Good. Very good. So I guess we've reached a moment of understanding between you and me. You know something, Maria? It turns me on when you are so understanding." Tommy smiled a demented grin as he walked away from the table, on his way to empty his tray into the trash can.

While still seated in her chair, Maria kept her eyes on him until he exited the cafeteria. When she could see him no longer, she turned, facing a wall opposite the entrance of the cafeteria, deep in thought.

If I can't have you, Tommy dear, then, my love, no one will, she thought with a demented expression on her face.

CHAPTER 12

ANOTHER WORKDAY CAME TO AN end, and Tommy exited the job and walked over to Crystal's place of employment to await her while standing on the side of the building where she worked.

A few moments later, Crystal came up to the lobby level on the elevator from the ladies' locker room in the basement. When she stepped off the elevator and walked through the lobby and the reception area, all her coworkers waved farewell to her. As she walked toward the glass rotary doors at the front of the lobby, she waved back before exiting.

She exited the building, and from the side of the building, Tommy saw her walk by twenty feet away. As she walked to the corner of Sixth Avenue and Fiftieth Street, Tommy began pursuing her from behind. Right behind him, Maria was pursuing Tommy. She stayed at a distance of fifty feet away as she crossed the street.

Why can't Tommy see that we would have so much if he would just open up his heart? she thought while following him.

While in pursuit of Crystal, Tommy had a feeling he was being followed, as he felt strange. He looked quickly over his shoulder. He saw other people walking about behind him, but no one looked familiar, so he continued following Crystal. Maria stayed well hidden among the crowd of people behind Tommy, staying on his trail.

Crystal all of a sudden felt as though she were being followed as she approached the subway. When she walked down the concrete steps of the subway, she quickly hid behind the token booth instead of going through the turnstile, trying to find out if she was being followed and who was following.

Tommy rushed down the concrete steps of the subway and toward the turnstile. He looked up and down the platform while staying behind the turnstile and saw a train in the station. He walked onto the platform, continuing to look for Crystal, while Crystal watched through the glass from behind a token booth. She couldn't believe it, but at the same time, she had expected it.

A moment after, Maria rushed down the same concrete steps and then walked slowly toward the turnstile, looking around for Tommy. Tommy was near the turnstile, on the side of the platform. Maria quickly ducked behind the token booth to hide from Tommy, careful not to be discovered.

Suddenly, Crystal turned around quickly and accidentally ran into Maria as Maria was looking through the window of the token booth, staring at Tommy as he stood on the platform, waiting for another train while looking for Crystal. He was aware of someone following him, and he felt it might've been Maria.

"Oh, I'm sorry for bumping into you," said Maria as she stepped back.

"No, I'm sorry. I'm the one who ran into you when I turned around quickly," said Crystal. Then she looked through the glass at Tommy standing on the platform as Maria looked at Tommy while wondering why this woman who had bumped into her was staring at Tommy. Maria thought she looked vaguely familiar.

"Hi. My name is Maria. What's your name?" Maria asked, looking at Tommy and then glancing over at Crystal.

"My name? Why do you want to know my name?" Crystal asked while wiping her forehead with a cloth, as she was perspiring.

"Well, I don't mean to pry, but I noticed you following that guy who's standing at the platform," said Maria, pointing through the glass of the token booth toward the platform.

"Me following him? He was following me! I have an order of protection against him, and you would think he would have put an end to this stalking business by now," said Crystal as she continued wiping her face and forehead with the cloth, growing more nervous and aggravated.

"Order of protection against him?" Maria asked as she and Crystal looked over at Tommy through the glass of the token booth.

"Yes, him! I've been trying to get rid of him for the past two or three months now, and—"

"Oh wow! You must be Crystal!" Maria said in disbelief.

"Yes, my name is Crystal. How did you know? And should I matter to you?" Crystal asked, and the next train arrived at the station as Tommy frantically looked up and down for Crystal, still thinking he was being followed by Maria.

Instead of entering the train that had just arrived at the station, he walked through the turnstile. Maria and Crystal stopped talking and continued hiding from Tommy as he walked by the token booth. Maria and Crystal went to the other side of the booth as he walked by. When Tommy looked back at the platform, he finally faced the fact that Crystal wasn't at the station, so he walked up the concrete steps and exited the subway. Maria and Crystal took deep breaths as they watched him leave the subway, walking up to the street.

"So, Maria—it is Maria, right?" Crystal asked.

"Yes," Maria responded, and she nodded once. She and Crystal were still behind the booth.

"How did you know my name and who I am?" Crystal asked with concern.

"Crystal, I don't know you, and I know you don't know me, but I've heard so much about you from Tommy. He told me about you because he's so much in love with you," Maria said as tears welled up in her eyes.

"I know he's in love with me, but I don't feel the same way. I even have an order of protection, as I mentioned earlier. I got the order of protection so he would eventually leave me alone. Even now, I could go to a cop on the corner of this block and present the order of protection to him, and Tommy would be arrested on stalking charges. You see, I don't know if you know about it or not, but Tommy is obsessed with wanting to be with me. New York law is very strict on antistalking laws now, so he could've been easily busted today. In a way, I wish I had been near a cop instead of coming down into the subway," Crystal told Maria as they walked away from the token booth and up the concrete steps to the street.

"Yeah, but why did you press charges?" Maria asked as they were approaching the street from the subway.

"Why did I press charges?" Crystal asked, not sure why Maria had asked her that question.

"Oh, I'm sorry. My question was, why didn't you press charges if he was obsessed with you in wanting to be with you?" Maria asked, correcting herself, as she and Crystal walked away from the subway.

"I don't know. I'm stupid sometimes. You know, I keep thinking that someday soon, he'll leave me alone, and all of this will be over with," Crystal said.

"Well, you know what? He's not giving up anytime soon. I know it because I could see it in his eyes. And he also said he wasn't going to stop," said Maria as they walked slowly up the block.

"I know, I know. That's the reason I have this order of protection against him. This time, I won't be the fool." Crystal smiled at Maria.

"You seem like a nice person, but in a way, I resent you," said Maria as they stopped walking, and other people passed by, coming and going.

"You resent me? Why?" Crystal asked as she folded her arms, wondering and curious for the answer.

"Well, I'm a little jealous of you. I mean, you are really beautiful. Long blonde hair, deep blue eyes, and—"

"Yeah, but, Maria, you yourself are beautiful. And I believe Tommy is obsessed with me, and I'm very much afraid. Let me ask you something. Are you interested in being with Tommy? I mean, I know it's none of my business, but I was just wondering. You kind of seem like you are." Crystal thought she wouldn't get much of an answer from her because of their recent meeting.

"Yes. Yes, I am," Maria replied as they stood on the corner down the block from the subway.

"Have you ever told him you are interested?" Crystal asked.

"Yes, I did. He already knows how I feel about him, and we've known each other for a few years as friends and coworkers, but like I said, even though he knows how I feel, he seems to have his sights set on you. I don't know. Sometimes when I think of what's going on with him and you, I feel like something terrible will happen if he doesn't stop this craziness. I wish there was something I could do to turn him around to be interested in me," said Maria as she folded her arms, feeling annoyed, as she looked down at the pavement.

"Maria, don't give up. Keep pursuing him, and maybe it will happen." Crystal put one hand on Maria's shoulder, and Maria looked back at her as she lifted her head.

"Hopefully. Hopefully soon," Maria responded.

"Maria, I have to go home now, all right? I wish you lots of luck—the sooner I'll be rid of him. I'm currently involved with someone now," said Crystal, and Maria's eyes lit up.

"Oh yeah?" Maria responded, feeling upbeat over what she'd just heard.

"Yeah, so if you see Tommy at the job, tell him I'm currently involved with someone. Tell him I now have a boyfriend, and he really needs to get on with his life. All right, take care, Maria." Crystal began walking away from Maria.

"You're right. You're absolutely right. Maybe he'll realize he has a brand-new chance to be with me," said Maria as she stood on the corner.

"Hopefully. We can only hope. I wish you all the best of luck with this guy, and hopefully, with everything that's been going on, in the end, everyone will be happy," said Crystal as she proceeded homeward, walking toward the bus stop across the street.

"Yeah, I hope so, Crystal," said Maria as she stood on the corner.

"All right. Take care, Maria! It was good meeting you! Wish you luck!" Crystal shouted as she arrived at the bus stop while a bus was approaching.

Maria ran across the street toward the bus stop as she saw Crystal at the end of the line, getting ready to board the bus.

Crystal turned her head briefly and noticed Maria approaching her from behind.

"Hey, Crystal! I just wanted to shake your hand and tell you how much I really appreciate the time that we were able to talk," said Maria as she held out a hand toward Crystal.

Instead of shaking hands with Maria, Crystal embraced her.

"Be very, very careful, Crystal! Don't be naive. Be aware of this guy. Please be careful," said Maria as they parted ways. Crystal boarded the bus, and Maria ran across the street back to the subway.

Before reentering the subway, at the concrete steps, Maria watched the bus exit the bus stop, and she felt it would be the last time she saw Crystal. Then she proceeded down the concrete steps of the subway.

<hr />

Tommy was on a Brooklyn-bound train. It entered onto the Manhattan Bridge. Tommy sat there puzzled, wondering where Crystal had disappeared to.

What the hell? I remember following Crystal to the subway station after she left the place where she works. I was following her from the time she left the building where she works all the way to the subway station. I saw her walk down the steps of the subway. I went down those same concrete steps she went down. I wonder if she discovered me following her, and maybe she hid herself, or maybe she exited the subway. But from what entrance? I don't know, he thought as he removed his black-framed glasses, rubbing his eyes. He laid his glasses on his right leg while watching the amazing New York skyline. Every building was lit up. As the train went over the Manhattan Bridge, over the Hudson River, the night sky was becoming dark. Evening was upon the city.

CHAPTER 13

THE NEXT DAY AT THE messenger center, Tommy was getting ready for his lunch break, and Maria saw him from over her shoulder while at her desk, surrounded by her paperwork.

"Tommy?" Maria called out, and he looked over toward her.

"Yes, Maria?" Tommy felt he didn't want to be bothered with her today.

"Can we have lunch together?" Maria asked as she spun her chair around counterclockwise toward Tommy. When she stopped the chair, she was facing him, looking directly at him, as he walked toward her.

"No, I don't think so," Tommy responded while taking off his work smock and walking toward his locker.

"Tommy, we must talk about last night," said Maria as she stood up from her desk.

"About last night? What about last night?" he asked while he threw his smock onto one of the carts in the corner.

"Look, why don't we talk over lunch? Lunch is on me." Maria laid a hand on his shoulder.

As he looked at her hand on his shoulder, there was a slight pause in the air, along with tension and curiosity. "Fine. I probably don't have much of a choice in this matter," he replied, and they walked out of the messenger center and toward the elevators to go to the employee cafeteria.

When an elevator arrived, they and other workers from the

basement, along with a couple of messengers delivering packages, entered the elevator. When the buttons for their destinations were pressed, the door slid shut, and the elevator went up. Tommy looked at Maria from the side of his eyes, as she looked straight ahead, smiling.

When the elevator reached its destination, Tommy, Maria, and a couple of other persons exited the elevator car, and they all walked toward the cafeteria. Tommy and Maria entered the cafeteria and walked over to the lunch line to pick out what they wanted to eat for lunch. They walked down the line, and all kinds of food lay behind the glass counter. When they had their trays of food, they went to the cashier to pay for their lunches. Maria paid for their lunches, and then they looked for a place to sit. They found a table and sat down, and Tommy stared at her, wondering why she wanted to talk about last night.

While Maria was eating a beef and bean burrito with her fork, Tommy didn't eat his taco; he continuously stared at her, expecting her to say something anytime.

"OK, Maria, here we are, having lunch together. What do I owe this moment to?" he asked as he just sat there, still not touching his food.

"Well, Tommy, before we discuss last night, I have a confession to make first," said Maria, wiping her mouth with a paper napkin.

"Go ahead. I'm listening." Tommy folded his arms against his chest as Maria stared at him directly in his eyes.

"All right. Here we go. I followed you last night. I followed you all the way to where Crystal works at Rockefeller Center. You know, across from the line of restaurants on Sixth Avenue." Maria bit into her burrito.

"OK," Tommy responded, trying to calm down.

"All right, so when Crystal came from out of the building where she works, I saw where you were, and as you were pursuing her, I was pursuing you," said Maria as Tommy picked up his bottled water from his tray.

"All right," Tommy responded as he took a sip of his water, still trying to calm down. "OK, so?"

"I can tell you why you couldn't find Crystal." Maria smiled.

"Oh yeah?" Tommy responded as he leaned a bit over the table. "Why couldn't I find Crystal last night?"

"Well, I—"

"I was thinking while on my way back to Brooklyn that maybe she discovered me following her, so she might've exited the subway from the entrance on the other side of the platform," said Tommy as he interrupted her, and he took another sip of water from his bottle, leaving his bottle of water half full.

"I won't tell you where she was, but I will tell you that I met Crystal last night, and you're right. She is so very beautiful. The long blonde hair and those bright blue eyes. Who could help but fall in love with someone who looks like that?" Maria asked, wishing she could look like Crystal. Then she smiled dementedly while Tommy shook his head, not believing what he was hearing. "Oh, better yet, who could help but be obsessed with someone like that? Especially when this beautiful woman is Crystal," said Maria with tears forming in her eyes.

Tommy listened and never said a word as he stared down at the table, at the half-eaten food on his tray.

"Crystal, and I were talking a bit last night, Tommy. And she explained to me that she is currently involved with someone else. Did you know that? She said she's involved at this time with someone else!" said Maria as her tears began to fall down her cheeks.

Tommy folded his arms as he sat back in his chair. "So? I saw him! It doesn't mean a damn thing!" he shouted, and he and Maria looked from the sides of their eyes, hoping they weren't making a scene in the cafeteria.

"Oh yeah? You saw him? So why don't you leave her alone?" Maria asked.

"Why do you have so much interest in her life? In my life?" he shouted in a whisper from across their table.

"What I'm trying to say is that I'm available, and she's not! I'm in love with you! And she isn't!" Maria shouted from across the table, and everyone in the cafeteria began to notice their arguing.

"I'm in love with Crystal!" said Tommy, getting ready to remove himself from the table but still seated in his chair.

"Look, I'm in love with you, and I know way deep down inside you, you're in love with me. Now, I don't know when you're going to realize it, but this is how I feel," Maria said.

"I'm in love with Crystal. And I don't care if she's with someone else. Because that's just temporary. Crystal and I will last forever and ever," said Tommy with a confident look upon his face, as though it were a natural fact.

Maria could see the obsession in his eyes while he spoke, and she felt her own obsessive feelings while at the same time denying she was obsessed. But her feelings toward Tommy were too deep to forget, just like his feelings for Crystal.

"Look, Maria, I'm not going to give up on Crystal. Somewhere, someday, sometime, I'm going to make her all mine," said Tommy as he drank the last of his water from the bottle.

"Tommy?" Maria called out as Tommy rose from where he was sitting, and she rose too. Maria picked up her tray and walked to the side of him. "Tommy, she doesn't want to be with you. Don't you get it? I am so much in love with you. Please, please find it in your heart to believe me. And then—" Tears rolled down her cheeks freely.

Tommy saw her tears of loneliness, which he knew well, combined with endless sleepless nights and many days of living with the frustration of being in love with someone but not being with the person.

"And then?" Tommy asked as he and Maria took their trays to the conveyer belt. When they reached the front entrance of the cafeteria, Maria turned, facing Tommy.

"And then find in your heart your feelings that you have for me," said Maria as she held both his hands.

"Maria, I believe you when you say that you're in love and that you love me, but I'm not in love with you, nor do I have any feelings for you other than the friendship we share, which may be in jeopardy soon. Now, if you don't mind." Tommy let go of Maria's hands and walked away, leaving Maria standing there at the entrance of the cafeteria, by the double wooden doors.

While Maria watched him walk away, she grabbed a chair from a nearby table and sat down. He entered an elevator when it arrived at the floor, and she stared at him as the doors of the elevator slid shut.

At the end of the day, Tommy arrived home. He entered the apartment, flipped the light switch in the living room, walked over to the recliner, and sat down after a long day at work and a long lunch with Maria. He stared at the telephone for a moment. He reached over, grabbed the receiver, and dialed the number of Crystal's residence.

Crystal's telephone rang as Crystal was coming out of the bathroom, wearing a huge bath towel. She'd just gotten out of the shower after a long day at work. She walked into the bedroom and answered the telephone on the side table next to her bed.

"Hello?" Crystal answered, and there was a brief moment of silence in the air. "Hello?" she said again nervously, but the silence was still present. "Hello? I know who's on the line, and if you don't speak up, I—" Crystal was frustrated.

"Hi. It's me—Tommy," said Tommy.

"Tommy?" She couldn't believe who was on the other end of the telephone.

"Yes. And I know about the order of protection you put against me, but I wanted—"

"You know about the order of protection, but what?"

"I know. I just—"

"I could have you arrested right now. Are you aware of this?" Crystal yelled.

There was a moment of silence. The silence was thick like a thick cloud up in the sky or a cheesecake someone would cut.

"Yeah, I know you could have me arrested right now, but I just wanted to ask you one question. Why did you go out with that other guy?" he asked, feeling nervous and trembling in fear of her calling the police on him and of what he was about to hear on the other end of the phone. He hoped she was about to confess her desire of wanting to be with him. While he was struggling to hold his phone as he sat on the edge of his recliner, his forehead broke out with beads of sweat.

"How do you know about the guy I'm seeing? Oh, wait a minute. Maria must have told you, right?" Crystal asked.

"Well, I was there," said Tommy as he wondered if he was doing the right thing in telling her that he had been there.

"Why are you stalking me?" she asked angrily, feeling terrified of the situation.

"No, no, I'm not stalking you. Maria told me about you seeing this other guy, and I know you and Maria were talking about me, and I—" Tommy wiped his face and forehead of the sweat that was forming.

"Tommy, understand something, all right? I believe that Maria told you about me seeing someone else, but I also feel you were stalking me. Anytime you follow me or pursue me the way you've been doing, it is called stalking! Get it? I am not in love with you, and I also do not love you! Please do not ever call me again, because if you do, I will most definitely call the police, and you will be picked up and placed in jail! Do you understand?" Crystal shouted. She felt as if she were going to pass out on the living room floor, so she sat down on the sofa for the remainder of the call. There was another moment of silence between them.

"All right. So in other words, I've been caught?" he asked while pacing about the living room floor.

"Yes, you have been caught. Next time, it will be the police who call you, you fucking bastard!" Crystal yelled, and Tommy didn't say anything. "So if you feel like you want to stalk me again, remember you're not too far from getting thrown in jail. All right?" she asked, trying to calm down.

"Crystal, why do we have to get the police involved?" he asked while removing his black-framed glasses from his perspiring face.

"Well, Tommy, I hate to burst your bubble, but the police are already involved. You have a copy of the order of protection, right?" she asked.

"Yes," Tommy responded, wondering where this was leading.

"Well, goodbye," said Crystal, and she hung up the telephone.

When Tommy realized she had hung up, he hung up his phone, rose from the recliner, went to the sofa, and lay in the fetal position on his side while he cried himself to sleep as he rocked back and forth.

The morning sun rose to a new day and another weekend. Tommy walked out of his apartment building to take care of last-minute errands. While he walked down the street, twenty feet away from Tommy, Maria came out from behind a car, watching Tommy and wondering where he was going. Tommy saw a check-cashing place, and he walked across the street to cash his check, make some money orders, and pay some bills.

When he entered the check-cashing place, Maria was right behind him. She stayed outside and looked through a little glass window on the door, staring at Tommy's every move. She watched him exit the check-cashing facility and cross the street. He walked over to a mailbox on the corner of the block, put a few bills he had stuffed inside envelopes into the mailbox, shut the hatch door, and then reopened it, making sure the bills had gone down to the bottom of the mailbox. When he was confident about his mail going to the bottom of the mailbox, he quickly turned around—and there was Maria right in front of him!

"Maria! You scared the shit out of me! Why are you here?" he shouted, trying to regain his composure because he was full of rage, as he stepped back.

"Tommy, I just wanted to be physically next to you. Is this a crime?" she asked as she smiled innocently.

"Well, according to our situation, it could be if you keep this up," said Tommy as he folded his arms as he tried to calm down, trying not to make a scene in public.

"Tommy, I want you in my life. And not only do I want you in my life, but I really need you, and you need me!" said Maria as tears flowed down her beautiful Peruvian face.

"You know what? I'm going to act as though I really want you, and then when I really get sick of you, I'll let you go. And if you continue pursuing me, I'll call the police. I'll get an order of protection, and it will be hand delivered to you by New York's finest. This is bizarre!" Tommy shouted as he stormed off.

He walked away from Maria and left her standing near the mailbox at the corner of the block. He walked into a five-and-dime store to find some things for his apartment, and everywhere Tommy turned around, Maria was right behind him. Driven by her obsession, which at one time had been love, she continued following Tommy, popping up her head in all the places where Tommy was.

Tommy walked about the shopping area stores, carrying a few shopping bags. On the way out of one of the stores, he noticed a hot dog vendor on the corner of the street, and he decided to take a break from shopping to buy a hot dog from the vendor. After he purchased a hot dog, he bit into it. It had mustard and onion sauce on it. He looked across the street after a bus went by, and he saw Maria across the street while he was chewing his hot dog. Watching him, she wet her lips with her tongue, being seductive to him.

After seeing her, he turned around as he finished the hot dog, feeling almost tempted to take her into his apartment and make wild love to her. He threw away the little bit of hot dog he had left into the garbage can on the corner a few feet from the hot dog vendor and proceeded to the supermarket to do some food shopping.

When he entered the supermarket, he grabbed a shopping cart, put the few shopping bags he had into the cart, and continued through the aisles of food. He walked up the first aisle as the store's stereo played music, looking at the canned vegetables and canned fruits.

"Ladies and gentlemen, this is your rocking radio DJ playing the hits of New York City! Do you remember when Blondie ruled the airwaves?" the DJ asked, and the song "One Way or Another" blared out on the supermarket stereo.

When Tommy picked up two cans of peas from the top shelf, there was Maria, behind the cans of peas. He didn't notice her while continued up the aisle, pushing his shopping cart, continuing his shopping. He walked into the next aisle, and Maria walked toward him from the opposite end of the aisle with her shopping cart. As she passed him, she smiled pleasantly while he stared at her, not believing that he was once again in her presence. He continued shopping, taking different foods from the shelves, going to the different aisles, and putting the gathered food in his shopping cart. His shopping cart was halfway full as he went toward one of the cashiers and joined the checkout line. He noticed an elderly lady passing around small food samples on a silver tray: little sausages with toothpicks stuck through them. She passed them out to customers in the supermarket while he stood in line, waiting for his turn to be checked out by the cashier.

Maria walked around with a shopping cart as the song "One Way or Another" finished, and the radio DJ put some commercials on. As she was walking about the store, she saw the elderly lady passing out the little sample sausages from the tray. When she walked over to the elderly lady and took one of the sausage samples, Tommy watched, still in line. As he watched Maria put the sausage into her mouth and chew it, she knew she was being watched by Tommy. She slid the toothpick in and out of her mouth as she swallowed the sample sausage, moving the toothpick slowly between her upper and lower lips as her lips were shut. Her lips were moist. Tommy just turned the other direction, avoiding her.

After being checked out by the cashier, Tommy exited the supermarket with his bags of groceries and the few bags he had from shopping at the other stores in the area and hurried to his apartment. Maria walked quickly, only a few feet behind, catching up with him. When he reached the front doors of the apartment building, before he grabbed hold of the knob to open the door, Maria leaped out in front of him.

"Now, Tommy, this is ridiculous. I mean, look at us, baby. I'm trying so hard to get your attention, and you're ignoring me," said Maria as she placed her hands on his waist, partially embracing him.

"Yes, I'm ignoring you, but I'm trying to tell you I don't want to be with you. My heart will forever be with Crystal," said Tommy as he showed a devilish smile.

He was irritating Maria, but she gave a half smile and laughed a little bit. "Tommy, I have to hand it to you. You're right. You're absolutely right." She removed her hands from his waist while stepping back a bit, stared at him, and then stepped aside, allowing him to proceed into the building to go to his apartment. She wore the expression of a lost child.

As Tommy opened the door, he glanced at Maria, wondering what she was thinking about.

"You're right about one thing: your heart. But those goddamn pictures on the edges of your mirror are the closest you're ever going to get to being with Crystal! And with that, someday you will walk up to me and say, 'Maria, I want you. I really want you! You were right! Forgive me, Maria!' And you know what? I will forgive you. I really will. I will forever love you, my sweet." Maria smiled halfway as she pinched his cheeks and kissed him on the lips with passion and length.

She slowly parted from his lips, feeling disgusted, and walked away. As he watched her walk down the street on her way to the subway, she turned and looked back quickly and then proceeded to the subway. As he entered the apartment building, he wondered what the hell that had been about.

When he entered his apartment, he walked into the kitchen to put the groceries away, and when he was done in the kitchen, he walked into the living room and lay down on the sofa. He removed his black-framed glasses and noticed the time: it was three in the afternoon. He let out a yawn while stretching, closing his eyes. When he shut his eyes, he remembered seeing Maria in the supermarket, sliding a toothpick in and out of her mouth slowly. And at the front entrance of his apartment building, Maria had stood right in front of him, blocking him from entering the building, begging to be with him as he'd continuously declined. Then she'd stolen a kiss from him.

The things that had happened to him that afternoon with Maria aroused him while he lay there on the sofa. But his heart remained true to only one woman, a woman who didn't want to be with him and didn't want anything to do with him, the one and only Crystal Farnsworth.

———————————

A few hours later, at Crystal's residence, the telephone rang as she was entering the living room.

"Hello? Crystal?" someone called out.

"Yes, this is Crystal. Jim?" Crystal asked, hoping it wasn't Tommy.

"Yes, Crystal, this is Jim. How are you?" Jim asked.

"I'm all right. How are you?"

"I'm doing fine. I'm sorry for not answering right away. It's just that you and your sister sound so much alike. I thought you were your sister."

"Yeah, I know. Everyone says that. Actually, my sister doesn't live here anymore," said Crystal as she sat down on the sofa.

"Oh yeah? Did y'all have a disagreement or something?" he asked while he looked out his window, imagining he was looking at Central Park in New York, as he was missing Crystal in New York.

"Ah, no. We haven't had a disagreement in so long. You see, she's getting married. My darling sister and her wonderful fiancé decided they would be better off saving up their money together by living together." Crystal was in the kitchen, and she sat down at the kitchen table.

"Seeing that they don't kill each other, right?" Jim asked, sitting by the windowsill, looking at a couple in a horse-and-buggy ride. He imagined the buggy entering Central Park as he closed his eyes, missing Crystal.

"Actually, they get along great, but you don't know a person until—"

"Until you live with him or her," said Jim as he politely interrupted her.

"Bingo!" she shouted, and she and Jim laughed. "Hey, Jim, how was your flight back to Dallas?" she asked as she smiled but, at the same time, cringed, missing him.

"It was all right. I'm sorry I couldn't stay a little longer in New York, but there was an emergency in the business, and I had to take care of it. Everything is all right now," Jim said.

"Oh yeah? What went wrong?" she asked, in front of her window, looking out from the living room.

"The computers were down, and they couldn't find any repairmen to work on them at that time. Since I know how to fix computers and they had deadlines to meet, I had to fly back a week earlier than expected to take care of the situation."

"I miss you," said Crystal as she lay down on the sofa.

"I miss you too, Crystal. Earlier in our conversation, I was sitting near my window, and sometimes as I'm sitting by the window in my living room, I feel as though I'm still at the hotel overlooking Central Park," Jim said.

"Oh yeah?" Crystal responded as she sat up quickly.

"Yeah. So how is my new favorite city doing?" he asked while looking out his window, which had a direct view of the tall buildings of the Dallas skyline.

"New York is doing fine, but we have a little rain tonight." Crystal was on her knees on the sofa, looking out her window in the living room.

"Oh yeah? We have a little rain out here in Dallas too. Crystal, I really had a great time with you during my stay in New York. Even though we only went out twice, it felt so right, being with you." Jim closed his eyes, feeling somber because of his feelings for Crystal.

"Well, I had a great time with you too, and I feel the same way about you," said Crystal as she rose from the sofa.

"I do have some good news, Crystal. I will be back in New York next month," he said as he rose from where he was sitting by the window.

"Next month? In November?" she asked as she went into the kitchen to look at the calendar that hung on the wall near the refrigerator, between the living room and the kitchen.

"Yes. It will be the week of Thanksgiving," said Jim as he rushed into his den and looked at his calendar.

"You have a business meeting during Thanksgiving?" she asked as she walked farther into the kitchen to make a cup of herbal tea. She reached into the cupboard for an herbal tea bag and a cup.

"Actually, no. I don't have any meetings that week in New York; I was hoping I could stay with you at your apartment during the holiday for the week if you like," he said, back at the window, looking out.

"Well, Jim, I was going to ask you if I would be moving too fast in asking if you could come to New York for the holiday and perhaps stay with me at my place. I think that would be great, Jim," said Crystal, and she and Jim laughed. She could not believe they would share the week together at her apartment during the holiday.

"Excellent! Crystal, I happen to like you an awful lot," said Jim as he laughed and smiled.

"I feel the same way, Jim. I like you and that Texan accent an awful lot," said Crystal, and she and Jim laughed together.

"All right, Crystal. I have to go now. You have a wonderful night," said Jim as he sat down on his recliner, still in his living room.

"OK, Jim, and you do the same. Good night, Jim."

"Good night, Crystal."

They hung up their phones. As soon as she hung up, the telephone rang again. Crystal just stared at it as she froze in place, thinking it could be Tommy calling her. The telephone rang a third time as she still stared at it, growing numb and more nervous with each ring. She looked at her caller ID, and it said, "Out of area." On the fourth ring, she answered it, and she smiled with relief that it wasn't Tommy.

"Hello? Jim?" Crystal said as her eyes closed for a few moments.

"Hello, Crystal. It's Jim. Sorry for calling you again, but I just wanted to ask you something. Is that guy still harassing you?"

"No, not since I got the order of protection against him. You know, the copy I showed you?" said Crystal as she stood by the bedroom door.

"Yes, I remember, Crystal. But do me a favor," he said.

"All right. What is it?" she asked as she went into the kitchen to turn off the stove, as the teakettle was whistling. She put a couple of teaspoons of sugar into her cup.

"If this guy ever makes you afraid or if you just need someone to talk to about this situation, please call me. Don't hesitate. I know I live all the way in Texas and I'm limited, but I'm concerned for your safety."

Crystal smiled halfway, thinking that Tommy was not really a threat in her life anymore. "Jim, I really appreciate your concern, but I'll be fine. I don't really see this going any further." Crystal took her herbal tea, sat down on her recliner, and looked out her window into the night sky lit up with the tall buildings of the city.

"All right, if you're sure. All right then. Take care, Crystal."

"All right, Jim," said Crystal as she rested her cup of tea on the side table.

"Good night, Crystal," said Jim, sitting on his bed in his bedroom.

"Good night, Jim," Crystal responded, and they once again hung up their telephones. Still in her recliner, she took in a moment of silence as she thought about the new man in her life, Jim Connors. She smiled as she picked up her cup of herbal tea, blew into her cup as some steam rose from the cup, and took a sip of her tea.

<hr>

Meanwhile, at Tommy's residence, Tommy was pacing about his apartment, talking to himself.

"Why doesn't Crystal want to be with me? God, I feel so alone! I want Crystal so badly!" Tommy shouted as he went in front of his mirror in the living room. "I'm not a bad person. I always conducted myself as a gentleman. Most men are animals or freaks of nature," he said as he looked into the mirror deeper. "I wouldn't say I'm the best-looking guy, but I wouldn't say I'm the worst-looking guy either."

Tommy continued looking at himself in the mirror, and in the mirror, he could see, on the side table next to the recliner, the telephone. He stared at the telephone momentarily.

"Why does she protest so much against me?" Tommy shouted as he walked into the bedroom. "I don't understand!" He looked into the mirror in the bedroom and then looked at the pictures of Crystal around the mirror. He just stood there and stared as though he were in a trance.

"I have her here with me, but then I don't," said Tommy, still looking at all the pictures, and then he walked back into the living room.

In the living room, he walked over to the side table, picked up the receiver of the telephone, and dialed the forbidden telephone number.

The telephone rang at Crystal's residence, but she didn't pick it up. Instead, her answering machine picked up the call. As soon as the answering machine picked up, Tommy hung up his phone as he wondered where she might be at that time at night.

At Crystal's residence, Crystal came out of the shower with a huge towel wrapped around her body and walked into her bedroom to get ready for bed at the day's end.

+‧+✦+✦+‧+

The next day arrived, and half the weekend was finished. After Tommy awakened, the first thing he did was reach for the phone on the side table near his bed. He called Crystal.

At Crystal's residence, the telephone rang while she was in the kitchen, making scrambled eggs and frying some bacon. Hearing the telephone ring, she rushed into the living room to answer the call.

"Hello?" Crystal said, wondering who it could be and wishing she'd looked at the caller ID first.

"Yeah, Crystal. It's Tommy."

"Why the hell do you keep calling me? I'm currently involved with someone else! I'm going to call the police if this shit doesn't stop! I swear to fucking God I will have you arrested. Do you fucking understand me?" Crystal shouted while she trembled.

"But, Crystal, I—"

"I don't give a flying fuck what you have to say! You are violating the order of protection!" Crystal shouted as she cooked the scrambled eggs on the stove, resting the cordless phone on her shoulder. She leaned her head to the side, holding the phone with her head, as she flipped the bacon strips in the other frying pan.

"Crystal! Now, look! You're seeing that other guy, and that is unacceptable! This is totally unacceptable! We belong together. You and me! If you want to call the fucking cops, go for it! But I'll tell you one thing: I'm not giving up! I'll never give up! And let your so-called new boyfriend do something about me! Let him try! Besides, he isn't much to brag about. I saw him! Oh, he may have some money, and he may have his BMWs," said Tommy, pacing about his living room floor.

"Wait a minute! How do you know he drives a BMW?" she asked, touched with shock and fear.

All of a sudden, there was a cold silence in the air that sent a chill down Crystal's spine, and then the operator came on in a recording.

"If you want to make a call, please hang up and dial the number. This is a recording," said the operator as Crystal just stood there, wide-eyed, stunned by his call. "If you want to make a call, please hang up and dial the number. This is a recording. If you want to make a call—"

Crystal stood there feeling numb from the call she had received from Tommy.

"Shit! He's been stalking me all this time still," she told herself as she hung up the telephone. "I know he was stalking me the last time I took the subway home from work. At that time, I ran into Maria, the girl who is in love with him. As I've been dating Jim, he has been there the whole time I was with Jim. Shit," she whispered to herself as she entered her bedroom and slammed the door shut.

⸻ ✦✦✦✦✦ ⸻

Later on, throughout the day, Tommy was cleaning his apartment. As he was cleaning, the telephone rang. He rushed to the side table next to the sofa to answer it.

"Hello?" he said, hoping it was Crystal on the other end of the line.

"Hello? Hi, Tommy," Maria said.

It took a moment before he recognized her voice. "Hi, Maria. What's up?" Tommy asked while dusting the furniture in the living room.

"I just thought I would call you to ask if you would be interested in going out with me tonight," Maria said, and a silence temporarily crept in as he stopped what he was doing.

"Well, Maria, I can't do that," he responded with his hands on his hips.

"Tommy, I feel very much alone, and I—"

"No, Maria! Wait a minute! You are a very beautiful woman, and any man who is pursuing you or is with you as a boyfriend is one helluva lucky man! You have a very sexy body, and you can get any man you want. Now, why don't you face facts, all right? I'm not giving up on Crystal. So leave me alone! Leave me alone!" he shouted into the telephone.

"Yeah, but, Tommy?" Maria responded, crying.

"Bye!" Tommy shouted, and then he hung up the telephone.

+ + ♦ + +

At Maria's residence, when Maria realized he'd hung up his telephone, she hung up hers and reached for a bottle of vodka that was next to the telephone on the side table. She picked up a small drinking glass and poured some vodka into the glass as she started to cry. After she poured some vodka into her glass, she put the bottle down on the side table, took a sip from her glass, and looked out the window in her living room, which overlooked her street where she lived. She walked toward the window to get a better view.

"Well, Mr. Tommy Landis, you may think it's over between you and me, but as far as you and I go, it's never going to be over. If I have to kill you to show you my love for you, then that is what I might have to consider," she mumbled to herself as she drank the rest of the vodka from her glass as she cried even more. As her tears rolled down her cheeks, she tasted the salt of her tears, feeling frustration and anger powdered with the pain of not having what she could not have.

The evening arrived. Tommy was eating a sandwich while watching television in the living room, when he heard a knock on the door. He lowered the volume on the television and went to answer the door.

"Hello," Tommy said.

"Hello. I'm Sergeant O'Hara with the Twenty-First Precinct," said the rough-voiced police officer.

"Oh, hi," Tommy responded. He had an idea why the officer was there.

"May I speak with Tommy Landis, please?"

"This is Tommy Landis." He really didn't want to hear what the officer was going to say.

"All right, Mr. Landis. How are you tonight?" Sergeant O'Hara asked.

"I'm all right," Tommy responded.

"That's good. Mr. Landis, I personally received a phone call from a young lady by the name of Crystal Farnsworth. She says you have been stalking her. She's alleging that you have been stalking her for a while now. And you make ongoing phone calls in spite of the order of protection that was served to you by my precinct about two months ago?" Sergeant O'Hara asked while standing at the entrance of the apartment.

"You see, sir, I—"

"Mr. Landis, you have a copy of the order of protection, and you were warned by the police who served the copy of the order of protection to you, not to mention all those times you called Miss Farnsworth, and she gave you numerous warnings. This is going to be the final warning, courtesy of Miss Farnsworth. The police are strictly against these final warnings, because we've warned you enough times, but this is what she wants. But the next time, we will just arrest you, and we won't need to ask her permission to do so. You could actually go to jail right now on charges of harassment, stalking, and violating the order of protection, but Miss Farnsworth wants to give you one more chance to move on with your life and leave her alone," Sergeant O'Hara said with his arms folded against his wide chest.

"All right, sir. No problem," Tommy responded as he wiped the perspiration from his face and forehead with a towel lying on the kitchen table.

"Do not call or stalk this woman again. Do you understand me?" Sergeant O'Hara said.

"Yes, sir," said Tommy.

"The only reason I'm not arresting you right now is because Miss Farnsworth insisted on this final warning. If there's a next time, I will bust you." Sergeant O'Hara reached inside his uniform jacket and gave Tommy an envelope with a letter inside with the final warning.

"Yes, sir. I understand well," said Tommy, and he went inside his apartment, entered the living room, and sat down on the recliner. The police officer entered the apartment and stood between the kitchen and the living room.

"I'm not a doctor or anything like that, but you should really consider counseling to take care of this obsessive problem you have," said Sergeant O'Hara.

"Sir, please understand my situation. I'm not obsessed. I'm in love. And I know that Crystal is in love with me," Tommy said.

"Mr. Landis, if that is true, then why doesn't she want to be with you, and why did she seek legal means of getting you away from her? Believe me, pal, if you proceed in doing what you're doing, next time, you will be sitting in jail. Right now you're a lucky guy. Take advantage of this chance that she and the police department gave you. Seek some counseling for your problem. Leave the lady alone. All right?" The police officer walked toward the front entrance of the apartment.

"Yes, sir," Tommy responded as he walked toward the door of the apartment.

"All right, good night," said Sergeant O'Hara as he exited the apartment.

"Good night," said Tommy as he shut the apartment door.

Tommy walked back into the living room, walked over to the recliner, removed his black-framed glasses, and rested them on the side table, next to the telephone. While standing in front of the recliner, he covered his face with both hands. When he removed his hands from his face, he wore an expression of bewilderment and derangement as he looked up at the ceiling while releasing a great yell of frustration.

"No! No!" he yelled out, still looking up at the ceiling. Then he walked to the bedroom, where he looked at the pictures hanging all around the mirror. He walked closer toward the mirror, looking at himself, starting to have hatred for himself for not accomplishing the task of being with Crystal.

When he was several inches away from the mirror, he started to laugh uncontrollably, as though he were watching a comedian onstage, and then he stopped suddenly as his expression changed from hysteria to rage once again.

"No!" he yelled out.

CHAPTER 14

T HE NEW YORK SKYLINE STOOD tall underneath the sun as the sun shone down on the city as Tommy entered the building where he worked. He walked through the lobby to the elevator bank to go down to the basement, to the messenger center.

When he arrived in the basement, a few of his coworkers greeted him in passing, but he never noticed them; he continued walking fast to the messenger center. When he turned the corner, he accidentally walked into Maria, who was just stepping out of the ladies' bathroom. Only a few steps away from the center, all of a sudden, he stopped where he was and turned around, facing Maria. He looked at her as she stood by the door of the bathroom. She stared at him, wondering why he was staring at her.

"You! You stay out of my way! Just stay out of my way!" he shouted, pointing at her.

"What? I was just coming out of the ladies' bathroom," she said, leaning up against the bathroom door while holding the key ring to the bathroom.

Tommy looked deranged as he turned around and proceeded to the messenger center with Maria and a few other people looking on. When Tommy entered the messenger center, he ran into the mailman, who was on his way out of the center with the special pickups he was taking out of the building.

"Excuse you!" the mailman said while trying to pass him, and he and Tommy looked at each other as Tommy walked slowly.

"Whatever!" Tommy responded as he continued walking toward his locker.

As Tommy proceeded toward his locker, he saw Louie sitting at Maria's desk. Tommy walked slowly toward the center of the room instead of going toward his locker, and Louie saw him and stopped what he was doing at Maria's desk. When Tommy noticed that Louie was looking at him, he decided to go back toward his locker. Louie continued staring at him as Maria entered the messenger center.

"Hi, Maria," Louie called out.

"Hi, Louie," Maria responded, thinking about why Tommy was upset with her.

"I have your paperwork ready," said Louie, still at her desk, on her chair. He spun around counterclockwise until he was facing Maria as she walked toward him.

"Thanks, Louie," said Maria.

"It's all right. Hey, Maria? What's wrong with Tommy boy?" Louie asked as he stared at Tommy, who was at his locker, putting on his work smock over his buttoned shirt.

"I don't know. Well, I have an idea," said Maria as she and Louie stared at him. "But then again, I don't want to say anything." Louie stood up from the desk, and Maria sat down on her chair as Louie stared at Tommy with his arms folded against his chest.

"Tommy, are you all right?" Louie asked as he slowly approached him.

Tommy continued getting ready to work, brushing his hair in front of the little mirror that hung on the back of his locker door, without saying a word in response to Louie. Louie grew more and more annoyed with Tommy for not responding.

"God damn it, Tommy Landis! Say something!" Louie shouted, right next to Tommy by his locker.

When Tommy put away his brush, he covered his face with both hands in front of the little mirror while looking partially at Louie, still standing next him, as his coworkers looked on, seeing what was going on, wondering why Louie was yelling at Tommy. Tommy slammed shut the door of his locker and slowly walked over to the carts. Louie was still standing near the lockers while Tommy began to load up one of the carts with the day's deliveries for the upper floors. Louie walked over to where Tommy was and came up right behind him.

"What?" Tommy said, knowing Louie was right behind him, as his coworkers went back to work, dispersing.

"Hey, Tommy, are you having a PMS moment today?" Louie asked with his hands on his hips, and then he put his right hand on the right side of Tommy's face. "Hmm. Whiskers? What is this? Growing a beard, Tommy?" Louie asked as he leaned over toward Tommy's side. Tommy was getting annoyed with his theatrical show.

"Hey, Louie, eat me! All right? Fucking eat me!" Tommy shouted as he walked over toward his locker.

Louie's mouth dropped open. He'd not expected what he'd just heard from Tommy's mouth, and he had mixed emotions as he pondered in disbelief, feeling a bit angered and, at the same time, feeling sorry for him. He walked over to him as Tommy opened up his locker.

"Tommy, I could fire you right now, but instead, I'm going to send you home without pay, and when you go home or wherever you go when I send you out of here, I want you to think about how you ought to act when you're at work. So take off your smock, and I'll see you in the morning!" Louie shouted, as he felt Tommy was ignoring him, and then he walked over toward the carts to continue loading them.

Tommy turned around, facing Louie. "Are you serious?" Tommy asked while he walked over toward Louie as Louie was filling up a cart with the day's mail and deliveries. Louie looked up at Tommy while organizing the small boxes in the cart.

"Yes, I'm serious. In fact, I'm dead serious!" Louie shouted with an unlit cigar at the corner of his mouth as he rose from the cart and stared straight into his eyes. "Now, if you don't want to get fired, get the hell out of here! I don't need your attitude bright and early in the morning! I'll have Sammy take your place today! So just go.

Leave, and I'll see you tomorrow morning! All right?" Louie said as he and Sammy continued filling another cart with the day's mail and deliveries.

Tommy momentarily stared at Louie while standing near his locker. "Fine! I'll go home! I'll come back tomorrow morning! I'll be back in the morning!" Tommy shouted as he removed his work smock and hung it back up in his locker.

Maria stared at him from the side of her eyes, hoping he wouldn't get fired. Louie momentarily walked away from Sammy and the cart while Sammy continued filling up the cart.

"Show up in the morning without that cocky-ass attitude! All right?" Louie said, at the point of his voice going hoarse, with the unlit cigar dangling from the corner of his mouth.

Tommy stopped at the doors at the entrance of the center, looking at Louie from across the center as Louie stood in front of his office door. "Right," Tommy responded sheepishly, ashamed of his current actions on the job and the way he was carrying on in front of Louie and his coworkers. As he stood at the entrance, staring at all his co-workers, they stared back. Louie was looking at him too.

"Bye, Louie," said Tommy, and he turned around and exited the messenger center as Louie walked quickly right behind him.

"Tommy!" Louie called out as he approached him. "I don't know what's going on in your life. That's none of my business, but whatever it is, get it straightened out, and come back tomorrow morning, all right? Here at the center, your coworkers, myself included, would like to see the same old Tommy Landis we all have known for the past three years, all right, Tommy?"

"All right, Louie. See you later." Tommy exited the messenger center with tears in his eyes as Maria watched from the desk with tears in her eyes.

"Thank God it's not busy today," said Louie as he walked back to load one of the carts with Sammy.

When Tommy exited the building, he wondered what he was going to do for the rest of the day. As he walked to the subway, in deep thought, he stopped midway. He decided to go to where Crystal worked, to see if he could speak with her. Even though he was taking a big risk, he walked the several blocks to the building where she worked.

When he arrived at the building, he sat down on one of the cement benches on the side of the building, awaiting her presence.

As the time moved closer to noon, Tommy began to pace about where he was hiding, still waiting for Crystal, hoping he wouldn't be discovered, as she suspected him of following her.

All of a sudden, he stopped pacing, slowly turned around, and noticed Crystal at a hot dog vendor cart. She was buying a hot dog and a can of soda. Tommy watched the vendor put mustard on top of the hot dog.

When she was given the hot dog and soda, she paid, and then she walked toward where Tommy was, to find a place to sit while she ate her lunch. When she found a cement bench to sit on, Tommy was behind a tree right behind the bench. As she was about to sit down on the bench, Tommy was inches from her. He stood there with his hands in his trench coat's pockets as she sat down on the bench.

"Crystal?" Tommy said from behind her.

Crystal was stunned, and she froze in place, not moving an inch, after hearing the unforgettable voice of Tommy Landis. Finally, she turned around and saw him standing behind the bench. Her expression was full of rage and disbelief, and she was frightened. When she turned, facing him, she didn't say a word as she finished the hot dog she had in her mouth.

"Now, Crystal, I know right this second, you could have me arrested by the cops, but I felt we should talk for the final time, and I promise I will never call you or bother you ever again, all right?" Tommy said, still standing behind the cement bench.

Wide-eyed and frightened, Crystal slowly nodded. He knew he would get through to her this final time. He sat down next to her on the bench, and when he sat, he smelled the sweet aroma of her perfume.

"All right, fine," said Crystal as she set down her can of cola on the concrete ground near the bench, and she covered her face with her hands in disbelief.

As Tommy watched her, he breathed in the sweet smell of her perfume as she slowly removed her hands from her face.

"I promise you, Tommy, this will be the final time. I should call the police right now," said Crystal as she looked Tommy directly in his eyes, pointing at his chest, touching his chest with her finger. "All right. Say your piece. Go ahead."

"Crystal, first of all, that guy you've been seeing? What makes him better than me? What do you see in him?" he asked, feeling a bit jealous and envious of her boyfriend and, at the same time, feeling a bit agitated as Crystal smiled. He could not believe she hadn't called the police yet.

"Well, Tommy, before I answer all these stupid questions, I'm going to say something first. I can't believe you've been stalking me all this time!" Crystal shouted as she threw her can of soda into the trash can near the bench.

"Well, Crystal, I have been following you, and you know something, love? I'm a much better kisser than he is." Tommy wore a bold look of confidence on his face.

Her eyes widened with fear as she slapped his face twice, once on each side, full of anger. Afterward, she gained back her composure. Tommy was stunned.

"I'm sorry," said Crystal while she looked at the other people around, not wanting to draw attention to her business. "Look, you said that there was something you wanted to tell me, that this would be the last time I would ever see you, and that I would never hear from you ever again," she said just above a whisper as she stood up from the bench.

"True. All true. I swear!" he whispered loudly as he looked up at her and smiled while he held up his right hand with an expression of innocence.

"Go ahead. I'm listening," she responded, still standing, as she looked at her watch, keeping track of time, because she had to go back into the building soon, as her break was almost over. She sat back down on the bench.

"All right, you know Maria, right? I assume you do," he said, and she nodded. "Well, Maria and I are now seeing each other." Tommy smiled convincingly, though he wasn't being honest with her.

"Oh really?" she responded, feeling free from his harassment in the present and in the future.

"Yeah. We were talking about spending some time with each other, and this morning at the job, we opened up our hearts to each other." Tommy smiled again, almost believing it himself.

"This is really wonderful! I'm so happy for you and for Maria," said Crystal as she smiled, feeling as if she had her own life again, with no interference from him.

"And you're really happy for yourself too, right?" Tommy asked as he smiled.

"Well, yeah. But I really do wish you and Maria the very best. I really do," said Crystal as she rose from where she was sitting.

"Thanks, Crystal." Tommy smiled and laughed a little bit, acting as though he really found had someone but wishing Crystal wanted him instead of the other guy. He continued smiling at her, impressed with the way she had fallen for it so easily, believing every word he said.

"I think it's wonderful that you and Maria hooked up together. When Maria and I met at the subway the other night, she told me she was very much in love with you." Crystal smiled halfway.

"Yeah, I guess it was meant for Maria and me to be together," Tommy said as he smiled halfway.

"Yeah, I guess. Things have a way of happening, right?" she asked as she looked at her watch again, not wanting to arrive back from lunch late. She laughed a little, feeling relieved after listening to Tommy's news about being with Maria now. "Tommy, I hope you and Maria are successful in the joining of the two of you. Unfortunately, lunch break is over now for me." Crystal and Tommy rose from the bench.

"Are you going back to work now?" she asked while they walked back toward the front entrance of the building where she worked.

"No, I took the rest of the day off work," he responded as he smiled, and then he walked away.

Crystal turned around, wondering why he'd just abruptly walked away. Then he stopped walking and turned around, facing Crystal, a few feet away from her.

"I took the rest of the day off because I wanted to talk with you and clear out my head of my foolish behavior toward you in the past, and I will face a new day tomorrow," Tommy said as he looked at his watch, and she nodded. "Crystal, have a pleasant day."

Crystal watched him walk away, wondering if this would be the final time she ever saw him or heard from him. She turned away and started walking toward the glass double doors. She turned around again while holding on to one of the glass doors, and then she entered the building as she looked at her watch again, on her way back to the reception desk.

As Tommy continued walking toward the corner, he wore a big smile on his face, plotting his next move on Crystal.

CHAPTER 15

THE NEXT DAY ARRIVED, AND Tommy entered the messenger center with a smile on his face, as though something had taken over his attitude from the previous day. He thought about yesterday, when he'd had some time with Crystal during her lunch break. While walking through the messenger center, he thought about the plan he'd come up with during his ride on the train on the way to work. The plan was set, and in the near future, he thought he might reap the rewards, if everything went according to plan.

As he entered the messenger center, Louie saw him as he was getting a cup of water from the spring water bottle in the corner of the center.

"Tommy! How's everything? How was your time off yesterday? Did you do a lot of thinking yesterday?" Louie asked. As Tommy drank the cup of water, Louie approached him in the corner of the center.

"Yeah, actually, I spent some time in Midtown yesterday afternoon on my way home. And yes, I did a lot of thinking. I had a lot to think about—or, should I say, a lot to rethink." Tommy and Louie laughed as though it were a new beginning at the job. "I had a pretty good day, and I owe it all to you. Thanks for the time off," said Tommy as he went toward his locker to get his work smock.

"Good. Very good, Tommy. I wish we could've worked together yesterday, but you know like I know—" Louie walked over to Tommy at the locker as Tommy was brushing his hair in front of the little mirror that hung on the back of the door of his locker.

"Shit happens, and then you die!" Louie and Tommy said it together, and they started to laugh.

"True. How true. All right, Tommy, we have a lot of mail today, as usual, so let's get on it," Louie said as he walked toward one of the carts in the corner.

"All right, Louie." Tommy slammed shut his locker door and proceeded toward Louie and the carts.

+ +++++ +

Crystal was at her workplace, at the reception desk, surrounded by her coworkers and friends.

"Hey, Crystal! You look so bloody happy today!" said Dawn as she sat down next to Crystal at the front desk, gathering up the day's paperwork, and Crystal looked at Dawn and smiled.

"Yes, I am happy. In fact, I'm relieved," Crystal responded, almost finished gathering the day's paperwork at the desk.

"Relieved? What? Oh, all right. Getting over your period for the month, right?" Dawn asked as she whispered in Crystal's ear, and they both laughed.

"No. You see, I was on my lunch break yesterday, and I sat down on one of the cement benches at the side of the building to eat my lunch, and guess who was standing right behind me," Crystal said as she looked toward the front, seeing if anyone was approaching the desk.

Dawn thought about it for a moment. "Who?" she asked, full of curiosity.

"Tommy Landis, that guy who's obsessed," said Crystal with no expression on her face, and Dawn was shocked.

"No!" Dawn replied, not believing it.

"Yes!" Crystal responded as she looked for a pen inside her desk.

"No bloody way. That obsessed nutcake!" Dawn responded.

"Look, Dawn, he was being honest with me yesterday about the things we were talking about. I think he just has a mental problem or something that could be just temporary. Unless he's one of those who has these problems and never snaps out of it. Then I would have a problem," said Crystal, and she thought about it for a second as she and Dawn just stared at each other.

"Crystal, are you telling me that you went and sat on one of the benches out there on the side of the building, and just like that, he was there?" Dawn asked while she was finishing getting the papers ready for the day.

"Yeah. I was about to sit down, and he was standing right behind me." Crystal took a sip of her coffee.

"Crystal, I don't know. This guy Tommy sounds real spooky to me," said Dawn, finding a pen inside her desk.

"I know. Believe me, he is spooky, but he told me that he was seeing this other woman and that he was going to leave me alone. And it's perfect because she works at the same job where he works. I met her once, and the night we met, she told me she was very much in love with him," said Crystal as she took another sip of her coffee.

"She is in love with him?" Dawn asked as she took a bite of her bagel with butter.

"Yeah, well, to each his or her own, all right? I wouldn't say he's attractive, but all people have a little good in them, even if they're a little crazy," said Crystal.

"Sounds right to me," said Dawn as she smiled along with Crystal.

"Anyway, he said that he and Maria—that's her name—were going to start going out together and that this was going to be the last time I saw him and heard from him." Crystal bit into whole-wheat toast with butter.

"So you have nothing more to worry about then?" said Dawn as she saw a few potential visitors enter the building.

"So far, I don't, but let's cross our fingers and hope he stays away from me." Crystal smiled but thought, *What if?*

"My fingers are crossed and my toes. I hope this guy really means what he says," said Dawn.

"Well, only time will tell," said Crystal as she raised her coffee cup.

Dawn met Crystal's with her coffee cup, and they toasted their coffees in the hope Tommy Landis had made his final appearance.

+ + + + + +

The master clock in the messenger center showed it was five minutes before five in the afternoon, and all the workers in the center were getting ready to go home as the day came to a close.

"Louie, this was a great day! Time came and went just like nothing," said Tommy, taking off his working smock, with his locker wide open.

"Hey, Tommy, I'll tell you one thing! Your attitude was one hundred percent better than yesterday! It's sure good to have you back!" Louie shouted as he put one arm around Tommy.

Maria looked at Tommy and smiled at him. Then he looked at her, and when he noticed her staring, he winked at her.

"Everyone have a lovely night! See everyone tomorrow!" Tommy shouted as he exited the front entrance of the messenger center.

Tommy went through the turnstile in the subway and onto the platform, waiting on a Brooklyn-bound train to arrive. He found a place to sit on the train and shut his eyes.

In his mind, Tommy was outside Crystal's apartment door. He knocked a couple of times, and Crystal looked through the peephole to see who it was.

"Who is it?" Crystal asked, as she wasn't sure who it was, and she looked through the peephole again.

Still without saying a word, he continued knocking. Crystal was still looking through the peephole.

"Who is it?" she asked again as she grew weary, not knowing who it was, because the peephole wasn't clear.

"Excuse me!" someone called out, and Tommy came back to reality. He was still on the train, Brooklyn-bound.

He looked up and saw a blonde-haired, blue-eyed beauty in front of him, but it wasn't Crystal. He moved over, allowing her to sit down next to him in the space that was available.

"Oh, excuse me," said Tommy as he moved over while putting on his Discman.

+ + + + + +

When Crystal arrived home at her apartment, she noticed a message on the answering machine, with the light flickering off and on. She entered the living room, turned on the light, took off her coat, and hung it up in the closet. As she walked toward the side table to the answering machine, she yawned because she'd had a long day, and she was feeling tired. When she was at the side table, she pressed the message-retrieval button on the answering machine.

Beep! "Hi, Crystal. It's Jim. I just wanted to say hi. How was your day? Good, I hope. My day went well. I just wanted to let you know that I was thinking of you and look forward to seeing you the week of Thanksgiving. All right, have a good night. Speak to you soon. Bye." *Beep!* The answering machine tape rewound itself to the beginning, as that was the only message on the machine.

As the tape rewound itself, Crystal sat down on the recliner and closed her eyes slowly, relaxing after the long day at work. With her eyes closed, she meditated, hoping she would really never see or hear from Tommy ever again and thinking about the man in her life, Jim Connors. She sat back in the recliner, smiling, with her eyes shut.

+ + + + + +

Tommy arrived home, entered his apartment, turned on the light, walked into the living room, took off his coat, and hung it up in his closet. When he hung up his coat, he had the feeling he wasn't alone. He walked farther into his living room, and he saw Maria stretched out on the sofa. He was in disbelief at what he saw. As he walked closer toward her slowly, he saw she was wearing tight blue jeans that outlined the beautiful Latin shape of her body, from her waist down to her beautiful feet, which were covered up in black socks, as her sneakers were on the other side of the floor, near the sofa.

Standing over her, he looked at her, from her feet all the way to her full, supple, moist lips, which begged him to kiss her. He felt tempted to, but his dedication to Crystal remained true. As he stood there, Maria's eyes opened slowly. As she slowly woke up, she smiled as she saw Tommy standing next to her. She stretched while still lying down on the sofa.

"Hi, Tommy. I kind of made myself at home. I hope you don't mind," Maria said as she sat up on the sofa. "I came by to talk with you about something I discovered on the way home today, but first, I ran into Crystal again at the subway, and do you know what she told me?" Maria smiled devilishly.

Tommy grew wary. The plans he had for that night were diminishing due to Maria's interfering. He placed his hands on his hips, feeling frustrated. "What did Crystal tell you today?" he asked. He didn't believe what she was saying. He knelt in front of her.

Maria held on to both his hands, which rested on top of her smooth, silky legs. Tommy held on to her hands, to her surprise, and she smiled, not believing his change of attitude toward her for the moment. She felt it wasn't going to last.

"Well, she said that you and I were seeing each other and that you are in love with me." Maria smiled again as she removed one of her hands from Tommy's hand.

Tommy was surprised by Maria's change of attitude toward him. *I never said I was in love with Maria*, he thought as she continued speaking and smiling.

"So, Tommy, you finally saw the light?" she asked.

"Yeah, yeah, I see the fucking light!" Tommy shouted as he took off his glasses and rested them on the coffee table as he smiled at her.

She beamed with love. She still didn't believe that her dream was going to come true. Little by little, she believed his confession to Crystal, but she thought maybe it was a plan to still pursue Crystal. Maybe he was using her as an excuse to see Crystal.

He waved his right hand through Maria's long, wavy dark hair. "Maria?" he said while smiling at her as the wheels in his mind kept turning.

"Yes, Tommy?" Maria responded. As he ran his fingers through her hair, he started kissing up and down the side of her neck, and she was getting aroused by his advances. "Oh, Tommy. I never thought you would ever want me," said Maria in total belief.

"Oh, you mean you were ready to give up?" he asked, stopping midway down her neck.

"Well, no," she responded as she opened her eyes wide. "But I still never thought, uh—" Maria closed her eyes as she was taken on a high she always had wanted to be on as Tommy put his index finger on her lips gently so she would stop speaking, and he continued kissing her on the neck slowly with little pecks.

"Oh, Tommy," Maria said again, still on the high Tommy brought her to, as he went upward, kissing her all the way up to her jawbone. When he arrived at her jawbone, he slowly stopped kissing her and just looked at her.

When Maria realized the kissing on her neck had stopped, she opened her eyes, and her eyes met his. As soon as their eyes met, they were fixed on each other, and she thought she was dreaming. As their faces drew closer, their lips flared up from the heat they were creating. When their lips met, their tongues intertwined blissfully. Tommy grasped her long black hair from behind her head while kissing her. Maria placed her hands on his waist, pulling him closer toward her, as the kissing continued slowly with heavy breathing. They kissed each other gently, and all of a sudden, with the handful of hair in his grip from the back of her head, he jerked her head back, and their lips parted abruptly. He quickly raised her to her feet from the sofa while he stood, and he pushed her toward the wall, still holding her by her hair.

"Tommy?" she said, not understanding what was taking place.

"Yes, my sweet?" he responded while holding her head back against the wall with the handful of hair in his grip.

"Why are you doing this to me?" she asked in a loud whisper, as she didn't believe this was happening.

"You ask me why I'm doing this? OK, my little bitch, I shall tell you why I am doing this. It's to make you understand, my little bitch, that

I do not in any way want to be with you! And what right do you have to enter my apartment?" Tommy asked as he still had her up against the wall in the living room.

"Tommy, I thought I—"

"I thought I—" Tommy spoke in an irritating, high-pitched voice, mimicking her.

"Tommy, I thought you really wanted me!" Maria cried as tears rolled down her cheeks.

"Tommy, I thought you really wanted me!" said Tommy, mimicking her again, as he smiled and laughed.

"Tommy, stop! You're hurting me!" Maria screamed, breaking away. She ran to the front door, and he was right behind her. When she arrived at the door, she opened it partially, but Tommy, right behind, slammed the door shut. She screamed when the door was shut, and a couple of tenants came out of their apartments to see who was screaming and where the noise was coming from.

After the door slammed shut, Tommy grabbed a handful of her hair as he slammed her against the back of the door while covering her mouth. He started kissing and biting her on the side of her neck.

"I'll tell you what, my little bitch. If you leave me alone, not only will I let you live, but I may even kiss you on the lips before I let you go," Tommy told her as he grabbed her hair and turned her head to face him.

While they looked at each other, he smiled in a demented fashion and quickly pressed his lips to hers, but she quickly declined his kiss and kneed him in the groin. As he backed away in a bent position, recuperating after the injury, she escaped his apartment. As she opened the door wide, the door swung and hit his head, and she fled the apartment. She ran down the steps of the building as Tommy slammed shut the door of his apartment.

"Ah shit!" He limped into the living room and lay on the carpeted floor in the fetal position, groaning with pain.

The next day, at the messenger center, the mood was somber. Maria was busy at her desk, still feeling what she had gone through the day before, not saying a word. Tommy was loading up one of the carts with the day's mail. When Louie entered the center, he immediately noticed that Maria and Tommy worked quietly, not saying anything or looking at each other from a distance.

"OK, everyone! I need everyone's attention!" Louie shouted as he put his unlit cigar on an astray on the counter.

Everyone in the messenger center came to the front of the center to hear what the supervisor had to say.

"All right, if everyone can finish up their work early—but the work must be neat and done in an orderly fashion—once everything is done, anyone with his or her work done—and each department must complete their own work—can go home early today! Only those who are done!" Louie shouted as he leaned up against the counter.

Everyone started to cheer, thanking Louie for what he'd just said. Maria quickly turned and saw Tommy loading up one of the carts in the corner. She rose from her desk and walked over toward Tommy while he was still loading up the day's mail into one of the carts.

"Tommy?" she called out.

"Yeah?" Tommy responded as he continued loading the cart.

"I want to apologize for entering your apartment without your permission, and I want to promise you that it will never happen again," said Maria, and she smiled as he looked up from the cart.

"You promise?" he asked as he looked at her while he continued loading the cart, almost finished.

"I promise and hope to die," said Maria as she held up her right hand, and she and Tommy laughed. She thought he looked much different from the man she had seen last night, who'd terrorized her in his apartment, as they shook hands.

"I forgive you, Maria," said Tommy as they continued shaking hands, and then he abruptly let go of her hand. "Oh, before I forget, I want to apologize for the way I treated you when you were in my apartment." Tommy held up both hands as he smiled.

"Tommy?" Maria responded as she put up one hand.

"No, really. I really treated you badly, and I'm sorry. I have this really bad temper, and I'm really sorry," said Tommy as he put down his hands and continued loading up the cart with the day's mail.

"OK, I forgive you. But you don't have to apologize for that one thing you did," said Maria as she smiled.

"One thing? And what's that?" he asked, about to finish loading the last bit of mail of the day into the cart.

"You don't have to apologize for kissing me. You kiss extremely well!" she whispered loudly to him as she leaned over the cart toward him.

"Maria?" Tommy responded as he rose from behind the cart.

"No, really, you do," said Maria as she moved closer, slowly pushed the cart out of the way, and put her arms around his waist. Everyone in the messenger center noticed what was going on between Maria and Tommy, and they realized they were being watched by their coworkers.

"Well, Maria, thanks for that compliment, but I want us to be just friends, and we're also coworkers. Isn't that enough for you?" He whispered because he didn't want to create a bigger scene than he and Maria already had. They knew all eyes were on them, even though the coworkers were acting as if they didn't notice what was going on.

"Your lips were so warm, sensual to the touch. And the timing of the kisses till our lips parted was perfect. Oh, Tommy, let me spend the night tonight, and I'll show you how much I want you," she whispered in his ear.

"No, Maria. I can't do that. I've told you a million times: I want Crystal," he whispered into her ear as he was leaving with his cart full of the day's mail, wanting to make the deadline so he could go home early.

As he left the message center, Maria watched him leave. She looked down at the tile floor, and then she looked up at the clock on the wall above the countertop; it was one in the afternoon. She walked back to her desk to complete her work for the day.

Ever since Maria had received Tommy's kisses at the apartment, she couldn't get enough of him. Even though he'd manhandled her and been rough with her, she still wanted to be with him.

CHAPTER 16

AT CRYSTAL'S WORKPLACE, CRYSTAL WAS on her way to lunch with Dawn, her coworker and friend. They left the reception area and went to the elevator bank. Crystal pressed the up button, and they waited for the elevator.

"So, Crystal, how is Jimbo?" Dawn asked, and she and Crystal laughed.

"Well, we are involved. But I guess you could say it's one of those long-distance relationships," said Crystal as she watched the elevator get closer to their floor.

"Oh yeah?" Dawn responded as the elevator door slid open, and they entered the elevator, with others following behind them. When they were inside the elevator, Dawn pressed the button for the floor they were going to, where the employee cafeteria was, and the elevator door slid shut as the elevator was on its way up. "Are you happy with that kind relationship? I mean, it's about twenty-five hundred miles or more from New York City," Dawn said.

"Am I happy with this situation? Yeah, I guess. It's just the beginning of the relationship or situation between us. I'm all right with it," said Crystal as they arrived on the tenth floor, where the employee cafeteria was.

When the elevator door slid open, Crystal, Dawn, and a few others stepped out of the elevator.

"I am happy, but it does get lonely at night," said Crystal as she and Dawn walked toward the entrance of the cafeteria.

"So you feel alone?" Dawn asked as they entered the cafeteria.

"Yeah. I'm a little lonely at night when I'm at home. Or when I'm on the subway and see couples holding hands, and I'm sitting there alone," said Crystal as they approached a line of employees, picked up their trays, and looked at all the different kinds of food on display over the counter and on the steam tables.

"Well, Crystal, I have a bloody answer!" said Dawn as she and Crystal stepped off the line momentarily.

"And your bloody answer is?" Crystal asked, expecting a serious answer, as she laughed along with Dawn.

"Call the nice man Tommy!" Dawn replied, wearing a devilish smile, being friendly.

"Dawn?" Crystal wore a half smile.

"Yes, Crystal?" Dawn responded as they walked back into the line for lunch.

"Shut the hell up!" said Crystal as she and Dawn were choosing their foods and putting items on their trays.

When Dawn and Crystal walked off the lunch line with their trays of chosen food items, they walked about the cafeteria, looking for a table. When they found a table and sat down, they started consuming their food while continuing the conversation.

"Dawn, I don't mean I can't bear it anymore, so I'm letting go of the loneliness bullshit, because I intend on keeping him. I'm keeping this guy in my life because he's tall, dark, and handsome and extremely nice!" said Crystal as she put a potato chip into her mouth.

"And rich!" Dawn added before popping a potato chip into her mouth as she smiled.

"Money has nothing to do with it. I do all right with the job I have and what I do for a living. I'm not rich, but I'm comfortable. I don't have to tell you that we're not rich working here, but we do get paid pretty well, and the benefits are great," Crystal said as she took a sip of her diet cola.

"Yeah, you are doing well since you received your promotion, right?" Dawn asked as she smiled sheepishly.

"That's right!" Crystal blurted out with a joking smile on her face as she bit into her pastrami sandwich with honey mustard, and they laughed together.

Another day at the job ended for Tommy. It was two in the afternoon, and some of the employees in the messenger center were coming together, getting ready to get off the job early, taking up Louie's offer. Tommy was among those people, but Maria still had some paperwork to finish. She was taking her time, preferring to be alone on the job.

As the few employees were leaving the center a little after two o'clock, Tommy walked behind the crowd of employees. Maria looked over her shoulder, watching Tommy leave early behind the crowd. Maria watched until she couldn't see him anymore when the elevator door slid shut.

One day, my sweet! One fine day, you will be all mine! she thought with a weird expression, feeling obsessive. Then she went back into the message center to finish her work at her desk.

After Tommy exited the elevator, he stopped midway in the lobby as he reached into his duffel bag, pulled out his camera, and put the camera in his coat pocket on the right side, so he could have easy access to it when the time was right.

He exited the building and continued on his way to the building where Crystal worked while he thought of the new man in her life. As he walked along Sixth Avenue, he looked and felt annoyed with the whole damn thing, continuing his journey.

Why does she keep rejecting me? Surely, deep down inside, she must feel some kind of feeling toward me, he thought while daydreaming back to the time when he and Crystal had met at the coffeehouse on Ninth Avenue in the Hell's Kitchen section of Manhattan.

I remember when we met at the coffeehouse. I was sitting in the lounge area, sipping on an Irish cream coffee, waiting for the chemistry between Crystal and me to kick in. Crystal Farnsworth is so incredibly beautiful that the movements of people and their talking around me stopped when she was in front of me. No one existed in the lounge except her and me with our Irish cream coffees! Everyone just faded into non-existence. I introduced myself, we were at the table, and we had some conversation. She owned a beauty from within that made me wonder how someone like her could have any interest in wanting to be with me. Oh, but I saw it in her eyes. She wanted me. I knew it would just be a question of when, Tommy thought as his daydreaming was starting to fade back into reality slowly. *I just can't see why she won't be honest with herself and with me.*

Fully back in reality, he rushed back to the corner of the street after a city bus almost hit him. After he regained his composure, he crossed the street. When he was crossing the street, he saw the American and Canadian flags waving in the air on the flagpoles in front of the office building, waving in time with the rhythm of the wind that swept across Sixth Avenue. Tommy hurried across the street toward the building where Crystal worked as he refocused his attention on Crystal. While walking toward the building, he glanced at his watch; it was two thirty in the afternoon. He began to feel a bit hungry and realized he had some time to kill, so he walked past the building. He saw a diner across the next street, on Seventh Avenue.

An hour later, Tommy walked out of the diner and back toward the building where Crystal was employed. When he arrived at the building, he kept himself well hidden. As he peeked through the glass of the rotary doors every now and then, he saw Crystal with her two coworkers at the reception desk. It wasn't too busy, and she was in open view, smiling, laughing, and looking just as sexy as she had the time they'd first met. As he continued looking through the glass of the rotary doors, he reached into his right coat pocket for his camera. Hoping he wouldn't be noticed, he focused his camera on Crystal. As he was focusing his camera lens, a gentleman from behind put his right hand on Tommy's right shoulder. Holding his camera, Tommy glanced over his shoulder and saw a tall, thin uniformed man as the gentleman removed his right hand from his shoulder. Tommy fully turned around and faced the uniformed man. Tommy realized the gentleman was a security officer working for the building. He wore an all-gray uniform, with a gray hat that resembled a police officer's hat. As Tommy faced the officer, he smiled at him.

"Why are you directing that camera through the glass and into the lobby?" the security officer asked, feeling a bit concerned about the matter.

"Well, I—" Tommy put the camera back into his right coat pocket.

"Sir, we have a strict policy here at the building that picture taking is not permitted in the building, on the property, on the grounds near the building, or anywhere around the perimeter," the security officer said.

"Oh, I'm sorry." Tommy was apologetic to the security officer as he smiled, and the security officer smiled back.

"No problem, sir. Just use today for future reference, all right?" the security officer said while still smiling.

"All right. Thanks," said Tommy as he backed away from the building slowly, still smiling.

"All right. Have a good day," said the officer, and then he went back into the building through the rotary doors, walking back into the lobby.

Tommy watched him from behind and then realized Crystal wasn't at the desk.

"Shit! Where did she go? God damn it!" he whispered to himself as he panicked quietly, frantically looking through the glass of the rotary doors, looking about the lobby area to see where she had gone.

All of a sudden, Tommy came up with an idea. He opened his duffel bag and took out a pair of sunglasses and a baseball cap. Then he closed his duffel bag and put on the sunglasses and the baseball cap. He didn't need the sunglasses that day, since it was cold and cloudy. He put away his black-framed glasses in his left coat pocket, put the duffel bag strap over his shoulder, and walked through the rotary doors and into the lobby. He walked through the lobby, looking around as though he were on the prowl. He waved to the security officer who'd confronted him earlier, and the security officer waved back at him, wondering what his intentions were as he walked toward the reception desk.

"Hi! How may I help you?" Dawn asked in her usual British accent as she smiled.

"Oh, hi. I usually come in here about twice a year—you know, meetings and whatnot. But there's usually a blonde-haired girl I sign in with. Is she working today? No offense to you." He looked around as he stood in front of the desk

"Well, Crystal is probably the one you're talking about," said Dawn as she smiled.

"Yes, that's her," Tommy responded as she smiled innocently, not knowing whom she was speaking to.

"She went on her fifteen-minute break, and she'll be back in about eight minutes," said Dawn as she looked at her watch.

"Hmm. I guess I'll be back." Tommy smiled and then walked away from the reception desk.

The security officer walked toward the reception desk as he and Dawn stared at Tommy exiting the building. Their supervisor came to the front desk, wondering who the man wearing a baseball cap and sunglasses and asking for Crystal was. Dawn, the security officer, and the front desk supervisor looked at one another as they watched the man leave the building.

"How odd," said Dawn as she smiled at her supervisor.

"Well, Dawn, welcome to New York City, USA!" said the supervisor as she and the security officer looked at Dawn and smiled.

When Tommy was several feet away from the building, he removed his sunglasses and walked over by the cement benches at the side of the building. In spite of the weather, he felt a bit cold. He sat down on one of the benches, opened up his duffel bag, placed his baseball cap and sunglasses in the bag, zipped closed his bag, and placed it on the bench next to him as he took a deep breath. He then covered his face with both hands while resting his elbows on his knees as he sat there wondering how long things would go on like this. The traffic was building up on the city streets, and the noise of the city grew louder with people in their cars.

Two hours later, Tommy was still sitting on the bench. He looked at his watch and noticed that it was a quarter till five, so he rose from where he was sitting, approached the side of the building, and awaited Crystal's exit.

Five minutes after five in the evening, Crystal left the reception desk, wearing her own clothes, and she had her Discman turned on, with the music loud, as she exited the building.

When she walked out of the building and onto the city sidewalk, Tommy already had his camera in hand. With no flash, he took some pictures of her. He took different shots of her at different angles, yet she didn't notice a thing.

Each snapshot he took of Crystal freeze-framed her beauty.

"Oh my God! I want to rip her clothes off! This is simply beautiful!" he mumbled to himself as he continued taking snapshots of her from a distance.

When she entered the subway, the transit jungle underneath New York City, Tommy didn't enter the subway. He turned around and walked away from the station, not only because he felt he had taken enough pictures but also because he wanted to go home.

As he walked to another subway station, he put the camera into his right coat pocket. Then he changed his mind, took the camera out of his pocket, and put it in his duffel bag, because he was afraid of damaging it, as he continued walking toward the subway station to go back to Brooklyn.

Later, when Tommy arrived at his apartment, he noticed the light on his answering machine was flickering, indicating messages had been left, as he shut the door of his apartment. He went to the closet in the small hallway and hung up his coat. When he arrived at the side table, he pressed the message-retrieval button.

The answering machine beeped, and the first message began.

"Tommy? This is your aunt Sylvie. I just wanted to call you to see how you are doing and to tell you that I love you. Talk to you soon. Bye for now."

Beep! The next message started.

"Tommy? This is Maria. When you get home, call me. All right? I'm at home. I believe you have my number, so call me. Bye."

Beep! The last message had played, and the tape began to rewind itself back to the beginning. He picked up the receiver of the telephone and called his aunt Sylvie as he sat down on the recliner while looking out the window next to the side table and sofa.

"Aunt Sylvie?" he said.

"Hi, Tommy boy! How are you?" Aunt Sylvie asked.

"I'm fine, except maybe for one thing," said Tommy as he rested his head on his right hand as his arm rested on the arm of the recliner.

"What is it, Tommy?" she asked with some concern.

"OK, it's like this. I'm in love with this beautiful girl," Tommy said as he sat straight up on the recliner.

"Well, what's so bad about that?" she asked.

"Aunt Sylvie, deep down inside, she's in love with me. But she won't admit it, and she is currently involved with someone else." Tommy took off his glasses, placed them on the side table, and started rubbing his face with his left hand.

"Wait a minute! Wait a goddamn minute! You mean to tell me that she is in love with you, but she's seeing someone else at the same time?" Aunt Sylvie asked.

"No. We are not involved, but she is currently seeing someone else. We went out on one date, and we didn't even finish that one date. It was only one date." Tommy began feeling edgy and started crying silently.

"Tommy, you two only went out once, and on that night, you only went out for half the date?" she asked.

"Yes. You see, we only had dinner, and then we were supposed to go straight to the movies afterward, but on the way to the movies, she told me it wasn't going to work out. So that was it." Tommy continued to cry silently, but she heard the strain in his voice.

"Tommy, it's going to be all right," said Aunt Sylvie as she realized he had been crying the whole time. "It's going to be all right because there are many more women in the world."

"I know, I know. I know this other girl, Maria. And she's drop-dead gorgeous and very nice, but—" Tommy couldn't finish what he was saying.

"But what, Tommy?"

"Aunt Sylvie, I don't want to be with Maria or anyone else," he explained, feeling a bit frustrated.

"But, Tommy, the other girl doesn't want to be with you. What can you do?" she asked, and there was a slight pause between them.

"I want Crystal!" said Tommy as he stood up from the recliner.

"Who's Crystal?"

"Crystal is the girl I went out with once, but we never finished the date."

"Oh, OK, right. But, Tommy, if she doesn't think it's going to work out, you're better off letting her go. Look, just let her go, and talk with that other girl, Maria. Maybe you and Maria will hit it off," said Aunt Sylvie, and a cold silence crept over the phone line as he breathed heavily into the telephone in the background. "Tommy, are you there?" she asked, thinking the silence and the heavy breathing in the background were weird.

"Yes, Aunt Sylvie, I'm here," said Tommy as he stared into space as though he were in a daze.

"Tommy, leave that girl Crystal alone. Please, Tommy, you don't need any problems right now. If she's not interested, leave her alone." Aunt Sylvie pleaded with him, hoping he would heed her advice.

"But, Aunt Sylvie, you don't understand! I'm in love with her, and she's in love with me!" Tommy shouted, and then silence once again ruled the telephone line.

"Tommy, you can do whatever you want, but you're asking for trouble if you don't leave this girl Crystal alone. It sounds to me like you're a little obsessed with this girl Crystal. Now, I could be wrong. I mean, I'm not a counselor. Leave her alone, Tommy. Please, Tommy, you have a long and wonderful life ahead of yourself." Aunt Sylvie started to cry, feeling helpless.

"Oh, do I? What kind of long and wonderful life do I have? I mean, I'm working at a dead-end job at a messenger center in an office building where the rich get richer off of people like me and others who work their asses off every day for a fucking living!" Tommy cried while he paced about the living room floor.

"Now, Tommy, be thankful you have a job!" she yelled out.

"Oh yeah? Well, isn't it like you to say something like that? And my own fucking mother just couldn't wait to abandon my little ass! The woman was supposed to be my mother, and she told me that she was going out to buy some ice cream and that I was to wait for her inside the apartment. But you know what?" he asked.

"I know, Tommy." Aunt Sylvie continued crying along with Tommy, reliving his pain of abandonment from his early childhood.

"She never came back! Never returned to the apartment! That bitch never came back!" Tommy shouted as he cried more and more into the phone.

"I'm so sorry, Tommy. She's my sister, and I just want to say sorry. And the best thing to come out of all of that was that I discovered you there in the apartment all by yourself and took you home with me, and then we had a pretty good life, right, Tommy? Didn't we, Tommy boy?" she asked, still crying softly, and silence fell upon them momentarily.

"Aunt Sylvie, yes, you did!" Tommy shouted softly. He felt overwhelmed with grief at his mother's walking out on him and at his yelling at the only mother he'd ever known, his aunt Sylvie, and he felt frustrated over not being with Crystal as he stood next to the sofa. "I really appreciate you, Aunt Sylvie. I really do appreciate you, but since the day my mother walked out on me, I don't know who I am or what I'm all about. I'm a stranger to myself." Tommy continued crying quietly, even though his aunt Sylvie already knew he was crying.

"Tommy, life will get better. I promise you. But you have to take control of it. And holding on to someone who has no desire to be with you is not only a waste of time but also a waste of your life. And your life could change for the worse if you try to hold on to something that isn't there. It just wasn't meant to be," she said while fighting back her tears.

"I know, Aunt Sylvie. You're right. You're absolutely right, but I know in my heart that Crystal does want to be with me. I wish there were some way I could show you, Aunt Sylvie." Tommy started feeling uptight with the phone call.

"Tommy?" she said, feeling frustrated with her nephew.

"Yes, Aunt Sylvie?" he responded, feeling tired of the conversation.

"Tommy, you are my favorite nephew, and I love you so very much, but—"

"Aunt Sylvie, what's wrong with me?" he asked, drying his eyes with a tissue from the small, square box on the side table near the window.

"Tommy, like I said, you are my favorite nephew, and I do love you so much, but this obsession thing that you have within you will eventually eat you up inside. It really will. I truly believe you need some counseling. Not later. Now!" said Aunt Sylvie.

"What? What are you talking about?" he shouted as he stopped crying and dropped the used-up tissue onto the carpeted floor.

"Oh, favorite nephew of mine, I do know what I'm talking about. You see, with your mother abandoning you at such a young age and with you going through life without a mother, well, it was apparent that you weren't happy, though you had the best of everything when you were with your uncle and me. But nothing could replace the love of a mother. When your uncle and I took you in, of course, you were among family, but like I said, nothing could replace the love of a mother. Nothing," his aunt said.

"That's true. You and Uncle Nick were always there for me, and I'll never be able to show enough appreciation for your bringing me into your home. I love you for that!" said Tommy as he smiled.

"Tommy, what your uncle and I did wasn't only because we're family or that it was our family duty but because we really do love you." Aunt Sylvie was crying again.

"Well, as far as counseling goes, I don't need counseling. I feel the way I do, and there's nothing on this green earth that's going to change that. Nothing." Tommy took a deep breath as he held on to his convictions, and the conversation with his aunt ended.

Tommy lay on his bed, and all of a sudden, the telephone rang. He reached for the phone on the side table in his bedroom, half asleep.

"Hello?" Tommy said, but there was no response from the caller. "Hello?" Tommy said again, but still, there was no response. "Hello? If you don't respond, I will, without hesitation, hang up my phone. Hello!" Tommy called out for the last time, thinking about hanging up on the mystery caller.

"Tommy?" A whisper came through the telephone line.

"Hello? Who is this?" he asked as he sat up in his bed as the darkness surrounded him in his bedroom.

"It's Maria, Tommy."

"Maria, you're calling me in the middle of the night?"

"Well, Tommy, it's not like we have to work tomorrow. It's still the weekend."

"I know it's the weekend. I don't need to be reminded by you, especially at this time in the evening."

"Yeah, but, Tommy, aren't we still friends?"

"Maria, for the moment, we are not friends, and that's because you don't want to be friends, remember? And at this moment, I don't care to discuss it, because I want to sleep! So if you don't mind, I would like to catch up on some sleep I missed because of this phone call. Good night!" Tommy shouted, and then he hung up the telephone at his side table, went back underneath the blanket, and lay down in the fetal position.

⁙

The next day, after eating a peanut butter sandwich and watching television, he decided there wasn't anything on, so he began pacing about the living room floor. As he paced, he talked to himself frantically.

"Why, why, why? Why doesn't she know how much in love we

could be? All we have to do is come together!" Tommy shouted as he hit his forehead with the palm of his right hand. "I just can't believe after going out only one time, she called it quits right in the middle of the date! It's so stupid! And on top of all of that, she's with someone new! Why does she have to be with someone else? Especially when she has me, who's interested in being with her!"

As he paced back and forth, the telephone rang. He rushed into his bedroom and stood in front of the mirror, looking at the pictures that still hung all around the edges, while the telephone continued ringing. He thought it might be Maria.

"Oh my God! I forgot about those pictures that were developing at the photo shop. I have new pictures to pick up today," he mumbled to himself as he started getting dressed.

After he dressed, he exited the apartment building and walked down the block to the photo shop to pick up the pictures. He entered the photo shop, and he saw an old man with whiskers on his face standing by the cash register, talking on the telephone.

"Look, sir, I have nothing more to say. Bye! Fine!" the old man shouted into the phone, dealing with an unpleasant customer, and then he hung up. When he placed the phone down behind him, he noticed Tommy by the entrance of the shop. "Tommy boy! Come in! You came for your pictures, right?" the old man asked as he coughed while covering his mouth.

"They're ready, right?" Tommy asked while he walked closer toward the counter.

"They are ready. And they look good too," said the old man, and he and Tommy laughed. The old man went into the back area to get the packet of pictures. He reached inside a blue milk crate, among other packets of pictures, and pulled out Tommy's packet from the crate. "Here it is! I found it!" said the old man as he rushed to the front, toward Tommy. "All right, that will be five dollars, my friend," said the old man as he laid down the packet on the counter.

"Five dollars it is!" Tommy shouted as he went into his pocket, pulled out a five-dollar bill, and gave it to the old man, and the man gave Tommy the packet of pictures in a plastic bag. "Thank you, old man Whiskers!" Tommy shouted as he smiled at him. He couldn't wait to go back to his apartment to see the love of his life.

"No, son, thank you," said the old man as he smiled while leaning over the counter.

"All right, have a good day, Whiskers," said Tommy as he exited the shop.

After leaving the photo shop, he walked back to his apartment building as he opened up the packet of pictures, revisiting the time when he had taken those pictures of Crystal when she was on her way to the subway after work.

He took them out of the packet, and one by one, he looked at them while still walking toward the building where he lived.

He arrived at the building and opened the steel front door with his back on the door while still looking at the pictures.

"Simply beautiful," he told himself as he walked up the stairs to his apartment. When he arrived at his apartment, he opened the door, entered, closed the door, and rested the pictures on the kitchen table. He went into the living room and walked over to the coffee table. He picked up a copy of a photography magazine, and as he sat down on his recliner, the telephone rang.

"Hello?" Tommy said, hoping it wasn't Maria.

"Tommy, it's your aunt Sylvie. Are doing all right?" she asked.

"Yeah," he responded while he rested the cordless phone between his shoulder and his ear as he looked over his magazine.

"Yeah?" she asked.

"Yeah, Aunt Sylvie. I'm fine. How are you?" he asked as he put the magazine on the side table and then picked it back up and began looking at the magazine again.

"I'm all right. I just called to see how you were doing. You know, after the conversation we had last night," she said with a slight whine in her voice.

"Actually, I feel a lot better, and I'm relaxing a little this weekend. I'm reading my photography magazine." Tommy wasn't reading the magazine at the moment but was skimming through it, looking at the pictures.

"Oh yeah? Since you feel a little better now, does this mean you'll leave that girl Crystal alone now?" Aunt Sylvie asked as he put his magazine down on the coffee table.

"I never said I was going to stop pursuing her," said Tommy as he picked up the magazine from the coffee table and began skimming through it again abruptly.

"Tommy, are you trying to be a photographer? I mean, that's what you always wanted to be, right?" Aunt Sylvie asked.

"Well, it's not just a hobby. I may consider taking this up as a career someday. Who knows?" Tommy smiled.

"Oh, OK, that's good. You're keeping yourself busy now." Aunt Sylvie felt somewhat relieved. "I'm glad you're doing all right now. So I'll call you soon, all right?"

"All right, Aunt Sylvie. I love you. And tell Uncle Nick I love him too. Bye." Tommy hung up the telephone and lay back in his recliner with his feet up and the magazine covering his face.

CHAPTER 17

ONE MONTH WENT BY. IT was November 20, not long till Thanksgiving Day, and Crystal was at JFK International Airport, waiting for her long-distance boyfriend, Jim Connors, to arrive from Dallas, Texas, to spend Thanksgiving week with her. She looked at her watch; it was ten thirty in the morning.

Oh, good. In five minutes, according to the flight schedule, he's supposed to arrive, Crystal thought as she looked over the flight information Jim had given her.

"Gate number three," she mumbled to herself as she looked at the gate where she was. "I'm at the right gate," she whispered to herself as she smiled.

At a distance of one hundred feet away, Tommy was hiding with his camera. He was adjusting his new zoom lens so he could focus on Crystal from a farther distance. While still adjusting the new zoom lens, he aimed the camera toward Crystal. As she walked up toward the gateway, he started taking pictures with freeze-frame precision.

At gate number three, the door flew open, and the commuters from the commercial jet airliner started exiting the terminal tube into the airport waiting area as loved ones looked for their beloved commuters. As the crowd of commuters came out of the tube, Crystal, among others searching for their loved ones, searched for Jim. Jim was looking for Crystal when he exited the tube. Jim swam through the commuters as Crystal swam through the waiting families and friends.

"Jim!" Crystal shouted as she saw him behind a crowd of commuters, just barely, and she waved her arms. Jim saw her, and he started waving back as he carried his suitcase, holding his briefcase under his armpit.

As the crowds disappeared, Jim and Crystal moved closer toward each other.

At a distance, Tommy continued taking pictures from behind as he saw Jim, Crystal's new boyfriend, embrace her. When Tommy saw Crystal and Jim embrace, he lowered his camera, which hung from a strap around his neck. As the camera dangled on his stomach, he leaned up against the wall in sorrow and bitterness.

Jim and Crystal continued embracing each other with warm kisses as the crowd around them slowly disappeared.

"So, Jim, are we ready to go?" she asked as he grabbed his suitcase, and she grabbed his briefcase.

"Yes, I believe we are," Jim responded as he kissed her on the lips again, and they joined hands and walked away from the terminal, hand in hand.

At a distance, Tommy was still leaning up against the wall, putting away his camera in his tote bag. He decided he was going home as Jim and Crystal walked hand in hand to the front entrance of the terminal.

Outside the front entrance, a row of taxis were present next to the curb.

"Why don't we take a taxi to your apartment?" Jim asked Crystal as they stood near where the line of taxis were parked, waiting for their next customers.

"All right. Let's try this one!" she shouted as she pointed one out.

Jim held up his right hand, hailing the particular cab they wanted.

The cab driver saw Jim with his right hand up and Crystal standing by him, and the female taxi driver drove to their assistance as Jim picked up his suitcase from the concrete sidewalk.

When the cab pulled up near the curb, from inside the cab, the driver popped open the trunk, and then she rushed out of the cab and assisted Jim with his suitcase and his briefcase, putting them in the trunk of the cab. As the driver of the cab was straightening out the things in the trunk, Jim took Crystal to the cab and opened the back door, and Crystal entered the cab as they smiled at each other. He was being a true gentleman. While he continued smiling at her, the driver slammed shut the trunk, and as she walked back to the front of the cab, she checked out one of the tires, making sure the tire wasn't flat or low on air. Jim entered the cab and slammed the back door shut. After the driver checked out the tire, she entered the taxi.

As the driver was on the radio before leaving the airport, Jim and Crystal just stared into each other's eyes. Jim towered a little over six feet tall and had piercing dark eyes that looked right through her. His shoulder-length dark hair swayed with the gentle breeze from the open window as the cab drove off.

"Where to, ma'am?" the cab driver asked Crystal.

While Crystal was giving the cab driver the address of where they were going, Jim just stared at her from the side and watched her speak as the cab entered onto the highway, leaving the airport.

＋＋＋＋＋＋

Meanwhile, Tommy entered a bus at the front of the airport, going to the nearest subway. He slid his card and sat down as the bus drove off, leaving the airport. On his way to the subway, he thought about how he could persuade Crystal to be with him. Endless thoughts ran through his mind.

I know she loves me, he thought as the bus drove on the highway to the nearest subway. *What did I do so wrong? Where did I go wrong?* Tommy thought about the time he and Crystal had met for coffee in Hell's Kitchen. Then he thought about their first and last date.

"I'm not bad looking," he said to himself as he looked into the rearview mirror of the bus while he knelt down.

The bus driver noticed him when he looked up at the mirror. "Hey, handsome, do you mind?" the bus driver asked, and Tommy slowly slid back into his seat, feeling embarrassed, as some of the tired passengers saw what was going on.

"Seventy-Fourth Street and Roosevelt Avenue! You can catch the number-seven train and the N, R, G, and F trains going to Manhattan!" the bus driver shouted into the microphone of the loudspeaker.

Tommy and another person stood up as the bus was pulling over to the curb at the bus stop, which was within steps of the elevated subway. Tommy and the other person stepped off the bus at Seventy-Fourth Street and Roosevelt Avenue. Tommy walked up the stairway of the elevated subway. As he was walking up the steps of the stairway to the number-seven train, he felt numb inside, not believing all of this was happening between him and Crystal. He didn't want to accept any of what was going on.

When he made it onto the platform of the seven train, he had tears in his eyes, as he was starting to cry over the ordeal, which was beginning to take a toll on him. But instead of making a scene in front of people, he fought back the tears, barely being successful, as he turned around, facing a billboard with some advertising on it.

———— ✦✦✦✦✦ ————

On the Upper East Side of Manhattan, in front of the apartment building where Crystal lived, Crystal and Jim stepped out of the taxi after Jim paid the driver. Then the driver stepped out of the cab, and they all met behind the cab as the trunk opened up. The driver rushed in front of Jim and Crystal, and as she was taking out Jim's suitcase, Jim grabbed his briefcase. Crystal took some money from her pocket and gave her a tip of five dollars.

"Crystal, I already gave her a tip when we were inside the taxi," Jim whispered as he leaned forward away from the driver, and the driver reentered her cab as they watched from behind.

"I know. I wanted to give her a little more of a tip. You know, with the holidays around, I'm in a real giving spirit," Crystal responded, and they embraced each other as the suitcase and briefcase rested on the sidewalk.

"Well now, just how giving are you today?" Jim asked as he smiled as they looked into each other's eyes. There was a slight pause, and then they laughed.

"Well, that depends," Crystal responded with a tone of seriousness in her voice as she snickered.

"Oh yeah? What does it depend on?" he asked with his dark eyes shining.

As Crystal noticed the flare in his eyes, her heart was melting away as the passion invaded the space around them. "It depends on the person I'm going to give myself to," she said as she smiled while looking down off and on, and they embraced with their bodies touching as they looked into each other's eyes more seriously. Their expressions remained serious but relaxed and, at the same time, more intense as their faces moved in closer toward each other. While their faces drew closer, so did their lips. As their lips drew closer, the heat on their breath became hotter, and the two of them felt it, which made it more intense. Finally, their heads tilted to opposite sides, and their lips met with a warm, slow kiss. As they kissed gently for a long time, they felt as if a kiss never had felt as right as it did at that moment.

When their lips slowly parted, they took a moment to look into each other's eyes. When they came back down to earth and their eyes left each other's sight for the moment, Jim picked up his suitcase and briefcase. He swung the briefcase strap over his shoulder while holding his suitcase, and he and Crystal walked toward the apartment building as he put his right arm around her shoulders as she put her arm around his waist.

+ + + ✦ ✦ + +

In Brooklyn, Tommy exited the train at the station where he lived and walked up the concrete steps of the subway. He exited the subway onto the street. He walked away toward his apartment building as he kicked an empty cola can on the sidewalk. As he kicked the abandoned can, he thought about the crumby day he'd had and how much crumbier it was going to be the next day, which made him even more depressed.

+ + + ✦ ✦ + +

Jim and Crystal sat on the sofa in the living room, holding each other's hands, looking into each other's eyes. She had her legs folded up on the sofa, with her body facing Jim.

Jim's shoulder-length dark hair was neatly feathered back on both sides of his head and neatly parted in the middle. He sat there looking at the most beautiful woman in the world, Crystal, with her long golden-blonde hair down her back, her sparkling baby-blue eyes shining brightly and seeming to look right through him, and her lips that sent signals to him of love.

"Crystal?" Jim said in a tone of voice that was nearly a whisper.

"Yes, Jim?" Crystal responded with the same tone of voice. She and Jim were covered behind a shade of love, with slight smiles on their faces. He picked up her hand and kissed it while she sat back in a subtle way into Jim's arms as they sat back on the sofa together.

"Crystal, about what I'm going to say—don't think I'm trying to make a move on you. But I—" Jim couldn't go further with what he was trying to say, as he felt numb with love for her.

"Yes, Jim?" Crystal responded as she looked up at him, smiling.

"Crystal, I'm in love with you. I really do love you. It just feels so right, and I know it's sudden, but I —"

Crystal interrupted him by placing her index finger on his lips, and he was unable to speak any further, delighted at her smooth interruption. "My love, I was going to say the same thing because that is how I'm feeling too," Crystal said as she removed her finger from Jim's lips and moved her hand through his silky, shoulder-length hair.

He was amazed and relieved at the same time. "Crystal, I'm speechless. I had some idea, but I'm glad you feel the same way," said Jim, and he and Crystal smiled with passion as he looked into her eyes as they cuddled closer on the sofa.

"Well, now you know! So what are you going to do about it?" Crystal asked as she looked up at him and smiled.

Jim put an arm around her shoulders as she threw her long blonde hair over his arm to one side, and with his other hand, he held on to her hand as they both sat back, enjoying each other's company.

"This is what I'm going to do about it," he responded as they looked into each other's eyes again. As their faces drew closer, their lips were flexing their tiny muscles, preparing for a moment of passion. Their lips met at an angle, and their tongues were exchanged back and forth through the heat of passion that only Jim and Crystal could feel. No one was going to come between them. Even Tommy wasn't powerful enough to enter between them.

+ + + ◆ + +

The next day arrived with some clouds. It was a cold, cloudy day, a typical winter day. Tommy was getting ready for another day at work.

When Tommy entered the messenger center without saying a word, Maria stared at him from behind while carrying some folders to her desk.

"Hi, Tommy," Maria called out as she sat at her desk.

"Hi, Maria," Tommy responded as he walked over toward Louie, who'd just finished loading up one of the carts with some of the day's mail. "Hi, Louie," Tommy called out, smiling halfway.

"Hi, Tommy. Say, Tommy?" Louie called out as he stopped what he was doing.

"Yes, Louie?" Tommy responded, a few feet away.

"Today you have more boxes than usual, so concentrate on taking them to the right departments, all right?" Louie said as he leaned over one of the carts.

"Yeah, sure," Tommy responded as he took one of the carts loaded by Louie to the front entrance of the center.

"Oh, Tommy? Someone called for you earlier, before you walked in this morning," said Maria. She had written down on a piece of paper the name of the person and the phone number at which the person could be reached.

"Maria took the name and phone number of the person who called for you," said Louie, sitting at the counter next to the carts.

"Oh yeah?" Tommy responded as he walked over toward Maria at her desk.

"Here it is, Tommy." Maria handed him the note with the information on it, and he read it.

To Tommy
Call 212-770-0784
Sandy Leonard

"Sandy Leonard, huh?" Maria asked as she wore a half smile with a concerned attitude, acting like a jealous girlfriend.

"Yeah, Maria. Lovely Sandy Leonard," said Tommy as he raised both eyebrows, turned around slowly, and walked to the cart with the day's mail as he put the note into his back pocket, folded up.

When Tommy exited the messenger center, Maria turned around, facing her desk, and threw her pen onto her desk, near the pencil holder, feeling annoyed with Tommy, his cocky attitude, and the whole situation of chasing him down and trying to convince him that they belonged together. She looked for something to occupy her mind.

After Tommy delivered the morning deliveries to the upper floors, before he went back to the messenger center, he stopped over by the pay phones in the lobby of the building. After setting the empty cart to the side, making sure it was out of the way of persons passing through the lobby, he reached into his back pocket for the phone number. He knew who it was: his counselor. He put a coin into the pay phone and then dialed the number on the paper.

"Hello. This is Sandy Leonard," she answered, in the middle of paperwork.

"Hi. This is Tommy Landis," he responded with one hand in one of his front pockets.

"Tommy Landis. Right. I called you earlier at your job. I wanted to schedule your next counseling appointment for this Saturday. Say, around eleven in the morning?" Sandy said while sitting at her desk in her office as she took a sip of her coffee.

"Ah, Sandy, are you a counselor, or are you a psychiatrist?" he asked, leaning up against the brick wall alongside the pay phones.

"Tommy, I am a counselor, not a psychiatrist. I'm a counselor who wants to help you. I want to help you deal with your problems of obsession, which you say is wrong with you, right?" she asked.

He was looking through space, barely listening to her. "Oh, right. Yes. Yes, I have this obsession."

"Excuse me. Please deposit five cents, or your call will be terminated. Thank you," said the recorded operator.

"Oh, I'll talk to you on Saturday, all right? I don't have any more nickels," said Tommy as he felt his front pockets for another nickel.

"All right, Mr. Landis. See you on Saturday," said Sandy Leonard right before the pay phone disconnected them.

After the call was terminated, Tommy hung up the telephone; grabbed his cart, which was empty; and rushed back toward the elevator to go back down to the basement messenger center to finish the day.

Saturday morning arrived with a cold, brisk, sunny day in store as Tommy entered a familiar building and walked toward the lobby desk.

"Hi, sir. How may I help you?" the desk attendant asked as he smiled at Tommy.

"Yes, I'm here to see Sandy Leonard. I have an appointment today," said Tommy as he picked up a pen at the desk to sign in on the sign-in sheet.

"All right. She's located on the tenth floor. Suite 10A," said the desk attendant while he looked over the guest roster while looking at his watch. "It's now a quarter till eleven, sir," said the desk attendant, noticing that eleven o'clock was his appointment.

"Thank you," said Tommy, and he laid down the pen on the marble desk and walked away toward the elevator bank.

As he approached the elevator bank, an elevator arrived at the lobby, the doors slid open, and a mass of people exited the elevator car. Tommy waited to the side until he was able to enter the elevator. When he finally entered the elevator, he pressed the button for the tenth floor as the elevator doors slid shut.

The elevator arrived on the tenth floor, and the elevator doors slid open. Tommy exited the elevator, and within fifteen feet of the elevator bank was the receptionist desk. The receptionist was typing away on her typewriter, with her computer on the side of her circular desk. He walked over toward her desk, and the receptionist saw him approaching.

"Hi. How may I help you?" the receptionist asked as slow, jazzy music played in the background somewhere in the waiting area, and he smiled at the receptionist.

"Yes, I'm here to see Sandy Leonard," said Tommy as he looked around while standing in front of the reception desk, feeling comfortable.

"All right. Just sign in right here. I'll inform her of your arrival." The receptionist handed him a pen and pointed to the waiting area.

When he was done filling out the form on a clipboard, he took the clipboard back to the reception desk. When he handed it back to her, she called Sandy Leonard to inform her of Tommy's arrival again and say he was ready to see her, and he went back to the waiting area to sit back down to wait.

Within minutes, Sandy Leonard, his counselor, entered the waiting area. "Tommy Landis?" Sandy called out as she smiled, and he stood up.

"Yes. And you must be Sandy Leonard?" Tommy smiled nervously while he faced her.

"Yes, I am. And I'm ready to see you now. So let's go into my office, OK?"

When they entered her office, Sandy shut the door behind them. "Have a seat, Mr. Landis," said Sandy as she went behind her desk to sit.

"Oh, you can call me Tommy," said Tommy as he sat down in one of the two chairs in front of Sandy's desk, and she smiled.

"All right, Tommy. Tommy, I will be recording this session. Is that all right with you? This will help me look into your situation deeper, all right?" she asked, and he nodded in agreement, so she pressed the record button. "So tell me, Tommy, about this obsession you think you might have," she said as she picked up her pen and flipped to a new page on her pad on her desk.

"Well, I met this beautiful girl from the personal ads in the newspaper. I wasn't desperate or anything like that. I just wanted to try out different ways of meeting women." Tommy crossed his right leg over his left leg.

"It's all right, Tommy. I mean, you are single." Sandy smiled.

"Yeah, right. Well, here goes the rest of the story."

"Go ahead, Tommy. I'm listening."

"All right. Where was I? Oh, OK, I remember now. I found this girl in the personal ads, and I called her and left a message in her voice box from the personal ads. I left my telephone number, and she called me back," Tommy said, reliving it as he told Sandy what had happened.

"Tommy, did you and this young lady make a date afterward?" Sandy asked.

"Yes. Well, we decided to meet over a cup of coffee first, and then if things went well during coffee, we would consider the first date. And we did." Tommy uncrossed his legs, feeling stimulated by the conversation.

"So you're saying that things went over really well while you and this young woman were drinking some coffee?" she asked, writing on her pad.

"It went better than I thought," he responded, visualizing the memory.

"Oh yeah?" Sandy responded with growing interest.

"Yes. You see, we made plans for that Friday night, and she gave me her phone number. And then a couple of days after, we arranged for our first date together," he said as his mind was in the coffee shop with Crystal. He wished to go back in time to make that meeting with her more positive, as he thought he could've been a little more aggressive.

"OK, you and this girl—what was her name?" Sandy asked as she stopped writing.

"Her name is Crystal." Tommy smiled.

"All right. You and Crystal went out on your very first date. How did it go?" Sandy asked.

"Well, it went great at dinner, but on the way to the movies, we stopped in the middle of Times Square, and she told me she wasn't attracted to me. She smiled and insisted I was a complete gentleman and a really nice guy, but she said she wasn't really attracted to me!" he yelled out as he stooped over while still sitting and covered his face.

"Well, Tommy—"

"Now, I'm no Romeo or the boy next door, but I'm not the boogeyman either!" said Tommy as tears streamed down his cheeks.

"All right, Tommy." Sandy passed him a box of tissues so he could dry his eyes. "Tommy, when she said that, how did that make you feel? I see that you are apparently hurt, because you're here crying, but give me a verbal description, in your own words, of how you felt, all right?" Eager to hear his pain, she looked at the recorder, making sure the tape wasn't running out.

"So you want to hear my pain? I'm not feeling good at all. I was in shock!" said Tommy as he crossed his right leg over his left leg quickly.

"All right, Tommy, what happened next after she told you she wasn't attracted to you?" she asked.

"What happened? I just stood there," said Tommy, again visualizing what had gone on. "I just stood there watching her walk away, until I couldn't see her anymore." Tommy's eyes were open wide, and he sat up straight, looking into space, while reliving it in his mind. "She disappeared in the waves of people coming and going on the streets of Times Square, and I couldn't see her anymore." As Tommy slowly came back to reality, he looked Sandy straight in the eyes. "You see, I—"

"Go ahead, Tommy. I'm listening to you," said Sandy, still recording the conversation and writing on her pad, as he looked into her eyes.

"Sandy, I love Crystal. I really do," he said as he grew more tense as he covered his face with both hands.

"Tommy?" Sandy called out as she put down her pen on her desk.

"Yes, Sandy?" Tommy responded as he partially uncovered his face.

"Tommy, does this woman Crystal feel the same way you do?" she asked, looking a bit concerned with him.

"Huh?" Tommy said abruptly.

"Was Crystal in love with you? You said she wasn't attracted to you."

"Well, I believe that deep down inside, she really does love me. But on the outside, she's just not showing it. That's all. That's all it is!" Tommy blurted out as he gave her half a smile, and she gave a sympatric smile back.

"Did she ever tell you in other ways that she was in love with you?" she asked as she began to write again.

"No. No, but she really wants to," he responded with confidence as he looked at his watch briefly.

"How do you know that?" she asked as she rested her pen on the desk, and he looked up at her slowly with a demented expression on his face.

"I just know, all right? I just fucking know! It's something you feel deep inside!" said Tommy as he pounded on his chest once and then rested his hand flat on his chest while leaning forward over Sandy's desk. Then he sat back down in his chair.

"OK, you're the one who called me, wanting me to make an appointment to see me, and you mentioned that you might be obsessed. What makes you realize that you might be obsessed with Crystal?" Sandy asked, interested to hear his answer, as she took a sip of water from her tall glass.

"I was speaking with a friend, one of my coworkers from the job, and he pointed out to me that this was an obsession I was feeling and that it wasn't love. He said, though, it might've been love at one time on my part, but my friend said the love I had from before for Crystal had turned into obsession. But to this day, I don't believe I am obsessed,"

Tommy said as he wiped away the tears from his eyes with a tissue from Sandy's desk.

"You know what, Tommy?" Sandy rose from behind her desk, walked toward her water cooler, grabbed a paper cup from the cup holder on the side of the cooler, and lowered the tab, filling the paper cup with cold water. "You know what, Tommy?" she asked again as she handed him the paper cup of water as he stared down at the carpeted floor.

"What?" Tommy asked as he looked up partially at her.

"Based on what you have told me about yourself and Crystal, I'm going to tell you something, and instead of becoming angry, you need to open up your mind and your eyes, all right? I understand that you were in love with Crystal, but now I think it's only fair that you should face the truth. You are obsessed with this woman Crystal. Now, tell me—I mean, it's obvious that you've called her numerous times, right?" she asked as she sat back down in her chair behind her desk.

"Well, yeah, I—"

"All right. You called her most of the time from your apartment, begging her, pleading with her to accept you?" Sandy asked as she leaned over her desk toward Tommy.

Tommy rose from where he was sitting and turned around, walking about the office with his back facing Sandy, and she wondered what was going to happen next with this case she was working with Tommy.

"I am not obsessed!" Tommy shouted with his back still facing her and his hands on his hips, facing the door.

Sandy stood up from her chair. "You are obsessed!" she shouted as she pounded once on her desk, and Tommy turned around abruptly upon hearing the pounding.

"No," said Tommy as he sat back down in front of Sandy's desk. "No! No, I'm not obsessed!" he yelled, covering his face with both hands. Then he knelt down as he looked down at the carpeted floor.

"Let me explain, Tommy!" Sandy shouted as she rose from her chair once again, still behind her desk. "Now, calm down, and I'll explain what's going on here, all right?" Sandy said, and as she and Tommy calmed down, she sat back down in her chair as Tommy rose and then sat back down in his chair. "All right, Tommy, I will explain why your friend and I say you are obsessed," Sandy said, but Tommy didn't respond. "When you fall in love with someone and that person you are in love with doesn't accept your love, that person doesn't want your love. That person is rejecting your love. But you feel you still have that person in your life, or you must be involved in that person's life, because you are so in love with her. But at the same time, she is still rejecting you and your love. So—"

"So?" Tommy responded, feeling impatient with her lecturing.

She ignored his attitude. "So this woman Crystal rejected your love, and she openly admitted that she is not attracted to you and doesn't feel anything for you, but still, you live in denial," Sandy said as he looked up and stared at her. "Obsession is when you're in love, she's not accepting your love, and you're not accepting her rejection. You feel she really does want to be with you, when she really doesn't want to be with you, and you still pursue her till this day." Sandy continued looking downward at the floor.

"Tommy, have you ever stalked Crystal? And be honest with me, all right? Because the day you're not honest with me is the day you're not honest with yourself. So have you stalked her before?" she asked. He stared at her, not saying a word, but she felt he probably did stalk Crystal. "You know, follow her to her job, when she leaves her workplace, or on her way home? Do you pursue her from behind all the way to where she lives or where she works?" she asked as she leaned over her desk, and Tommy looked up again.

"Yes. Yes, I pursue her but not in a stalking way. Not in the way you're describing. I follow her from behind at a distance because I really feel that deep down, she really wants me. She loves me." Tommy smiled sheepishly, feeling sure of his feelings and what he was saying, as Sandy wrote down notes on her pad.

"Tommy, you need to take a few steps back and take a look at what's going on around you and inside you. You need to leave that woman alone and move on with your life. And you can do it." Sandy smiled halfway, trying to encourage him.

"Sandy, I am not obsessed. Really. My friend was full of shit! And you? You don't even know me! You don't know me!" Tommy shouted as he stood up, and Sandy rose from her desk.

"Calm down, Tommy," said Sandy as she held up both hands. "Look, obsession has a few different stages. Just hear me out, all right? I know you probably want to run out of here and leave, and that would be simple, but you can't run away from your problems, especially this problem! You need to face it! Head-on! And fucking deal with it!" Sandy yelled without realizing at first what she'd just said, and Tommy looked stunned.

"Oops! I'm sorry, Tommy. I wish I could just make you understand this obsession you have. It's not a game. And some people can even get hurt or, worse, die. It turns everyone's life upside down," said Sandy as Tommy calmed down and gave her his full attention.

"Obsession has a few stages. The first stage involves never-ending telephone calls. An obsessed person keeps on calling and calling and calling. Begging and pleading for the other person's presence, acceptance, and affections. The person being called tells the obsessed person not to call."

Tommy thought of the times he'd called Crystal, begging and pleading for her love and acceptance over and over, as he looked at Sandy as she continued explaining.

"But this person stills calls. The second stage is stalking. Stalking her where she lives, where she works, or both," Sandy said.

Tommy was in another world, thinking of all the times he'd stalked Crystal, most of the time when she was leaving her place of work and going home to her apartment.

"In the third stage, the obsessed person doesn't feel he is getting through to the person he's obsessed with, so the obsessed person kills the person he's obsessed with and then commits suicide, or the obsessed person kills the person he's obsessed with and ends up in a mental hospital for the rest of his life if they have an extra bed available," Sandy said, hoping she was getting through to him.

He stood up again near his chair, and Sandy also stood, behind her desk, as they looked into each other's eyes. Tommy looked down at the carpeted floor and then looked back at her with a weird expression on his face, as though he realized that what Sandy was saying was true, but there was a battle brewing inside Tommy. The denial part of him was battling the part of Tommy that wanted to face reality, and the denial was quickly overcoming him. His denial seemed to be stronger.

"Tommy?" Sandy called out to him as he just sat there looking into space, trance-like, flying in his own little world of realistic fantasy. He was looking at her as though he were looking right through her, and she began to feel somewhat frightened; he didn't blink, not once. "Tommy, are you all right?" Sandy asked as she moved away from her desk and walked up to him where he was sitting in front of her desk.

All of a sudden, he stood up. "I have to go," said Tommy, and he rushed out of her office. In the hallway, he walked quickly as she walked quickly right behind him, trying to catch up with him. When she caught up with him from behind, she grabbed his right arm.

"Look, Tommy, you can't spend your life avoiding this!" said Sandy as she turned him around to face her as they stood in the center of the reception area as everyone watched. "Because this thing only gets worse! It never gets better!" Sandy shouted as she stood by the receptionist desk.

The receptionist and others throughout the reception area were startled by the abrupt exit of Tommy. Sandy walked over by the glass doors, while Tommy went over by the stairwell exit to go downstairs to the lobby to exit the building.

Tommy opened the door of the stairwell, ran through the lobby to the front entrance of the building, and made his exit out of the building. He ran across the street, with a car almost hitting him. The car came to a screeching halt as he continued running, with onlookers helping themselves to a little excitement via Tommy Landis.

CHAPTER 18

I T WAS A COLD AND frosty Thanksgiving morning in New York City, and Crystal was just waking up at her Upper East Side Manhattan apartment. Getting out of bed, she stretched while yawning slightly, wearing nothing, as a slight glare of the morning sun came through the light black curtains, showing off her beautiful body in the dimly lit bedroom. Her boyfriend, Jim, still lay in bed, sleeping on his side, with his back facing Crystal. His face and the front of his muscular nude body faced the fogged-up window on the other side of the bedroom. Crystal made her way to other side of the bed, watching Jim as he continued sleeping nude, covered up underneath the blanket. As she moved in closer toward him, she smiled with temptation written all over her face. She lifted up the blanket from the end of the bed, but in the middle of lifting the blanket, she quickly changed her mind as she thought about going underneath the blanket and joining him in bed. As she pulled the blanket up, she moved toward the upper part of the bed, as she wanted to cover the upper part of his beautiful, muscular body. When she bent down, trying to pull some of the blanket upward to cover him, before she could accomplish the task, Jim lunged at her, dragging her into bed. Surprised, she screamed, and he laughed loudly.

"Aah!" Crystal screamed as she and Jim play-wrestled in bed with each other, both laughing. On her knees, she swung her pillow at him as he was on his knees, and he fell back with the force behind the swing of the pillow.

+·+++++·+

Tommy was just getting out of bed in his Brooklyn apartment. Wearing pajama pants and no shirt, he walked to the window in the living room. While he looked out the window at the street below, at the entrance of the building, tears rolled down his face. He saw people rushing on their way to spend the holidays with their families. Tommy pulled down the window shade, avoiding the holiday cheer, looking at the floor. He made sure the window shade was all the way down to cover his depression from the world. He noticed that the other two windows' shades needed to come down in the living room as well, plus the ones on the window in the kitchen and the window in the bedroom. He made sure every window shade was pulled down.

Afterward, he reentered the living room, and he looked around the apartment slowly. The whole apartment was dim and quiet, and a feeling of isolation crept upon him.

All of a sudden, the telephone rang, and he quickly turned around toward the telephone on the side table in the living room, realizing he hadn't disconnected the telephone line. He decided not to answer the call while he continuously stared at it, and the answering machine picked up the call.

"Tommy? It's Aunt Sylvie! Please pick up the phone!" said Aunt Sylvie, who felt distressed that her only nephew was home but not answering the telephone. "Oh well, I tried. Tommy, happy Thanksgiving. I love you very much. I was wanting to invite you over to spend the holidays here at my house with the whole family like every year, but I'm sad to say this will probably be the first Thanksgiving you're not at home with your family. If you change your mind later in the day," Aunt Sylvie said, and Tommy was tempted to pick up the receiver at the moment but then declined as he knelt in the corner of the living room, near one of the windows, "maybe later tonight, and that would be fine with your uncle and Aunt Sylvie. Oh, and some of your cousins are supposed to be here later today. Well, anyway, sorry we didn't connect. If we, your family, don't see you anytime today, happy Thanksgiving. At least call us tonight, all right? Bye. Love you."

Beep! The answering machine tape rewound itself to the beginning of the message just left on it, and the light flickered on and off as Tommy sat there in the corner of the living room, near the window, with his head between his legs. The living room grew depressingly more dim due to the coming thunderstorm and the window shades pulled down at every window in the apartment.

Back at Crystal's apartment, Jim came out of the bathroom after taking a shower, with a big towel wrapped around his waist. Steam followed him and hovered above and behind him as he entered the bedroom.

He walked over toward Crystal as she was putting on blue jeans and a red sweatshirt bearing two big letters, *OU*, representing Oklahoma University.

"Hey, Jim!" Crystal shouted as she looked at him as he slowly walked toward her wearing nothing but a towel wrapped around his waist, showing off his muscular bare chest, muscular arms, and firm, slightly muscular legs, which had some hair.

"Hey, baby!" he shouted as he picked her up off the floor, and he and Crystal swirled around as their eyes were locked onto each other. Their lips were flaming with passion and desire.

It was the kind of passion that made one's lips swollen with desire. They were just inches away from the passion that grew inside them and could ignite at any time. Slowly, their inflamed lips drew closer, and their heads tilted in opposite directions, preparing to invade some personal space. Neither one minded the invasion, because when their lips met, it was like a cosmic collision, and they were in ecstasy. No more trying to figure each other out. No more taking the time to see if there were any sparks. Jim and Crystal knew how they would create sparks of their own. It was there on both sides, and both Jim and Crystal looked beautiful as they continued kissing slowly and passionately.

+‚+‚+‚‚+‚+‚+

On a television set at Tommy's apartment, the Macy's Thanksgiving Day Parade was on. Tommy was lying on the couch, watching the parade. As he watched the giant floats stroll down Broadway in Manhattan, he felt a bit somber.

"Why doesn't she find me attractive? I feel so alone," he whispered to himself while looking up at the ceiling as he grabbed one of the pillows from the couch and put it over his face.

+‚+‚+‚‚+‚+‚+

Back at Crystal's apartment on the Upper East Side in Manhattan, Crystal and Jim were having a brunch she'd prepared, showing off her cooking skills.

"Crystal, you cook so goddamn good!" Jim shouted.

"Yeah? You like it?" Crystal asked as she put her coffee cup down on the kitchen table after taking a sip.

"I've never had eggs Benedict cooked like this before. This is really good," said Jim as he took a sip from his coffee cup.

"Thank you, Jim. I'm glad you like it. My mother taught me well," said Crystal as she wiped her mouth with a white paper napkin.

"Well, you give your mother my compliments." Jim sat back in his chair while he stared at her as though he were in a trance. He was falling more in love with her.

"Is something wrong, Jim?" she asked as she stopped chewing her food and froze in place, wearing half a smile on her face.

"No, no, there's nothing wrong. Definitely nothing wrong with you," said Jim as he leaned over the kitchen table while sitting, and Crystal leaned over the table while still sitting as well, meeting Jim halfway in the middle of the kitchen table Their lips met in the middle of the kitchen table, and they kissed passionately for a long time.

⁘⁘⁘⁘

Tommy was coming out of his bedroom as someone knocked at the door. He rushed toward the door, looked through the peephole, and then opened it. A short Chinese man was at the door with a bag of hot, fresh Chinese food.

"That will be six dollars," said the deliveryman as he smiled at Tommy, who smiled halfway back at the deliveryman, while he handed Tommy the bag of Chinese food.

Tommy reached into his pocket, gave the deliveryman six dollars, and then reached into his pocket again and pulled out another dollar bill for a tip.

"Thank you, sir. Thank you very much," said the deliveryman as he smiled at Tommy graciously before walking away from the apartment, and Tommy shut the door.

After he closed the door, he walked into the kitchen and placed the bag of Chinese food on the kitchen table. He walked to one of the cupboards, reached for a plate, and then went back into the living room with the plate and the bag of food to continue watching the parade on television.

⁘⁘⁘⁘

Crystal bent down, placed the turkey in the preheated oven, and adjusted the temperature on the oven before closing the oven door. Then she went to the kitchen sink to wash her hands as Jim entered the kitchen. While she was washing her hands, Jim sneaked up behind her. He slowly wrapped his arms around her lean body as she continued washing her hands, and she felt something.

"All right, you!" said Crystal, and she and Jim laughed.

"Well, Crystal, I'm so much in love with you," said Jim as he hugged her from behind, and she rested the back of her head on his chest.

"Jim, I love you too, and I'm also in love with you." Crystal slowly turned around as she smiled, facing him, and he smiled along with her as she placed her arms on his neck. "My mother will be coming over in just a few hours. And my mother is going to adore you, Jim," said Crystal as she smiled.

"Oh yeah?" Jim said, and then he kissed her on the nose.

"Yes. And I'm going to have to watch her." Crystal smiled and gave Jim a quick peck on the lips as they broke their embrace, and she walked toward the refrigerator. "Are you making the salad?" Crystal asked as she shut the refrigerator door, and she walked into the living room.

"Yes, I am. And the sweet potatoes and the mashed potatoes," said Jim as he folded his arms upon his chest and leaned up against the kitchen sink, admiring the woman he was in love with. He stared at her.

While Crystal walked toward the terrace's sliding doors, she quickly spun around, looking directly at Jim, who was still in the kitchen, smiling.

"All right! I have a boyfriend who knows how to cook! This is good!" said Crystal as she went to pick up the receiver of the telephone to call her sister, Darlene.

✦✦✦✦✦

Tommy threw away the leftover chicken bones from his dinner into the trash can in the kitchen. He walked back into the living room quickly, grabbed the remote control from the couch, and turned on the television to see what was on.

"There are a lot of things to watch, but I'm not really in the mood," he whispered to himself, going through all the channels on the television. When he'd seen enough, he turned off the television and threw the remote control back onto the sofa as he sat down on the recliner. Then he rose again, as he felt the need to pace about. He paced back and forth in the living room, feeling a bit restless, as he thought about Crystal being with the other man.

I want Crystal so bad I can taste it on my lips. If she would just give me a fucking chance, I know she would be pleased, he thought as the telephone rang. He walked over to the side table to answer the phone call.

"Hello?" Tommy said, wishing he hadn't answered the call.

"Hello, Tommy. It's Maria."

"Hi, Maria," he responded, still wishing he hadn't picked up the call.

"How are you, Tommy? Happy Thanksgiving." Maria sensed that he probably didn't want to be bothered.

"Happy Thanksgiving, Maria," said Tommy as he removed his black-framed glasses and sat down on the recliner, covering his face with one of his hands while listening to Maria, barely responding.

<hr />

Meanwhile, back at Crystal's apartment, Crystal was in the kitchen, preparing the mustard tray, with pretzels all around the tray, surrounding the three mustards: spicy brown mustard, honey dijon mustard, and Grey Poupon mustard.

When she was finished setting up the mustard tray, she took the tray into the living room. Jim took two glasses of eggnog seasoned with nutmeg sprinkled on top. Crystal set down the tray of mustard and pretzels on the coffee table, Jim placed the two glasses of eggnog down, and he and Crystal sat down on the sofa as the doorbell rang.

"Who can that be?" Crystal asked as she looked at her watch while she rose from where she was sitting. Jim also rose, and she walked toward the door to answer it. When she arrived at the door, she looked through the peephole and saw Darlene and her fiancé.

Crystal opened up the door, and her sister smiled.

"Surprise!" Darlene shouted. She was holding a large bowl, and her fiancé, standing next to her, was carrying a couple of bottles of soda. They both were smiling.

"Wow! This is a surprise! You're early," said Crystal as Darlene and her fiancé entered the apartment. "And we're glad you could make it," added Crystal as she shut the door when they entered.

* * * * *

Tommy was still sitting on the recliner in the living room, still conversing with Maria on the telephone.

"Maria, why do you want to come over?" he asked.

"Well, it's Thanksgiving, and well, why should you or I be alone for the holidays?" Maria asked.

"Maria, that is my decision to be alone for the holidays, all right? Do you understand me?" he asked as he rose from the recliner.

"No, I don't understand! I don't understand how someone could be so pigheaded! Bye!" Maria shouted before hanging up her phone and terminating the call.

"That bitch!" Tommy shouted, hanging up his phone.

* * * * *

Darlene and her fiancé, Peter Knobbs, were introduced to Crystal's boyfriend, Jim, and four of them enjoyed conversing in the living room, with Darlene and Peter sitting on the love seat and Jim and Crystal sitting on the couch on the other side of the coffee table.

"Peter and Darlene, this is my boyfriend, Jim Connors. He's from, and still lives in, Dallas, Texas," said Crystal. Darlene shook his hand, and then Peter shook his hand. "Jim, this is my crazy sister, Darlene, and her fiancé, Peter Knobbs," said Crystal as they continued shaking hands and smiling at each other.

"It's nice to meet y'all finally. Crystal has told me so much about both of you. And congratulations on your engagement, and happy Thanksgiving," said Jim as he sat back down on the couch next to Crystal as everyone smiled at one another.

"Thank you. Happy Thanksgiving to you," said Peter as he sat back down.

"Happy Thanksgiving, Jim," said Darlene as she joined Peter on the love seat.

As everyone relaxed in the living room, Crystal went back into the kitchen to get some eggnog for Darlene and Peter.

"So you're from Texas? Do you come to New York often?" Darlene asked.

"Yes. I'm one of the owners of an insurance company in Dallas, and we do a lot of business out here on the East Coast, mostly in New York," said Jim as he took a pretzel and dipped it into one of the flavored mustards on the coffee table.

"That's good," Darlene responded as she took a pretzel from the mustard tray on the coffee table.

"Welcome to New York again," said Peter as he smiled at Jim, and Jim smiled back. "Nothing like jolly ole New York!" Peter added.

"True. I notice you have a British accent," Jim said as he sipped his eggnog.

"Oh yeah, I forgot to tell you that Peter is originally from Liverpool, England," said Crystal as she returned to the living room with the additional two glasses of eggnog and gave one glass to Darlene and the other to Peter as she smiled. Then she sat back down on the couch.

"Yeah? Liverpool, England? So what about those Beatles?" Jim asked Peter, and they both smiled and laughed.

"Darlene, let's go into the kitchen," Crystal said, and she and Darlene stood. Jim and Peter were right behind the girls.

"Peter, are you into football?" Jim asked as he grabbed the remote control for the television.

"Sure," said Peter, next to Jim, standing between the living room and the dining area, facing the television.

Jim and Peter went back into the living room and sat down on the couch while Crystal and Darlene were in the kitchen. Jim and Peter took pretzels from the tray and dipped the pretzels while watching a football game.

A couple of hours into the Thanksgiving holiday, Crystal began to set up the dining table. Jim and Peter were still watching the football game on the television in the living room. As Crystal set up the dining table, Darlene helped her. During the commercials, the doorbell rang.

"Jim, can you please get that? I think it's my parents!" Crystal shouted from the kitchen.

"All right," Jim responded as he rose from where he was sitting alongside Peter to answer the doorbell as it rang again.

"Thanks, Jim!" Crystal shouted as she peeked from the kitchen and dining area as Jim approached the door.

When Jim reached the door, he looked through the peephole before opening the door. He recognized Crystal's parents, as he had seen pictures of them before throughout Crystal's apartment. Jim opened the door, feeling a bit nervous but, at the same time, proud.

"Hi, Mr. and Mrs. Farnsworth," said Jim as the Farnsworths entered the apartment.

"Hello," the Farnsworths responded as Jim shut the door behind them. Mr. and Mrs. Farnsworth entered the living room with four pies, and they rested them on the coffee table as Jim reentered the living room behind them. Mr. and Mrs. Farnsworth removed their coats, and Jim took their coats and hung them up in the closet in the hallway close to the living room. After hanging up the coats, he reentered the living room.

"Would you like something to drink?" Jim asked Mr. and Mrs. Farnsworth as he walked toward the kitchen.

"Yes, we'll have some eggnog, please," said Mr. Farnsworth as he looked over to his wife, and she nodded in agreement. Then he and Mrs. Farnsworth sat down on the love seat. Peter rose from the couch while Darlene was coming out of the bathroom in the hallway, and Crystal entered the living room from the kitchen.

"Hi, Mom and Dad! Happy Thanksgiving!" Darlene and Crystal shouted as they met their parents in the living room. They hugged their parents when their parents rose from where they were sitting on the love seat.

"Oh, Mom and Dad, I want to introduce you to my boyfriend, Jim Connors," said Crystal as she took him by the hand quickly as she stood by the kitchen, close to the dining room, and then they walked into the living room.

"Mom and Dad, this is, of course, my fiancé, as you already knew," said Darlene. She and Peter were holding hands.

"Peter Knobbs, to be exact, right?" Mr. Farnsworth asked as he and Peter shook hands.

"Yes, sir. Right you are. Happy holidays, Mr. and Mrs. Farnsworth," said Peter as he and Darlene smiled at them and at each other.

"Happy holidays, Peter," said Mrs. Farnsworth.

"Happy holidays, Mr. and Mrs. Farnsworth," said Jim as he extended his right hand to Mr. Farnsworth.

"Happy holidays to you, Jim," said Mr. Farnsworth as he and Mrs. Farnsworth smiled at Jim. They felt pleased to have the opportunity to meet Jim, who was involved with their daughter Crystal.

"All right, it's time to eat!" said Crystal as she tapped her wineglass lightly with a fork at the dining table. Everyone left the living room and entered the dining room, joining Crystal, and she and Darlene continued setting up the table.

"Crystal, I can help you," said Jim as he walked toward the kitchen.

"Relax, Jim. Darlene and I are doing fine." Crystal smiled and kissed him on the cheek, and then Jim went back to the dining table to sit down with everyone else. Mr. Farnsworth sat at the head of the table, and Mrs. Farnsworth sat next to him.

Crystal brought out the golden-brown turkey on a serving plate from the counter in the kitchen and placed it on the dining table. Darlene was right behind her with two large bowls. One bowl held mashed potatoes, and the other held stuffing.

After Crystal placed the turkey on the table, she grabbed one of the bowls from Darlene and placed it down, and then she went back into the kitchen as those at the table talked among themselves.

When Crystal arrived back in the kitchen, she grabbed a large bowl of tossed green salad and a few bottles of assorted dressings. Darlene reentered the kitchen and grabbed a large plate of corn on the cob that had been kept nice and warm on top of the stove, as the oven was still hot from the turkey cooking inside.

After Darlene placed the large plate of corn on the cob on the dining table, she quickly went back into the kitchen to check on the pies, which were on the counter near the refrigerator. There were two pumpkin pies and two chocolate pies. When Darlene saw that everything was all right, she quickly went back into the dining area, rejoining the family.

When everyone was seated at the dining table, Crystal's father, Mr. Farnsworth, who was seated at the head of the table, stood up as he bowed his head. Everyone followed his lead, and Mr. Farnsworth began to pray before eating. Jim and Crystal held hands underneath the table.

"We give thanks to God up above for the food we're about to receive. In his name we pray. Amen," said Mr. Farnsworth.

"Amen," said everyone at the table.

"Let's eat," said Mr. Farnsworth as he smiled, and they all picked up their wineglasses and toasted him as they smiled while he began to carve the golden-brown turkey.

Later on, when Peter and Darlene were leaving, they were the last to go. Crystal shut the door behind them.

"Jim?" Crystal called out as she was locking the door.

"Yes, Crystal?" Jim responded as she joined him on the couch.

"I love you so much. And my family loved you too." Crystal was amazed how fast they had taken a liking to him after meeting him for the first time.

Jim placed an arm around her as she rested her head on his chest. "I'm glad. I really am because I loved everyone in your family. Your family really treated me well, and it felt so right when I was with your family tonight. I'm really grateful we all hit it off really well, in spite of my being a little older than you. I noticed that when you brought it up to your parents, it didn't even matter to them," said Jim.

Crystal took off her sneakers while listening to Jim, and she placed her tired feet, covered up in socks, on the coffee table. Jim had his sneakers off too. He placed his sock-covered feet up on the coffee table next to Crystal's feet and put his arm around her again as they both sat back on the couch, and she rested her head on his chest.

"Jim, my father and the rest of my family don't care how old you are. The only thing they're concerned about is how well you treat me. Especially since this thing that's been going on with that guy Tommy. You know, the harassing and the stalking. As long as I'm happy—" Crystal stopped speaking momentarily as she lay there in his arms while she looked into his eyes.

"Well, Miss Crystal Farnsworth, are you happy?" Jim asked while looking directly into her eyes, and a moment of silence fell upon them as their eyes were locked on each other.

"Am I happy? More than you'll ever know," said Crystal as she sat back up. "Now, we haven't known each other that long, but it is Thanksgiving, and I am so thankful we met that one day at my job. And to answer your question, yes. Yes, I'm very happy. And you treat me extremely well." Crystal moved in closer toward Jim, which brought their faces closer.

"I am very happy to be with you, and I never have met or been with a more beautiful woman in my life than you, Crystal Farnsworth," said Jim as he smiled at her.

"Oh yeah?" Crystal asked as she also smiled. She moved in closer while he embraced her tighter, and they both felt the excitement grow between them. "Oh yeah?" Crystal asked again purposely as they gently kissed as their lips came together softly.

As their lips parted, he looked deep into her eyes. "Yeah," Jim whispered into her ear, and their lips moved in closer for another round of ecstasy. As they kissed passionately, they rose from the couch at the same time. Their bodies melted into one as they continued kissing.

When their lips parted, Jim took Crystal by the hand, and they walked into the hallway that led to Crystal's bedroom. They entered the bedroom, and Crystal turned around and shut the door.

The next day arrived, the day after Thanksgiving. Pigeons flew through the frosty air, and frost rested upon Crystal's bedroom window. Crystal lay in bed, underneath the blankets, resting her head upon Jim's muscular bare chest. He cuddled Crystal in his arms as they both lay there underneath the blankets.

While lying there, Jim opened one eye, looking at her from the side of his eye. "Hey, baby?" he said in a sexy whisper as he smiled while she started to awaken slowly.

"Hmm?" she responded as she opened her eyes and looked up at Jim.

"Did I wake you?" Jim asked.

"No. I've been awake off and on. What's wrong?" she asked, rubbing her eyes.

"Don't you have to go to work today?" he asked, and they both looked over at the alarm clock radio on the side table near the bed. It was six thirty in the morning.

"No, I'm not working today. I'm off the whole weekend because of the holiday; the building is closed for the holiday," Crystal said.

"No kidding. That's great," Jim responded while he lay there in bed on his side, with his arm resting on his side, as she sat up.

"Yeah, it is," said Crystal as she kissed him on the lips.

"That means we'll have more time together. This is wonderful," said Jim as he turned onto his back. Crystal lay back down, and they cuddled up to each other as they felt the morning chill.

While they cuddled up to each other with their arms wrapped around each other's nude body, Crystal took a deep breath and then exhaled slowly. "Yes, it is wonderful," she said as she and Jim lay there in bed together, looking up at the bedroom ceiling, engaged in a love that was all their own.

Tommy woke up with a streak of loneliness looming over him. After he rose out of bed, stretching and yawning, he entered the living room. He looked out the window and saw that it was a cold, cloudy, and dreary day, with a bit of frost around the window. He wiped away a little bit of the frost with his hand to look outside, and he saw a few buses and cars roaming about the deserted streets in front of his apartment building. Because of the holiday weekend, the slick, wet streets were a deserted wasteland, as families continued gathering together on the festive holiday weekend.

All of a sudden, the telephone rang on the side table in the living room, and he jumped, feeling a bit startled by the unexpected phone call. He'd been relishing the moment of silence. The telephone rang again, and the disruptive sound from the telephone broke through the stillness of solitude that hung over him as he walked over to the side table to answer the phone, wondering who it might be.

"Hello?" Tommy said. He thought it might be Maria again.

"Tommy? This is your aunt Sylvie. Where were you for the holidays? We were waiting for your call, hoping you might've been on the way over or something," Aunt Sylvie said as Tommy sat there in silence on his recliner, sitting upright, not saying a word. "We waited for your response yesterday, since the time I left my message. Well, anyway, we all—you know, your family—were hoping you would show up for the family. Everyone was asking about you, and everyone was really wanting to see you," said Aunt Sylvie. Her voice had a slight crack in it.

"I'm sorry, Aunt Sylvie. Tell the family I'm sorry for not showing up for the holiday and for not calling. I know there's no excuse." Tommy rose from the recliner and walked back toward the window, looking outside.

"It's all right, Tommy. So where were you yesterday? Were you at home all by yourself for the holidays?" she asked with more of a crack in her voice, which came from years of heavy smoking, and a moment of an eerie silence crept over the apartment.

"Yes! Yes! Yes! All right? Is there something wrong with that? I was by my-fucking-self! Is that all right with you and my lovely family?" Tommy shouted as he turned from the window and walked to the middle of the living room.

"No! No, there's nothing wrong with that! It's just that the holidays are supposed to be a time when family spend some time together and—"

"Whoever said that that's the way it is? And besides, ever since Mom deserted me, man, I don't know about the family thing. I don't know." Tommy, thinking about his mother, began to cry silently. He put down the telephone receiver on the couch while he wiped his eyes of the tears he'd been shedding for years, and his aunt knew he was crying, as there was a moment of silence. Then he picked up the cordless phone from the couch while he continued standing in the middle of the living room.

"Tommy? Are you still there?" Aunt Sylvie asked, wondering if he'd hung up the phone.

"I'm here, Aunt Sylvie," said Tommy as he walked back toward the frosty window at the corner of the living room.

"You know, Tommy, your uncle and I have been there for you all your life, and for you to speak that way to me on the telephone is unbelievable! No respect. No goddamn respect!" Aunt Sylvie shouted as her husband tried to calm her down, comforting her, as she was upset.

"I said thank you! I said goddamn thank you! What more do you want from me? Shall I rip out my fucking heart and show you how thankful I am that you and my uncle took me in? Or should I ship my heart to you in a care package with some fruit and cheese inside and have it sent to you by Christmas Day?" Tommy shouted.

"Tommy, don't getting fucking smart with me!" Aunt Sylvie responded, gasping for her breath, and Tommy began to feel concerned for her health.

"I'm sorry. It's just that I—" Tommy stopped midway through what he was saying.

"I know, I know. It's that girl you're head over heels for, right?" she asked, smoking her almost-finished cigarette.

"Yes. You see, she's going to call me anytime now. Really, she will," said Tommy as he felt a bit optimistic all of a sudden.

"Tommy, get off it. Listen to me! Get off it! Get off it right now,

Tommy!" Aunt Sylvie responded, gasping for her breath again, and Tommy again noticed and began feeling ashamed.

"Huh?" Tommy responded, not knowing what else to say, only wishing the call would end soon.

"Tommy, let me ask you something. Are you currently in counseling?" she asked as she began feeling weak, and her husband felt concerned, wanting to end the call soon, while he stood next to her.

"I was," said Tommy as he sat back down on the recliner.

"All right. So are you still in counseling?" she asked, hoping for a positive answer.

"No. I'm not in counseling anymore."

"Why the hell not? You need it, Tommy!"

"Well, I went once." Tommy grew impatient with the conversation.

"You went only once? Going only once isn't going to help the way it should. Tommy, you really need to go to counseling more than once. I wish you would reconsider and go back to counseling. You have a problem. A major problem, and it sounds like this problem is obsession. Actually, I think it is obsession. I mean, I'm no counselor or doctor, but this sounds a lot like obsession. You need to take care of yourself. Your uncle and I really care about you a lot. And we still love you very much." Aunt Sylvie fought to hold back her tears.

"I know you do," Tommy responded, feeling embarrassed.

"Promise me! Promise me you'll get more counseling!" she cried as she burst into tears.

"OK, all right," said Tommy as he rose from the recliner and walked toward the mirror that hung on the wall at the other end of the living room. When he arrived in front of the mirror, he placed the cordless phone next to his ear again while staring at himself in the mirror.

"Let me hear it!" Aunt Sylvie shouted, feeling frustrated with the conversation, and Tommy was feeling the same.

"All right. I promise," said Tommy as he continued looking at himself in the mirror.

"Promise what?" she asked.

"I promise I will go back to counseling," said Tommy as he looked down at the carpeted floor and then quickly looked back up at his reflection in the mirror.

"Promise?" she asked again as both felt the tension.

"Yeah, I guess," said Tommy, and he quickly turned around opposite the mirror and looked straight ahead toward the three windows at the other end of the living room. He looked straight ahead into space, wide-eyed, not blinking, as he dropped the cordless phone to the floor.

"Tommy? Tommy, are you still there? Tommy!"

CHAPTER 19

THE FOLLOWING MONDAY AFTER THE Thanksgiving weekend, Tommy was at the counselor's office, seated in the waiting area, listening to the smooth jazz coming from one of the speakers near the reception desk, as he waited for the counselor.

"Good morning, Sandy. Tommy Landis is in the waiting area, wanting to see you," said the receptionist as she directed Sandy with her eyes to where Tommy was sitting.

"Yeah, all right. Wish me luck," said Sandy, and she walked toward Tommy in the waiting area.

"Tommy?" she called out, holding a clipboard, as she approached him.

"Oh, hi, Sandy Leonard. I'm sorry about the last time I was here. You know, when I ran out of here like a bat out of hell?" Tommy was nervous about being back in counseling, feeling helpless, as he stood up.

"That's quite all right, Tommy. Let's go right into my office. Shall we?" Sandy asked while she carried her clipboard at her side and smiled at him, making him feel at ease.

"All right," said Tommy as he followed her to her office, walking right behind her.

◆◆◆◆◆

A yellow taxi pulled up to the curb at John F. Kennedy International Airport. When it came to a complete stop at the curb, Jim and Crystal exited the cab, and the driver exited from the driver's side. While Crystal and Jim walked to the sidewalk, the driver walked to the trunk of the cab, and she took out Jim's suitcase and briefcase.

"Here's fifty dollars. Keep the change," said Jim, and he and Crystal walked toward the entrance, with Crystal carrying his briefcase and Jim carrying the suitcase. They entered the lobby of the airport, walked to the security screening area, got in line, and waited their turn to go through the security screening. Jim set his suitcase on the floor, while Crystal still held his briefcase, but then she felt her hand getting tired, so she put the briefcase down on the floor next to the suitcase.

"Crystal, I had a great time over the holiday weekend with you and your family," said Jim as he put his right arm around her waist, and she put her arm around his waist as she smiled at him.

"I wish you could move to New York, so we wouldn't have to live so far apart," said Crystal as she smiled halfway with wishful eyes.

"Well, Crystal, I was going to save this as a surprise, but I suppose I'll tell you now what I'm trying to do. When I arrive back in Dallas, I will see if I can transfer to the northeastern branch division of my insurance company and see what I can work out with them, all right? How does that sound, baby?" Jim asked as she embraced him tightly. "I know this long-distance thing sucks, especially with this holiday weekend we had. We've grown so much closer in a short period of time," Jim said as they walked down the line little by little toward security as he pushed his suitcase with his right foot.

"Yes, I know it's been a short time, but we do love each other," said Crystal, and they kissed each other. "That would be great if you can get the transfer from Dallas to New York City. I really will miss you." Crystal and Jim hugged each other while still waiting in line at security.

"Next!" the security screener shouted as the last person went through the screening, and Jim and Crystal looked at each other.

"Are you coming with me to the terminal?" Jim asked as he picked up his suitcase and briefcase. He put the suitcase and briefcase on the conveyer belt, he and Crystal emptied their pockets, and she placed her purse on the belt as well.

"Of course I'm going with you to the terminal," Crystal responded as she put some spare change into a bucket as Jim was going through the metal detector. Crystal went through the metal detector behind Jim and met him on the other side as Jim was taking his shoes off the conveyor belt. Crystal did the same, and they put on their shoes. Jim pulled the suitcase and briefcase off the conveyor belt, and as soon as he placed them on the floor, he and Crystal tied their sneakers.

"Yeah, I guess the terrorist attack changed everything as far as the airports go," said Crystal as she and Jim looked at each other and grabbed the suitcase and briefcase.

* * * * * *

"So, Mr. Tommy Landis, how was your holiday weekend?" Sandy asked, sitting behind her desk.

"Oh, it was all right, I guess. I was off the whole Thanksgiving weekend from the job. I'll be back at work this afternoon, whenever I leave here. How was your holiday weekend?" Tommy asked as he sat back in his chair, getting comfortable.

"Pretty good, thank you. My parents came from California, and my brother came over too. Yeah, we all had a great time. I put up my Christmas tree yesterday."

"Oh yeah? I thought about putting up mine this week, but I don't know." Tommy looked down at the carpeted floor.

"Oh really?" she responded as she took a sip of her coffee from her coffee cup.

"Yeah, but, Sandy—" He covered his face with both his hands as he bent over while still sitting on his chair.

"Yes, Tommy? Go ahead; talk. I'm listening," said Sandy as she gave him every ounce of her attention.

"I really was a little lonely over the Thanksgiving holiday weekend. It was a long weekend!" said Tommy as tears welled in his eyes.

"Well, Tommy, why were you alone over the holiday weekend? Why didn't you go to your mother's or another relative's place or something?" she asked Tommy, feeling his pain of being alone with an obsessive problem, as he lifted his head slowly and looked straight into her eyes.

"My mother left me when I was six years old," said Tommy, and Sandy was shocked, relating the new revelation to the obsessive behavior and feeling his grief.

"I'm sorry to hear that, Tommy," said Sandy, writing in her pad.

"Yeah, me too," said Tommy, still looking directly into her eyes, as though he were looking through her. Then, suddenly, he looked back down at the floor, feeling somewhat ashamed that he didn't come from a better family than that. Then he looked up into Sandy's eyes again with tears streaming down his cheeks.

"Don't you have any relatives you could've gone to for the holidays instead of being all alone, especially for the whole weekend?" Sandy asked, writing down notes for further study on his problem on her clipboard.

"My aunt Sylvie," he responded as he smiled halfway.

"Your aunt Sylvie?" she asked as she looked at him.

"Yes, my aunt Sylvie." Tommy sat up and leaned forward with his hands joined together in front of him as he smiled again, and Sandy smiled back nervously, seeing something positive for the first time in his sessions with her.

"Well, why didn't you go to your aunt Sylvie's for the weekend or at least for the holiday?" Sandy asked, looking through some papers on her desk, next to her clipboard.

"I felt like staying at home in my apartment," said Tommy, remembering what he had been doing at that time.

"Oh yeah? What did you do at home for the holiday weekend?" she asked, still writing on her pad, and she laughed at the funny expression on his face.

"I was fine. I ordered some Chinese food on Thanksgiving, and I watched that movie that's usually on only for the holidays, *March of the Wooden Soldiers*. And then I watched a marathon of the original *Star Trek* show." He smiled.

"Oh yeah, the one from the sixties," she responded as she joined him in smiling.

"I watched the whole damn thing till the next morning." Tommy crossed his right leg over his left leg with both hands cupped over his knee.

"I guess we could say you were pretty content over the holiday, right?" she asked, interested in hearing what his response would be.

"Yeah, sort of." Tommy uncrossed his legs, feeling somewhat uncomfortable because he was still lonely and was thinking about Crystal throughout the session with Sandy.

Sandy noticed his facial expression change immediately in response to her last question. "You were happy during Thanksgiving, but what?" Sandy asked, but he just shrugged, not answering her, while he looked down once more at the carpeted floor. "What wasn't making you happy that day?" she asked as she continued writing on her pad and took a sip of her coffee. "Oh, I'm sorry. Did you want some coffee or tea? I don't remember if I asked you or not," she said as she rose from behind her desk.

"No. That's all right. No, thank you." Tommy held up his hands, not wanting her to go to the trouble.

"Are you sure? All right." Sandy sat back down behind her desk. "So as I was asking you, were you happy, or was there something that should've happened but didn't that night?" she asked, and the sound of silence filled the air between Sandy and Tommy across her desk.

Then, all of a sudden, Tommy clapped his hands, startling Sandy. "Amazing! Simply amazing!" Tommy shouted, joining his hands together as they rested on his lap, while his eyes lit up.

Sandy sat there stunned at Tommy's sudden outburst, not knowing how to respond to him, being careful. "What's so amazing, Tommy?" Sandy asked as he was calming down somewhat.

"It's quite amazing how quickly you picked up on how my holiday went, without being there. How about that, Sandy Leonard?" he asked with a wild look in his eyes.

"Tommy, I just guessed. That's all. I'm trying to help you in some way. And in some way, you're very unpredictable," said Sandy, and he began to laugh.

"I know, but you do have a talent. You definitely have a talent." Tommy sat back in his chair with both legs stretched out forward and crossed.

"Thank you, Tommy. So I'll ask you the same question, which you never answered. What didn't happen on Thanksgiving night that should've happened?" Sandy asked once again as she put down her pen on top of her pad.

Tommy removed his black-framed glasses and rested them upon Sandy's desk, close to him. Then he placed both hands over his face while leaning forward in his chair. Sandy looked down at her desk, at her paperwork from the session, and then she looked back at Tommy.

"Tommy?" she called out, and then he looked up at her while still partially covering his face, keeping his eyes mostly covered, as Sandy thought of a way for him to open up with her. "Was it because that young lady Crystal didn't call you?" Sandy asked, feeling sorry for him.

Tommy didn't look up at her but nodded in response to her last question, and then he covered his face again with both hands partially.

"Tommy, Crystal didn't call you because she didn't want to. Crystal has gone on with her life, and maybe you should do the same." Sandy leaned forward over her desk as Tommy looked up at her.

"Yeah, but you don't understand, Sandy!" Tommy yelled out as he leaned forward.

"Tommy, I am a counselor. I've been in this business a long time. I don't mean to sound insensitive, but I've spent my whole life helping those just like you and others with other problems. And I know an awful lot about obsession. Believe it or not, you have all the major symptoms of someone who's obsessed," said Sandy as Tommy rose from where he was sitting.

"What makes you so sure I'm obsessed, other than those college degrees hanging on the walls in this office?" Tommy asked while looking around her office at all the college certificates that hung on the wall behind her and the wall on his left. Then he looked back at her as he put back on his glasses and sat back down.

"Tommy, I'm really sure you have obsession, because you have all the classic symptoms, all right? Hey, look—" Sandy stopped midway, rose from behind her desk, walked over to him, and knelt beside where he was sitting. "Look, obsession is in existence when a person doesn't accept rejection from a person who's rejecting him. And no matter how much this person pursues the one he's being rejected by, the other person won't except him, no matter what. And in turn, the obsessed individual doesn't accept the rejected feelings of the person. There are constant telephone calls and stalking—you know, constantly following the one who's doing the rejecting. Then, when the obsessed person is tired of continuing phone calls and stalking, he eventually ends up in a mental ward or kills the person he's obsessed with. Sometimes the obsessed person even kills himself too. Tommy, you can't make someone be attracted to you." Sandy rose from where she was kneeling at the side of Tommy's chair, and she sat partially on her desk as Tommy listened, not responding yet.

"Ah, come on!" Tommy shouted as he quickly rose, turned around, and walked toward the door slowly with his hands on his hips.

"I've seen it all before, Tommy, and if you don't let her go, this will be the story of your life!" Sandy shouted as Tommy just stared into space, still with his back facing her as he faced the door. "Tommy, I'll say it again! If you do not let this woman Crystal go, this will be the story of your life!" she shouted again.

He slowly turned around, looking down at the carpeted floor. When he'd fully turned around, he just stared at her, as though he were looking through her. As Sandy noticed the cold, unblinking stare, a chill ran down her spine, and she slightly shivered at piercing dark eyes coming through the black-framed glasses.

"Tommy?" Sandy called out to him as she stood at the front of the desk, staring at him, not knowing what he was going to do.

Tommy gave half a smile, and then his mouth opened up partially. At first, he mumbled in a low tone, and then he quickly stopped himself.

"Love—" Tommy stopped, still staring at Sandy.

"Go head, Tommy. I'm listening," said Sandy, feeling inquisitive because of Tommy's weird actions and somewhat intrigued.

"Love of the twisted. Love of the twisted! There! I said it!" Tommy whispered loudly as his eyes grew wide, and Sandy wondered what had made him say that.

"Love of the twisted? Tommy, what made you say that?" Sandy whispered softly, shocked, as she went behind her desk and sat down on her chair as Tommy gave half a grin and then laughed while he walked toward her desk.

When he arrived at her desk, he leaned over it, covering half the desk. "Love of the twisted," he whispered again but this time softly, as he was somewhat calm. He smiled as she just stared at him with her mouth open a bit, seemingly a bit bewildered.

"Love of the twisted?" she whispered to herself while looking down at her desk, realizing the symptoms of obsession in front of her eyes.

All of a sudden, still leaning over her desk, he laughed hysterically out loud as he looked up at the ceiling of Sandy's office.

CHAPTER 20

CRYSTAL ARRIVED HOME AT HER apartment in her semiposh area on the Upper East Side in Manhattan. When she entered her bedroom, the telephone rang. She rushed to answer the phone that rested on the side table near her bed.

"Hello?" Crystal said into the receiver of the phone, but there was no response on the other end of the line. "Hello? Jim? Jim, is it you?" she asked, hoping, but as each second passed, she grew more horrified, wondering who might be on the telephone. She heard a slight giggle in the background, but it wasn't clear who might be on the phone.

"Love of the twisted," Tommy whispered slowly into the receiver of the telephone.

"Who? What? Who is this?" she asked, thinking she knew who it was. "Tommy? Tommy! Why are you calling me?" she shouted, pacing nervously about the bedroom floor and then into the living room, as she panicked, not knowing how to respond.

"Love of the twisted," Tommy whispered again but this time in an aggressive tone of voice, and then he hung up the telephone.

Tommy was standing at a pay phone on a corner where he lived, and then he walked away.

* * * * *

After Tommy hung up the telephone, Crystal heard a dial tone, and she looked at the receiver of the cordless phone. She hung up her phone from her bedroom; she lay down on her bed. Lying on her back, she closed her eyes slowly, and soon she fell asleep.

As Crystal fell asleep, she began hearing a voice in her dreams. She heard a voice mumbling and saw a huge, growing white light in the distance from where she was standing. When she walked forward, the voice became clearer. Suddenly, she stopped walking and listened intently.

"Love. Love. Only love," said the whispering voice from the distance.

As she wore a cautious expression on her face, she began to walk forward slowly, one foot in front of the other, and as she walked forward carefully, the whispers sounded louder and clearer than before.

"Love," the voice whispered.

Crystal stopped once again. Within a foot of where she was standing, in front of her stood someone wearing a black robe with a black hood on the back of the robe, over the shoulders. The person Crystal was facing was facing her. But the mysterious person tossed the black hood up, hiding his identity.

"Love," the whispering voice called out once again, coming from the hooded person in front of Crystal.

Crystal walked forward slowly, a bit frightened of the unknown figure standing in front of her with a glowing white light behind. When she approached the figure, the hooded person put both his arms up in front of his body, in the shape of an X, while his head looked downward as the hood dropped downward.

"Love? Love?" said the person as he kept his head looking downward, sheltering his identity with the big black hood, as she wondered what all of this meant.

"Love?" Crystal asked as she looked for a response from the hooded one in front of her.

"Love? Love?" said the hooded one as he lifted his right hand slowly.

Crystal walked two steps backward, not knowing where she'd end up next, as she wasn't feeling safe at the moment.

The hooded one slowly lifted his left arm, bringing it to the same level as the right arm in the air, while Crystal became more suspicious of what was taking place.

The hooded figure reached for his big black hood and began removing the hood slowly.

"Love. Love of the twisted! Love of the twisted," said the hooded unknown as he finally removed the hood from his head.

Crystal couldn't believe her eyes when the hood was finally off. "Tommy? Tommy, is that you?" Crystal shouted. She still couldn't believe the view before her, and she started stepping back.

"Love of the twisted!" Tommy shouted with his arms folded.

"I have to get the hell out of here!" Crystal told herself, and she turned to run away. But before she turned fully around, Tommy appeared in front of her, and before she could scream, Tommy covered her mouth with his right hand, keeping her quiet, as he put his face right in front of her.

"Love of the—" Tommy stopped, looking straight into Crystal's crystal-blue eyes.

"Oh my God," said Crystal, terrified of the moment that was overtaking her, as he went toward her ear. He still had his right hand over her mouth, keeping her quiet.

"Twisted! Love of the twisted," Tommy whispered into her ear.

Feeling overwhelmed with fear and desperation, she bit into his hand, and when he was forced to let go of her mouth, she let loose with a roaring scream.

Back to reality, coming out of the disenchanting nightmare, Crystal awoke, still lying on the bed, still on her back.

When she awoke, the telephone rang on the side table next to the bed.

"Oh my God," said Crystal as she looked at the telephone as it continued to ring. She hesitantly answered the phone, expecting to hear the evil and demented voice of Tommy Landis.

"Hello?" Crystal said with fear in the back of her mind, still a bit shaken from the nightmare she'd had moments ago.

"Crystal?" someone said.

"Oh, hi, Mom. How are you?" Crystal asked as she quickly sat up in her bed, brushing her hair straight back with her other hand, as she smiled with relief.

✦✦✦✦✦✦

Tommy paced about the living room floor in his apartment with tears forming in his eyes.

"Why doesn't she see the truth in the way she wants to be with me? I know deep down, she really does want to be with me. Now she's seeing some fucking rich guy! And I'm just a fucking mailroom clerk in an overstuffed office building!" Tommy shouted to himself while approaching the mirror in the living room. When he was in front of the mirror, he stood there looking at himself.

"There's no future with a fucking loser like me! I certainly can't provide a future for her, so how could I possibly be angry that she's seeing some rich guy who can give her everything she desires in life?" Tommy told himself, still looking at his reflection.

"Why settle for a cheeseburger, when you could order a New York sirloin steak instead?" Tommy asked himself as he moved in closer toward the mirror, nodding. "Though cheeseburger and steak are both made from beef, I guess she would rather have the steak than the burger!" Tommy shouted at his reflection as if he were talking to another person. He paused, catching his breath.

When he stopped talking for a moment, he turned around and walked toward the sofa to lie down. He lay down with his hands behind his head as he stretched out with his eyes shut.

"But I know one thing for sure: if I can't have her, nobody will have her. Not only will I take her, but I'll take her soul! Then and only then will she be all mine!" Tommy shouted as he remained on the sofa with his eyes shut. While exhaling, he smiled, wearing a wide grin upon his face with confidence, knowing where he stood with Crystal Farnsworth for the first time.

✦✦✦✦✦

"Hey, Darlene, it's Crystal."

"Hey, Crystal. What's up?" Darlene asked.

"I just woke up from a short nap, and I had the weirdest dream," said Crystal, still sitting up in her bed.

"Oh yeah? What did you dream about?" Darlene asked, wearing a headset to talk with her while she was washing the dishes.

"Well, Darlene, I wouldn't say this was a dream—more like a nightmare. Let me tell you what happened."

Darlene stopped what she was doing and sat down at the kitchen table. "All right, I'm listening," said Darlene.

"OK, I had just arrived home from the airport after dropping off Jim, who is on his way home to Dallas. When I arrived home, I felt a little tired, so I went to bed to take a nap, but before I went to bed, someone called me on the telephone," Crystal said.

"Oh yeah?" Darlene responded.

"It was a man whispering into the telephone, saying, 'Love of the twisted.'" Crystal turned around, placing her feet on the floor and sitting straight up.

"Love of the what?" Darlene asked.

"Love of the twisted. Can you believe that?" Crystal asked as she looked over toward the answering machine in the living room, sitting straight up on her bed in her bedroom, as tears welled in her eyes.

"Tommy. This sounds a lot like Tommy," Darlene said.

"I thought the same thing. It could've been him, but he has a copy of the order of protection, so I don't think he's that stupid," said Crystal, wiping her eyes with a tissue from a square box on her side table, careful not to smear her makeup.

"You're right. You are absolutely right, but, Crystal, don't be naive with this whole thing. He's not stupid, but he is crazy and obsessed, and I heard that obsessed people are somewhat creative, so you might want to consider moving into a new apartment," Darlene said.

"Move? Move out of this apartment? No. Absolutely not! I can't run from this problem! And leave this apartment I love so much." Crystal rose from the bed, walked into the living room, walked to the window, and placed her left hand on the window, feeling how cold it was. "Darlene, I can't move out of this apartment. If he keeps on pursuing me, I—" She stopped, thinking for a moment.

"You what? He could kill you, my sister, and then what?" Darlene asked.

Crystal turned around slowly, imagining her sister was right in front of her. "I won't let it go that far," said Crystal as she walked away from the windows and toward the kitchen.

"Oh yeah? So now you have the talent to tell the future and everything that will happen to you?" Darlene shouted.

Crystal turned around quickly and then looked down. "No. No, I can't see into the future, but I wish I could." There was a pause between the two sisters as Crystal imagined that Darlene was present in her apartment. "Do you want to hear about my nightmare?" Crystal asked as she sat down on the couch and imagined Darlene sitting next to her in the living room.

"Yes. Yes, I do," said Darlene as she listened intently.

"All right, as I mentioned earlier in the call, I had this nightmare. I was surrounded by darkness in my bed, trying to get some sleep. All of a sudden, a huge white light appeared in front of me, and then there was a mumbling voice near me, but I didn't know exactly where the voice was coming from. So I walked forward slowly about twenty feet from where I was standing. When I stopped walking, a person stood twenty feet away, wearing a black robe with a black hood over his head. While he looked downward, he was mumbling."

"OK," Darlene responded as she continued listening, thinking she probably had just had a bad dream while sleeping.

"So at that point, I saw where the mumbling was coming from. So I approached the black-hooded person, and the closer I got to the person, the louder the mumbling became. When I was within five feet of the person, the mumbling was clearer than before. I listened very carefully to what the person was saying, and he was saying, 'Love of the twisted,' while remaining underneath the big black hood connected to the black robe. And when the black hood came off and the person revealed his true identity, it was Tommy! I wanted to run up to him and kill him! If I'd had a knife or a gun, I would've killed him, Darlene!" Crystal yelled out. She and Darlene had tears in their eyes.

"Crystal, if you don't deal with this situation more seriously, he will eventually kill you. That's why I suggested moving away to another apartment. Maybe not out of New York but maybe to another apartment," Darlene said once again as she felt her sister's pain.

"I can't leave this apartment," said Crystal, drying her eyes with another tissue from another square box on the side table next to the couch.

"The voice you heard on the telephone last night was the voice of Tommy Landis, but you have to remember that this call came right before you had that nightmare. What I'm saying is that when you go through something dramatic right before you fall asleep, sometimes you will dream something pertaining to whatever was going on before you went to bed. But then again, this could be a sign that maybe you should heed. Take notice, and do something." Darlene was running out of things to say to encourage her sister.

"Darlene, I got the order of protection. Isn't—"

"Yeah, and that's good. But it's not good enough. Very good for the beginning, but the police aren't going to be there twenty-four hours for you. There are times when you have to do other things as well, and that's why I've suggested, many times now, moving out to another apartment."

Crystal was on the couch, in a daze, feeling as if Darlene were right next to her, but she was really on the telephone. There was a moment of silence penetrating the air between them over the telephone.

"Hello?" Darlene called out, not knowing if Crystal had hung up the telephone or if they had been disconnected.

"I'm here, Darlene. And you are right, but you see, I can't do any more than what's already been done. I put out an order of protection not too long ago. I'm not going to inconvenience myself by moving into another apartment and, especially, moving out of here, because I've lived here for a long time. That is pretty much all I can do for now, according the police department near where I live," Crystal said.

"I know, Crystal, that you can only do so much for now, but I'm concerned, you know? I'm very, very concerned over this whole damn thing. You have to be very careful out there. Just be aware all around yourself. Every time you step off the train, going to work or going home, look around yourself, and be alert! I don't put anything past this weirdo," said Darlene.

"I understand. You're right. I will be more alert, and pretty much, I've been alert. I just hope he gets a life soon and leaves me alone." Crystal reentered her bedroom, and she hung up the phone after Darlene hung up her telephone.

She took off her sneakers, placed them on the floor near the bed, and lay down.

—————————— ·•••••· ——————————

Tommy arrived home at his apartment. When he entered his apartment, he turned on the light switch in the living room, walked into the living room, removed his glasses, threw them onto the recliner, and then covered his face with both hands, drowning in frustration and loneliness over not being with Crystal.

"What the hell am I going to do?" Tommy asked himself as he removed his hands from his face. With a look of horror on his face, he imagined Crystal and her new boyfriend in front of him. An illusion was building up right in his living room.

The new boyfriend, Jim Connors, was wearing a black tuxedo, while Crystal was wearing a virgin-white wedding gown and holding a small bunch of flowers. They walked down the aisle as though they were king and queen for the day in his apartment. Jim, looking handsome, and Crystal, looking radiant, continued walking down the aisle as Tommy stared into space in a daze with thoughts of horror and despair as tears rolled down his face.

——————— ⊰✦⊱ ———————

The next day arrived, and a cloudy day took hold as Tommy entered the messenger center. His demeanor was as though he were a walking zombie. Maria saw him walking by her as she was at her desk.

"Hi, Tommy," Maria called out while sitting at her desk as she stared at him, but he walked by without saying a word or noticing her existence.

After Tommy put on his work shoes and smock, he slammed shut his locker and walked toward one of the carts full of the day's mail. Louie was by the counter, doing some paperwork, and he noticed Tommy taking one of the carts. Tommy had on his work shirt and smock, but the smock was unbuttoned and wrinkled.

"Hey, Tommy! Your smock is a little wrinkled. It's all right for today, but at least button up your smock!" Louie shouted as he grabbed the other cart from the other end.

"What? What, Louie?" Tommy asked as he let go of the cart from his end.

"Button up your smock, please. Be more presentable for the upper floors. You're not a goddamn new employee!" Louie shouted as he leaned over the edge of the counter next to the cart.

Tommy buttoned his smock, and he tucked his white button-down shirt into his jeans as well. "There. Are you happy now?" Tommy shouted at Louie, and Louie's cigar fell from the corner of his mouth, as he was shocked at what Tommy had just said. Maria and the other coworkers were just as shocked over the scene. "OK, my work shirt, or smock, is buttoned now. Are you happy now?" Tommy shouted again as he grabbed the cart from his end.

Louie picked up his fallen cigar from the floor. He blew on it, stuck it back in his mouth unlit, and put his hands on his hips. "Tommy, I need to see you in my office right now," said Louie as he walked away toward his office.

Tommy trailed behind, taking his time.

Louie turned around, facing Tommy. "Right now!" Louie shouted, and Tommy immediately hurried behind Louie as they walked toward the office.

After they entered the office, Louie shut the door behind Tommy. When the door was shut, Louie and Tommy were face-to-face, just staring at each other.

"Tommy, I don't know what trip you're on, but your vacation ends right here right now. And the shit stops right now!" Louie shouted as he turned around.

"But, Louie," Tommy said, and Louie turned back.

"Shut up! Just shut the fuck up! I've heard everything you had to say for the last month to a month and a half! And lately you haven't been quite the person we all have known for the past three years. Now, I don't know if you've noticed, but everyone here is sick and tired of this fucked-up attitude you have. I don't know if you changed or if there's something going on in your personal life that isn't going so good." Louie sat on the edge of his desk as Tommy turned his head, facing him from the side, with his arms folded. "Maybe you just have a fucked-up personal life, and maybe whatever is going on completely changed you from the person you used to be! I don't know. I'm just disgusted at this point in time! I'm not a goddamn counselor, but I strongly urge you to see one! Today I'll give you one last chance. Now, if you screw up again, the next one will be on you, all right?" Louie asked.

Tommy nodded, agreeing with Louie.

"Now, get the hell out of my office, and get your ass to work!" Louie shouted, and he and Tommy went back to work, walking toward the carts at the corner of the center.

Louie was on one side of the cart, and Tommy was on the other side of the cart. They stared at each other. Tommy looked down into the cart and then looked back at Louie as Louie just stared at him, wondering what he was thinking, with his unlit cigar dangling from the corner of his mouth.

While still staring at Louie, Tommy straightened up, and then he walked toward his locker. Louie watched Tommy walk toward his locker, wondering why but, at the same time, not shocked.

When Tommy arrived at his locker, he opened it and then took off his work smock. Louie took out his unlit cigar and threw it into the trash can at the corner near the counter behind him as Tommy took out a plastic bag from the bottom of his locker. He began filling the big black plastic bag with his personal items from inside his locker.

"Where are you going?" Louie asked as he leaned over the cart while Tommy was filling his bag.

"What does it look like I'm doing?" Tommy asked with his back turned toward Louie, still filling his bag. He looked over his shoulder at Maria, who was looking at what was going on from the side of her eyes.

After Tommy cleared out his locker, emptying it of his personal items, he slammed shut the door for the final time, and the sound echoed throughout the messenger center. Everyone looked on as he picked up the plastic bag and turned around, facing Louie.

"Hey, Louie?" Tommy called out.

"Yes, Tommy?" Louie responded as he looked at him, knowing what was about to happen. It was quiet in the center.

"I quit! You can keep this fucking job!" Tommy shouted.

Maria was sitting at her desk, covering her face with both hands, not believing this was going on. As Tommy walked toward the entrance of the messenger center, Maria kept her face covered with her hands, with her elbows on the desk. Louie followed Tommy from behind.

"Tommy, wait!" Louie called out as he quickly grabbed his arm from behind, making Tommy turn around.

"What?" Tommy asked, partially turned around, not resisting Louie for the moment. "Let go!" Tommy shouted as he shrugged off Louie's hand from his arm.

"Tommy, you've been here for three years. And you're even due for a promotion in one more year. Don't do this to your job! Don't do this to me! Don't fuck up your life," Louie whispered as he pointed at him.

"Don't fuck up my life? My life is already fucked up! I don't have Crystal!" Tommy shouted as he laughed slightly. "I'm already fucked." Tommy swung the plastic bag over his shoulder and stormed off out of the center, and Louie closed the door at the entrance.

"Crystal? Who's Crystal?" Louie asked himself as he turned around and walked toward his office in the back.

Maria watched from the side of her eyes, knowing full well who Crystal was.

When Louie entered his office, he slammed the door shut, and the slamming echoed throughout the basement.

Maria looked toward the entrance, wishing and hoping Tommy would change his mind and come back to work, but as time went on, he never did, and Maria covered her face again with her hands, with her elbows on her desk, while a couple of the workers from the back went toward the belated deliveries in the carts to deliver them to the upper floors.

A train arrived at the station where Tommy was. When the train stopped at the platform and the doors slid open, Tommy entered the semicrowded train; meanwhile, at his apartment, the telephone rang, and the answering machine picked up and recorded a message.

"Tommy, this is Sandy Leonard. I need to see you soon. All right? I want you and I to keep up the appointments. I want to advise you that it would be prudent and beneficial for you to keep all of your appointments with me. Call me as soon as you can. Bye, Tommy."

Beep! The answering machine tape stopped and then rewound itself back, saving the message.

When the train was going over the Manhattan Bridge, Tommy could see the Brooklyn Bridge, with a magnificent view of the skyline, minus the World Trade Center towers, because of what had happened on September 11, 2001. Tommy looked down at the floor of the train, remembering the Twin Towers. He removed his glasses and covered his face with his hands, remembering a friend who'd died on the eightieth floor on that dreadful morning.

After a little while, Tommy arrived at the station near where he lived, and when the train stopped completely and the doors slid open, he exited with his plastic bag full of his belongings from his locker. Instead, of going straight home to his apartment, he went to the deli on the corner. When he entered the deli, the bell on the door rang loudly.

"Husson!" Tommy shouted as he approached the counter.

"Tommy! How is everything? I haven't seen you for a while now!" Husson smiled, wearing his white apron, standing next to the cash register.

"Yeah, I've been very busy lately," said Tommy, looking over the menu above the counter.

"Oh yeah? Me too," said Husson.

"I would like to order a salami and provolone hero with extra mayo and no lettuce and tomato," said Tommy as he looked through the glass where the meats and cheeses were kept refrigerated.

"All right, Tommy." Husson put mayonnaise on both sides of the hero bread after he sliced it open.

"All right, Crystal. Break time," said one of her coworkers.

"All right. I'll get my purse before I go. See you in fifteen minutes," said Crystal as she exited the reception desk.

She exited the building and approached the fountain area on the side of the building, where the cement benches were. It was sunny and breezy, and when she sat down, she basked in the sunshine as the sun's rays poured down from the skies above the buildings along Sixth Avenue.

With her eyes closed, she took advantage of the time she had on her break. One of her coworkers sat next to her on the cement bench. Crystal opened her eyes and saw Dawn sitting next to her.

"What's up, Dawn?" Crystal asked as she and Dawn smiled at each other.

"Nothing much. So how are things between you and the dark-eyed prince with dark hair?" Dawn asked, and she and Crystal laughed.

"Great. We're doing great. Everything is actually coming together little by little. I had him stay with me during the Thanksgiving holiday weekend, and my family came over, and everyone met him. Everything went really well." Crystal smiled softly.

"Oh yeah?" Dawn responded as she smiled.

"Yes. They loved him big-time. More than I thought in the beginning, and he loved them as well. We all had a great time on the holiday weekend," said Crystal, enjoying the sunshine.

"That's good. Crystal, I admire you," said Dawn as she felt a little embarrassed.

"Why?" Crystal asked, and she and Dawn laughed.

"You just received a promotion not too long ago from the job, so you're making tons of money. And on top of that, you met a wonderful and handsome businessman who's well established in his business and also unattached to anyone. And now you have this pretty good relationship with him. Long distance for now, but it looks good to me. Man, you have it all, and that is so cool!" Dawn smiled.

"Yeah, but you're missing just one other thing," said Crystal as she and Dawn rose from the cement bench, as their break time was over.

"Oh yeah? What did I leave out?" Dawn asked as they walked toward the entrance of the building and entered.

"You forgot to mention that there's a crazy stalker on the loose who's after me!" said Crystal as she and Dawn rushed back to the reception area.

"Tommy, this is Sandy Leonard. I need to see you soon. I want to keep up our appointments, if you would like to. I would like to advise you that it would be prudent and beneficial for you to keep coming to see me. Call me as soon as you can. Bye, Tommy."

Beep! The answering machine rewound itself to the beginning of the tape, and then it stopped. Tommy was on the couch, eating his salami with provolone hero, in deep thought. After listening to the message Sandy Leonard had left on his answering machine, he continued eating his sandwich.

The next day arrived, and Tommy exited the elevator and approached the reception desk at his counselor's office.

"Hi. I'm Tommy Landis."

"Oh, all right. Have a seat, and I'll let Sandy Leonard know you're waiting to see her," said the receptionist, and Tommy walked over toward the waiting area while the receptionist called Sandy Leonard to inform her of his arrival.

✦✦✦✦✦✦

Crystal was at the reception desk in the busy office building where she worked. When business died down, Crystal picked up the receiver of the telephone and called the police department near where she lived to see if she could do something about Tommy's interference in her life.

"Thirty-first precinct. How can I help you?" the police officer at the desk asked.

"Yes, my name is Crystal Farnsworth, and I—"

"Excuse me? What was your name?" he asked.

"My name is Crystal Farnsworth, and I would like to speak with Officer Clemens, please," she said, wishing all of this would end soon.

"All right. What does this pertain to?" the police officer asked as he was looking through some paperwork.

"A follow-up call pertaining to my order of protection," Crystal said, hoping that it wouldn't get busy at her job while she was speaking on the telephone and hoping that she would not get caught by her supervisor.

"All right. Hold, please," the police officer said, and she transferred the call to Officer Clemens's office.

"Officer Clemens."

"Hi. This is Crystal Farnsworth. You assisted me in obtaining an order of protection against an obsessive man who lives in Brooklyn, and I—"

"And this man's name?" Officer Clemens asked, going through her order of protection files.

"His name is Tommy Landis." Crystal hoped for no interruptions from her job as she looked around the lobby, and her coworkers wondered what she was doing.

"Mr. Tommy Landis from Brooklyn. Ah, OK," Officer Clemens responded, going through her files on the computer as she had the phone receiver on her shoulder. "Here we go." She found his file, and it appeared on her screen. "All right, I found his file, and this is a follow-up call, right?" the officer asked.

"Yes. Can I place you on hold for a moment, please? I'm at my job," Crystal said, and she placed the officer on hold.

"Mr. Tommy Landis?"

"Oh, hi," Tommy responded as he raised his right hand while still sitting in a chair in the waiting area.

"All right, Mr. Landis. Come with me, please," said Sandy, and she and Tommy walked to her office.

"Dawn, can you take over for me while I continue talking to a police officer on the telephone?" Crystal asked as she rose from where she was sitting, and Dawn took over at the desk, while someone took over what Dawn had been doing prior.

"OK, no problem," said Dawn, and she and Crystal smiled at each other, as Dawn knew what the call to the police was about.

"Officer Clemens, I'm sorry for that hold. I'm presently at my job," Crystal explained.

"That's quite all right. OK, Miss Farnsworth, is there something he has done recently to you that violates the order of protection?" Officer Clemens asked, reading the order while speaking to Crystal.

"Well, he hasn't done anything for the moment, but I received a phone call from someone. I don't know if I can prove that it was him, but—"

"Maybe a whisper? Carefully disguising his voice?" the officer asked.

"The voice was disguised well," said Crystal as she grew more confident that the caller was him. At the same time, she knew it was going to be hard to prove that it was Tommy.

"Oh really?" the officer said as she put down the order of protection on her desk. "Well, when this disguised voice spoke, what did it say?" The officer took a pen from the pencil holder and started writing on her pad, recording the conversation between herself and Crystal.

"When I received the phone call, the caller said, 'Love of the twisted,' in a whisper," said Crystal as she smiled at her coworkers, wishing the call would end soon so she could resume working at the desk.

"Love of the twisted? Hmm." Officer Clemens thought about it while sticking the end of the pen in her mouth.

"Tommy, the last time you were here in my office, you said something that sort of baffled me. I wrote it down in my report from the last session we had. You said, 'Love of the twisted.' Can you please explain what this means?" Sandy asked, sitting behind her desk with her pad and pen, writing down the current interview, as Tommy sat in the chair in front of her desk.

"You want me to explain what I meant when I said, 'Love of the twisted'?" he asked while he laughed at her.

"Crystal, sounds like Tommy Landis to me, according to the history of the order of protection. And you are right. As far as proving it was Tommy, we can't at this time, but for now, just be alert. There isn't really anything we can do at this point. Even though you have the hookups on your telephone at home, he might've used a pay phone on the street. I don't think the number that popped up on your caller ID was his number, was it?" the officer asked.

"No. It definitely wasn't his phone number. All right. Thanks anyway," Crystal replied, hoping she was being understood.

"Now, I know it's a bit hard to deal with, but hang in there for a while longer. Sooner or later, he'll screw up, and I'll be there personally to book him, and we'll put him away for a long time. All right?" the officer said as she was putting away the order of protection back in his file.

"All right. I guess we can only hope for the best," said Crystal as she smiled halfway.

"Yes. But like I said, sooner or later, he'll screw up, and then we'll have him in our hands. All right?" Officer Clemens said as she smiled.

"All right. Thank you for your time, Officer Clemens. Goodbye," Crystal responded before hanging up her telephone.

"Goodbye, Miss Farnsworth," said Officer Clemens before she hung up the telephone.

———— ✦✦✦✦✦ ————

"Try to reach down inside yourself, Tommy. For what reason would you want to say something like that?" Sandy asked as she stood by her office window to the right of her desk, looking out the window, which overlooked the Hudson River, as Tommy, still in his chair, listened to her question.

"Crystal is the love of my life. And it's crazy that we as humans would do pretty much anything to be with the person we're in love with. That's the twisted thing about love." Tommy smiled slightly while he looked down at the carpeted floor.

"And obsession. Aren't love and obsession a bit twisted, Tommy?" Sandy asked while she stood behind him, looking at the top of his head.

He began to feel a little anxious. "Wait a minute! I know about love being a little twisted, but obsession? You have the wrong freak!"

Tommy shouted as he looked up at Sandy, who was still standing behind him. She was looking out the window at a few ships sailing across
the river, and then she quickly looked down at him again.

————— ✦✦✦✦✦ —————

"All right, sir. You're going to the twenty-second floor," said Crystal as
she made a pass for the guest to place on himself.

"Thank you, Crystal," said the visitor as he placed the sticker on
his suit blazer.

"Have a good day, sir," said Crystal, and she looked over at Dawn,
who was a few feet away, at the other side of the desk. "Dawn, thanks
for taking over while I was on the phone with the police officer," said
Crystal as she smiled at Dawn.

"No problem, Crystal. I totally understand. Is that nut still stalking
you?" Dawn whispered as she leaned over while gathering some of her
paperwork for the day.

"I don't know, Dawn. But recently, I received a phone call with
some whispering, and the caller disguised his voice on the other end
of the phone. If I was going to bet my life's fortune on it, I'd say it was
Tommy. He was saying stupid things over the telephone," said Crystal.

"Oh yeah?" Dawn responded with amazement, but she was not
too surprised.

"Yeah. So on top of stalking me, he calls and plays these stupid
little games over the telephone. It's a psycho thing that's going on,"
said Crystal as she pointed toward her head.

"It sure is." Dawn laughed, and Crystal joined in on the laughter.
"Unbelievable, Crystal. I don't know how you deal with it. If it were me
in the same situation, it would drive me to the point of going crazy. I
don't know how you deal with it. I would go absolutely out of mind,"
said Dawn as she sat back, getting ready to sign someone in at the
desk, shaking her head.

————— ✦✦✦✦✦ —————

"So how are things going at your job?" Sandy asked, sitting behind her desk.

"What job? I quit yesterday," said Tommy, standing near the window, looking down at the city streets, looking at all the people coming and going with their busy lives. He wished he had a life. A different life like everyone else's.

"Tommy, why did you quit your job?" Sandy asked as she drank some coffee from her coffee cup as it turned cold.

"Why did I quit my job? I had problems on the job. And sometimes, if you don't mind me changing the subject, I feel like Crystal is taking up my whole life! And I just don't know what to do about it!" Tommy shouted as he approached Sandy's desk, and when he arrived at the front of the desk, he slammed both his hands down on the desktop.

Sandy was startled by Tommy's outburst, and she jumped and stood up. "Tommy, you're feeling a bit frustrated."

"Well, no shit, Doctor," Tommy responded sarcastically as he turned around, facing the door.

"What I want to do is prescribe some depression medication, and I suggest indefinite counseling here with me. All right? You need to cope with this situation. You need to know how to deal with this problem, Tommy. You need to deal with this roller-coaster ride we call life," Sandy said, writing on her clipboard.

"Yeah, so you're going to prescribe something, like Prozac or something? But I can tell you that it won't change my feelings about Crystal." Tommy sat back down in the chair in front of the desk.

"Tommy, as far as getting over Crystal, that's on you, but the Prozac or whatever I give you will help you cope and deal with your life, even without Crystal. I personally know how it is to get into a rut." Sandy sternly looked at Tommy while he looked up at her.

"Yeah." Tommy looked around the office, still seated in his chair.

"So I'll prescribe something to you for your depression, and I believe medical insurance will cover the bill—but you mentioned you just quit your job," said Sandy, looking through her papers in his file.

"Yeah, I quit, but my medical benefits are still good for another month," Tommy said, wearing half a smile.

"Oh really? Well, that's good. Well then, use it while it's there. All right?" Sandy asked while writing out his prescription. When Sandy finished writing down the prescription for Tommy, she handed it to him over the desk.

Tommy took the prescription she'd filled out for him and read it.

"In the meantime, look for a job, and let this be a new beginning for you. When you arrive back at your apartment, just take a deep breath, and think to yourself that this will be a new beginning. All right?" She rose from behind her desk as Tommy rose from where he was sitting. "Thanks for coming in today. I'll be in touch with you soon to schedule a new appointment, and we'll meet again, all right?" She held out a hand, and his hand met hers.

As they shook hands, for the first time, Tommy finally thought about moving on with his life and leaving Crystal far behind him—for the moment.

CHAPTER 21

THE DAY HAD COME TO an end, and when Crystal was properly relieved by a coworker, she went to the ladies' locker room. When she left the reception area and went up the escalator, a man to the side in the lobby was watching her while holding up a newspaper, shielding himself, wearing a pair of sunglasses. When he lowered his newspaper slowly, he removed his sunglasses and saw Crystal coming off the escalator.

After a little while, Crystal exited the front entrance of the office building and started her journey home to the Upper East Side in Manhattan.

As she walked fast past the big cement fountain at the side of the building, Tommy was hiding, wearing a pair of black sunglasses and a long black trench coat.

After she walked by, he waited until she was at least fifty feet away, and then he pursued her from behind. Dawn, one of Crystal's coworkers, was right behind him on her way home, though she had no idea who was five feet ahead of her. But as she walked quickly behind Tommy, she noticed the man following Crystal. She had no idea who the man was. As she looked ahead over his shoulder, she saw Crystal some distance away from him. Crystal was walking toward the subway, going home. Dawn watched the man in front of her follow Crystal, and she remembered seeing a man in the lobby wearing the same attire the man in front of her was wearing. She realized who the man might be: Tommy!

Thinking quickly, Dawn rushed past Tommy and ran toward Crystal, leaving Tommy behind. Tommy wondered who had brushed right by him, silently panicking, feeling he might be discovered soon.

"Hey, Crystal! Crystal!" Dawn shouted.

Tommy panicked upon hearing the woman call out to Crystal, and he stopped the pursuit and quickly walked toward a busy crowd of pedestrians, blending in, as he didn't want to be discovered. He walked across the street on his left side.

When Crystal heard her name being called out, she quickly turned around and, pulling off her headphones connected to her Discman, saw a familiar face.

"Dawn?" Crystal called out. She smiled but wondered why Dawn was out of breath. Dawn wore a worried look on her face as she called to Crystal again while approaching her as Crystal stood where she was.

"Hey, Dawn. What's up?" Crystal asked as Dawn walked up to her.

"Crystal!" Dawn called out her name again while trying to catch her breath. "Crystal, there was a man following you from behind. Really. I saw him."

"What?" Crystal asked as she turned off her Discman, not believing what she'd just heard.

"Crystal, there was a man following you. At first, I saw him in the lobby. And then I saw him as you were going up the escalator on your way to the ladies' locker room. The whole time, he's been watching you," Dawn said as Crystal kept shaking her head in disbelief at what she was hearing.

"And then, when you were walking out of the building on your way home, he was behind you at a distance, and I was behind him. I was on my way home, not realizing at first that I was right behind him!" Dawn said.

As they continued talking, they didn't notice the mysterious man in the trench coat in the midst of the crowd of people on their way home. Crystal and Dawn looked around while standing at the corner.

"He must've run away in that direction." Dawn pointed across the street to her right, which was Tommy's left side. "Yeah, he must've run when I was calling out to you. You think maybe it could've been Tommy once again?" Dawn asked as Crystal was putting on her headphones.

"I think it was Tommy," said Crystal as she thought about it for a moment. "I know it was Tommy again. Well, Dawn, I appreciate you telling me about this. You might've saved my life. Thanks, Dawn." Crystal and Dawn hugged each other, and then they together walked to the subway, on their way to their homes.

• • ✦ ✦ ✦ ✦ • •

The evening arrived, and Tommy was sitting on his recliner, watching television. All of a sudden, the telephone rang. Tommy leaned over to the side table next to his recliner and reached for the telephone.

"Hello?" Tommy said.

"Hello, Tommy. How are you?" Maria asked.

"Maria?" Tommy wondered why she was calling.

"Yes, this is Maria," she responded, hoping he didn't hang up on her.

"Hi." Tommy sank deeper into his recliner, as he felt somewhat uncomfortable with the phone call.

"I'm sorry to hear about what happened this morning at the center," said Maria, talking slowly.

"You're sorry? What are you sorry for?" he asked, wanting to hang up on her.

"Well, you know how Louie is. I was just apologizing for him," said Maria, feeling sorry for him.

"So Louie wants me back at the messenger center?" he asked, reluctant to go back to work at the messenger center.

"No. No way. By the way he was upset the whole day until the time everyone went home, I doubt it. I don't think he wants to see you again after what happened." Maria started to laugh with tears in her eyes while remembering how upset Louie had been and how he'd looked the whole day.

Tommy laughed along with her as they continued talking.

----------◆◆◆◆◆----------

The next day arrived, as the sun rose behind the Manhattan skyline as the concrete empire of buildings stood tall, Tommy was inside Sandy's office. She and Tommy were having another session.

"Tommy, I'm sorry I called you late last night on short notice," said Sandy.

"That's all right," Tommy responded as he smiled halfway.

"So how's your job search going?" she asked as she smiled.

"I haven't really looked around yet." Tommy was embarrassed by his current situation.

"All right. You need to plan for a new way of life as soon as you can, Tommy." Sandy was seated at her desk, and he sat in front of the desk.

"I quit my job. So?" said Tommy with folded arms.

"All right. Were you planning at some point to find another job?" she asked.

"I don't know. I have some money saved in my savings account at the bank for now," said Tommy as he looked down at the carpeted floor.

"How long will that last?" Sandy asked while she leaned back in her chair.

"Get off my back!" Tommy shouted as he rose quickly from where he was sitting. He walked toward the door and leaned against the wall with his back facing Sandy, who rose from her desk and walked over toward Tommy while he continued to stand against the wall with his back facing her.

"Tommy, I haven't known you long, but I do know about the problem you have at this time. I really do know about the problem you have, this obsession. I know the havoc it can bring to one's life. Both to the victims and their families and to the person who is obsessed." Sandy turned his body around to face her.

"Well, if I'm obsessed, then so be it. I feel at this point, it's overcome my life, and I'm into this life way too deeply; there's nothing that can help me now. All I can do now is hope that this thing we call obsession eats me up quickly and that this whole damn thing ends soon. And if there's pain, maybe God will have mercy upon my soul, and maybe he might just forgive me," Tommy said while looking down as Sandy stared him and listened to a bitter man speak.

"Yeah, but, Tommy?" she called out to him, wishing he would listen to what she'd been saying, and he looked up at her.

"Goodbye, Sandy Leonard. Thank you for trying to help me," said Tommy as he opened up the door and exited the office. In the hallway, he turned around quickly, shut the office door, and continued on his way to the receptionist area.

After he shut the door, Sandy looked up at the door as she listened to the cold silence that filled her office, this time not chasing after him.

"Goodbye, Tommy. Good luck, wherever this trip takes you," Sandy whispered to herself as she leaned up against her desk, rethinking the sessions she'd had with Tommy, wondering if she could've done more. But she knew she had done all she could.

Crystal entered her apartment and shut the door behind her. She entered the living room, turned on the light with a flick of the switch on the wall, removed her coat, opened the closet, and hung up her coat. After she shut the door to closet, she walked toward the middle of the living room, and the doorbell rang. She quickly rushed toward the door to see who was there. She peeked through the peephole, recognized who it was, and quickly opened the door.

"Darlene. How's everything? Come in," said Crystal, and Darlene entered the apartment.

"Oh, nothing much going on. Can we talk?" Darlene asked as she and Crystal entered the living room.

Darlene removed her coat, and Crystal took her coat to the closet in the hallway and hung it up. Darlene went to the couch with Crystal behind her.

"So what do you want to talk about, Sis?" Crystal asked as she smiled, and Darlene smiled back. Suddenly, Crystal rose quickly to close the front door all the way.

After Crystal shut the door all the way, she reentered the living room, rejoining her sister, as their expressions became more serious.

"Crystal, I know we have had numerous conversations about Tommy, but I truly think and feel that your life is in grave danger," said Darlene, holding her sister's hand.

"Danger? Darlene, aren't you being a little melodramatic about this whole damn thing?" Crystal asked as she rose and parted hands with Darlene as the telephone rang. "Let me answer this call. I'll be just a quick moment. All right?" Crystal rushed to the other side of the side table to answer the telephone.

"Hello?" Crystal answered as she looked over at Darlene.

"Crystal, it's Jim. How are you?" he asked as he smiled.

"I'm doing all right. Hey, Jim, I have my sister, Darlene, here with me right now, and we're talking right now. Can I call you back later?" Crystal asked as she smiled at Darlene, and Darlene cracked a half smile while looking down at the carpeted floor in the living room.

"Sure. Tell Darlene I said hello, all right?" said Jim.

"OK, I will. Goodbye," said Crystal.

"OK, bye," said Jim, and he and Crystal hung up their phones.

After Crystal put down the receiver, she quickly rejoined her sister on the couch, rejoining their conversation. "All right, Darlene, what in the world do you mean when you say *danger*? Do you know something I don't?" Crystal asked.

"Well, Crystal, think about it for a moment. What does *danger* mean?" Darlene asked as Crystal's and her smiles converted to more serious looks.

"Well, *danger* means to me something fatal or threatening to life. I don't know," said Crystal, wondering where this was leading.

"You're right, Crystal. You're absolutely right. Something or some-one threatening your life. This is the danger I'm talking about."

"Oh, all right. You feel that Tommy will kill me, right?" Crystal asked as she rose from the couch, and Darlene looked up at her, still seated on the couch.

"Bingo! You got it!" Darlene answered as she rose from where she was sitting as Crystal sat back down on the couch. "Crystal, I love you. You're my sister—my only sister—and maybe I don't want to lose you." Darlene knelt while she began to weep, and they embraced each other, with their arms wrapped around each other tightly.

"Darlene, I love you too. I understand and appreciate everything you're telling me. Don't think I don't. I really do," said Crystal, con-soling Darlene, as they continued embracing each other with their eyes closed. "Do you want something to drink?" Crystal asked, and Darlene nodded, so they went into the kitchen.

———————— ✦✦✦✦✦ ————————

Tommy arrived home, and when he entered his apartment, the tele-phone rang. On the way to answer the phone call, he flicked the switch on the wall, and the light came on.

"Hello?" Tommy answered, wondering who it might be.

"Hello, Tommy. It's Maria. Where did you go? I was trying to call you earlier, but you weren't home."

"I went to take care of something in Manhattan. Why?" Tommy asked.

"I was just wondering. That's all." Maria knew it wasn't any of her business, and there was a slight pause between them.

"OK, so is there anything else you needed to ask me, or is there another reason for this telephone call out of the blue?" Tommy asked as he grew impatient with the conversation while he removed his glasses. He rested his glasses on the side table, where the telephone was, and rubbed his eyes, feeling sleepy.

"Tommy, you don't want to talk to me?" she asked, and silence crept between them momentarily while she smiled, twirling her shoulder-length black hair with one of her fingers.

"Look! Why do you persist in pushing yourself onto me? I don't want you anywhere near me! Not even on the telephone!" Tommy shouted.

Silence filled the air again, and each one thought the other person had hung up the phone as the silence grew so thick that one could have cut it with a butter knife.

"Why do you persist?" Maria asked as she clenched her teeth, feeling insulted by his comments.

"Huh? What?" Tommy asked, feeling somewhat confused as she used a little mind-bending technique on the suddenly upside-down conversation. "I'm the one who's persistent? How do you figure? Persisting in what?" he asked, wondering what she was trying to say.

"You persist in trying to be with Crystal, when she has no intention of ever being with you!" she shouted.

"First of all, how would you know what's going on in my life? And even if you have any idea what's going on in my life, that's none of your goddamn business!" he shouted as he pointed a finger toward the mirror in the living room.

"Yeah, but, Tommy, I—"

"Yeah, but what? Bye!" Tommy shouted.

After he hung up the telephone, he sat down on the recliner and covered his face with both hands, wishing this twisted nightmare would end soon.

♦♦♦♦♦

"Darlene, I really understand what you were saying earlier about Tommy. But I will be all right. I don't foresee anything like what you mentioned earlier happening to me." Crystal drank some orange juice, feeling confident about what she'd just said to Darlene, as they walked out of the kitchen and toward the couch. They sat down and continued the conversation.

"But, Crystal, I have a strange feeling about this guy. He isn't wrapped too tightly, if you know what I mean," said Darlene as she pointed to one of her temples while drinking the rest of her orange juice with the other hand.

"I know what you mean. After work today, while I was on the way to the subway, on the way home, Tommy was stalking me from behind," said Crystal as she set down her glass of orange juice on the coffee table.

"See? That son of a bitch!" Darlene shouted in a whisper.

"But at the same time, a coworker of mine was right behind him. She ran past him, and when she reached me, she informed me as I was approaching the corner of Sixth Avenue. She told me he was behind me at a distance, and she'd been walking right behind him," Crystal said.

"See? See that?" Darlene shouted, desperate for her sister to do something more than what she was doing.

"I know. But I already checked in with the police department, and so far, I haven't heard anything from them. He might be a touch crazy, but I don't think he's stupid enough to waste his life stalking and carrying on. This won't last forever, Darlene." Crystal reached for her glass from the coffee table and drank the rest of the orange juice from her glass.

"Well, he's not stupid. He's just obsessed with you. My sister of mine, I hope you're right about this not going on forever, because it sure feels like it will," said Darlene as she sat back on the sofa with her arms folded, feeling wary of the situation.

———————— ✦✦✦✦✦ ————————

Tommy lay on his bed, still in his clothes, on his back with his hands folded behind his head, with his head on the pillow. He looked up at the ceiling, wearing no glasses, with the lamp on the side table illuminated. He just stared up at the ceiling, in deep thought, plotting his next move and where he would like to make it.

———————— ✦✦✦✦✦ ————————

The weekend arrived, and Crystal called Jim as she sat up in bed, wearing nothing but a long T-shirt that said, "I love NY."

"Hey, Jim, I'm sorry I didn't call you back last night. You see—"

"Your sister, Darlene?" Jim asked.

"Yeah. She and I were talking, and before we knew it, time came and went so fast, and it was late." Crystal laughed a little.

"Yes, I know how that is. I wanted to let you in on something I found out yesterday, which was why I called last night," he said as he smiled.

"Oh yeah? What?" Crystal asked as she smiled and sat up straighter in bed.

"I got my transfer!" Jim shouted with a tremendous smile on his face.

"You did? Oh my God! That's so cool!" Crystal shouted with excitement.

"Yes, Crystal, that's real cool, but it's not in New York," said Jim as he looked out his living room window, watching the traffic below his apartment, as the skyline in metropolitan Dallas shimmered with the lights coming from the buildings.

"It's not?" Crystal asked as she frowned.

"No. The transfer will be to New Jersey." Jim was sure she wouldn't mind.

"All right. Where in New Jersey?" she asked anxiously.

"Oh, I'm just over the river, in Jersey City. So I'm not far from you at all."

"This is so cool! We'll be able to see each other more now!" Crystal felt overwhelmingly excited.

"Exactly my thoughts, love! I miss you so very much!" Jim smiled, walking away from the window with one hand in his pocket.

"I miss you too, Jim," said Crystal, looking down at the carpeted floor, while walking about the living room, thinking about the mishaps of Tommy Landis and his craziness in her life. She would have given anything to be safe in Jim's arms that morning.

"Crystal, is that guy still bothering you? You know, stalking or calling you?" Jim asked, as he sensed what she might've been thinking during their conversation.

"Truthfully?" she asked.

"Truthfully," he responded softly and patiently as he laid down his heart, showing how much he cared.

"Well, he still stalks me, but you see, the last time he did it, I couldn't even prove it. Even though I informed the police of what happened, they said there wasn't really anything I could do, because I have to see him stalking me and not hear it secondhand from someone telling me he's right behind me. You see, a coworker informed me on the street when I was on my way home, but when I turned around, he was gone. But according to one of my coworkers, he was behind me, at a distance. And my sister, Darlene, thinks he's going to kill me if I don't do anything else. But I have been doing something about it. But lately he's gotten sneakier and more cunning. Anyway, I was trying to explain to Darlene last night that the police couldn't do anything about the last incident, the one I just told you, because it was word of mouth. It kind of sucks right now, but there's nothing I can do right now but hope for the best," Crystal said as she grew frustrated, partially covering her face with one of her hands.

"So when will you have the proof? When he, God forbid, kills you?" Jim asked, feeling helpless.

"Jim, you sound like my sister! I don't want to talk about this anymore!" said Crystal as a tear rolled down one side of her face, reaching her lips.

"OK, all right. I'm sorry I made you cry. I just care about you, and I feel somewhat helpless right now. I'm in Dallas, and you're up there in New York," Jim said as he sympathized with Crystal and her problem.

"Jim, I'm sorry. I know you love me. So no apology needed. It's just that we have to sit it out and see what happens, all right?" Crystal took a tissue from the tissue box on her side table.

"All right, baby. I love you very much," said Jim as he went into his bedroom and imagined Crystal on his bed.

"I love you too. I really do love you," said Crystal, imagining him in front of her in a pajama pants, with no shirt, showing his muscular upper body.

"I can't wait to see you, my sweet." Jim smiled.

"I can't wait to see you again, babe," said Crystal, looking as though she were in a trance, hopelessly in love.

"Soon. Real soon. I promise you. Crystal, I have to take care of some errands right now, so we'll talk again soon, all right?" Jim smiled while sitting on his bed.

"All right, babe. But when is your transfer going to happen?" she asked as she rose from where she was sitting and walked toward one of the windows in the living room.

"Well, if things go the way they're supposed to go, it will be in one week!" Jim said, as excited as Crystal.

"Excellent! When you come out, we have to celebrate!" said Crystal as she turned around, facing the inner part of the living room.

"Definitely. I'm looking forward to it! OK, talk to you soon. Love you," said Jim.

"Love you too, Jim. Bye," said Crystal as she walked toward her side table.

"Goodbye," they both said, and they hung up their telephones.

After Crystal hung up, she walked back into her bedroom and lay down on her bed, on her back with her hands folded behind her head, wearing a big smile on her face.

* * * * * * *

Tommy was in his bed, under the blanket, lying on his back, looking up at the ceiling, calculating ideas. Many thoughts came and went through his mind. As though in a trance, he continued going over what to do with the current situation between himself and Crystal. While he continued swimming in his thoughts, he sort of knew he was a little obsessed, but at the same time, part of him felt that he and Crystal were meant to be in some way, even if they didn't end up romantically involved. In a moment of isolation, he spent the whole weekend pondering what his next move would be.

CHAPTER 22

A WEEK LATER, ON MONDAY MORNING, Crystal arrived at her place of employment as Tommy was at home in his apartment, pacing about the living room floor, trying to deal with his life. He quickly turned toward the television set as he grabbed the remote from the side table next to the recliner. He turned on the television and flipped through the different channels, looking for a program that could stimulate his mind and catch his interest and, at the same time, relieve his mind of the anguish that dwelled within. He saw an infomercial featuring a couple of people discussing the topic of mental problems. One of the problems they were discussing was obsession, which caught Tommy's attention. Tommy turned up the volume as he continued watching.

"Hi. I'm Dr. Leslie Choice, and my guest is Dr. Max DeFault. We're here today to discuss one of the mental problems we've discussed earlier, and that problem is obsession. Dr. DeFault, how are you?"

"I'm fine. Just fine."

"Good. That's good. Now, what can you tell our viewers about obsession?" Dr. Choice asked as she smiled.

"Dr. Choice, I specifically deal with patients who are obsessed."

"Now, Dr. DeFault, you say you treat patients who are obsessed. Is this obsession about love and rejection, or are there other kinds of obsessions you also deal with?" Dr. Choice asked.

"Well, as you know, there is more than one type of obsession, and of course, the most common kind of obsession is the love-and-rejection kind. But I deal with patients with all kinds of obsessions. Another one is obsession with a certain type of food. You know, pizza or other junk foods. One might have an out-of-control sweet tooth. Or be a neat freak. Everything has to be in the same order. In the refrigerator or around the home. A compulsive disorder and constant repetition until the person thinks something is perfect. The same old routine. And then there's love." Dr. DeFault smiled.

"Ah, love! That's *amore*! Probably the most common form of obsession, right?" Dr. Choice asked as she smiled halfway.

"Yes."

"Now, what's interesting about this particular form of obsession is that there are stages of this problem. Can you tell the television viewers those stages and symptoms of obsession when it comes to love and obsession?"

"Sure. The beginning stage is when a person doesn't accept the rejection of the person he's in love with."

"OK, that's when the obsession moments begin, right?"

"Yes. That's the first stage. After the obsessed individual has been rejected by the person he's in love with, the person who's obsessed does not accept the rejection; thus, that person goes through the first stage of this particular obsession."

"All right. I believe I'm getting what you're saying," said Dr. Choice as she smiled, making sure she knew what he was saying.

"It's a pretty deep-rooted form of obsession. The first stage is, of course, making telephone calls. Never-ending, ongoing phone calls," he said.

Tommy continued watching as though he were in a trance while the two doctors spoke about the ins and outs of obsession.

"Well, anyway, the obsessed person calls the person who rejected him, the one the obsessed person is in love with. The obsessed person calls, begging, pleading, and trying to convince the other person that they belong together. However, maybe the person who rejects isn't attracted to the person who's been rejected, or maybe the chemistry or whatever just isn't there," Dr. DeFault said as he crossed one of his legs over the other, getting comfortable.

"Uh-huh." Dr. Choice felt she was learning something for the first time.

"So the person who's obsessed continues begging and pleading, saying that they are no good if they are not together and that the obsessed person needs the other person in his life. No other person will do, even though the other person is still rejecting him. It must be this certain person, and the obsessed individual will not accept the fact that the other person is not attracted to him."

"Amazing. Simply amazing. Now, is there another stage to this obsession thing with love and rejection?" she asked, and her body movements showed she was really into the interview conversation while still seated in her chair.

"Yes. The telephone calls tend to run their course. The calling gets rather old and boring to the person who's obsessed. So the obsessed individual moves to the next stage of his obsession. And the next stage is stalking. Wherever the victim in question is, so is the obsessed person. Perhaps within arm's reach but most times at a distance. The victim in question will be followed home, to work, or wherever the victim goes. Wherever the victim is, anywhere, at any time," Dr. DeFault said, and the studio audience members were amazed at what the doctor guest was talking about.

"This is a very scary moment for the victim at this stage, right?" she asked as the studio audience looked on with interest.

"Oh, it is. It is. And believe it or not, this obsession thing happens to women as much as men," he said as he smiled.

"Oh yeah?" she responded, surprised.

"Oh yes." Dr. DeFault removed his glasses and began to wipe them with a handkerchief.

"Get out of here. Who would have thought? Women just as much as men? This is simply amazing," Dr. Choice responded with both hands in the air, bewildered by what her guest had just said.

"Yes, it is pretty amazing. And once he or she gets frustrated because things are moving slowly in the stalking department, he or she will move on to the third stage. But before moving to the third stage, this person will still use fear, intimidation, and threats to detain the victim."

"So what is the third stage of this kind of obsession?"

"This is the final stage. An end or closure to this obsession ride. The victim of the obsessed person is killed by the obsessed person because the victim chooses still not to be with the pursuer, and in most cases, the obsessed person kills him- or herself right after killing the victim. But in some cases, if the obsessed person doesn't kill him- or herself along with the victim, he or she eventually gets caught by law enforcement or, in rare cases, turns him- or herself in, going to prison or to a mental institution for the remainder of his or her life. In some cases, the obsessed person commits suicide while serving his or her time in prison or in a mental institution."

"It's a shame that some victims wouldn't go to the police after all of that," said Dr. Choice.

"Well, actually, most victims do go to the local authorities, and they do report these things that go on. But on the other hand, there are victims, men or women, who hesitate in calling. Either from laziness, or they simply think this obsession thing will just go away or stop. Hey, look, the longer the victim delays in calling, the longer he or she helps to keep the obsession alive. And that's the truth," Dr. DeFault said.

Tommy just sat there as the doctors continued discussing the topic of obsession, sitting on his recliner, looking straight ahead, in deep thought.

***

At an Uptown Manhattan subway, Crystal walked up the concrete steps from the East Eighty-Sixth Street station, on her way home to her apartment. When she arrived at the corner of the block, she walked around the corner, and from out of nowhere, Tommy shoved Crystal into a dimly lit alley.

As Tommy held her up against the graffiti-covered brick wall, he placed his right hand over her mouth to keep her from screaming and drawing attention as he placed a butcher knife to her throat. Crystal's eyes grew wide, filled with terror, as she saw Tommy staring at her while he pressed the ice-cold blade of the knife against her throat.

"Hey, Crystal. I'm so sorry it came down to this, but you left me no choice. Now, here's what we're going to do. We're going to your apartment. Yes, we are going to your apartment, and—"

She interrupted him, taking his hand off her mouth. "Tommy? Why are you doing this? This doesn't make sense. Please, whatever you do, don't hurt me, Tommy," Crystal whispered, pleading with Tommy, while she cried and shook her head, disapproving of the situation.

"No! No. If you don't cooperate with me, I'll kill you right here right now. Get it?" Tommy whispered into her ear, and she was too shocked to respond as he covered her mouth again with his right hand. "I want to ask you something, love. Must we be so rude to each other?" he whispered into her ear as he pulled back her head. While her head was tilted a little back against the brick wall, she nodded slowly, indicating she understood.

"Now, on the way to your apartment, I'm going to go inside your coat with the knife in my hand, and the knife will be placed against your back. If you decide to get stupid with me and try to free yourself from me, I have some news for you: you won't make it, because I will kill you right there on the spot you stand on. Get it?" he asked as he wore a deranged and desperate look on his face, and she nodded slowly as he removed his hand from the back of her head, letting go of the handful of hair in his grip.

"All right, now that we understand each other the way a man and a woman should, shall we go?" Tommy asked as he held the knife with his left hand inside the back of her coat, pressing it against her back, and grabbed one of her arms, trying to pull her along to start walking to the apartment up the street.

"Tommy? Please, Tommy, don't," Crystal whispered, pulling back, hesitating for a moment.

"Remember, my little bitch, no cooperation, no life. So let's go," he whispered as he had her against the brick wall again.

As she stood away from the brick wall, she stared at him, looking into his demented eyes, while he touched with his fingertips her firm, average-sized breasts with one hand.

"No! Don't touch me!" Crystal shouted as she became even more terrified and stepped away while she thought about the times she had gone to the police and filed an order of protection against him. Maybe she hadn't been on top of it like she'd thought. She remembered Darlene suggesting during their conversations about Tommy what he might do if things became worse.

Crystal started shaking nervously, feeling horrified at the situation, which was increasingly looking ugly. When she pulled back, Tommy pulled the blade to its side, placing the sharp tip against her spine.

"I'll cripple you, you fucking bitch," Tommy whispered as they walked out of the dimly lit alley and proceeded to the apartment.

As they walked, behind them at a distance, Maria followed, watching what was taking place, careful not to be discovered by Tommy's insanity. Maria had been watching since the beginning, when they had gone into the alley, and she couldn't believe it. She believed Tommy had finally flipped.

"He's gone mad. I can't believe how low Tommy has become," she whispered to herself as she continued hiding from a distance as Tommy and Crystal continued walking toward the apartment building together side by side, looking like a loving couple. Tommy wished that was a reality.

As Tommy and Crystal approached the apartment building, two elderly women exited the building. Maria wasn't far behind, but she kept her distance, watching intensely the crazy situation.

"Hi, Crystal!" said one of the elderly women as she and her close friend, the other elderly lady, were walking out of the building, and they smiled at Crystal and then smiled at the man who was with her.

Crystal gave the other two elderly women a half smile, wishing she could tell them who this man was and what he was doing to her, but she feared she might get stabbed, shot, or just plain murdered, and if she involved the two elderly women, he might kill them too. Tommy gave a big, wide grin at the two elderly ladies, becoming increasingly nervous at the interruptions, wishing that none of this ever had happened, including the time when he'd met Crystal.

"Hi, Nancy, Edna," Crystal called out as she smiled halfway at the two elderly women.

"Who's your new friend?" Nancy asked while she smiled, and she looked toward her friend Edna.

Crystal was embarrassed because not long ago, she'd introduced them to her boyfriend, Jim Connors, and now she was seen with Tommy, who was not even a friend, let alone a boyfriend.

"Oh, this is Tommy. Tommy Landis. Tommy, this is Edna and Nancy. Tommy is a friend of my boyfriend, Jim Connors," said Crystal, and Tommy smiled while laughing halfway, pressing the sharp blade of the knife to her back, reminding her of what was waiting for her if she got out of line and didn't cooperate with him.

"Hi, Nancy, Edna," said Tommy, annoyed with Crystal for calling him by his name. He continued smiling halfway as he wondered when they were going to continue their trip to her apartment.

Edna noticed Tommy's arm inside Crystal's coat, as though he had his arm around her but inside her coat. "OK, Crystal. Nice to meet you, Tommy," said Edna as she smiled at Tommy and Crystal.

"All right, Tommy," said Nancy, and as she and Edna walked away, Tommy felt relieved.

"All right, Crystal. Shall we proceed?" he asked as he smiled devilishly, with evil intentions awaiting them upstairs at Crystal's apartment.

Edna and Nancy looked back at them while they were entering the apartment building.

"I thought she was involved with that young man from Dallas, Texas. What was his name?" Edna asked.

"I believe you're talking about James," Nancy said.

"Yes and no. I believe his name was Jim," said Edna.

"Yes. Yes, that's him," Nancy responded excitedly as she smiled while they walked toward the corner.

"And now she's seeing this young fellow," said Edna. "Well, I guess young couples don't stay together long these days. They come and go now."

"Yes, they sure do. I guess the world has changed," said Nancy, and they laughed while looking at each other.

"Yes, it has," said Edna as they went across the street to the next block.

At the apartment building, in the lobby, Tommy and Crystal went into an elevator, with the blade of the knife at her back, inside her coat. When they were inside the elevator, the doors slid shut, and Crystal pressed the button hesitantly for the floor where her apartment was. Quickly, the elevator left the lobby level. As the elevator car was on its way to its destination, Tommy was thinking that this was his destiny, and he nodded slowly.

Meanwhile, Maria entered the lobby of the apartment building after watching through the glass of the outer metal-framed door and seeing Tommy and Crystal enter the elevator. She rushed toward the elevator bank to see where Tommy and Crystal got off the elevator, to see which floor she needed to go to. After she pressed the call button on the wall for an elevator to arrive in the lobby, she turned around and saw, on a marble table, a house phone. She wondered if she should call the police and not only end his punishment toward Crystal but also maybe end her obsession with him. Suddenly, another elevator arrived in the lobby, and when the doors slid open, she entered.

Tommy and Crystal stepped off the elevator and walked toward her apartment. Crystal physically struggled with Tommy as they walked closer toward the apartment, and getting frustrated with her, he swung her up against the wall next to her apartment door, with his butcher knife up against her throat. This time, the blade was touching her throat, and she felt the coldness of the blade against her soft neck as the lights from the ceiling in the hallway shone down on the blade.

The blade was pressed so hard against her neck that it made a red line against her skin.

"What?" Tommy asked as he stared deep into her eyes.

When Maria stepped into the elevator, she saw the two elderly women Crystal and Tommy had been talking to. They were approaching the elevator to enter, so Maria held the door for them. The two elderly women entered, and then the elevator door slid shut. Maria pressed the button for the floor she was going to.

"Ah, young lady? Can you press the button for the fifth floor, please? Thank you," said Edna, and she and Nancy smiled at Maria while she pressed the button for the fifth floor.

"Let's go. And don't try anything stupid, all right? Huh? Because I won't hesitate in killing you," said Tommy as he and Crystal proceeded to the front door of the apartment.

Edna and Nancy exited the elevator on the fifth floor. The elevator door slid shut, and the elevator proceeded to Maria's destined floor.

"Nancy?" Edna said, and they stopped after walking a few steps out of the elevator. "I don't know what it is, but I don't feel right about that young man who was with Crystal earlier downstairs when we ran into them at the entrance of the building. It's just a gut feeling. I don't know."

Edna and Nancy proceeded to their apartment. When they arrived at the front door, while looking for the keys in her purse, Edna looked at Nancy. She unlocked the front door.

"Well, Edna, it's really none of our business. But if something is truly wrong and something happens to Crystal, God forbid, I don't think we'll ever forgive ourselves. So later on, if you want, we can visit Crystal at her apartment and make sure everything is all right. OK?" Nancy said as she placed an arm around Edna as she unlocked the door with one of her keys from her key chain. The door opened, and they entered their apartment and shut the door behind them.

When the elevator stopped on the floor where Crystal's apartment was, Maria stepped out of the elevator. In the hallway, she saw many apartments as the elevator door slid shut. As she looked around, she listened for voices and sounds of struggling between the two of them. She approached the first apartment, which was opposite Crystal's apartment. As a dog was barking loudly and uncontrollably, she heard Tommy's voice faintly in the background of the barking. The familiar voice of her ex-coworker Tommy became louder as she slowly walked forward in the hallway.

Meanwhile, inside Crystal's apartment, Crystal was standing next to Tommy as he held on to her wrist. He saw a chair he wanted her to sit on, and he found a role of duct tape on the countertop, underneath the cupboards above. He stared at Crystal seductively, from her baby-blue eyes to her long, sleek blonde hair to her breasts to her feet. He looked at her as though he were in a daze. Then he walked to the kitchen table, grabbed one of the chairs, placed the chair in the middle of the kitchen, and sat her down forcefully. He slapped her on the right side of her face, and then he slapped her on the left side of her face with the back of his hand. He started wrapping the duct tape around her ankles and the legs of the chair, taping her legs to the chair, as he smiled at her.

Afraid and angry at him for what he was doing to her, while he was still smiling at her while on his knees, she slapped him on the face twice, once on each side of his face. When she slapped him, she took the smile off his face, and he stood up. His face not only was red but also bore Crystal's handprint. His eyes grew with rage and disappointment at the way things were going.

With both his hands clenched tightly, he shrugged off the sting of the unexpected slaps in the face. He smiled again, and he began to tie her wrists together with duct tape. Afterward, he threw the roll of duct tape onto the countertop and stared at her as she looked down at the tile floor. He walked in front of her, placed a finger underneath her chin, raised her face up slowly, and smiled at her. He nodded slowly as his smile faded away, and with a closed fist of fury, he punched her on her right cheek. With the impact of the punch, she almost fell off the chair. He laughed, while she was barely coherent after he punched her in the face. He placed another chair next to her chair and sat down as he took a deep breath.

"Crystal?" he said as he laughed.

"What? What do you want from me?" Crystal asked as she started to cry.

Tommy just looked at her; he saw the right side of her face was bruised from the punch, and he started to feel bad, seeing what he'd done to her. "All I ever wanted was you!" he yelled while he jumped off the chair.

"Yeah, but, Tommy, I'm not attracted to you, and you're doing all of this to me? This isn't going to make me attracted to you!" Crystal shouted while she looked at the duct tape wrapped tightly around her ankles and wrists. She struggled to speak, feeling nervous and dreading what was going to take place.

"Oh no? Maybe if I remove my glasses and brush down my hair instead of brushing it back, maybe that would make me more attractive?" Tommy shouted while standing in front of the mirror in the living room as he brushed his hair with a brush he had found in her bedroom. When he was finished brushing his hair, he smelled the brush, which was filled with the scent of the shampoo Crystal used whenever she washed her hair.

Meanwhile, in the hallway, Maria was still looking for the right apartment. She moved slowly and cautiously past each door, hoping to find the right apartment soon, listening intensely for the voice of Tommy or Crystal from behind the door of an apartment.

"Tommy, you will never get away with this," said Crystal, still feeling the pain from the punch.

"Oh yeah?" Tommy responded as he walked away from the mirror in the living room and back into the kitchen, where he stopped within a few inches from her. "Is your boyfriend going to be your knight in shining armor and rescue you from the grip of Tommy Landis?" Tommy shouted in a dramatic tone of voice, bent over slightly, within inches of her face. She slowly turned her face, meeting Tommy's gaze from the side.

Crystal wore an expression of disgust, anger, and resentment on her face as he smiled at her with a devilish grin. She suddenly smiled slowly. She soon had a big smile on her face, and Tommy didn't know what to think. He kept smiling but showed disbelief, feeling somewhat comfortable with her smile. He felt amazed by her surprise smile and the change in atmosphere with her supposed new attitude. He started to feel that she was finally seeing things his way. He stood straight up with a big smile on his face while unzipping his blue jeans slowly. As she disgustedly watched, her smile slowly faded. As he still smiled, he bent down slightly once again, this time right in front of her. Their faces were within one or two inches. She smiled again and then laughed slightly, and his grin grew wider as he began to feel more comfortable with her in her apartment.

All of a sudden, she spit in his face.

"You bitch!" Tommy yelled out as the saliva dripped down his face and fell in one long string to the floor. He pulled back his right hand and slapped her on the right side of her face with the back of his hand, and she let out a loud scream as she fell onto the floor, still seated and tied to the chair.

Still in the hallway, Maria heard Crystal's scream, and she realized which apartment the scream had come from, as she was only a few apartments away. She rushed to the front door of the apartment and gently laid her ear on the door, listening, trying to make sure before entering.

"You fucking animal! You want to spit in my fucking face?" Tommy yelled while he slapped her again abruptly, this time on the left side of her face, as she was still on the floor.

"No! Please stop!" Crystal cried out, bleeding from her bottom lip.

"Well, hey, you're getting beat up, but you should still have some dignity," said Tommy as she looked at him with a cold stare, as though she hadn't heard what he'd just said. Her stare seemed to go right through him. "You're supposed to be a fucking lady!" Tommy yelled, standing a few feet away, as he stared at her with a wild look on his face.

"Go to hell!" Crystal shouted, lying on her side on the floor. Tommy helped Crystal, who was still tied to the chair, sit up straight, and he tightened the duct tape while she sat on the chair.

"Wait a minute. Hold on!" said Tommy, and he stood there quietly for a moment, thinking for a few seconds. "If you will just be my lady, I will give you the world. I will give you the whole goddamn world!" Tommy shouted as he faced her. "But you say you're not attracted to me." Tommy turned around, facing the wall, and then he faced her once again slowly. "What do you want me to do? Huh? What can I do for you to make you change your mind?" Tommy asked while bending down slightly in front of her with a desperate tone of voice, at the point of almost begging.

She turned her head away. She felt disgusted yet scared as she looked off to the side of the kitchen, showing that she was ignoring him, as he continued speaking to her.

"Please hear me out," Tommy pleaded as he moved in closer to her. He was so close that if he'd moved an inch closer, his face would have touched her face. She continued looking toward the side of the kitchen as he kept staring at her.

While still sitting there in the chair, she positioned her legs together as she saw him right in front of her. He stood up straight with his legs stretched apart while he stared at her as she made sure again her legs were positioned together for what was about to take place.

All at once, she threw both of her legs up between Tommy's legs, right into the groin area.

"Ahhh!" Tommy yelled as he fell onto his knees, screaming in agony and pain. Crystal sat back on the chair, still bound by duct tape, and with one kick to Tommy's mouth, he fell back in more pain.

"Shit! I can't believe this is really happening. I don't know why he doesn't give up on wanting to be with her. I wish he wanted me that much," Maria whispered to herself as she continued to listen from the front door of the apartment, in the hallway.

Tommy rose from his knees on the floor as Crystal loosened herself from the duct tape. She ran to the front door and tried to unlock the lock, but she noticed he'd jammed it with a foreign object. As Tommy rose from the floor, he saw Crystal trying to unlock the door, trying to escape the hellish fate that awaited her. He rushed over to her at the front door, grabbed her by the hair, and dragged her as she staggered with him toward the chair.

"Ever since the day we met, you've managed to make my life a fucking hell!" Tommy shouted as he sat her back down on the chair, and he leaned up against the wall between the kitchen and the living room, still in pain from Crystal's kick in the groin area and in the face, as Crystal gave him a "Go to hell" look.

"Go to fucking hell, bastard!" Crystal yelled out.

There was a moment of silence, and outside the apartment door, Maria could hear only her own heavy breathing and her heartbeat pounding at the suspense of what was taking place behind the door of the apartment.

The silence was broken by the sound of the telephone ringing in the living room. As the telephone rang a few times, Crystal and Tommy first looked toward the living room and then looked at each other. After a couple more rings, the answering machine picked up the call.

"Hello. This is Crystal. Please leave your name and number, and I'll call you back."

Beep! The answering machine tape rewound itself, positioning itself to take the phone call.

"Crystal, it's Jim."

Tommy and Crystal looked at each other again, and Tommy noticed her eyes lit up with a sense of hope and love as she listened to Jim's voice on the answering machine. Tommy felt slightly uncomfortable while listening to Jim's voice on the machine.

"I just wanted you to know that I have already moved to Jersey City, New Jersey, just across the river from you. So I no longer live in Dallas. I love you, and I shall call you in the morning and catch you before you go to work. See you soon. Goodbye for now. Love you."

Beep! The answering machine tape rewound itself, saving the message, and after the tape finished rewinding, the red light flickered, indicating a message was there.

"Well, I guess you have a concerned boyfriend. You know, I could be a much better boyfriend than he is. If you'd give me a chance to show you," Tommy said on bended knee while he looked her in the eye. "If you would just give me a chance, I could prove it to you!" said Tommy as he tried to hold her hands, and he started wrapping her wrists together again, even tighter than before.

"Stay away from me!" said Crystal as she pulled back with disgust. "Just stay away from me!" She pulled her hands away from his. "I should've never responded to your message in my voice mailbox from the personals in the newspaper. I never thought it would end up like this," said Crystal as Tommy was starting to show signs of remorse and guilt. "If I had only known ahead of time that something like this could happen." Crystal looked down at the kitchen floor.

"Crystal, spend your life with me. Please, please, please," Tommy begged as he tried to hug her while she was still seated on the chair.

Maria was still listening from behind the apartment door, in the hallway. While listening, she grew more and more frustrated with the situation as it escalated, and with each passing minute, she wondered if she should call the police and end the whole fiasco, but she still listened, glued to the door, still wanting to be with him.

"I'll never go with you! Not now and not ever!" Crystal shouted, still bound by duct tape wrapped around her wrists and ankles, still seated on the chair in the middle of the kitchen, as Tommy wore a concerned look on his face.

"Well, Crystal, I'm truly sorry about all of this. I am truly sorry you feel the way you do. Is there anything I can do or say to change your mind?" Tommy asked with a sincere look on his face.

Crystal just turned her head in the other direction, defiant in answering his questions, which made Tommy even more irritable, vulnerable, and frustrated. He walked over to her, this time being alert as he watched her legs.

"Well, my little pet, you told me to go to hell a while ago, and I have no doubt that's where I'm going. But I refuse to go there alone." Tommy grinned with a spaced-out look on his face, and Crystal began to worry, silently panicking to herself but being careful not to show it.

In the hallway, Maria was on her knees, still listening to Crystal and Tommy. She wanted to pull him out of the apartment to deal with him, but she feared he would kill her too, as she was a witness to what was taking place.

Crystal stared at Tommy as he stared into space. "Tommy, you really need to think about what you're saying. There are many girls out there you can be with. What about Maria? You know, that woman who works where you work? She's very interested in being with you. You just need to change your attitude. Maybe change your look somewhat or develop a different personality, and seek better and different ways to make it better for yourself." Crystal was using psychology on him while she trembled with fear.

"Shut up! Shut the fuck up!" Tommy shouted.

"But, Tommy, I—"

"Shut up! Shut up!" Tommy shouted as he walked toward the kitchen window.

"I was only trying to help you, and—" Crystal spun around on her chair, trying to convince him to change his mind and see that what he was doing was wrong, while he went behind her over to the kitchen window.

"You want to help me? Let's do it! Come on! You want to?" he asked, standing right behind her, pressing the knife on her neck gently but hard enough that the blade made a red mark across her neck.

All of a sudden, he removed the knife from her neck and placed the tip of the knife on the duct tape, ready to cut her loose from the bondage, as he was asking her for a favor.

Silence filled the kitchen. An odor came from Tommy's body, as he was perspiring, and she looked at him with disgust.

"Tommy, the only way you're ever going to touch my body is if you kill me," Crystal said with a smirk on her face, and Tommy's eyes grew larger with anger and frustration. "I would never, ever allow you to fuck me while I'm alive!" said Crystal, filled with anger and disgust. Immediately, she wondered if she should've said that, as she feared for her safety.

Tommy stared at her with cautious eyes, amazed at her abrupt attitude, while he grabbed a butcher knife from the knife stand on the countertop next to the stove. "You know, Crystal, that's not a bad idea," said Tommy while he pointed the butcher knife at her, standing to the side of her, inches from her face.

———————— ·+·+·+·+·+· ————————

In Jersey City, New Jersey, Jim Connors, Crystal's boyfriend, exited his new apartment building. Outside on the street, he waved down a taxi to go to New York, to Crystal's apartment, to pay a surprise visit. When he saw a cab slow down, he rushed over toward it, and the cab pulled over to the curb. When the yellow cab stopped at the curb, Jim opened the passenger door and entered the taxi.

"Where to, Mac?" the cab driver asked as Jim slammed shut the door of the cab.

"I'm going to the Upper East Side in Manhattan," said Jim, and the cab drove off, on its way to New York City. As the cab drove on, Jim gave the driver the address of where he was going as they were approaching the tunnel.

———————— ·+·+·+·+·+· ————————

"Hey, Peter, I'm going to my sister's apartment for a couple of days. Is that all right with you, babe?" Darlene asked while she and her fiancé, Peter, were watching television in their living room at their apartment.

"Yeah, sure, love. But does she know of your plan to come visit?" Peter asked as she was drinking a can of beer.

"No, she doesn't know I'm coming over. I figure I'll surprise her and cheer her up because we had a disagreement about something, and I figure I'll make it up to her for a couple of days," said Darlene.

"Does it have to be tonight? Why not tomorrow night? Then we could cuddle up tonight with some romantic music, and then we—"

"No. Sorry, love, but my sister needs me right now. I don't know. There's something about tonight. I just have a bad vibe about tonight." Darlene looked into Peter's eyes, frightened. "It's something about tonight. And it really feels bad. This nut is out there somewhere, and there's no telling when he will attack her." Darlene looked out the living room window and then turned around and walked back toward her fiancé. "I just think that a couple of days will be good for my sister and me, and I will feel much better too. I won't feel so paranoid about this situation," said Darlene as she grabbed her suitcase above the closet in the bedroom.

As Darlene began to pack her suitcase, Peter went into the bedroom to join his fiancée. When he entered the bedroom, she shut the door as they continued talking about Crystal.

After a little while, Darlene finished packing. She walked over to the front door of their apartment with Peter right behind her, carrying her suitcase filled with some of her belongings.

"OK, love, I will call you as soon as I arrive there, all right?" said Darlene, and she kissed Peter on the lips.

"Shall I call you a taxi?" Peter asked as she stood by the door of the apartment. As she entered the hallway of the building, holding her suitcase, it felt a little light.

"Thank you, babe. Bye," said Darlene, and she started walking down the steps.

"Be careful, love," said Peter right before he shut the door.

+ + ♦ ♦ + + +

At Crystal's apartment, Tommy was still speaking with Crystal, who was still tied up on the chair, torturing her with small talk, prolonging the horror that was about to happen.

"So is there anything I could do or say that might—"

"Get out of my face!" Crystal shouted as she turned away her head to the side.

He moved himself away from her face, and then he leaned over toward her ear. "Crystal. Crystal Farnsworth," he whispered slowly, and then he repeated her full name slowly in a whisper.

She turned her head slowly, looking straight ahead, with her eyes wide open. When she turned her head, her baby-blue eyes met his eyes as he grinned at her. Still grinning, he began to drool, and some of the saliva spilled from his bottom lip and fell in a long string down to the kitchen floor. Between watching him drool and what he looked like when he grinned, she began to feel sick.

"Crystal. Crystal Farnsworth. Look at me," he whispered once again, and she turned her head slowly toward him. When their eyes met, his devilish grin began to fade. "Love of the twisted. Love of the twisted," Tommy whispered while bending over slightly in front of her.

While she continued watching him, her mouth fell slightly open, as she recognized those words and the whispering, crackly voice from the phone call she'd received recently. She was between fear and grief.

"Love of the twisted!" Tommy shouted, and Crystal's eyes grew with remembrance once again, as she was shocked, though she expected this demeanor from him.

"You bastard!" Crystal shouted as she leaned forward.

Tommy stood straight up as his grin was wiped from his face by her shout. He turned around to face the counter and reached for the duct tape. He took the duct tape from the countertop and started to wrap the duct tape around the knuckles of his right hand while staring at her as she looked down at the kitchen floor.

"You know what, Crystal? I've just decided something," said Tommy as he ripped the end of the duct tape with his teeth. "Yeah, I just came to a conclusion over this whole fucking thing! If I can't have you—"

Maria listened closely with her ear to the front door of the apartment, never blinking, as she couldn't believe what she was hearing.

"Then no one in the whole wide world will have you. Absolutely no one." Tommy laughed and smiled.

Crystal looked at him with disgust on her face.

Jim was still in the back of the yellow taxi, on his way to Crystal's apartment. As he looked out the window of the cab, he noticed they were in a traffic jam on their way to the tunnel. As he and the cab driver waited in the midst of other cars, he took a deep breath, as he began to feel a little impatient.

"Excuse me. Is there a way around this mess?" Jim asked as he leaned forward toward the driver.

"No, this is it. We're sorta stuck here. There's not a lot I can do at this moment. But don't worry about the meter to the fare. I stopped it from charging any further until we go again," said the cab driver as he sat comfortably back in his seat, smoking his cigar with his window rolled down.

"Oh, all right. Thank you," said Jim as he sat back and looked up, feeling even more impatient. He hoped Crystal was doing fine, but he was afraid of her situation with the obsessed Tommy Landis, and he hoped Tommy wasn't anywhere around her.

"Attention, ladies and gentlemen! We have a sick passenger on board the train. As soon as the paramedics arrive, we will proceed uptown on this train! Attention, ladies and gentlemen!" said the train conductor.

Darlene looked up at the intercom while the conductor continued speaking. "Wonderful." Darlene sighed as she looked at her watch.

"Thank you for your patience," said the conductor as she looked up at the intercom while she sighed once again.

Tommy stared coldly into Crystal's eyes while slowly caressing her face with his left hand, placing his hand softly all over her face. When he was finished touching her face, he directed his index finger underneath her chin, pushing her chin upward until she looked upward. Then, all of a sudden, he punched her with his right hand, which had duct tape wrapped around his knuckles. Feeling the blow unexpectedly, she was stunned, feeling the pain of the punch but feeling somewhat numb to her surroundings, as her head turned to the side with the force of his punch. When she turned back, facing Tommy, he punched her again, this time sending her to the kitchen floor, near the kitchen window, still bound by duct tape at her ankles and wrists.

Maria jumped from the noise as she heard the punch from outside the apartment, and she too was stunned.

"Help me! Somebody, please help me!" Crystal yelled as she cried from the pain of the blows coming from Tommy while she lay on the floor.

Tommy smiled, feeling pleased with what was taking place, as he walked over toward her. When he was next to Crystal, he turned her onto her back and got on top of her. When he was on top of her, he began to strangle her with his hands wrapped around her throat.

"You bitch! You motherfucking bitch! It didn't have to come to this! It didn't really have to come to this!" he yelled while looking at her. Her face was dark red from the entanglement of his hands. She cried, coughing from the suffocation of being strangled. He removed himself from on top of her, walked toward the counter, and opened up a couple of drawers underneath the counter. He found another butcher knife in one of the drawers. He held it up to his eyes. *So shiny and so sharp to the touch*, he thought.

Holding the butcher knife, he slowly walked over to Crystal, who was still lying on her back as she painfully stared at him, hoping he would at some point kill her and let her be in peace.

Tommy stood by her side with his hands on his waist while still holding on to the butcher knife. He knelt down and then got on top of her again. He stared down at her momentarily, into her eyes, as she remained frozen, still stunned by what was going on. She didn't know what was going to happen next. Without smiling, he waved the butcher knife slowly back and forth as the reflection of the light shone on both sides of the knife. As he continuously waved it slowly in front of her face, her eyes followed the shiny, pointed blade as they grew enlarged with unspeakable fear.

"Tommy, what in the world are you doing in there?" Maria whispered to herself as she looked around the hallway, making sure no one was watching her.

Tommy was still on top of Crystal, still waving the butcher knife slowly in front of her while the blade shone from the dim kitchen light. Suddenly, he stopped waving the knife and stopped smiling. With both hands, he clenched the butcher knife tightly as he raised the knife upward slowly, pointed directly at her heart. He raised the knife over his head while looking into her eyes. Tears rolled down her bruised cheeks, and she was perspiring on her forehead. She licked her lips, which were dry and cracking.

"Tommy, please don't do this. Please don't. Tommy?" Crystal begged as she trembled with fear while he raised the knife slightly higher, getting ready, as his eyes grew enlarged, not believing any of this was taking place, which made him even angrier.

"Love of the twisted. Love of the twisted," Tommy whispered.

Crystal now sensed that no hope existed. Tommy Landis, the guy who'd answered her personal ad in the newspaper, had finally lost his mind, and she was about to lose her life and never see her boyfriend, Jim Connors, or sister, Darlene, ever again.

"Oh my God. Oh my God!" Crystal shouted as she closed her eyes slowly.

"Yes, my love! Love of the twisted!" Tommy shouted as his eyes filled with unforgiving rage from within.

"Love of the twisted?" Maria asked herself as she continued listening, and she began to tremble at what she was hearing behind the front door of the apartment.

"Tommy? No! No!" Crystal yelled out as she saw the madness in his eyes.

"Love of—" Tommy brought down the butcher knife full speed directly into the heart of Crystal Farnsworth, the woman he was in love with and the woman he was obsessed with till the end.

"No, Tommy," Crystal whispered with her final breath. With her final word, she lay there in a pool of blood.

"The twisted!" Tommy shouted.

CHAPTER 23

S *HIT! WHAT'S GOING ON INSIDE?* Maria thought as she heard Crystal's final words.

Tommy removed himself from Crystal's bloodied dead body as she lay there in a big pool of her own blood. She lay there motionless and still as though she were sleeping, leaving the present day for the next day. Tommy placed the blood-covered butcher knife on the countertop, not concerned that the police would see the knife covered in blood or discover his fingerprints on the handle. He showed no fear that he would be discovered or connected to the murder of Crystal Farnsworth, because as far as he was concerned, his life was over as well. If he ended up in prison for the rest of his life—and he knew there was a good chance of that—it wouldn't matter much to him, he thought. While walking through the living room, he tripped on something and made a loud noise, startling Maria, who continued listening near the front door of the apartment. As she panicked, hoping she wouldn't be discovered by him, she saw a janitorial closet across the hall. She rushed over to the closet to hide from Tommy, in case he came out of the apartment. After she entered the closet, she kept the door of the closet slightly open to see if Tommy came out of the apartment, thinking that Crystal wouldn't be coming out anytime soon. She almost felt a bit guilty for not calling the police when she should've, but on the other hand, she thought maybe he would let Crystal go once and for all and come to her.

Tommy reentered the kitchen on his way out of the apartment. When he reached the door to leave, he turned his head and glanced over at the motionless and half-naked body of Crystal Farnsworth, and he almost passed out. He grabbed quickly at the doorknob to prevent his fall, and he refocused on leaving the apartment, with some blood on the bottom of his right sneaker.

Tommy exited the apartment and closed the door, not locking it, because he didn't have the key to the apartment. As he closed the door gently and quietly and stood at the front door in the hallway, Maria watched from inside the janitorial closet, with the door open slightly. While Maria continued watching in horror, an elevator arrived on the floor, but instead of going down with the elevator, Tommy ran toward the stairwell and ran downstairs instead. He exited the floor in a fury, wanting to leave it all behind him, as Maria continued watching him.

After seeing Tommy run downstairs, she exited the closet. At the same time, another elevator arrived, and when the elevator doors slid open, Edna and Nancy exited. Edna and Nancy saw Maria closing the closet door, and they felt it was odd that there was someone in the building who didn't look familiar. They'd lived in the building for many years, and they'd never seen her before. Edna and Nancy stared at Maria as she entered the elevator before the elevator doors slid shut.

"My, she was in a hurry," Edna whispered to Nancy while the elevator doors slid shut as they walked toward the apartment of Crystal Farnsworth.

When Tommy reached the lobby level via the stairwell, he exited the stairwell and ran through the lobby, and upon leaving the building, he hurried down the street, on his way to the subway, homebound, as the elevator landed in the lobby.

When the elevator arrived in the lobby and the door slid open, Maria stepped out and ran through the lobby and onto the street through the entrance, careful not to be discovered by Tommy. She looked toward the corner of the block to her right and saw Tommy walking fast, almost running, as he turned the corner, where the subway entrance was.

Seeing Tommy turn the corner, she walked out from the entrance of the building, walking fast. *What's going on with Tommy and the mess he created?* Her heartbeat quickened as she approached the corner of the block, but when she arrived at the corner, she could no longer see Tommy. She curiously looked around, wondering how fast he had gone to the subway, thinking to herself.

Edna and Nancy stood in the hallway at the entrance of Crystal's apartment. Nancy pushed the front door open. Before they entered the apartment, Edna knocked on the door, announcing that they were entering, hoping Crystal heard the knocking, but there was no answer. They stared into each other's eyes, thinking the worst.

Edna knocked on the door again as they entered the apartment and stepped into the kitchen.

"Do you think that young girl was inside this apartment at all? Or how about that young man Crystal was with when they arrived at the building?" Edna asked anxiously as she stared wide-eyed at Nancy. Then they both looked at the front door, which was back against the wall of the kitchen, as it was open. "Do you think Crystal brought that man into her apartment?" Edna asked.

"Well, you know how younger couples are nowadays. They're very sociable. You know, they have many friends all over the place. The younger generations are very transient nowadays. You know, here, there, and everywhere," Nancy replied as they slowly walked farther into Crystal's apartment through the kitchen. It was dim.

"We can't stay here," said Edna, as she wanted to leave and not pry into Crystal's affairs in her apartment.

"No, no. It's all right. We're not intruding at all. You see, we're concerned neighbors. We've known Crystal for a while now, and we're just here to make sure she is all right. OK?" Nancy asked.

They held hands as they walked through the kitchen into the living room. When they arrived in the living room, they looked around quickly, and when they were satisfied that no one was present in the apartment, they turned around and walked back into the kitchen to leave the apartment. On their way out, when they reentered the kitchen, they noticed at the other end of the kitchen, over by the window, between the stove and the wall, a blanket lying on the floor. Immediately, Edna and Nancy saw their nightmare.

"Oh, Crystal! Crystal!" the elderly women yelled out as they saw blood coming out from underneath the blanket. They looked around the kitchen, hoping it wasn't Crystal.

They walked over to the blanket lying on the floor with what seemed to be blood coming from it. When they arrived at the blanket, Edna bent down near the blanket and lifted up a corner to see if anyone or anything was underneath the blanket. Even though they had an idea of who it might be, their faces filled with disbelief and shock. When Edna lifted up a piece of the blanket, she and Nancy saw the still body of Crystal Farnsworth lying in a pool of blood.

"Edna!"

"Nancy!"

The elderly women yelled out in response to what they'd just seen underneath the blanket.

"Oh my God! Nancy, do you see what I see?" Edna yelled out as she covered her face with both hands, shielding her vision from the grisly sight.

"It can't be Crystal! It just can't be," Nancy responded as she and Edna looked at each other and then slowly looked back together at the bloody body of Crystal Farnsworth.

In a moment of desperation, Edna bent down slightly, grabbed one end of the blanket, and uncovered Crystal's body, removing the blanket. "Good God!" said Edna as she sat down on one of the kitchen chairs, feeling as though she were going to pass out, while Nancy continued standing.

"Edna, what are we to do?" Nancy asked, as she felt vulnerable in the situation. "Well, we ought to call the police, and we have to remain calm, all right?" Nancy said, and Edna nodded, agreeing with Nancy.

"Yes. We must remain calm and call the police. She was such a nice girl," said Nancy as she and Edna began to cry.

Edna called 911 from her cellular phone.

Tommy was on his way home on the train, underneath New York City. Maria was looking for a taxi to go back to Brooklyn, to Tommy's apartment, hoping she'd arrive at Tommy's apartment before he did.

"Need a car?" a cab driver asked Maria as she was walking around looking for a taxi.

"Yes. I'm going to Brooklyn," said Maria as she opened the door to the back of the cab and entered the taxi. "I'm in a hurry to Brooklyn." She slammed the door shut, and the back tires of the cab peeled out as it drove off into the night, on the way to Brooklyn, as Tommy was on his way back to Brooklyn via the subway.

At Crystal's apartment building, an elevator approached the floor where Crystal's apartment was. When the elevator door slid open, Darlene stepped out of the elevator, carrying a suitcase. She walked toward the apartment of her sister, and as she got closer to the apartment, she noticed something strange come over her. She saw that the front door of the apartment was wide open, which was unusual. The more she thought about that, the faster she moved toward the apartment as her heart raced with nightmarish thoughts. Breathing heavily, thinking the worst, unaware of what had gone on at the apartment with her sister, she entered the apartment.

"Hello! Crystal?" Darlene called out as she walked into the kitchen. She saw two elderly women standing near a blanket, and then she looked at what had been underneath the blanket. Darlene's eyes widened with frantic, horrific disbelief. She felt as if she were in the beginning stages of a nightmare.

"What the hell? Crystal! What the fuck happened? I can't believe this!" Darlene yelled out as she frantically dropped her suitcase onto the kitchen floor and ran toward her sister's motionless body as Crystal lay there in a pool of blood. "What happened?" Darlene knelt down next to her deceased sister as she cried heavily while looking up at the two elderly ladies, Edna and Nancy, whom she knew, as Crystal had introduced them a long time ago. While she looked for answers, the two elderly women didn't remember who she was.

"We're neighbors of hers. Are you a relative? Because you look just like her," Nancy said as Darlene knelt beside her deceased sister's body and then looked up.

"Yes, I am a relative. I'm her sister. My name is Darlene," she replied, and Nancy and Edna looked at each other with sad expressions on their faces. "Can one of you please tell me what happened here? Are the police on their way?" Darlene asked while she cried continuously, trying to get a pulse from Crystal's wrist and then her neck. Her body was still semiwarm.

"Darlene, the police are on their way, and as far as what happened here, we saw a young man enter the building through the lobby with Crystal. They were on their way up to her apartment," Edna said slowly.

"Did you say a young man was with her?" Darlene asked, looking down at her sister, as she covered her sister's body fully, up to her head.

"Yes," Edna answered.

"Well, it's either the new boyfriend, or maybe it was—" Darlene thought out loud.

"And we also saw a young woman on this floor as well, just outside the apartment. Close to the outside door of the apartment," Edna said as she and Nancy rose from where they were sitting.

"OK, you've mentioned that there was a younger man with my sister. Can you tell me what he looked like?" Darlene asked as she looked up at the two elderly women.

"Yes. The younger man was shorter than the other man she was with in the past in her apartment," said Nancy.

"Other man? Oh, Jim? Jim was here recently. He's tall, with dark hair and dark eyes." Darlene described Jim to the elderly women while still on her knees next to the body of her sister.

"No. No, the gentleman who was here today with your sister was short. Shorter than the other gentleman," Edna said.

"And he was wearing black-framed glasses. And had not that much hair," said Nancy as she remembered.

"Black-framed glasses, shorter, and a little bit of hair? Oh my God. Oh my God!" Darlene covered her face with her hands.

"Oh dear. Oh no," said Edna and Nancy, worried about how Darlene was reacting to what they were saying.

Darlene looked up at them, wide-eyed, as horrific thoughts went through her mind. "Oh God, that was Tommy Landis," Darlene mumbled to herself as she looked down at her deceased sister.

"Tommy who?" Nancy asked Edna, because Nancy wasn't sure of what she'd just heard.

"Tommy Landis. Tommy Landis was the guy who was obsessed with my sister, and finally, he killed her because he knew he couldn't have her. She didn't want anything to do with him," Darlene said.

The two elderly women looked at each other. They had sympathy for Darlene, who continued crying.

All of a sudden, it was quiet. Darlene felt as if she were going to pass out at any time, while Edna and Nancy tried to console her. They too were on their knees, embracing her.

"No!" Darlene shouted as she cried hysterically in a fit of rage and sorrow.

Darlene was still on the floor in a kneeling position, holding on to Crystal's cold hand, crying in disbelief over the whole ordeal. She thought back to the time when she and Crystal had met Tommy when he arrived at the door and the time when she had tried to convince Crystal to do more than what she was doing. Now she looked down at her sister lying in a pool of blood.

"Oh, Crystal, I told you! I told you!" Darlene cried out, dealing with the realities of life without her sister.

＋＋＋＋＋

Tommy was still on the Brooklyn-bound train, looking down at the floor of the train while sitting on the cold plastic seat. From another car of the train, four teenage boys wearing thick gold chains around their necks walked into the car Tommy was in. All four boys looked over at Tommy as Tommy continued looking down at the floor. They walked right by him while talking among themselves, on their way to the next car of the train. Tommy watched them leave his car and enter the next car. Seeing them leave, he breathed a sigh of relief that they hadn't started trouble with him, robbing him or, worse, killing him. But that didn't really matter to him because of his current situation, having killed Crystal, he thought. The four teenage boys in the next car stared at him momentarily as he continued looking down at the floor, thinking to himself.

Unexpectedly, one of the boys turned around and reentered the car where Tommy was. As the teen approached him, Tommy panicked to himself, hoping no problems would arise. Feeling somewhat uncomfortable, he started moving about in his seat as he wondered what the teen wearing the gold chains wanted with him. The teen walked by Tommy, looking down at the floor as if he were looking for something, while Tommy continued looking down at the floor as well. After the teen walked by, Tommy felt relieved, hoping the boy would keep moving along away from him, because he didn't want trouble, especially right now, because he was already in a lot of trouble. As he looked up at the teen, the teen bent down quickly, looking toward the floor, within inches of Tommy.

"My keys!" the boy said as his heavy gold chains swayed back and forth against his chest, and he called out to his friends in the next car, smiling, holding up the small ring of keys.

Tommy looked down at the floor with relief as the teen walked right by him, never acknowledging him, while placing the set of keys

362 R O B E R T   B I G A O U E T T E

in his pocket. The teen exited the car where Tommy was and reentered the next car, rejoining his friends. After Tommy saw the teens walk away, he regained familiar feelings about what had taken place earlier at Crystal Farnsworth's apartment. While remembering, he covered his face with his hands while leaning over slightly while still sitting.

⋅✦✦✦✦✦⋅

At the apartment, two police officers arrived.

"Hello?" said one of the officers as he knocked on the door while they looked inside.

"Yes, come in," said Darlene. As she watched the police officers enter the apartment, she walked toward them with streams of tears flowing down her cheeks.

"Ma'am, I'm Officer Harris. And this is my partner, Officer Shelby. We received a call about a stabbing in this apartment," Officer Harris said as he pulled out a big pad while looking around.

Darlene turned around and walked toward the body of her dead sister. "I know who the killer was!" she yelled out. She still felt numb from her sister's sudden death.

"Oh yeah? You know who the killer was?" Officer Harris asked as he, his partner, and Darlene stood near the body of Crystal Farnsworth.

"It was Tommy Landis! That fucking bastard!" Darlene blurted out as she covered her face with both hands as she cried hysterically.

"Now, ma'am, what's your name?" Officer Harris asked as he opened up his big pad.

"My name is Darlene Farnsworth. I'm Crystal's sister," said Darlene as she and the two officers looked at her dead sister on the kitchen floor underneath the kitchen window.

"All right, this is your sister, Crystal Farnsworth, I believe you mentioned earlier?" Officer Harris asked as he stepped away, and he called an ambulance to pick up the deceased from the apartment.

"And you mentioned a man by the name of Tommy Landis. And this man killed your sister, Crystal Farnsworth? He was the killer who murdered your sister, you said?" Officer Shelby asked as he wondered how she knew. She sounded convinced that it was a fact.

"Yes. Oh yes!" Darlene quickly responded as her eyes widened. She had a convinced tone of voice and look on her face.

"Well, I understand that this is your sister, but how do you know it was Tommy Landis? Were you here when she was murdered?" Officer Shelby asked while writing on the pad.

"Well, it's obvious the murder took place in the kitchen in this apartment," Darlene responded with her hands on her hips.

"All right, we've already established that fact," said Officer Shelby as Officer Harris rejoined them after calling for an ambulance.

"OK, getting back to your question about how I know it was Tommy Landis. No. No, I don't know as far as seeing what actually happened, because I wasn't there at the time of my sister's murder, but I—"

"But I was in the building during that time," said Edna.

"Me too. We both were in the building at that time," said Nancy. She and Edna were sitting on kitchen chairs at the kitchen table while listening to the conversation between the police officers and Darlene.

When the two elderly ladies responded, the two police officers just looked at each other.

＊＊＊＊＊＊

The taxi raced through the streets of Bensonhurst in Brooklyn as the driver tried to find out where Maria's destination was.

"OK, we're approaching Bay Parkway here in the good ole borough of Brooklyn, USA. I remember when Brooklyn used to be some great place to live," said the cab driver to himself in a whisper, reminiscing about his childhood days in the old borough.

The cab approached scenery familiar to Maria.

"This is it!" Maria shouted, interrupting the daydreaming cab driver, as she pointed to the apartment building she remembered as the building where Tommy lived.

"OK, lady!" the cab driver shouted as he pulled over to the curb in front of the apartment building.

As Maria stepped out of the cab, she felt a gentle breeze. She reached into her pocket and paid the cab fare to the driver, also paying him a tip of five dollars. When she stepped back, the cab drove away, and a gentle breeze blew back her long dark hair behind her shoulders as she stood near the entrance of the dimly lit alley. While she looked around, calmness lurked in the atmosphere.

It's so quiet in this neighborhood, she thought as she continued looking around while standing in place. She looked back behind her down the lonely, dimly lit alley. Then she looked up at the window next to the fire escape, which was Tommy's bedroom window. She walked slowly through the alley while still looking up at Tommy's bedroom. As she approached the old fire escape, in the building across the alley, looking out the window, the same neighbor who'd seen her the last time she sneaked inside was watching her again.

Without hesitation, she jumped onto the ladder of the fire escape, pulled herself up, and started climbing. The stranger across the alley watched with interest and shook his head, wondering what was going on across the alley.

✦✦✦✦✦

"All right, your name is?" Officer Harris asked.

"My name is Edna, and my good friend and roommate's name is Nancy. We saw Crystal before she died. She was with a young man at the entrance of the building prior to entering the lobby. Nancy and I saw her earlier today," said Edna, and she and Nancy looked at each other and then at the officers.

"All right, Edna, can you or Nancy describe what this young man Tommy Landis looked like?" Officer Harris asked as he wrote on his pad.

"Sure, we can! He stood at five foot seven and had a skinny to medium build and a little bit of hair. And he wore these old-looking black-framed glasses. Like the black-framed glasses Buddy Holly wore," said Nancy.

"Believe me, he was no Buddy Holly! More like Woody Allen," said Edna, and she and Nancy agreed.

Darlene looked even more convinced than before. "That's him! That's the fucking bastard! That fucking bastard!" Darlene yelled out as she again cried hysterically, and Officer Harris walked over to Darlene and consoled her.

CHAPTER 24

A T THE APARTMENT BUILDING WHERE Tommy lived, Maria was on the fire escape, at the window of the bedroom. She tried to lift the window, hoping it wasn't locked from inside, and it slowly started opening. She gently opened the window.

After she opened the window, she crawled through and entered the bedroom. The bedroom was cold and dim. She closed the window gently and slowly. After she shut the window, she walked over toward the bed, and when she reached the bed, she stopped where she was. She quickly turned around, walked back toward the window, and quickly pulled down the window shade, as she didn't want anyone to discover her inside the apartment. The neighbor across the alley saw the window shade being pulled down over the window. Then the neighbor could see only a silhouette behind the shade, moving about the bedroom. Having lived there for many years, he knew that a young man lived in the apartment, and no other person did. Plus, the woman looked suspicious climbing through the bedroom window and entering the apartment in that way. The neighbor went onto the fire escape to make himself more comfortable as he continued watching Maria from the other side of the shade. When he sat down on the fire escape, he grabbed his black cat, who was sitting on the windowsill, still watching the young lady in the apartment across the alley.

A light came on as Maria flicked the switch on the wall. She walked over to the closet, took off her coat, and hung it up in the closet as she made herself at home. Then she walked over toward the bed, but quickly, she turned, walked back to the closet, reached into her coat pocket, pulled out a two-piece lingerie set, and threw it onto the bed as she smiled with only one thing in mind: having Tommy Landis in bed with her before the night was over—or before the police reached him for the murder of Crystal Farnsworth.

She walked to the bathroom, removed her sneakers and socks, and started to undress herself as she turned on the hot water in the bathtub. She noticed, at the corner of the tub, a bottle of bubble bath. She removed her sweatshirt and looked at herself in the mirror as she dropped her sweatshirt onto the floor. While looking in the mirror, she saw her shapely golden-brown breasts, with her nipples pointing, while she continued thinking about Tommy, turned on by the slightest thought of him. Still looking into the mirror at herself, she removed her jeans as she held on to the sink for balance while taking them off. After taking off her jeans, she removed her panties. Standing there nude while still looking in the mirror, with even higher hopes of being with Tommy Landis that night in bed, she grew more and more excited in the moment. Finally, she would make her fantasy come true and make it a reality. As she stopped the water from running, she poured some of the liquid bubble soap into the tub and swirled the hot water, making bubbles. She laughed out loud, swirling her hands faster and faster, making more and more bubbles.

She entered the tub with one foot first and then the other, and when she was fully in the tub, she knelt down. Soon her whole golden-brown nude body was submerged in the steamy, hot, soapy water, and she was completely covered with the big, clear bubbles. As she leaned back and relaxed, she closed her eyes, feeling like this was too good to be true, as she felt Tommy might see things her way, and that night, they would be together.

✦✦✦✦✦✦

"Ladies and gentlemen, there's a little congestion ahead of us. We'll start moving again shortly. Please be patient. As soon as we get the signal, we shall proceed. Thank you," said the train conductor over the intercom speaker as the train Tommy was in came to a screeching stop in the middle of the tunnel while Tommy looked down at the floor.

"Wonderful! Wonderful! Wonderful!" Tommy shouted, and then he began to pace about the car of the train.

A few other commuters noticed him being tense and pacing about and looked at him with caution, not knowing what was going to happen. The commuters found him a little bit odd as he walked over toward the side door all the way in the back of the train.

"God damn it! Let's go!" Tommy yelled in frustration, because the train hadn't moved yet, and with everything that had happened that day, he just wanted to be home, away from the whole world. He rested his head on the sliding door of the train.

Back at Tommy's apartment, in the bedroom, Maria was standing in front of the mirror with a big towel wrapped around her nude body as she brushed her long, thick dark hair while she smiled.

"Tommy, I'm going to make you a happy man," Maria whispered to herself as she removed one of the pictures of Crystal from the edge of the mirror. As she stood in front of the mirror, she noticed that all the pictures around the edges were pictures of Crystal, and she smiled devilishly as she studied all the pictures of Crystal coming to and going from her job. There were even a few pictures of her walking out of her apartment building, going wherever she was going.

Maria's devilish smile turned into a sheepish smile as she took down one of the pictures of Crystal. She looked at it and then flung it over her shoulder, and it landed on the edge of the bed. The picture was of Crystal coming home from work on a particular evening.

At the apartment where Crystal had been murdered, two paramedics placed Crystal's body in a body bag on a stretcher. Once she was on the stretcher, the two paramedics picked up the stretcher and walked toward the door, exiting the apartment. Jim Connors, Crystal's boyfriend, was about to knock on the door of the apartment just as the paramedics exited the apartment with Crystal in the body bag on the stretcher. As they passed Jim, he was confused, and he made sure he was at the right apartment.

"Oh my God! Crystal!" Jim shouted as he ran into the apartment. When he arrived inside, he saw two elderly women and a young woman standing near a bloody blanket with a puddle of blood underneath.

As he walked closer toward the pool of blood, the two elderly women, Edna and Nancy, were leaving the apartment. They wondered who the young man who'd just entered the apartment was.

"Jim? Jim Connors? Crystal's boyfriend?" Darlene said, slowly remembering him from the Thanksgiving dinner with the family.

"Yes, I'm Jim Connors. And you are Darlene, Crystal's sister," said Jim while he looked at the pool of blood on the kitchen floor. "Darlene, where's—" Jim stopped as tears formed in his eyes, because he knew he was about to hear the worst nightmare of his life.

"Crystal? She's dead, Jim," said Darlene, crying. She looked down after looking straight into Jim's eyes.

"No! No way! I just spoke to her! I just transferred to New Jersey from Dallas! We had plans! We had plans one day to be married. She can't be!" Jim shouted, covering his face as he cried. He thought about the two medics who'd passed him earlier in the hallway.

He looked outside the apartment into the hallway and saw the paramedics standing by the elevators, waiting for an elevator to arrive so they could go down to the ambulance. One of the lobby attendants was operating the elevators manually. Without thinking twice, Jim ran out of the apartment into the hallway and rushed over to the medics.

"Excuse me! Excuse me, sir! Sir, I'm Crystal Farnsworth's boyfriend, and I find myself in disbelief that my girlfriend, Crystal, is dead. I heard she was murdered!" said Jim with tears in his eyes.

"Yes, we were told the deceased's name was Crystal Farnsworth," said one of the medics, looking at his paperwork.

"And you are her boyfriend?" the other medic asked as one of the elevators arrived, with one of the lobby attendants operating it manually.

"Yes, my name is Jim. I was her boyfriend. If it's all right with both of you, may I see her face one last time? Please? I really would appreciate it," Jim said, standing near the stretcher.

"Gee, I don't know. We're not supposed to do this," said one of the medics.

"It's not part of the procedures, but since you are her boyfriend and you're going through this hard time right now, all right. We understand, but are you sure you want to see her this way?" the other medic asked as he signaled to the lobby attendant for a little more time before going down. He pulled the stretcher away from the elevator and over to the side, away from everyone, giving Jim and Crystal some private time.

"Yes, I'm sure. I need to see her for the last time, please," said Jim, so one of the medics unzipped the body bag down to her neckbone, and then the medic left him alone with her. "Crystal!" Jim cried while he looked at Crystal for the final time. He stared at her blonde hair drenched in blood. So much blood was in her hair that it was as though she never had been blonde. "I just talked to her not too long ago, and now she's—" Jim cried as the medics zipped up the body bag.

Then the medics took the stretcher with Crystal's body into the elevator as Jim watched from the hallway. He watched until the elevator doors slid shut, still crying. Then Jim looked back at the front door of the apartment, wishing he'd never left her side and gone back to Dallas. He saw Darlene crying hysterically at the front door, and then he looked down at the carpeted floor and continued to cry. Edna and Nancy stood a few feet away from the apartment, seeing the tears everyone was shedding over the death of Crystal Farnsworth.

◆◆◆◆◆

Tommy exited the subway, on his way home to his apartment, as Maria was on her knees on the bed, wearing her black satin and lace lingerie, awaiting Tommy's arrival, while she smiled. The neighbor across the alley, still on his fire escape, watched her silhouette. While she was on her knees on the bed, he could see her body form in silhouette behind the shade over the window. He still had his cat with him, and the cat purred in his arms. While watching her sexy form through the window shade, he wore a perverted smile on his face.

A key went into the lock. Tommy turned the key both ways, unlocking the front door. Then he opened the door quickly and entered. Maria quietly and quickly closed the door to the bedroom and turned off the light as Tommy shut the front door of the apartment. Inside, the apartment was dim, and he rushed into the living room, turned on the light with a flick of the switch on the wall, and threw his coat onto the recliner. Then he walked toward the bedroom slowly, anticipating taking a nice, hot shower and getting underneath two blankets in his big bed for the final time, until the police picked him up on charges of murder.

When he opened the door to his bedroom, the light from the living room partially shone into the bedroom, and he saw someone on his bed. Someone was sitting there on her knees—a woman wearing lingerie. She was not totally recognizable yet. As he moved closer toward the bed, many things were on his mind at one time, making his mind unclear. Suddenly, he noticed who it was, much to his surprise.

"Maria!" Tommy said as he stepped backward, taking one step toward the entrance of the bedroom.

Maria sat on her knees at the foot of the bed, wearing the black lace lingerie. Her long dark hair was to one side, over her left shoulder, and her pointed, aroused breasts were swollen somewhat from her sexual desire of wanting him. He stood there stunned yet tempted to have just one night of escapades with her. After what had happened earlier in the day, when he'd killed Crystal, with the police on their way, he was surprised to see Maria on his bed, trying to lure him in boldly.

"Maria? Maria, why all of this? Why are you here? I mean, I know why you are here, but—" Tommy walked closer toward the bed, tempted by her beauty. With the sweet scent of the perfume she wore, lightly sprayed, she smelled seductively alluring.

"Tommy, if you haven't noticed, I want your love. Take me now. Take me now, please. I waited here for you." Maria reached out for him with both hands, and she touched his hands. She slowly and gently took both of his hands and placed them on her breasts. "Yes, Tommy. I'm all yours!" said Maria as she shut her eyes and tilted her head upward, still feeling as though she were dreaming, as she had ever since she'd entered the apartment.

Tommy pulled back and stepped back away from the bed. He kept going back all the way to the door of the bedroom. "I can't. I can't, Maria. I still love Crystal Farnsworth. Maria, I still want Crystal in my life." Tommy leaned up against the wall while looking down at the carpeted floor. He knew he would never see Crystal again. He exhaled heavily. He was tired. Then he covered his face with both hands.

As Maria watched, she grinned because she knew the truth, but at the same time, maybe he was just too far gone, she thought as she continued watching with wonder.

<hr>

"Jim, I'm sorry," said Darlene. As she stood at the entrance of the apartment where Crystal had lived, she watched the paramedics enter the elevator with the stretcher with Crystal's body lying on it.

"No, Darlene. I'm sorry. This was your sister, and I'm so sorry," said Jim as he and Darlene embraced each other, comforting each other and sharing each other's grief, as they bid their final farewell to a woman they'd loved as the elevator doors slid shut.

"Darlene, I'm taking a taxi back to Jersey City. Would you like to share a taxi with me, and we'll have more time to talk?" Jim asked as they walked together.

Darlene looked behind her, making sure the front door to the apartment was closed, as they walked together toward the elevator, leaving the familiar apartment for the last time, until Darlene went back to collect Crystal's belongings in a couple of days.

"I would like that very much. Thank you. But I have to do

something first," said Darlene, and she went back toward the apartment to get her suitcase inside the apartment as Jim waited by the elevators.

When she exited the apartment, she remembered she had an extra key, so she locked the door. She then picked up her suitcase and rushed toward the elevator, where Jim was waiting for her, as she wiped her tears, missing the only sister she'd ever had. Jim wiped his tears as he continued missing the biggest love of his life, and together they shared the misery. As Darlene approached Jim, an elevator arrived.

"Jim?" she said.

"Yes, Darlene?" Jim asked as they approached the elevator as the doors slid open. Darlene took out a handkerchief from her purse, and he took one out from his back pocket as they entered the elevator.

"Crystal, really, really did love you. She talked about you all the time," said Darlene as the elevator doors slid shut.

As Darlene and Jim continued talking, they felt the weight of each other's stare as the elevator went to the lobby.

"I felt her love in so many ways, Darlene. I really loved Crystal very much. I just can't believe the whole damn thing happened," said Jim as they embraced each other again.

Darlene reached for the elevator buttons and pressed the automatic stop button as the elevator was several floors away from the lobby. While they embraced each other, they felt the numbness in their hearts, and passion flared between them.

As they looked at each other slowly and cautiously, the hidden passions flourished between them, and their faces drew closer. Their lips touched uneasily, and then they kissed with a bit more passion and a lot more steam. Each of them gasped, catching his or her breath, while their forbidden hearts beat faster and faster as they mended each other's misery, knowing that it could not go any further than the elevator, out of respect for Crystal. Darlene pressed the button for the elevator to proceed the rest of the way to the lobby.

When the elevator reached the lobby level and the doors slid open, Darlene and Jim stepped out of the elevator and walked arm in arm through the lobby. The lobby attendants stared at them from the sides of their eyes. They had watched it all on their monitors showing footage from the camera in the elevator.

After they exited the apartment building, Jim hailed a taxi, and when the taxi drove up to the curb, Jim opened the back door of the cab. Darlene entered the cab, Jim followed, and they proceeded on to their destinations.

CHAPTER 25

AT THE POLICE STATION a few blocks away from Tommy's apartment, it was just another night in Brooklyn—until the telephone rang, and the officer at the desk answered the call.

"Precinct 101. How may I help you?" the officer at the desk asked.

"Yes. This is Officer Harris from precinct 775. How are you?" Officer Harris asked, trying to pass all the formalities.

"Down here, we're all fine. So what's up?" the officer at the desk asked, wondering what this call was about.

"Well, sir, we have a cold-blooded murder on the Upper East Side in Manhattan, and we have a couple of witnesses. In fact, they are neighbors who live in the same building. They said they saw a five-foot-seven male. He was seen wearing a pair of black-framed eyeglasses, and he was skinny to medium in body weight." Officer Harris described the suspect in question to the desk officer.

"All right," the desk officer responded as he wrote down the description on a pad at the desk.

"Now, according to the description by the witnesses and sister of the deceased—"

"What's the name of the deceased?" the officer at the desk asked as he politely interrupted, feeling a bit lost in the conversation.

"Her name was Miss Crystal Farnsworth." Officer Harris sighed, feeling sad about the murder.

"Crystal Farnsworth. I'm going to check on the order-of-protection list. Can you hold, please?" the officer at the desk asked while he looked through the order-of-protection files. The name Crystal Farnsworth sounded familiar to him. Finally, he found the file.

Crystal Farnsworth. She put an order of protection against a Mr. Tommy Landis. Tommy Landis? the desk officer thought.

✦✦✦✦✦

"Tommy? Love of my life?" said Maria while she laughed as Tommy tried to deny what was taking place in his bedroom.

"Maria, you need to leave right now!" Tommy shouted as he quickly approached her while she still sat on her knees at the foot of the bed.

He grabbed her by the arm, but Maria pulled back in her defense, and his smile became a look of weariness.

"Hey, I'm not leaving!" she yelled with a devilish smile.

"You have to leave right now!" Tommy shouted again, this time with desperation, as he grabbed her arm again, but again, she pulled back, forcing his hold off of her.

"No," said Maria as she smiled again.

"Maria, if you don't leave right now, I'll call the police!" Tommy shouted, pointing toward the door of the apartment. His neighbors down the hall were opening the doors of their apartments, listening to what was going on.

"The police! The police? You want to call the fucking cops?" Maria asked with a demented expression on her face and her hands resting on her shapely hips.

"Yes! You can believe me. I will call. I will call the cops!" Tommy shouted, thinking the police were probably on their way to pick him up for the murder of Crystal Farnsworth. "So leave, and there won't be any problems. All right?" Tommy asked as he walked toward the entrance of the bedroom, pointing out of the bedroom.

The man across the alley was still watching. As he watched Maria's silhouette through the window shade, he listened intently to the yelling back and forth while the drama continued. The man's cat was still in his arms as they sat on the fire escape.

———— ✦✦✦✦✦ ————

"All right, Officer Harris. Oh, by the way, my name is Officer Higgins. Now, as far as the murder of Crystal Farnsworth, there is an order of protection out on Tommy Landis from Crystal Farnsworth, if that means anything," said Officer Higgins while he read the order of protection. "Had numerous complaints against Tommy Landis—harassing over the telephone, and he has stalked her numerous times."

"Officer Higgins, I really appreciate your help and your time. I recommend we pay a visit to Tommy Landis's residence and bring him in for questioning; he is pretty much a suspect in this. He seems to be the biggest lead we have at this time," said Officer Harris.

"I agree. I'll send a couple of our officers to his place of residence right now," said Officer Higgins as he grabbed his radio.

"All right. I'll be there soon. I'm leaving right now, on my way over," said Officer Harris.

"All right. See you there," said Officer Higgins, resting the receiver of the phone on his shoulder while gathering the paperwork on his desk.

"OK, bye." Officer Harris hung up.

After the officers hung up, Officer Harris exited his office at his precinct in Manhattan, on his way to Brooklyn, to Tommy's place of residence.

———— ✦✦✦✦✦ ————

"I mean it, Maria! I will call the police on you, bitch!" Tommy shouted as he walked through the living room and picked up the cordless phone. He held on to it, hesitating because of the crime he'd committed earlier that evening. He walked back to the doorway of the bedroom and stood still, showing the cordless phone to her, wishing none of this was happening, feeling exhausted. "I mean it! God damn it! I mean it! I will call the fucking police!" Tommy shouted, and the neighbors out in the hallway worried about what they were hearing.

"OK, right, whatever! And while you're at it, you might as well hide somewhere in the apartment, because the police are probably looking for you." Maria smiled while calmly laughing.

Tommy wondered what she'd meant by that. While he approached her, she rose up from her knees and started jumping up and down on the bed.

"Maria, why would the police want me?" he asked, worried and trying to figure out why she would say something like that, wondering what she knew.

"Well, maybe I know something you know," Maria responded while she continued jumping up and down on the bed as she smiled at him with a quirky smile of wishful thoughts.

While he watched her jump up and down, he grew desperate. As a look of depression showed up on his face, Maria's grin grew wider and wider. The neighbor across the alley wondered what was going on as he watched through the shade and saw the silhouette of her jumping up and down on the bed. He watched continuously from the fire escape with his pet cat.

+ + ◆ + +

Sandy Leonard, Tommy's psychiatrist, was at her home. She entered the living room, carrying a plate of cheese and crackers on a tray. When she was near the sofa, she set the tray down on the coffee table, and then she sat down on the sofa. She grabbed the remote control from the side table, turned on the television, saw that the news was about to start, and put down the remote control on the coffee table. While watching the news, she put a slice of cheese on one of the crackers.

"This is Channel One News. I'm Wanda Nabors. There was a murder tonight on the Upper East Side in Manhattan. Right now, live, we have one of our roving reporters there at the scene. Tammi?"

The screen switched to show Tammi in front of the apartment building where the murder had taken place.

Sandy watched the news while eating her cheese and crackers, shaking her head after hearing about the murder, as she continued listening with interest.

"Hi, Wanda. I'm standing in front of the apartment building on the Upper East Side here in Manhattan, and right above me, there was a murder here tonight. This is where it all took place not too long ago tonight. Police officers and detectives are here at this moment, conducting an investigation," said Tammi.

"Tammi, are there any suspects?" Wanda asked.

"Well, at this moment, they have one suspect, a man who lives in Brooklyn. It was said by one of the detectives that the woman who was murdered was stabbed in the heart, and there was duct tape wrapped around her wrists and ankles. Tape was found on her wrists and ankles as well as on the floor by the chair, where possibly she was sitting, and she might've been held captive for some time before she was murdered here at the apartment. The victim's name is Crystal Farnsworth. Her family was notified, but the police officers mentioned that her sister, Darlene Farnsworth, was here at the apartment after she was murdered. She was one of the few who discovered the body of her sister."

Upon hearing the name Crystal Farnsworth, Sandy choked on the cracker and cheese slightly. She'd heard the name Crystal Farnsworth from one of her patients, Tommy Landis. She couldn't believe what she'd just heard on the news, and she knew the connection.

Oh my God! Crystal Farnsworth? She was that young lady Tommy was obsessed with. Did he kill her? she thought as the news program continued. She continued watching and listening.

"This is Tammi Wang reporting."

"Tommy, how stupid are you? Or better yet, how stupid do you think I am? Huh? Tell me. Tell me! Huh?" Maria was on her knees again on the bed.

He just stared at her bouncing, watching her golden-brown breasts jump up and down. He didn't believe what was taking place.

"Yes, Tommy?" Maria smiled sheepishly, expecting Tommy to give in to his and her temptations.

"You're definitely sexy. And you're definitely smart. And most definitely, you're sick! You are one sick bitch! The only woman I will ever make love to will always be Crystal Farnsworth," said Tommy, covering his face with his hands, feeling frustrated again, knowing he would never experience sex with Crystal.

"Say what? Did you just say that the only woman you would ever make love to was Crystal Farnsworth?" Maria asked while smiling halfway.

"Why are you so surprised?" Tommy asked with a calm smile on his face as he snickered a bit.

"Well, Tommy, I am a bit surprised. Actually, I'm shocked," said Maria.

"Oh yeah? You shouldn't be. You know how I feel when it comes to Crystal. My Crystal." Tommy continued to smile.

"Oh, I know how you feel. I really do know how you feel, Tommy boy. Especially from the times we talked about her in the past." Maria smiled briefly, growing impatient was the trivial moment.

"OK, why do you feel so surprised?" he asked as he folded his arms while leaning up against the wall, wearing a big smile, facing Maria as she sat at the foot of the bed.

"Well, Tommy boy, I just can't help myself." Maria rose from the foot of the bed and stretched her legs, showing off her firm golden-brown legs and her red toenails and fingernails. When she was done stretching, she went back onto the bed, and she knelt on the bed, facing Tommy. "I mean, how could someone, like yourself, make love to a dead person?"

Tommy's smile disappeared as he began to sweat and tremble.

"How does one make love to the other when the other is dead?" she whispered as she slowly raised her head and looked straight at Tommy with a sarcastic smile on her face. Her eyes looked cold, as though she were looking right through him, and it sent chills up his spine, as he knew she was right.

When she was through speaking, a look of fear appeared on his face, along with perspiration. A look of concern was on his face, and then quickly, his expression changed to nonreality.

"Crystal is not dead, Maria. But if you keep speaking the way are, you might be the one who is dead at the end," said Tommy as he pointed at her.

"Uh-huh. Yeah right!" Maria responded with a half smile.

"What the fuck are you talking about? Huh? She's not dead!" Tommy yelled in desperation.

She started to laugh as he approached her in a threatening way. "Tommy, I'll tell you what. Allow me the opportunity to be the woman in your life, your girlfriend, and I won't tell a soul. I won't tell a soul, not even the police, about what happened at Crystal's apartment, all right? Think about it, all right?" Maria wore a half smile on her demented face as Tommy stood at the foot of the bed.

"There's nothing to think about! You don't know much about anything!" Tommy shouted as he walked away from her.

"Hey, Tommy, you can't walk away from this. And you definitely can't walk away from me. Hey, Tommy boy! You can't run and hide from me! Don't deny it! Don't fucking deny me!" Maria shouted as she rose onto her knees again on the bed. "And don't—" Maria stopped to catch her breath.

Tommy stopped where he was in the living room with his back facing her as the silence crept from a distance. Their lives felt a bit different than they'd ever felt before, for they realized the end was about to come.

In a fit of rage, Tommy hit the wall in the living room with both his fists.

"Tommy, let's get together, and I won't mention anything about what happened with Crystal Farnsworth." Maria was desperate.

Tommy turned around and walked halfway to the bedroom. "Maria, no one will believe you. No one in hell will believe you! Oh, all right! I'll admit it to you! Yes! Yes, I killed my lovely, wonderful Crystal! Are you fucking satisfied? I fucking killed that bitch because she denied my happiness in spending the rest of my life with her! She denied me totally. I wanted her with all my heart. But each time, she kept denying me and denied us." Tommy began to cry. "At least now no one will ever have her! I may not have her physically in my life, but at least I'll keep her close to my soul. Yeah. I own her fucking soul!" Tommy shouted, and then he laughed.

Seeing Tommy laughing hysterically, Maria brushed away her tears, and she began to laugh hysterically too.

"No, believe me, Maria, no one will ever believe you. Don't be a fool!" Tommy yelled as he pointed at her, and then he walked away toward the cordless telephone in the living room.

"Tommy! Tommy, wait!" Maria shouted as she held up a hand, still on her knees on the bed.

He froze in place near the side table, where the cordless phone was. While he stood there in place, he slowly turned his head and saw Maria pointing a nine-millimeter handgun directly at him. With the handgun pointed at him, he turned his whole body slowly and walked toward the entrance of the bedroom, in disbelief at everything that had happened since he became obsessed with the notion of being with Crystal and, at the same time, trying to convince Maria to leave him alone. It seemed that whatever problem he had, Maria had the same thing wrong with her, he thought.

"Oh shit!" the neighbor across the alley said with his telescope on the fire escape.

"Maria. Maria, put down the gun. Put it down, please. Please," Tommy begged, taking small steps toward the bedroom door.

"Stay where you are! Don't come any closer than where you are! You don't need to be any closer than you are! You don't need to be any closer to me! We can talk a little bit more maybe, but don't come any closer toward me!" Maria shouted as she pointed the gun directly at him.

The neighbor across the alley still watched Maria's and Tommy's silhouettes, with Tommy's window shade still down, and he saw Maria's silhouette point the gun at Tommy's silhouette.

"Tommy, I don't know, but I still believe that we can be a happy couple. We could get married and have children. Maybe a boy and a girl or two boys or two girls." Maria momentarily daydreamed aloud while still pointing the gun at him, and as he listened, he casually started to walk away. "Tommy!" Maria shouted as she waved the gun at him.

"What the fuck do you want, huh?" Tommy shouted as he turned around just outside the bedroom, and he began slowly approaching her.

Seeing Tommy walking toward her in a fit of rage, Maria kept the gun pointed at him. She squeezed the trigger, and the gun went off twice. Tommy saw the bullets coming toward him as if in slow motion, and he soon met his fate. The two bullets went into his heart, killing him instantly, and he fell to the floor.

The neighbor across the alley heard the gun go off, as did the neighbors in the hallway, and one of the neighbors called the police. As the neighbor across the alley saw gunfire through the silhouettes, he stood there in disbelief. His cat jumped at the sound of gunfire, and he ran inside their apartment.

Maria, still on her knees, lowered the weapon and stood up from the bed in disbelief, not believing what had just taken place in the bedroom of Tommy's apartment. She felt stunned while still holding the gun downward. She could smell the smoke from the gun.

Partially off the bed, she leaped off the rest of the way and walked over toward Tommy's unmoving body. He lay on the floor motionless in a pool of blood. The blood was soaking the living room carpet, slowly making its way toward the entrance of the bedroom.

She approached Tommy's body, knelt down next to it, lowered her head onto his chest, and listened for a heartbeat, not yet realizing he was dead, though she saw the blood, not facing reality. As she rose up, she slowly started to cry, and she lay, while still on her knees, over his deceased body.

"Oh, Tommy! Tommy, Tommy, Tommy!" Maria shouted over and over as she wept over his motionless body. The neighbors in the hallway were all stunned by what they'd heard and seen.

After a few minutes, she got dressed, and then she walked over toward the front door of the apartment. When she reached the door, she opened it slowly, but before leaving, she listened carefully. Not only did she hear police sirens, but she also heard a group of people coming from downstairs. She had the door open a crack, and she saw a few people who lived on the same floor looking at the apartment, wondering what was going on inside. She quickly but gently closed the door; rushed to the bedroom window, passing the body of Tommy; opened the window; and looked down from the window as she felt for the gun, making sure it was with her. Then she quickly ran back to the door of the apartment and locked it. Just then, there was a knock on the door. She immediately ran to the bedroom, but before going through the window, she paused. She rushed back into the living room, knelt down, and kissed Tommy goodbye on his warm lips. The police were trying to pry the door open, so she ran to the window and leaped onto the windowsill. When she was on the window, the gun dropped to the carpeted floor without her noticing, and she took the ladder of the fire escape down to the sidewalk in the alley as the neighbor across the alley watched her in amazement.

After Maria jumped off the ladder onto the sidewalk, she quickly and quietly ran toward the streets.

As she was escaping the alley, the police busted the front door of the apartment. As the landlord ran up the stairs behind them, the police entered the apartment.

When Maria ran into the street, she reached for the gun in her jeans, but it wasn't there.

Oh my God! Where's the gun? I was going to throw it into the garbage can, but I lost it in the apartment. God, I hope they never find it. Shit, she thought as she went across the street and started walking down the street.

As the old man who lived across the alley watched her, she turned her head and saw the old man. He was at Tommy's building, where the police were at Tommy's apartment. As soon as Maria saw him, he quickly went into the building to look for the police. She saw him enter the building, and she walked away, not thinking anything of it, on her way to the subway.

As four police officers, with the landlord behind them, entered the apartment, they noticed a body on the carpeted floor in the living room, in a pool of blood, lying there motionless. They approached the still body, expecting the worst. As they moved closer to the motionless body, they saw that he had been shot twice in the chest. It looked as if he'd been shot in the heart. His eyes were open. The landlord shook his head in disbelief, knowing who his tenant was, as the body of Tommy Landis lay there on his back.

"Officers, this is a fine tenant of mine, Tommy Landis. I'm the landlord of this building. This was one of my tenants," said the landlord, and the police officers just looked at one another, remembering that they once had brought an order of protection to him from a young woman he had been stalking in Manhattan.

While the police officers shook their heads, remembering the order of protection, the old man from across the alley walked tiredly up the steps, hoping he would reach the police on time, hoping they hadn't left yet.

"So this is Tommy Landis," said Officer Harris as he knelt down next to his body to check his pulse, though he and the others knew he was dead, based on the blood on the floor. He looked around Tommy's still body, and then he closed Tommy's eyes. "This whole thing is connected! He murdered Crystal Farnsworth in Manhattan, at her apartment. He was obsessed with that young woman Crystal Farnsworth, I believe strongly, and when he knew he was never going to be with her, he killed her. And now he's been murdered by someone else," said Officer Harris as he stood up.

"That's her. Do you think the order of protection wasn't working for her, so she came here to kill him and take care of it herself because she couldn't deal with it any longer?" another officer asked.

"No. Crystal Farnsworth, the woman Tommy was obsessed with, who had an order of protection against him, was already dead a few hours," Officer Harris said as he looked around the apartment. He noticed a pair of black-framed eyeglasses a few feet away from Tommy's body. He walked over and picked up the glasses from the carpeted floor.

"So if it wasn't Crystal Farnsworth, who killed Tommy Landis?" the officer asked with his hands on his hips.

"No. Tommy killed the girl in Manhattan and then came back to his apartment, and then someone killed him. Maybe it was the boyfriend. I'm sure we'll find out soon. But I do know one thing: this is definitely Tommy Landis." Officer Harris held up the glasses as they all looked at them.

"I already told you this is Tommy Landis," said the landlord, and all the police officers looked at the landlord.

Just then, the old man walked into the apartment slowly. As he walked closer toward the police officers, the police officers noticed him, and one of the officers walked over toward him.

"Well, it's obvious that the murderer of Tommy Landis isn't here at this moment, but there were no witnesses to this murder, just like the murder of Crystal Farnsworth," said Officer Harris as he picked up the black lace lingerie off the floor in the bedroom, looking at it and wondering how it could be connected.

"I saw everything! I saw the whole damn thing!" said the old man from across the alley. The officers and the landlord all looked at the old man, who seemed to be the only apparent witness to what had happened in Tommy's apartment.

Officer Harris saw the mirror in the bedroom, with all the pictures hanging from the edges all around the mirror. The pictures were all of Crystal Farnsworth. He started taking them off the mirror as proof of Tommy Landis's obsession with Crystal Farnsworth, and he placed them in a bag as evidence on the case as the other officers stared at the old man while listening to what he was saying. The old man wore a long-sleeved plaid shirt and an old pair of jeans and was still approaching them, moving closer toward the body of Tommy Landis.

"I saw the murderer, and she had a gun. I saw the gun through the window shade, in the form of a silhouette. When she left the apartment, she climbed through the window and went down the fire escape from the bedroom, and she entered the same way," said the old man.

As Officer Harris was listening, he looked over toward the bedroom window, and there on the floor below the bedroom window was a nine-millimeter handgun. Officer Harris walked over toward the window while taking a white handkerchief from his pocket, and he picked up the gun with the handkerchief and placed it in another bag as evidence in the murder of Tommy Landis, as the weapon that had killed Tommy Landis.

Officer Harris then went back into the living room and approached the old man and the other officers as he took out his pad.

"All right, sir. Your name is?" Officer Harris asked the old man.

"Oh, my name is Joe," said the old man.

"All right, Joe. We may have to use you as a witness to the murder of Tommy Landis. I will need your phone number, and we will be in touch with you soon. All right?" Officer Harris asked.

"Oh, sure. All right," Joe responded as he shook his head while shrugging.

A subway train was heading toward Manhattan with Maria inside. Maria was sitting there quietly, thinking deeply. She'd shot Tommy in the apartment. She could see it in her mind: when she fired the handgun, the bullets went through his chest and into his heart as if in slow motion, with blood squirting out. It was etched into her memory for the rest of her life. The look upon her face was of horror and guilt when she realized what she had done, but she was in a calm state of mind. As he fell to the carpeted floor in slow motion, she placed her hands over her face. She knew that as long as she lived, she would live with that moment. She didn't care if the police found out, if they hadn't found out already. She remembered the old man who'd stared at her when she left the building. She looked around the train and saw other commuters staring at her, so she quickly changed her expression, not wanting to draw attention to herself.

"Shit," Maria said aloud at what she was thinking. She grew weary, and then she let out a quick giggle. Some commuters noticed and quickly turned around, staring at her again, and a few commuters were getting annoyed with her. She giggled to herself, and then she turned her head, looking out the window, as the train continued its trip.

+ + ◆ ◆ + +

Joe was still speaking with the police officers, primarily Officer Harris, at the apartment, when his New York Yankees cap fell onto the floor in the living room.

"Officer Harris, I found this a couple feet away from his body," said one of the officers as he handed a notepad to him.

"A pad with some poetry written on it," said Officer Harris. He quickly flipped through it, reading a few of the pages. It was filled with poems, as though it were a minibook of poetry. Then he flipped to the front of the pad. "All right, I guess this must be the title of this poetry book: *Love of the Twisted.* Hmm," Officer Harris said to himself, thinking out loud, looking at the title. "*Love of the Twisted*? This whole thing is a bit twisted."

Officer Harris shook his head as he threw the pad onto the sofa while walking toward one of the windows in the living room, near the side table. The pad lay faceup on the sofa, showing the name *Love of the Twisted* on the cover.

"All right, so we've identified the deceased as Tommy Landis. He is also the one who murdered Crystal Farnsworth," Officer Harris said, and the other officers agreed, while he was writing on his pad. "And we have Joe, who will help us as the witness and help us locate the murderer who killed Tommy Landis. Hold on. I remember speaking with the sister of Crystal Farnsworth, Darlene Farnsworth. She mentioned that she spoke with Crystal on a couple of occasions about a young Peruvian American woman who worked where Tommy worked. And this woman was obsessed with Tommy, according to what Darlene said."

Maria was still on the Manhattan-bound train, going to her apartment in Manhattan. As she sat there on the train, near the window, she was perspiring, with sweat beads building on her forehead. She couldn't erase the memory of killing the biggest love of her life, Tommy, in a crime of passion. She was thinking to herself, trying to somewhat justify what she had done, while wiping her forehead with a handkerchief she had taken out of her back pocket. As she continued wiping her forehead and face, removing the perspiration, she noticed a little boy sitting next to his mother, sucking on a lollipop, sitting opposite Maria. The little boy stared at Maria while his lollipop was still in his mouth.

CHAPTER 26

ONE WEEK LATER, MARIA WAS at her desk at her job in the messenger center below the office building. She filed some of the day's paperwork, getting it ready for her supervisor, Louie.

"Hey, Maria!" Louie shouted from across the messenger center.

"Yes, Louie?" Maria shouted as she turned her head, looking at Louie.

"Are you caught up on the day's paperwork yet?" Louie asked as he approached her from across the office.

"Yes, Louie. We're almost there," said Maria as she slowly turned her head toward the front door of the center, as she felt something was about to take place. She quickly turned back, looking straight at Louie, feeling a bit anxious. She smiled, and Louie smiled back with his unlit cigar dangling from the corner of his mouth, not suspecting a thing about what had been going on or what was going to happen. As she looked back at the door at the front of the center again, she saw two police officers with Officer Harris, who was now Detective Harris, because he'd just been promoted to detective. Detective Harris wore a trench coat with a suit underneath.

One of the police officers knocked on the door, and Louie looked over toward the doors and saw two police officers and another man wearing a trench coat.

"Oh shit! Who's in trouble now?" Louie mumbled to himself as he approached the doors, and he let them into the center. "Hi. I'm Louie, the supervisor here at the messenger center. Is there something I can assist you with?" Louie asked.

While the officers and the detective were looking around, they noticed a woman at the desk. The detective remembered the description the old man had given him, and she fit that description. Louie looked to where the officers and the detective were looking, in the same direction.

"Louie?" the detective asked, feeling convinced they'd found the person who'd killed Tommy Landis.

"Yes?" Louie responded as he grew nervous because they were looking at Maria.

"We're looking for Maria DeBlanco," Detective Harris said as he looked toward Maria. As she overheard the detective and the policemen talking with Louie, she listened to her own downfall.

"That's Maria over there." Louie pointed in the same direction they were all looking, and the two policemen and the detective walked over toward Maria at her desk.

"Maria DeBlanco?" the detective asked, and she stood up from her desk, with Louie behind the police officers.

"Yes? Are you going to arrest me? If you go back to—" Maria stopped as one of the police officers, who had handcuffs ready, turned her around.

"OK, read her rights, and let's take her in and book her," said Detective Harris.

As she quickly turned around, avoiding the handcuffs and the arrest, Louie shook his head, not believing what was going on. As he went to his office, she saw him leaving her alone with the officers and the detective, and she knew it was her last day at the job.

"Hold it! If you go back to the apartment, you will see Tommy! Tommy Landis is alive! He's not dead. Believe me, he's not dead," said Maria as the officer turned her around again.

"You have the right to remain silent. Anything you say may be used against you in a court of law. If you can't afford an attorney, then the state will have one for you," said the officer as he handcuffed her while she was mumbling to herself and giggling out loud. "Hey, Harris, maybe we should take her to Bellevue Hospital instead of jail right now, because she seems sick at the moment," said the officer as the detective approached her, facing her.

"All right. I guess we'll let the hospital check her out first before we take her to central booking. Maria DeBlanco?" Detective Harris called out to her, and she didn't utter a word, but she stopped giggling. "Miss Maria DeBlanco?" the detective said again. He looked at the two officers, as she never uttered a word and had no expression on her face. "All right. Take her now," said the detective.

Maria stood back and started laughing wildly, as though she were watching a stand-up comedian at the exclusive Caroline's Comedy Club. It was the kind of laughter that sent chills down people's spines. The officers had her sit down in her chair at her desk while Detective Harris got on his cell phone and called a mental health center, Bellevue Hospital, to come pick her up to examine her, because of her sudden and peculiar behavior.

While Maria was still laughing hysterically and mumbling to herself, moments after the detective called Bellevue to pick her up, two men in all-white clothes entered the messenger center. Detective Harris directed them to Maria as one of the officers removed the handcuffs, and one of the mental health aides put a straitjacket on her. The sleeves on the jacket crossed across the chest and stomach area to keep her from hurting herself or others. When they were slipping the straitjacket on her, she continued laughing while wondering what was going on; she didn't have a clue. When she was fully in the straitjacket, she was still laughing and mumbling to herself, talking even faster. No one understood what she was saying. Louie was staring from his office, still not believing what was going on. She continued mumbling to herself as the two mental health aides took her out of the messenger center with the two police officers and the detective. After they exited the building, Louie shut the door of the messenger center.

When Maria was in the back of the white van, one of the mental aides slammed shut the back door of the van, and she looked out the side window, with her face up against the window, looking sad and hopeless, not knowing if she was going to be all right or if she was in the beginning stages of mentally illness. As the white van drove away, starting their journey to the mental facility, Maria still had her face pressed against the glass of the window as she thought about her fate that awaited her.

Some time passed, and then Maria was at the mental center, sitting on a chair in the middle of an isolated room. The walls and floor were padded with thick mats, and a female doctor carrying a clipboard walked around her, observing her, while she sat there on the chair, still in a straitjacket, wearing no expression on her face. She remained quiet and looked around the room with her eyes as her head stayed still. She sat there in a daze, and she would giggle a little every now and then.

"Maria, how are you feeling today?" the doctor asked while she continued walking around Maria, circling her, as she asked questions as Maria twitched. "Maria, how are you feeling?" the doctor asked again, and Maria twitched again as the doctor wondered what was going on with her.

"I—" Maria stopped.

The doctor stopped where she was as two nurses looked through the square glass on the door. "Yes, Maria? Go ahead. I'm listening to you," said the doctor as she continued walking.

"I did it! I did it!" Maria shouted as she smiled.

The doctor continued walking around Maria, writing down on the clipboard what she was saying and what her responses were, so that she and her staff at the hospital could evaluate her. "You did what, Maria? What did you do?" the doctor asked as she stopped where she was again, so she could study Maria's reactions to her questions.

Maria looked up with sorrowful eyes. "I wanted his love. I really wanted his love. That was all I ever wanted. I swear. That's the truth. I just wanted his love." Maria began to cry.

The doctor started walking around Maria again. "Maria, what went wrong? Where did all of this go wrong?" the doctor asked as she continued writing everything down on her clipboard. Then she stopped walking and stood right behind Maria as Maria's blank expression changed to a frantic look.

"What went wrong? What went wrong, you ask? Well, I'll tell you what went wrong!" Maria paused for a moment.

As the doctor stood behind Maria, she placed her right hand on Maria's right shoulder, calming her down, as she felt the tension from her body. Maria was trembling a little. Two nurses and two police officers heard what was going on as they watched from behind the door, through the small, square glass window.

"I will tell you what went wrong. Crystal Farnsworth! Fucking Crystal! Crystal! Fucking Crystal," said Maria as she grinned while showing just the whites of her eyes, as though she were in a trance. "That fucking bitch! Tommy. My love, Tommy. Tommy Landis killed Crystal, and I killed Tommy. I fucking killed Tommy Landis! But really, I really didn't mean to. I really didn't mean to. Really, really, you have to believe me. I didn't mean to kill him. You see, I killed Tommy." Maria cracked a smile and then laughed hysterically. "I fucking killed Tommy Landis."

The doctor continued walking around Maria. Maria sat on the chair, still wrapped up in the straitjacket, with tears rolling down her cheeks.

"You see, I just wanted him and I to be married and to have babies. We could've been a very happy family. I don't know about the house, you know, with a white picket fence out in the country. I know we could've been happy. Very happy. I just wanted to be his wife," said Maria while smiling.

"Uh-huh," the doctor responded as she took a deep breath while she continued writing down observations.

"That was all I wanted! He was all I ever wanted. No one had to die. No one! No one," she whispered as she looked serious, shaking her head. Maria started to cry hysterically, trying to get out of the straitjacket she was wrapped in. As she rose from where she was sitting, the female doctor tried to restrain her so that she didn't hurt herself.

Detective Harris was behind the door with the two nurses as he heard the confession of her killing Tommy Landis in his apartment. He thought to himself as the two nurses were talking among themselves about what was taking place in the room. The female doctor was still restraining Maria, trying to get her to sit back down on the chair.

OK, Tommy Landis murdered Crystal Farnsworth because he was obsessed with Crystal, and she didn't want to be with him. And Maria murdered Tommy Landis because he didn't want to be with her. Maria was obsessed with wanting to be with him, but he rejected her, so she killed him, and now here we are in a mental facility. Hmm. This is getting more and more interesting by the moment, Detective Harris thought as he watched the two nurses join the doctor in restraining Maria to sit back down on the chair.

"Maria, calm down!" the doctor yelled while both nurses held her down, and Maria sat down slowly on the chair. The doctor was in front of her with a needle, preparing to administer a drug to calm her down. Maria saw the needle and panicked as the nurse was about to put it into her arm.

"No! Don't drug me up! No, please don't do this! No! No!" Maria yelled as her eyes bulged out while the nurses and the doctor tried to restrain her. One of the nurses placed the needle in her arm.

Everything in Maria's mind went blank. A dark space came into view as she was sedated.

⁓✦✦✦⁓

"This is Wanda Nabors, and I'm on location with the Channel One van. At this time, I'm in Brooklyn. I'm in front of an apartment building where someone was shot to death. The victim was shot right in his apartment. Believe it or not, this murder is somehow connected to the murder that took place about a week ago, when a young woman by the name of Crystal Farnsworth was murdered by an obsessed man by the name of Tommy Landis in her Upper East Side apartment building in Manhattan. Throughout the investigation, the police and detectives found out it was Tommy Landis who murdered Crystal

Farnsworth. It's been said by those who were investigating that when Tommy Landis killed Crystal, someone witnessed everything, from the time Crystal was taken into her apartment until the time she was murdered, after which he fled the apartment. The witness was at a distance. And listen to this: Tommy Landis was obsessed with Crystal Farnsworth, as we already know, but the witness to the murder of Crystal Farnsworth was obsessed with the murderer, Tommy Landis. The police have identified this woman as Maria DeBlanco.

"When Tommy Landis fled the scene here in Manhattan, he went home to his Brooklyn apartment, but when he arrived here at his apartment, he found a surprise waiting for him. Maria DeBlanco was in the apartment, waiting for him. According to the investigators in the depths of the investigation, Tommy Landis arrived home at his apartment right after he murdered Crystal Farnsworth, and according to a witness who lives across the alley in the neighboring building, the woman in the apartment, Maria DeBlanco, who witnessed the murder of Crystal Farnsworth and reportedly was obsessed with Tommy Landis, killed Tommy Landis when he arrived home in his apartment. Tommy Landis apparently didn't want to be with her, and she didn't take no for an answer, obviously. She killed him. She used to be a co-worker of his at the job where he worked before he got fired.

"The whole thing got started when Tommy didn't accept the rejection of Crystal Farnsworth. He became obsessed with her to the point of killing her. Maria was pursuing Tommy Landis while he was pursuing Crystal Farnsworth before he killed her. And after Crystal Farnsworth was murdered by Tommy Landis, Maria DeBlanco murdered Tommy Landis. According to investigators, he didn't want to be with her, so she killed him here at his apartment. So this was an obsession triangle, classic to the very end."

"Wanda, this sounds like one of those crazy stories that will be around for a long time," said an anchorperson at the news center.

"Yes, this will be here for a while," said Wanda.

"So Maria DeBlanco is the sole survivor of this whole ordeal. Where is she at this moment? In prison?" the anchorperson asked.

"Well, the police made the arrest and picked her up where she worked, but they noticed she was acting peculiarly, so they sent her to a mental health facility in Manhattan, where she confessed to killing Tommy Landis. However, mental health staff found her to be mentally ill, so she won't be fit to stand trial. She was evaluated, and it was confirmed that she is indeed mentally ill. She's currently being taking care of and will be getting the necessary treatment."

"All right, this was clearly love gone wrong, and bingo—it's obsession. Right?"

"This clearly was a case of obsession run amok. It was love by one party that turned into obsession. For Maria DeBlanco, the obsessed woman who was pursuing Tommy Landis, it was love from the past. She had been in love with him for two years, according to coworkers of Maria and Tommy, so it was love from the past to the present. It turned into an obsession because Tommy Landis didn't want anything with Maria DeBlanco, except to remain friends and coworkers. This was a crazy and unique situation as far as pop culture goes. Anyway, this shows how love can get a bit twisted at times. I'm Wanda Nabors, live in Bensonhurst, Brooklyn, New York, for Channel One News."